SCAVENGYR HUNT
Book I of the Tyrning Cycle

COPYRIGHT

INTRODUCTION

I began research for the *Tyrning Cycle* in 2011, the year before <u>Ring of Truth</u> was published. At that time I envisioned another stand alone novel, one revolving around mythemes—myths and legends common to many cultures across the globe. The world ending in cataclysm, like Ragnarok or Armageddon, is one example. Thanks to the popularity of *My Fair Lady,* many of us are familiar with the Pygmalion myth from Greek mythology. The Greek version of that mytheme may owe its roots to similar African stories.

One of the most culturally pervasive mythemes is the existence of an "axis mundi," which translates as "world axis" or "center of the world." It is sometimes called the Omphalos, the world navel, and is the physical intersection of heaven and earth. Some world navels are well-known places, like Delphi for the Greeks. A large number of cultures, and religions, have an axis mundi. In North America there is Baboquivari Peak, sacred to the Tohono O'odham Indians. The Foundation Stone in Jerusalem, under which lies the Well of Souls, is a well-known world navel. Mountains are frequently believed to be axis mundi. Mounts Fuji in Japan, and Kilimanjaro in Tanzania are examples, as is Mount Kailish, sacred to a number of religions, located in Tibet.

Cuzco, in what is now Peru, was a world navel to the Incans. Uluru—also known as Ayers Rock—in Australia is an axis mundi to several Aboriginal tribes. "Te Pito O Te Henua," which according to some sources may have been the original name of Easter Island, is literally translated as "the navel of the world."

Pulling focus from the physical to the metaphysical, it was also of interest to me that the axis mundi is a well-known concept in both yoga and tai chi. On a micro-scale, the spine is sometimes considered the axis mundi of the human body. From a macro perspective, it is the human body itself which is the axis mundi between heaven and earth.

Winner! Axis mundi it was then. It's a great concept, and I knew it would work perfectly with any version of Joseph Campbell's hero's journey. I've been a huge fan of Mr. Campbell's work for decades, and I think the hero's journey provides a wonderful rollercoaster ride of a narrative.

I also knew the novel would have three of my Trues as the book's tent poles. First, a True Hero (or Heroes, and "Hero" is gender neutral in my opinion) must prevail. I've always been a superhero guy. Sorry for all of you who are more psychologically nuanced, but with apologies to the Hulk, Daredevil, and the Punisher, you can keep the anti-heroes. I am a straight up King Arthur "right makes might" person. Don't try the reverse with me, it won't sell. Doesn't mean the Hero can't do bad things or make mistakes. After all, warts and self-serving decisions are part of any Journey.

Second, True Love has to win. Like Westley and Buttercup in William Goldman's masterwork, *The Princess Bride*. If I flip on the television and the last fifteen minutes of *Notting Hill* is on, I'm going to watch it. Every time. Consider yourself forewarned.

Third, True Choice must exist. Free will—without exception or caveat. For everyone. The good guys, the bad guys, and the folks who really aren't sure where they belong until they've actually made their decisions. Without free will there is no Journey. Absent choice we are merely automatons performing our steps in some prescribed dance of life.

After making a substantial beginning into diagramming the necessary scenes, I realized I had a problem. World-building was too big an enterprise for one volume. In searching for a solution I went back to my bookshelves, to look at some old friends. I noticed I had a handful of trilogies in my library. Among them were C.S. Lewis's <u>Cosmic Trilogy</u>, and John Ronald Reuel Tolkien's <u>Fellowship of the Ring</u>. I began doing research on the trilogy format. Playwrights were early adopters, with <u>The Oedipus Cycle</u> by Antigone and <u>The Oresteia</u> by Aeschylus written millennia ago. Dante Alighieri used the trilogy framework in the beginnings of the fourteenth century for his epic poem, <u>The Divine Comedy</u>.

I am not inferring I believe my writing to be of the caliber of those giants. I was interested in their choice between a serialized format and that of a trilogy. I decided a trilogy would fit the <u>Tyrning Cycle</u> perfectly. Although it was the right decision, here's what I have to say about it—Yikes!!!! (yes, with four exclamation points).

When I was in my early teens, my folks were apparently concerned my brothers and I might grow into feckless youth. Or maybe just your basic run of the mill idiots. So they did the best they could for us. National Geographic specials were required viewing. They tried to teach us how to play bridge. We had informed discussions concerning current events around the dining room table. One Christmas, as a group present, we received a three-dimensional chess game. My brothers became proficient at the game. I was terrible at it. I never could figure out how a move on one level might advance or destroy my position on one of the other two levels. I have never felt so stupid in my entire life. That record stood until forty years later when I thought I could construct all three books of a trilogy.

Writing this trilogy—for me, anyway—is roughly equivalent to putting together a three-dimensional jigsaw puzzle.

One in which you could swear some cosmic prankster has removed half of the border pieces. At least half. It was easy to get overwhelmed, and I did. Frequently.

Enter epiphany. I finally realized the entire project had to be addressed as a single epic. I had to finish the borders for all three-levels of the puzzle. So I stopped and wrote the end of Book III. Then I wrote the ending of Book II. After that I was able to fill in the character arcs and major turns for all three books.

I used to skip "Forewords" and "Introductions" because I assumed they were boring and I wanted to get right into the good stuff. I read them all now, because I realize authors sometimes provide insight into their work that enhances the reading experience.

True Hero, True Love. True Choice. This one's all about Time, folks.

I hope you enjoy the Journey, there's plenty more to come.

Tim.

ACKNOWLEDGMENTS

To Mom. This series isn't going to be your customary book club fare. As one of the characters says, "Our worlds are not all Disney, some parts are very Grimm." Just remember—I'm your favorite son. I know you'll read the book, you'll enjoy the literary and mythological themes, and you'll be proud. I love you.

To Dad. We feel your absence everyday. I'm not sure I have ever met someone who sought the center more than you. Oh, and I totally blew some of my inheritance traveling—doing research for the Tyrning Cycle. It was spent to acquire knowledge, which I'm pretty sure would have been okay with you.

To my three brothers. Please feel free to buy dozens of copies of this book at full retail price, and hand them out as presents to your friends and business associates. You may proceed worry-free this go-round. Unlike Ring, your names appear nowhere in Book I.

To my Scavengyr beta readers (in alphabetical order): Christie Greer, Laura Haynie, and Diane Holitik. Thanks for your constructive criticism. More importantly, thank you for your repeated encouragement along the way. It's an awful bleak Gehenna of a place to be sixty thousand words in on Book I, with legitimate doubts as to whether you are actually smart enough to finish the puzzle.

To KHT. Thank you. You read. You encouraged. You abetted. And you listened. A lot. Most importantly, however, you showed me that "y"s are in fact magykal.

To the UnFading Spirit. Thank you for (hopefully) guiding my mind and my hand. Sometimes I fear I may be more than a little spiritually deaf, but I do try each day to 'Seek the Center'. Regardless of the name you may call the UnFading One, I hope this book will help you do the same.

PANTHEON OF THE MOIETY

———————

AMARANTOS

———————

PRINCIPES

CHRONOS

AURORA

SOL

LUNA

———————

RULING COUNCIL OF THE MOIETY

—————

ARCHON
The Alberich
King of the Tuatha Dé Danaan

SENESCHAL
The Marid
Suleyman of the Djinn

PARLIAMENTARIAN
The Raja Jinn Peri
King of the Malay Faeries

The Márku
Empress of the HuldreFolk

The Proteus
Regent of The Olympians

—————

HUNTS SCHOOL ADMINISTRATION AND FACULTY

PRINCIPAL
Chiron

HUNTSMISTRESS
Lilith Empousa

HUNTS TEACHERS
Professor Daedalus Hardcastle
Doctor Delphi SilverTongue
Professor Sprite Elphinstone

HUNTS FINALIST TEAMS

AILE
Turkish Realm
"group of people who live together"

MERKEZ
Aile Prime Direction
"Center"

KUZEY
"North"

GÜNEY
"South"

DOGÜ
"East"

BATI
"West"

AYLLU
Incan/Mayan Realm
"sib or clan"

YAXKIN
"Center"
Allyu Prime Direction

XAMAN
"North"

NOHOL
"South"

LIK"IN
"East"

CHIK"IN
"West"

BÙLUÒ
Chinese Realm
"tribe"

ZHONG
"Center"
Bùluò Prime Direction

BEI
"North"

NÁN
"South"

DONG
"East"

XÍ
"West"

HAK"ÉÍ

Navajo Realm
"group of people related by blood, marriage, law or custom"

ULH-NE-IH
"Center"
Hak'éí Prime Direction

NAHOOKOS
"North"

SHÁDI'ÁÁH
"South"

HA'A'AAH
"East"

E'E'AAH
"West"

KABILA
Swahili Realm
"tribe"

KATI
"Center"
Kabila Prime Direction

KASKAZINI
"North"

KUSINI
"South"

MASHARIKI
"East"

MAGHARIBI
"West"

OMADA
Greek Realm
"party, group, or team"

BORRAS
"North"
Acting Omada Prime Direction

NOTOS
"South"

ANATOLIA
"East"

DYSI
"West"

QUINT
"Five"

PLEME
Serbo-Croatian Realm
"tribe"

SREDINA
"Center"
Pleme Prime Direction

SEVER
"North"

ISTOK
"South"

JUG
"South"

ZAPAD
"West"

SHUZOKU
Japanese Realm
"tribe or family"

CHUUSHIN
"Center"
Shuzoku Prime Direction

KITA
"North"

MINAMI
"South"

HIGASHI
"East"

NISHI
"West"

SLÄKT
Swedish Realm
"group of people related by blood, marriage, law or custom"

MITT
"Center"
Släkt Prime Direction

NORD
"North"

SÖDER
"South"

OST
"East"

VAST
"West"

"Before even the breath of a beginning, the UnFading Spirit is. She first created her Seneschal—When."

— *LEX IMMORTALIS*

CHAPTER ONE

"Happy Birthday, Loser!" Barton's voice was easy to identify, even over the shotgun clatter of the gravel as the pickup peeled out. Nasally and constricted—like helium escaping from a balloon—Barton's voice was his sole physical imperfection.

"This is some seriously jacked up shit," Tal muttered to himself, as he pulled the burlap bag off his head and stood up—slowly. His left ankle wobbled on him, promptly sending a level-six pain message to his brain. As he shifted weight to his right side, Tal gave himself the once over, analyzing the data. Immediate swelling, but the leg remains load bearing. Probably a high-ankle sprain, he decided. At least it's not broken. His new Levis hadn't fared as well. One of the back pockets was zipped off, and both knees had small tears. His right elbow was oozing from a walnut-sized strawberry, and there was gravel imbedded in the meat of both palms. It's a miracle I'm not bleeding in a dozen different places, he thought. I mean, really, who throws someone out of the bed of a moving pickup truck?

He took a studied look around, assessing his location. Not good. The assholes had dumped him at a beat down defunct gas station out in the middle of somebody's back forty. Tal could almost imagine a couple of tumbleweeds rolling by, except he knew tumbleweeds weren't indigenous to the Arkansas Delta. Mosquitoes the size of small raptors—yes. Tumbleweeds—no.

Chipped where it hadn't already peeled off into curlicue shavings, the remnants of the dirt-encrusted white paint on the station's clapboard walls looked more like eczema than paint. The decades had been equally unkind to the oval "Sol's Gas" sign, creakily swinging in the fitful morning breeze. The sign had a dozen or so rusted out divots, no doubt the result of generations of twenty-two target practice. Both of the station's front windows had long ago been robbed of their glass, replaced with rough-hewn two-by-four "X"s nailed across the splintered wooden frames. Tal felt goose pimples populate both his arms as he looked at the windows. They looked like large dark eyes staring straight at him, through him. It wasn't hard to imagine they were even sizing him up. Must have hit my head too, he decided.

A wrought iron fence ran lengthwise behind the gas station, the rusted-iron spear points a head taller than his stepfather. The fence itself extended a pretty good ways in both directions. There was a driveway to the left of the gas station that led to a padlocked gate. The gate wore a big hand-lettered sign zip-tied to it that read:

LUNA'S TIMELESS TREASYRES
KEEP OUT! DON'T COME IN HERE! I'M NOT KIDDING!
TRESPASSYRS WILL BE ~~DRAWN AND QUARTERED~~ ~~DISEMBOWELED~~ SLAYN!

Okay, that sign ups the strange factor a couple of levels, Tal thought. Luna needs a how-to book on customer relations, and it wouldn't hurt her to use spell-check. Looking through the fence, he could see heaps of haphazardly piled junk. Corroding car chassis, refrigerators, treadmills, and construction materials. Luna and Sol are quite the pair. She thinks junk is treasure, timeless treasure at that, and Sol's brilliant business plan had been to put a gas station in the middle of nowhere. Great!

"Tal S-S-S-Smith."

Tal whipped his head around to see who was whispering his name. Nobody. No one.

"Tal S-S-S-Smith."

He turned back quickly toward the road. Nobody. No one. Must be the wind, he decided.

"Tal S-S-S-Smith."

He turned another ninety degrees. Nobody. No one.

"Tal S-S-S-Smith. Go to the Ladies-s-s-s' Room. Now!"

Tal turned again, this time back toward the station. Nobody. No one. There was some thing, though. He hadn't previously noticed the air hose at the near corner of the station, but the hiss of escaping air drew his attention. And there's your rational explanation, Tal told himself. There's nothing unusual about air hoses, there's one at every gas station in the world. Besides, even if an air hose knew my name, why would it tell me to go to the Ladies' Room? And why am I even having this conversation with myself?

As he walked back toward the road to start the trek home, Tal quickly reviewed the morning's events. After breakfast, his Mom had dropped him off at school early so she could get the twins over to the elementary school. She told him she'd pick him up right after the last afternoon bell, and reminded him not to be late because she had to get home right away to start cooking his birthday dinner.

Barton and his brace of hyenas had been lying in wait for him in the photinia hedge overgrowing the parking lot. While the other two grabbed him, Barton threw a burlap seed sack over his head, and then they'd manhandled him up into the back of Fail's Ford truck. Even blindfolded, Tal had been able to keep up with where they were going. Sorta. They'd gone south out of town on the old state highway. He couldn't be sure how far—it must have been at least five or six miles. Then they'd taken a right turn onto an unpaved road. He'd heard the small rocks pinging off the truck's skid plate. There had been two additional right turns, then he heard the tailgate being lowered, and shortly after that one of the asshats put a boot in his ass, and pushed him out the back of the still moving truck.

That's when Barton had started yakking. "I told you, Loser, if you couldn't figure out a way to look stupid on your own, that it would be our job to help you. This is us, helping you. By the time you get back to town, you'll have an unexcused absence. And guess what? You're going to get one every day from now on—until you're expelled." Tal had heard Barton turn back toward his pals. "There's a pity boys, Einstein's gonna have him a hard time even getting into junior college after he flunks his senior year."

Tal heard the two sycophants guffawing at all the appropriate places during Barton's monologue. The *Idiot's Guide to Being A Bully* must have a whole chapter on how to laugh like a moron, he thought.

"Not to worry," Barton continued. "A smart young man like yourself shouldn't have any trouble landing a minimum wage job working at any one of the many Sellars' family fast food restaurants. Just remember Loser, keep your piehole shut about our 'assistance.' I've got a pink slip already filled out with your step-pappy's name on it."

Then he'd heard them all laughing again as the truck spun out, peppering him with dirt and gravel. Counting the time on the highway, and the turns they'd made off the main road, Tal figured he must be somewhere about ten miles from his house. He pulled his cell phone out of his front pocket. No coverage. Of course, they knew that when they picked this place. Great, he thought, even if I really hoof it, I won't make it back until well after lunch.

Lunch! Damn it! My lunch date with Elle. She said she hates it when people are late. The chick is intelligent…and funny…and smoking hot. And she thinks I'm cute. She also thinks I've stood her up. *Happy freakin' eighteenth birthday to me!*

The wind strengthened, whipping Tal's legs together before tugging him sideways. As he turned, he saw something that looked like a little white flag flapping at the far end of the station. No, not a flag. An envelope stuck on the glass of the service bay door. I'm going to be late anyway, he decided, as he gingerly limped over the service island, and headed toward the mechanic's area.

When he got to the envelope, he saw it had words printed on it.

DO NOT OPEN THIS UPON PAIN OF DEATH
(OR WORSE.)
UNLESS YOU ARE TAL SMITH.

"I see Mr. Barton Sellars IV, is a little melodramatic," Tal said, peeling the envelope off the glass. 'Death (Or Worse.)' Actually that's kinda funny, he thought. What's worse than death? Tal lowered himself gingerly to the curb and opened the envelope. Inside was a sheet of letterhead with a funky crest containing a weird looking compass. The words, '**Hunt School,** *est. #B.C.*' in embossed gold lettering were printed immediately under the crest. What's up with "# B.C.," he wondered. The paper contained a message, printed in the same hand:

> It is imperative that you go to the Ladies' Room immediately. You cannot be late for the first day of the Tyrning Year. Dust yourself off a little. You look like you've been thrown out of a moving vehicle.
>
> Sincerely,
>
> The Service Bay

"The Service Bay?" And what's up with this "Tyrning Year?" Barton gets style points for creativity, Tal thought, but his spelling is as bad as Luna's. He glanced both ways in case Barton was pulling some hidden camera punk. Nobody. No one.

Several minutes later, the nearest of the two gas pumps started dinging, as if somebody was pumping gas. Tal got up— laboriously—and hobbled over to the pump. He peered through the scratched glass, at the display that normally messaged gallons and dollars. Instead of numbers, the following message slowly scrolled up:

> I was told you were an exceptionally intelligent Munedan. It's time you start showing it, worlds depend upon you. Go to the Ladies' Room. Right now. And really—dust yourself off a little.
>
> Sincerely,
>
> Gas Pump No. Unus

Tal stood there, mouth agape, as he watched the words scroll up and out of view. All kinds of questions flashed rapid-fire. "Munedan?" What's up with the spelling out here? Has my life come to this? Even a gas pump gets to be the boss of me? A scratched up, out of order gas pump at that. A scratched up, out of order gas pump named Unus. There's some serious melodrama going on with that whole "worlds depend upon you" thing. Tal started feeling around for the bump on his head. I must have sustained a concussion when they threw me out of the truck, he thought. It's the only possible rational explanation.

At that moment, the other pump dinged. Tal took two steps over to it, and watched as more words scrolled up:

> You don't have a concussion, and this is not a game, Tal Smith. This is a Tyrning Year. You must bind the contract. Go to the Ladies' Room—now! But first, dust yourself off a little.
>
> Sincerely,
>
> Gas Pump No. Duo

Tal stood nonplussed as he watched those words also scroll away. Duo? That's two in Latin. Okay, makes sense. Unus is one in Latin. These two good old boy Southern gas pumps have named themselves "One" and "Two" in Latin. What am I doing standing here, he asked himself. I should have already started the hike back to town. Eye on the prize—there are college scholarships to win, and then there's the whole thing about making something of myself. Who am I kidding? There's no way I'm getting back in time for lunch with Elle. She'll probably never speak to me again. I probably won't even make it back before Mom is supposed to pick me up after school. How am I going to explain missing school?

The jackasses had him in a dead-end box. There was no way he could afford college without a scholarship. Dead end. Once Barton found out Elle liked him, he'd screw that up. Dead end. If Tal said anything about the bullying, Barton would have Pell blackballed and they'd have to move again. Dead end.

Going back didn't seem to be a viable option. What was it Dr. Wilt said—that it was the journey that was important? Tal wasn't sure he agreed with that premise, and he certainly wasn't sure that any important journey started in a Ladies' Room. Gas Pump No. Unus did say that worlds depended on him. Really, Tal, asked himself, when did you start doing things because a gas pump told you to? Now, he decided.

He turned around to look at the station, and saw a small curved arrow sign that read, "Bathrooms." He walked slowly around the corner of the building and saw the Ladies' Room sign. He dusted himself off—a little. Then, after knocking twice to make sure it wasn't occupied, he slowly opened the door, stepped in, and flipped the light switch on. As soon as he did, the metal door jerked out of his hand, and slammed shut behind him.

"HOLY CRAP!"

CHAPTER DUO

Tal was looking at a Greek temple…and an Egyptian pyramid…and a Moroccan minaret…and a Northern European gothic cathedral…and a half-dozen other structures conflated into one ginormous alabastrine building. He'd never been in a Ladies' Room, and hadn't known what to expect—a couple of extra stalls, nicer two-ply toilet paper, maybe even some seasonally appropriate potpourri. Certainly not a creamy white marble building that incorporated architectural elements from all over the planet.

Between Tal and the superstructure was a large lawn. It was rectangular, roughly about as long and as wide as a couple of football fields. The grass was lush and cut tight in an alternating diagonal pattern, like a giant rectangular putting green.

At the far end of the lawn, just before the building, was a fountain. Actually, Tal thought, the word fountain was inadequate. It was the king boss daddy of all fountains. The dang thing looked like it must be about a hundred feet in diameter. The initial attention getter was a central water jet as big around as a sewer culvert shooting a solid tube of water hundreds of feet into the air. From there, his eyes were pulled to several dozen carved figures surrounding the center jet, with water erupting from countless openings, at every possible angle. The fountain lay at the foot of a double-tiered set of wide white marble steps that led up to the building's front entrance.

Gargoyles jutted up from the building's eaves. It appeared from the portion of the building Tal could see that they were spaced every thirty feet or so. It looked like they marched around the roof of the entire structure. Each was a representation of the same misshapen four-legged grotesque, although in different poses. They were similar to the gargoyles Tal had studied in World Civ last year, but there were differences too. The first difference was their color. These gargoyles weren't pitted out grey limestone. They were carved out of a polished blood-red stone that made them pop against the pure white of the building and its matching white roof tiles. Plumes of smoke wafted up from their nostrils. The hot water or heating system must vent through them, Tal decided. There was something else different about the gargoyles. Their slick stone surfaces seemed to be under tension.

Tal turned around to look back at the bathroom wall. It wasn't there. No light switch, no door, no wall, no gas station. Only a cotton field that seemed to stretch to the horizon. Most surprising to him wasn't the fact the building wasn't there. Most surprising to him was he wasn't at all surprised the building wasn't there. Well, Dorothy, you're not in Arkansas anymore, he thought.

He began listing the passably semi-sane possible explanations for what was happening. Severe concussion remained far and away the leading contender. Followed—not very closely—by wormhole, alien abduction, both the invention and utilization of a fully functional transporter device in the form of a ladies' bathroom, and death. Death, with heaven being a truly odd place. Can't go back the way I came, he decided. That leaves forward as the only possible way home.

"Hunts School," he mumbled to himself as he stepped stiffly out onto the lawn. "Place must have a heck of an endowment." As he walked toward the school, Tal could see the front double doors were pulled wide open. They were at least three stories tall, about a foot thick, and made of dark wood. The arched entry area to the doors was about twenty feet deep, and its entire surface was covered with intricate carvings of gold-colored words and hieroglyphs. The main doors opened to the fountain entrance from the Greek temple portion of the structure. The minaret was to the left, thrusting several hundred feet toward the clouds smattering the blue-shot southern sky. The gothic cathedral module was to the right.

He could see small parts of other buildings as well. Off to the rear left of the main structure a covered sidewalk led to a scaled-down replica of the Taj Mahal, and to the right a similar sidewalk ended in a Viking longhouse. At the farthest edge of his vision he could see a sports stadium. There was something else back there too, it looked like it was a four-sided pyramid. What are those things called, he asked himself. Ziggurats. That's it.

A ziggurat. Go figure. As he neared the fountain he walked past the first group of students. They were all chatting a mile a minute and no one paid any attention to him. He'd been born in New Orleans, and a couple of Pell's jobs had been in Southern areas, so he thought it a little curious as he passed group after group that here, within a stone's throw of the Mississippi River, he didn't hear a single drawl or even a y'all.

As he got closer, he could see there were hundreds of students milling about, maybe as many as several thousand. Nemeton High doesn't have but three or four hundred students. Where did all these teenagers come from? A gong sounded. Tal felt its deep bass thrum through his entire body. Everyone stopped what they were doing, and started migrating up the steps. Tal followed suit, and as he approached the open doors he noticed three supersized guys standing guard by each of the doors. All six of the dudes were bare to their waists, and wore black silk trousers. They had symbols tattooed in black across their faces and chests, and wore bright yellow scarves tied across their temples, the scarves trailing halfway down their backs. And they were blue. Not robin's egg blue, closer to an indigo. Those freaks have dyed themselves like Easter eggs. Extremely muscular Easter eggs.

They must take their security here at Hunts School serious, Tal decided. Serious and freaky. And blue. Those guys' training program has to include steroids. Human beings can't physically get that big by pumping iron. As the students walked by, the guards stood mute and immobile, massive well-defined deltoid to massive well-defined deltoid. At least they stood still until Tal walked by. He could swear there was the tiniest flinch by one, and that another looked a little surprised. Must be my imagination, he thought as he stepped across the brightly lit threshold—and smack into a hillock-sized wall of flesh.

"Hi. I'm Borras." Dinner roll sized incisors gleamed as an earnest grin blossomed across the broken landscape of the giant's face.

"Nice to meet you, uh, Borras," Tal replied. Dang, he must be well over seven foot tall by three wide. It's like meeting three new people at the same time.

"I've met pretty much everybody at school," Borras said, looking him up and down. "I don't think I've ever seen you before."

"Uh, this is my first day." First and last, Tal thought, but I might as well find out if he has a working cellphone, or even better, maybe he has a car and will give me a lift back to Nemeton.

The large land mass of a person gave him a long, appraising look.

"I don't always look like this," Tal said defensively. "I tried to dust myself off a little."

Borras's attention was clearly on something else. "So…what you're saying is that you are a new underclassman?" he asked Tal hesitantly.

Stranger and stranger, Tal thought, as he was jostled by one of the dozens of students moving apace through the hallway. "Nope. I'm a Senior," he responded. When the giant looked sideways at him he continued, "Senior. As in, senior year. You know, the last one before you graduate?"

Borras let out a low whistle. "This is the Tyrning year. The Hunts Rules clearly prohibit any student substitutions who might be contestants after the fiftieth year, with 'limited exceptions.' " He walked around Tal, checking him out a little more thoroughly. "To the best of my knowledge, in the history of Hunts School there's never actually been a 'limited exception.' " Borras paused for a second before continuing, "Oh well, 'Seek the Center'. That's supposed to be our ultimate goal. Give it up. I know it's not Omada, so which group are you joining?"

Several thoughts flashed through Tal's brain: Fiftieth Year? Group? What is he talking about? "Umm, as far as groups, I'll go with…the Honor Society?" You're screwed bucko, he told himself. Nobody is letting this whack job have a cellphone, much less a car. No way.

Borras's oversized mouth turned downward into a thinking frown. "Honor Society? There's no Honor Society in the remaining nine squads. Pretty sure there wasn't one in the original three hundred sixty Hunts qualifying teams."

Tal couldn't even think of how to fashion a reply. So he just stood there.

"No offense new guy, but mouthbreather really isn't a good look on you," Borras said laughing.

"So I've been told," Tal replied, before firmly closing his mouth, and attempting to wipe a little more dirt off his shirt.

"Come on, which team? There's no need to be secretive. We'll all be finding out in Orientation in about eighteen minutes. Which group?"

Tal remained as confused as moments before. "I guess I don't have a group."

The outsides of the giant's eyebrows arched upwards while the insides scrunched down. He paused for a moment, absent-mindedly rubbing his chin with his left hand. "You're saying you have been admitted to Hunts School during a Tyrning year, and you are not bound to a team?"

Clueless, Tal simply shook his head.

Borras stood there staring at Tal for another few seconds, and then apparently reached some decision. "Omada is at four, one member below full complement. It has been millennia since a four-person team won the Tyrning. I'll take a chance on you. If nothing else, it's a good defensive strategy. If I don't grab you some other team may get the new weapon."

"The new weapon?"

"You. You must have some serious magyk to be admitted during the Tyrning year." The giant evidently saw Tal's befuddlement. "Right, you just got here so you wouldn't know about the opening. The Hunt last year was the most brutal in the history of the school. Our folks weren't ready emotionally to deal with it last year, after what happened to Kentro…well, after what happened. Anyway, there's no need to go into that now. The Hunts Rules say we have until the start of the first Journey to pick a replacement for our roster spot."

What are the Hunts Rules, Tal wondered. Who is Kentro, and why did he get expelled from school?

"So what do you say, new guy? Bind the contract?" Borras asked, extending his ham-sized nutmeg colored right hand.

"Bind the contract," Tal thought. I've heard that recently. "I don't know Borras. I mean I really appreciate the offer and everything, but we just met, and I'm not even sure where I am. Or why I'm here."

"I get it," Borras replied. "You want to weigh your options. That's fair. We both know it's the single most important decision you'll ever make. Kind of a hard decision to make on the spur of the moment."

Okay, Tal thought, I take school way more seriously than most anybody I've ever met, but that's ridiculous. The "single most important decision," I'll ever make?

"Normal procedure is team vote, but after we lost Kentro, I became the Acting Prime Direction. The Hunts Rules say Primes can make emergency personnel decisions. Since you are unprecedented—unquantified—and unbound, I am declaring an emergency. There's clearly a reason you're here."

"How do you know that?"

"Because Hunts School has been in existence for thousands of years, and you are the first 'limited exception' ever."

Thousands of years? And how do you "lose" a teammate, Tal wondered.

"The Prime is permitted to make command decisions, including a state of emergency declaration, so I have the authority to bind you. I guess. We're about to find out, aren't we?" Borras's arm, which looked like the arm of a construction crane, extended toward Tal. "So what do you say—bind the contract?"

Where am I, Tal asked himself. I walked into that Ladies' Room, and it's like I landed on an alien planet. I attend Nemeton High, not Hunts School. I have no idea where I am, or how to get home. Yet here I am, talking to an extremely pleasant—and very large—lunatic about binding some contract. Tal reminded himself that every time they'd moved throughout the years he'd prayed for his family to land someplace where he could fit in. A place where he could make the kind of friends you keep for a lifetime. He decided that if he'd wanted the new friends to also be sane, he should have prayed with more specificity. "Oh well, it's not like it's a life and death decision," Tal replied.

"Not always," Borras replied. "Will you bind the contract?"

Tal remembered where he'd heard the phrase. Gas Pump No. Duo told him to bind the contract. Am I really going to do what a gas pump told me to do? Tal decided when he got home tonight, he would pray much much more specifically.

What the hell, he decided. "Yes. I'll bind the contract," Tal said, sticking out his hand. It was quickly enveloped by Borras's massive paw in what Tal fervently hoped was some bizarre ritualistic South Arkansas handshake. Because it was either that or he and Borras were now going steady. "Did it work?"

"That remains to be seen. Okay, let's talk about your name. Of course you'll be Quint."

Tal laughed. "Right. I have a name Borras, it's Tal."

Borras looked puzzled. "I know of no language in which Tal means 'five.'"

Now it was Tal's turn to be lost. "Why would it have to mean five? It's my name, Tal is short for…"

In less than a heartbeat Borras had clamped his left hand firmly over Tal's mouth, and effortlessly lifted Tal over his head with his right arm, carrying him to a little alcove off to the left side of the crowded hallway. The whole time, Borras's head swiveled rapidly, looking first one way, and then back the other, scanning, looking to see if anyone else had been paying attention to their conversation. After satisfying himself they hadn't, Borras put his boulder-sized face scant inches from Tal's. In a whisper that sounded way more serious than if he'd been yelling, he said, "What are you, a Dunser or something? I don't know why the geas doesn't prevent you from saying it, but regardless, didn't your parents tell you NEVER, NEVER tell anybody at this school your psuche name? That includes even me, and the other members of the Omada."

Tal knew it. He knew it was too good to be true. The gas station, this building. He didn't know how they'd done it, but this entire thing was some type of elaborate setup by Barton Sellars and his crew. Even the whole "bind the contract" nonsense. Borras isn't crazy, he's just jerking the new kid around. "Okay, I get it Borras," he said angrily. "This is probably your version of a snipe hunt, but I'll bite. Why shouldn't I tell anybody my sushi name?"

Borras's surprise stretched all the way to the farthest outposts of his face. He then began speaking slowly as if Tal's command of the English language wasn't so good, "It is best you not speak of the Snype Hunt with disrespect. Hundreds of teams lost comrades. It was the biggest bloodbath in Hunts School history. And it's pronounced 'psoo-khay' name. No one at this school may know your psuche name because then they might be able to figure out who you are, what you are, and gain power over you, and through you, your group…"

Borras stopped abruptly, and started smiling. "Okay good one, you had me going Like anybody in all of the Folk Realms wouldn't know what a psuche name is. You are quite the jokester, Quint."

"I'm not kidding Borras," Tal replied. "I don't have a clue what you're talking about." "Folk Realms," must be some new video game, Tal decided.

Borras hesitated a moment, but finally realized Tal wasn't joking. "Wow, we read about Folk like you in ninety-seventh year Folk Civilizations. You're a feral Phrygian, aren't you? That's why you qualify as a limited exception. There's never been one of your people at the Tyrning Hunts. You were sent away at birth to be raised by she-wolves, weren't you? You don't have fleas do you?"

"No, I don't," Tal replied, deciding the conversation really couldn't get much weirder. "I was raised by my mom and stepfather, who are not wolves. As far as my name, I'll keep it, thank you. It's Tal…"

"Sshh!" Borras interrupted. Several other students stopped their conversations to see what was going on. Borras began again, this time back to the fierce whisper, "Until the Hunts are concluded, you must never tell anyone your psuche name. Me included."

And so it goes, Tal thought. Always the square peg in a round hole, never quite fitting in. Even at this freak show, I'm the odd man out. The twins don't care about moving all the time. They're only in the first grade, and it doesn't matter where we move, their best friend always moves with them. "The only name I have is the name my Mom put on my birth certificate."

"Birth certificate?" Borras asked, the color fleeing from his face.

Yes sir, the boy's friendly, Tal thought, but he's a few clowns short of a circus. "Yep. So exactly how does one go about getting a bazooka name?"

"Psoo-khay name. During their Naming Ceremony each Folk child selects which Avatar of Legend they will be. Then if you are chosen to compete during the Tyrning Hunts, and your team wins, your team becomes those Avatars and they rise to prominence again for that Tyrning." Borras stopped and stared intently at his new friend. "You really don't know any of this, do you?" Borras asked.

"Don't have the vaguest idea what you're talking about," Tal replied.

"And you aren't a feral Phrygian, are you?"

"Nope, not even close. I got my first name, and I got my family name. That's it."

"A family name? I need to ask you something. You're probably going to think I'm crazy—"

Too late for that, Tal thought.

"And I'm really not trying to offend you," Borras continued. "Are you absolutely sure you're supposed to be here?"

"The Air Hose, a note stuck to the Service Bay door, and both Gas Pump Nos. Unus and Duo told me I was supposed to come here. I could see maybe one gas pump being wrong, but two? There's simply no way."

"What are you talking about?" Borras asked.

"The Gas Station. You know. Back across the front yard." Tal could see it wasn't registering. "Sol Oil. You have to go into the Ladies' Room to get here?"

As other students continued to move around them Borras became as still as stone. "Are you saying you came through the Crossing?"

"If by the Crossing you mean a boarded up old gas station, yeah. How else do you get here?"

"Students are only permitted to come and go using the Prime Omphalos."

"Well, not me. I used the girls' powder room."

"When you went through this gas station, you had no difficulty seeing the school, or stepping onto the school property?"

"I could have done without the part where the creeps threw me out the back of a moving truck, but otherwise no," Tal said laughing. "What's the matter?"

"Nothing," Borras said, as the frown left his face. "For a minute there—as nuts as it sounds—I thought you might be, well I thought you might be—Munedan." Borras started laughing, "I know, crazy huh?"

Tal instinctively started laughing too. That's twice today I've heard that word used. The smart move here is to play along until I can find out what's going on, he decided. "Munedan? That's whack. You're lucky I don't go get a ladder, and come up there and punch you in your big old already smashed up nose."

"Sorry, I know it's impossible."

"What were you thinking? Me? A Munedan? Here? Never going to happen." Gotta change this subject, Tal decided. "So— my team name?"

"Oh yeah. Hunts Rules specify replacements are assigned numbers. So you're Quint." Seeing that Tal still wasn't up to speed, he added, "Quint. You know—five."

Borras speaks Latin, Tal realized. Quint is five in Latin. Thank goodness. At least I'm not on an alien planet. "Quint it is," he replied, resolving that he needed to get a copy of those Hunts Rules. Stat.

CHAPTER THREE

"Sshh, Tal. There's no need to cry."

"I s-s-saw him, Mommy, I saw him again."

"I've looked in the closet and under the bed three times, sweetie. There's no one else here," Thea said, as she gently ran her fingers through her four-year old's tousled, damp blonde curls. Sweat-fear damp, she thought.

"I told you, he's invisitable unless you look at him sideways."

Tal had been crying so hard he was having trouble getting more than a couple of syllables out at a time. Dieseling, Thea's mom used to call it. "I don't understand, Tal."

"Sideways," the boy repeated, as he turned his head, and cut his eyes far to the right to show her he was looking out of the corner of his eye.

Thea realized her four-year was talking about his peripheral vision. An oddly specific detail for him to remember from a nightmare. "What does he look like?"

"He doesn't look like anything," Tal sniffled. "He don't have no face. He's never had no face."

"It's 'he's never had "a" face,' Tal." She started stroking his back. "You know everyone has a face, sweetie."

Tal shook his head. "Not him. And he says really mean things to me, Mommy."

Thea was indignant. Even if it was only a nightmare beastie, it had no call saying mean things to her precious boy. "What does he say to you?"

"He says I'm nothing. Then he says he's going to steal my face. That somebody gave my face to him. But he don't talk like we talk, he talks inside my head."

Before she could correct his grammar, Thea felt the icicle of a chill begin in her chest, right behind her heart, and work its way all the way up to her head. "Sshh, Tal, everything's going to be okay." She stood up, and smiled to encourage him. "Tell you what I'll do, soldier. I'll make another sweep of your perimeter, and from now on we will always leave your closet door open."

"Always?" he asked.

"Always."

"Always open, and with the light on?" Tal asked.

"Yes. Always open, and with the light on," she added.

"Forever?" Tal asked.

Thea nodded again, before getting down on one knee and looking under his bed. She then crossed the room, opened the closet door, and turned on the light before returning to sit beside her son. "There. It's all clear. Good to go?"

Tal nodded, the last of his tears drying as they inched their way down his chubby cheeks. Thea sat there for a couple of more minutes, urging him to lay back down as she resumed rubbing her only child's back.

Even after she was sure he was asleep she sat on his bed, thinking. About the pieces of a jigsaw puzzle that had been doled out one per year for the last three years, and the many pieces still missing. This had happened—well, something had happened—every year on Tal's birthday, she thought, as she continued to massage his back. Even though Tal hadn't been able to explain it in detail verbally the previous years, he'd woken up screaming from an epic nightmare on his birthday every year. It happened at almost the same time each year, right around midnight on the

22

birthday itself. She'd even had to let him sleep in her bed before he could go back to sleep. In previous years, there had only been garbled syllables of the story she'd just heard. She'd gleaned from his hoarse screaming that it involved some faceless specter coming and going from the closet, and hiding under his bed. At first she'd written it off as a basic childhood fear of the dark. Tal was a bright, inquisitive child, with an imagination that pretty much remained locked in hyperdrive. It made sense his subconscious was as active as his waking mind. But he'd never before said the thing had spoken to him. Inside his head— telepathically. About stealing his face.

Thea continued to turn the pieces in her mind, trying to find the sides that made sense logically, turning the corners trying to find the pattern. I need more information, she concluded, I need some additional pieces to figure this out. One thing is clear—we can't stay here any longer. It knows where to find him. They would have to abandon the only home Tal had ever known. Some unnatural thing was stalking her child, and they needed to disappear. After I make that happen, I can start researching, trying to find enough puzzle pieces to figure out how to protect him. Nothing was more important to her than protecting Tal. Not this house, nor her job at the hospital. She was the only protector he had, and she wasn't going to let him down. She started making a mental checklist. Contact Angie in the morning and let her know they'd be out of the house by the end of next month. That would give her another paycheck to cash, and sufficient time to give the hospital well more than two weeks notice. Money was going to be a huge problem, they'd barely been getting by as it was. She'd find a way for the two of them to make do. She always had.

Thea surveyed Tal's room, only so much would fit in her small Toyota wagon, so they wouldn't be able to take their furniture, and most of their other stuff wouldn't fit either. Just as well. Since she was clueless as to the nature of the thing haunting Tal, she had to assume it might be like a bloodhound. That it could track them through their belongings. There was nothing in the room they absolutely had to keep, it could all go to the Goodwill. Her eyes stopped on Tal's child-sized guitar leaned up against the far wall. She'd gotten it for him, along with some lessons, on his second birthday. He'd started out merely slapping the strings, but it quickly became apparent he had an aptitude for the instrument. He practiced on it almost every day. His ax, he already called it, after hearing some of the older boys at the guitar store use the term. He even had calluses on his fat little toddler fingers. She would get rid of everything that tied them to this place, except for the guitar. She couldn't do that to him.

She stood slowly, and tiptoed to the bedroom door before stopping and turning around. "Good night, Taliesin," she whispered. "As soon as we get settled someplace safe, I promise I will spend every spare moment studying to figure out what that thing is—and how I can kill it."

CHAPTER FOUR

'You're nothing.'

"That's not true," Tal whispered. He was curled up on his bed, knees pulled into an upright fetal position. Although his head was turned toward the window, his eyes were cut sideways. Toward the open closet door. At the faceless apparition lurking just inside.

'Many times we have had this conversation, Dust Child. Your heart tells you I speak the truth. Your life has no value and no meaning. They are a complete family without you, you're only a complication. No one will miss you if you give up. Just go ahead and say the words. Say, "I'm nothing." '

"No. You're not even real," Tal replied. "Dr. Burton says you are merely a figment of my overactive imagination."

'LIE!' the specter screamed inside Tal's head. 'Reach over to your desk, and get your pocketknife out of your backpack. I'll show you what to do. There's no need to wait another year. Do the world a favor, and I will take your face now.'

"Shut-up!" Tal yelled, shaking his head in an effort to dislodge the voice from within his brain.

'No matter. One year hence is your Day of Choosing. That day your face is mine, as my reward.'

"I'm not worthless. I'm not worthless,..." Tal heard himself repeating hours later, as a claxon began blaring in his head. An insistent, repetitive claxon. Blaring, blaring.

"Of course you're not worthless," Thea said as she gently began shaking her eldest child. "Tal, wake up. Honey, wake up."

"It's not true."

Thea started shaking him a little more urgently. "Wake up, Tal. You need to wake up, now!" She turned her head to the open door. "Pell! Pell, I need you in here, please."

"I'm not..." Tal said, before slowly opening his eyes. "Oh, uh, Mom? Hey. What's up?"

"Not you sleepy head. The alarm has been going off for ten minutes."

"Sorry, I didn't hear it."

"What's happening?" Pell asked as he ran into the bedroom.

Thea markedly cut her eyes over to the open closet door, before turning back to her son. "Tal, did you have your bad dream again?"

"Get real, Mom. I'm way too old to have bad dreams. I stayed up too late reading, that's all."

"Get up and get dressed. We'll meet you downstairs. The twins are already down there ready for school. We'll barely have time for seventeenth birthday pancakes."

"On my way," Tal replied as he scrabbled out of the bed, and headed toward the hall bathroom.

After he heard the bathroom door click locked, Pell turned to his wife. "Well?"

Thea nodded in response.

"Are you sure?"

"His sheets are sopping wet."

"You still believe it was that thing?"

"I'm more sure now than ever before."

"How, Thea? How? We did everything that freaky mystic legends website said to do. We left everything behind.

Everything. Our clothes, our dishes. We sold the car, everything. We brought nothing with us."

"I don't know how, Pell, but it's followed us here." She bent forward, burying her face in her hands. "I know it took forever to get the new job, but I'm sorry, we have to do it. We have to leave everything. Again."

Pell walked to the bed, and held his hand out to her. As she took it he pulled her up from the bed, and wrapped his arms around her, breathing her into himself.

"I am so afraid for him, Pell. Every birthday for seventeen years. He's eighteen next year. The age of majority is a common theme in all of the literature, it's always a critical juncture."

"The 'Day of Choosing,' you said it was called."

"Yes," she replied, starting to shake in his arms. "I'm so scared, I…" Thea couldn't even finish her sentence, her words dissolved into tears.

Pell wrapped his arms around her even more tightly, and whispered in her ear. "It'll be okay, Thea. He's going to be okay."

CHAPTER FIVE

So far, so good, Tal thought, as he stood in the hallway working his way through the unfamiliar combination for his hall locker. He got it open on the second try, and stood there a moment deciding which books he needed to take with him for homework. Calc for sure. Math was one of his strengths, so he was good with his class schedule starting off each day with Calculus. The intro this morning had covered known territory so he'd been able to add to the class discussion on the formula for angles of inclination, without appearing to be a know-it-all. And, he reminded himself as he shut the locker and spun the lock, the hot redhead across the room had noticed he could hold his own on the math front. So, from his ectomorphic semi-geekish perspective, things were looking up. For a change. Finally.

"Uhhh!" Tal grunted, spittle spraying, as the right side of his face got slammed sideways into the battleship gray locker.

"Welcome to Nemeton High, Loser." Both the greeting—and the full body locker slam—were courtesy of the Barton Russell Sellars, IV gang. It hadn't taken Tal but a couple of classes this morning to hear about Barton. The school's alpha male, economically and anthropologically. Based upon Tal's prior school experiences he'd been expecting some type of intimidation encounter with Barton. Sooner rather than later, based on his substantial experience in being bullied. Tal felt like he'd experienced every permutation of bullying at some time in his life. Sometimes the confrontation was purely verbal, but more often than not there was some type of physical beat down as well. Tal knew better than to try to resist, it simply provided ramp up friction for the bullies. He had promised himself that if the Nemeton High iteration involved a beating that Barton wouldn't get any reaction out of him. That promise was made prior to Barton lifting Tal off his feet, and throwing him against the hall locker so viciously it knocked the breath out of him.

Barton spun Tal around, and arm-barred him against the locker, using his forearm to press deep into Tal's throat. Tal could feel his face swelling as the blood being pumped into his cranium couldn't escape to recirculate. "So, Unwanted New Person. I like to read, I'm sure you do too," Barton said casually, his high-pitched voice whistling a little. "I've read dozens of medical treatises on the phenomenon of bullying. In some cases, it's a result of abusive parents. Often, the bully is a low-functioning individual, or has deep-seated insecurities." Barton paused to press his arm harder into Tal's windpipe. Tal was now having difficulty even drawing shallow breaths. "Not me, Loser. My parents love me, and my family owns this town and everyone in it. I have the second highest grade point at this school, and any chick I want is happy to do me. I think you'll find that I'm chock-full of fucking self-esteem."

Wonder how come he hasn't offed Number One, Tal thought, as he heard, as if from a distance, little gurgling sounds coming from his own mouth.

"Simple truth, Loser, is that I hit others because I get off on it."

Great, Tal thought, the head dick at this school is an honest to goodness teenage psychopath. Actually, he might be a sociopath. A sociopathic salutatorian, what are the odds of that? Nice alliteration, Tal. Why am I even having this discussion with myself when I'll be blacking out in about twenty-five seconds? Twenty-four...twenty-three...

Gunnar Haslip, Barton's first lieutenant, chimed in. "There's only one rule you need to remember—Barton runs this school." He paused a moment, before adding, "Also, you have to do whatever Barton says."

That's two rules, Tal thought. Clearly math is not Gunnar's strong suit. He decided to keep his mouth shut, particularly since his face felt like a tick about ready to pop. His tongue was swelling, filling the inside of his mouth. Unconsciousness was on the imminent event horizon. And statistically, death—which of course meant shitting his pants— was approximately thirty seconds behind. Nine...eight...

The third member of the triumvirate, Fail McDermott, took his turn. "And don't be answering no more questions like in class today. We don't need some new stupid dipshit Mr. Wizard smartass asshole showin' our asses up our stupid senior year. Making us look all like stupid ass dumbasses, and everything like that."

Three...two...

Suddenly Barton stepped away from Tal, who promptly fell on the floor—limbs akimbo—gasping for air. As his eyes began to focus, Tal watched as the trio strutted off down the hallway. He wondered if it was a basic rule of bullying that every bully group had to have at least one numbnuts galoot. Fail McDermott certainly occupied that position here at Nemeton High. What kind of person is so proud of flunking out of their first attempt at being a high school senior that they make it their nickname?

Oh well, I survived the first day, Tal thought. It's gotta get better from here on, right?

"Chicken pot-pie and green bean casserole," Pell said as he pushed himself back from the dining room table. "Good work Thea, that's two of the three major food groups."

"And there's karo nut pie for dessert."

Pell promptly scooted back up to the table. "A hat trick, then. Dinner was great, thank you."

"You're welcome," Thea replied, as she sliced and plated the pie. "I thought we'd celebrate, it being a first day for all four of my guys. Pell, you go first. How was work?"

"Everyone seemed real glad to have me on-board, and I'll be the only chemical engineer at the plant. Little early to know for sure, but we may have finally found a home."

Thea went next, while she methodically slid the pie plates around the table. "I like the elementary school. I met a couple of moms with children the twins' age, and they said they'd introduce me around. Principal Davis said she thinks she might have a part-time spot for me as the school nurse."

Pell swallowed his mouthful of pie before responding. "Sounds like a good start for everyone."

"Tal?" Thea asked.

"Yes, Mom?"

"You're awfully quiet."

"Just tired I guess."

"Tell us about your day."

"You know, it was school. No big deal."

"No big deal?" Pell asked. "From the kid who loves school more than any other kid in the history of the world? Is there something we need to talk about Champ?"

"No, I'm good," Tal replied. "May I be excused from the table? I have some homework to finish."

"Sure, son," Pell replied. "See you in the morning."

After watching her eldest son slowly walk up the stairs, Thea turned back to her husband. "Karo nut is his favorite. He barely picked at the crust."

"He'll adapt Thea, he always does."

"I know. It's just we have each other, and so do the twins. Every time we move he seems to be more alone, more unwilling to even try to make new friends."

"It's been hard on all of us, Thea. His birthday's next week. Maybe this year we will be able to celebrate the end of his nightmares."

When Tal got to the bathroom he made sure the door was locked before carefully pulling his t-shirt off, and looking at his back in the mirror. Well, it's got all of your basic bruise components. Couple of different shades of purple, a light green, and the mandatory jaundice yellow. It's kind of shaped like Australia. Great, only six more continents of bruises to go, and I'll have a complete set.

I can't tell Mom and Pell, he decided. Pell caught a break getting that random headhunter call about the chemical engineer opening, and I've seen the name "Sellars" on at least half the buildings in town. Including the chemical plant.

Keep your mouth shut and gut this year out, he told himself for the umpteenth time. Early admittance scholarship decisions are made based primarily on test scores and grades through junior year. Both my ACT and SAT scores are off the chain. All I have to do is maintain my GPA for the fall semester, and I'll have my pick of full-rides. And my pick will be some place where studying hard and learning matters. Some place far, far away from Barton Sellars, and all the Barton-Sellars-like haters. Some place where the Faceless Spook will never think to look for me.

CHAPTER SIX

"We left a present in your locker to celebrate your second day, Loser. We like to think of ourselves as an alternative kind of Welcome Wagon." Tal could already detect a pattern in the Sellars' gang's cadence. Barton started. Gunnar was next. Then came Fail, although Tal presumed that Fail didn't always get a turn. Maybe he's more of a mook than a galoot, Tal thought.

Gunnar chimed in on cue. "Yeah. Packed a late lunch for ya. Couple of day old road-kills in your backpack. Mighty thoughtful of Barton don't you think?"

"It ought to set up real nice by the time school's out," Barton added chuckling.

So Fail didn't get a turn this conversation, Tal thought.

Barton concluded the morning lecture. "Don't even think about touching it until then, Loser. Got it?"

"Tal, what happened to your backpack? It smells awful."

"Um, yeah, sorry about that Mom. I must have spilled some milk in there yesterday and didn't realize it until this afternoon."

"I'll try to wash it out, but you're going to have to be more careful. Your new jeans, the shoes, everything—they're all going to have to last for awhile until we get back on our feet again. The move has us a little strapped."

"I understand."

CHAPTER SEVEN

"I'm going outside to shoot some hoops with the twins for a few minutes before I take them to school. Come on, we'll play some two on two."

"Thanks Pell, but Mom's going to run me over to school early," Tal replied. "I need to study for a math test."

"Maybe after school, then."

"Sure."

The crew was waiting for him when he walked in the front door.

"Ready for the math test, Loser?"

As Tal expected, Gunnar got to go second. "I bet you got here early to study. Didn't you?"

Tal remained silent.

"Well, we can't have that," Fail said. "Barton says today you have to miss every other question."

Well at least Fail got a turn today, Tal thought. Focus Tal, they're messing with your plan for the rest of your life, and you're worried about gang patterns and sequences.

"We'll know if you don't follow instructions. Barton helps Ms. Johnson grade all of the tests."

Gunnar got an eat shit look from Barton. Because it wasn't his turn to speak, Tal realized, as the pack sauntered off. I have to figure out some way to neutralize their interference. I can't let them crater my grades this term, or I'm screwed.

CHAPTER EIGHT

"Here's your lunch, Tal. I made your favorite."

"Two peanut butter and jelly sandwiches?"

"A three-course meal, actually," she said smiling. "Two PB&Js with the crusts cut off, a bag of fritos, and an apple."

Tal took the sack and put it in his backpack. "Mom?"

"Yes?"

"You know I love you, right?"

"I know that, sweetie."

"Would it hurt your feelings terribly if I asked you to quit drawing a smiley face on my lunch sacks?"

"No, son," Thea replied smiling, as Tal grabbed his lunch sack and headed out the door. As she cleaned up the kitchen from the morning's onslaught, she mused about how all boy-Moms must have similar experiences—moments when sons shatter their Mom's hearts into a million sad shards, while at the same time swelling that same heart until it almost bursts with pride. And then she switched focus, and started thinking about what other protective wards she'd read about that she might hide in a drawing on his lunch sack every school day to keep him safe from unnatural terrors.

"Scoot over, Loser."

Tal had hoped the cafeteria was neutral territory—his hope had been misplaced. He moved over to allow Barton space to sit.

"We've decided that in the four days you've been at Nemeton, you've gotten a little chunky. Barton has decided to put you on a diet." It was clear Gunnar had been reprimanded for yesterday's violation of the bullyfication pecking order.

"Yeah, so hand it over," Fail said, grabbing Tal's lunch sack and handing it to Barton. Fail is on a roll, Tal thought, that's two days in a row they've let him speak. "Look, Barton, there's even a happy face on the bag."

Barton rummaged around in the bag, and then handed it to Fail. "Throw this crap in the trash. Except for the apple. I'm sure Ms. Hopkins is going to enjoy the shiny red apple. Apparently, I brought it from home especially for my favorite teacher."

CHAPTER NINE

"Everything all right in here, Barton?"

"Sure, Coach. We're giving the new kid some tips to help him out. Wouldn't want him to get hurt out there."

"Thoughtful, Sellars, but you ladies can have book club on your own time. This is my time. Now, hurry up and get changed. We're scrimmaging today."

"Gotcha, be right out." Barton watched to make sure Coach Ross left the locker room, before turning back to Tal. "So here's what you'll be doing today, Loser. Every time I get the ball, I'm driving the lane. Every time I drive the lane, you're going to try to take a charge. And every time you try to take a charge, I am going to knock you flat on your bony ass. Got that? What's the matter Mr. All High and Smarty, cat got your tongue?"

Tal did nothing, said nothing.

"Good. I see what we have here is not a failure to not communicate. Smart boy, you're learning."

"I'm calling the Principal tomorrow, Pell."

"Tomorrow's Saturday and you can't do that to Tal."

"You saw him when he got home. He could barely walk up and down the stairs."

"It'll embarrass the hell out of him if you Mother Hen him. He's going to be eighteen next week."

"Pell, something's going on at that school."

"I agree, Thea. But you don't think it has anything to do with the...well, you know, with the other?"

"There's no way I can know for sure, but no. Not during daylight hours. Unless I missed something."

"Sweetie, you've done everything humanly possible to research the thing," Pell said as he leaned back into his easy chair. "As I recall, the first time I ever saw your exceptionally fine ass you were at a Starbucks slamming a latte. Tal was out cold in your lap, and you were using the free internet for some late night research."

Thea smiled wanly. "It was a non-fat latte, and I will thank you appropriately for the ass compliment when I have a little more energy."

Pell laughed. "Did you just give me a booty rain check?"

"Yes, I did," she replied. "It's been going on forever Pell, and I'm tired. Early on, it was every waking moment I wasn't at work or taking care of Tal. Mother's Days Out, vacation days, all of it spent either online or actually at a library looking at some of the older texts that hadn't been placed online yet. I was pretty much one of the walking dead when you walked in for coffee that night."

"Pretty much one of the walking dead—with an exceptionally fine ass."

Thea laughed. "Ease up tiger, you already have your rain check."

Pell paused for a moment before continuing. "You don't think it has anything to do with Tal's father do you?"

Thea stood, and walked over behind her husband's chair, leaning over to wrap her arms around his neck. "I love you, Pell. There is no finer man on this planet, and I couldn't be any more crazy about you. I told you the first time you inquired about Tal's father the subject was off-limits, and we would never ever speak of it."

He turned his head sideways a little so he could look back over his shoulder at her. "I've always kept my end of that deal, and I intend to keep on keeping it. I'm only trying to explore every possibility for ways to help Tal."

Thea walked around in front of him, and motioned for him to move his legs so she could sit in his lap. "I know, and I thank you, but that's a dead end. Okay?"

He nodded his acquiescence.

"I'm really frightened, Pell. I think next week is critical."

"Because of what you found in New York City? The old parchment?"

"Yes. Actually, it was vellum—which helped to date the writing."

"Didn't you think it a little odd you couldn't find any of that same information on the internet?"

"Yes."

"Or that there was a yellowed business card in the exact spot on the shelf where a small town New England library card catalog said there was supposed to be a book about arcane creatures?"

"Yes, Pell. Of course I did. I found it all incredibly odd. And, well, contrived. What was I supposed to do? Ignore the only lead I'd ever found after years of searching?"

In response, he simply stroked her hair, then ran the back of his hand softly down her jaw line.

As she relaxed into the strength of his caress, Thea found now that she'd started the old story, she was unable to stop in the middle. She'd told Pell the entire tale, word for word, many times but it comforted her this evening to go back through it again. "That card was lying there all by itself on the shelf. There's no telling how long it had been there. It wasn't merely yellow with age, I think it must have been made out of vellum as well."

Sucked back into the story, Pell wanted to help in the retelling. "When you picked it up and looked at it, the card was blank," he said, as he gently stroked her cheek.

She nodded.

"This is my favorite part of the whole story." Pell saw her puzzled look. "Oh, all the rest of it is a fantastical tale, mind you, but this part—this is the heart of the matter. Where True Love never quits. It finds a way over, or around, or through any obstacle. It never stops seeking fulfillment, and always finds its way. The part where True Love never doubts its own existence— not even for a second—will always be the best part of any story, as far as I'm concerned, Thea. Always."

She paused and kissed the back of his hand, whispering "I love you, Pell," before resuming the tale. "Blank. I know the card was blank when I first picked it up. I looked at both sides any number of times. I got on my tiptoes and looked on the rest of the shelf to see if there were any more pieces of paper. There weren't. I blew the dust off the card. I cleaned it using my sweater sleeve. Blank—whatever it was made of—it was blank. I remembered leaning up against the shelving, exhausted. Done in, I think is more appropriate. I'd pulled a double-shift at the hospital, Tal was sleeping when I got off duty so I'd left him with Ellen at the twenty-four hour daycare. I went to the grocery store and only bought half of what we'd needed, because that took most everything I had in my account until I got paid again. And I needed the rest of my cash for gas. I never used credit cards or bank accounts because they were traceable. Yeah, done in is what I was."

"Your nadir," Pell added. "You had reached your personal nadir."

Thea smiled at him. "Yes, Mr. Vocabulary, I'd reached my personal nadir. Maybe even a half a step lower, if possible."

"It's not," he said softly, "but go on."

"I collapsed against the shelving and ended up on the ground, sobbing. Really heaving, and sobbing. It'd been just Tal and me for years. I never got to make any friends, he never got to make any either."

"Because you were always moving," Pell interjected.

"It wasn't only that. It was partly because I always knew we would be moving soon. But it was also because I suspected anyone—everyone, actually—as possibly being hooked up with our enemy. I sat there on the floor in the back of that old dusty library, praying—eyes squeezed hard shut praying—to anyone or anything who might be listening, to please help me take care of Tal, to keep him safe. When I finally caught my breath, and opened my eyes, I noticed I still had the card clenched in my fist. It was damp all over from where I'd cried on it."

"And it was no longer blank…"

"No, it wasn't. On one side, written in flowery purplish-ink letters, were the words, "M. Ryss." On the other side, in the same flowing script was, "HC SVNT DRACONES—Royal Stationers & Cartographers, 777 Shamb Hala Court, New York City."

"Here Be Dragons," Pell added.

"Right. Of course, I didn't know the Latin until I looked it up later that day."

"One of those stray factoids I picked up in World History," Pell said. "They used to put it on the edges of maps. Any area that was unknown, or unexplored, was potentially the home of dragons. And giants. And any number of other terrible dark things." Pell looked at his wife with a wry smile, "I think one only has to travel a few inches inward to find such a place—in every human heart."

In his lap, Thea was completely motionless for at least a five-count. "Strong, handsome, and this evening, you're also Erato's mouthpiece. Doesn't get much hotter than that Pelleas Smith."

"Thanks, Gorgeous. Finish the story. I always hope maybe there's some detail we've missed before."

"Right. Okay, the writing faded away, as quickly as it had appeared. I wrote it down on the palm of my hand to make sure I didn't forget it. As soon as I got home, I went back to sleuthing, trying to find even a single reference to a business by that name or anything similar. I googled every version of "M. Ryss," I could think of, thinking I might could scare up a telephone listing, but again—nothing. I bought a couple of New York City maps, one showing streets and the other mass transit information. Still nothing. I realize that in a pretty short period of time we've come to believe the internet is the fount of all wisdom, and that that's not necessarily so, but Pell, it was like any reference to that information or that individual had been scrubbed."

"Or had never existed," Pell added.

"I almost gave in to that conclusion several times, except I was holding a really old blank business card in my hand. It didn't look or feel like some type of prank. So I kept at it. I was chasing stray threads down the online rabbit hole late one night and somehow ended up on a blog about the history of the New York subway and elevated train systems, and boom. There it was in a video about the Suicide Curve of the Manhattan Railway Company's Ninth Street El. A video shot by none other than Thomas Edison himself."

"And on the wall of a building was a painted advertisement for 'Allcock's Porous Plasters.' " Pell enjoyed the story so much, he couldn't stop himself from chiming in.

"Yep, and all the way down to the bottom right-hand corner of that ad was an arrow pointing downward that said…"

"HC SVNT DRACONES—Royal Stationers & Cartographers. M. Ryss, Proprietor."

"You got it," Thea added.

"I forgot, what year was the Edison video shot?"

"The YouTube upload said it was dated, '1899.' "

"Right. More than a century ago."

"I get it, Pell, I do, but there were several plausible explanations. The business card itself was obviously older than the video. The library was several hundred years old itself, and the card could have been sitting at the library for decades. Also, for all I knew, 'M. Ryss,' might have been a family name. He could have been 'M. Ryss' the fourth, or fifth."

"I remember the next part from the very first time we discussed it," Pell said. "I never knew at one place on its route that the New York City elevated train was almost a hundred feet above the ground."

"I was surprised too," Thea said. "The Ninth Street El was about that high when it reached 110th Street. Because of the escarpment in what is now Morningside Park, they engineered the track to take a hard curve at 110th Street to take it up Eighth Avenue. I watched the video repeatedly until I figured out the sign was on the side of a building facing the park. New York was only a hard day's drive from where Tal and I were living, so I scheduled myself to work four doubles, with three straight days off, so Tal and I could have the time and the money to take the road trip. When we got to the city, I didn't have any trouble getting to 110th Street and Ninth Avenue. But there were tall buildings on several sides, facing the park. And no sign of a street named 'Shamb Hala Court.' "

"Because there wasn't one," Pell added.

"Because there wasn't one," Thea repeated in agreement. "Tal and I had about walked our legs off, canvassing the same couple of blocks for hours, when I saw a discrete little name plaque on an old red brick building."

"You couldn't find it because 'Court,' didn't mean court, like a short street. It was used in a different context," Pell said. "Like a large mansion, or a palace or something."

"Exactly," Thea replied. "That red brick building was 777 Shamb Hala Court."

"We've looked at the map and at satellite images a zillion times since you and I first hooked up. There are high rises in that area, and there's Morningside Park. There is no small building anywhere around there."

"I know that, Pell. My brain acknowledges there's presently no such place as 777 Shamb Hala Court. But I'm telling you on that day, when I went looking for it, when Tal and I needed it to be there, there was a place called 777 Shamb Hala Court, in New York City."

"I believe you, Thea," Pell replied softly. "I have always believed in you."

Thea again paused to smile at her husband, before continuing. "The building really wasn't much, it's no wonder I didn't see it the first few times I walked past it. It's hard to describe its appearance."

"Seedy?" Pell asked.

"No, definitely not that. More like a nice Sunday go to meeting dress that has seen better times. Still classy, but…"

"Tuckered out?"

"That's it. You could tell by looking at the building that it was hundreds of years older than the business card."

"We've talked about this part, Thea. It doesn't work historically. Henry Hudson didn't sail up the river until the early 1600s, and that was all the way down at the far end of Manhattan. There couldn't have been any European buildings in that part of New York City until well after then."

"I'm telling you the building's aura, or whatever you want to call it, was…ancient."

"I know, it's one of many anachronistic details in the story."

"I took Tal's hand and we walked up the steps to the front door. There wasn't a doorbell, but there was an oversized brass doorknocker shaped like a compass. It was an odd sort of compass, though. In addition to the four cardinal directions, it also had an arrow angled diagonally to point inward toward the door."

"Toward the center."

"Right. That's the part that actually contacted the door when I used the knocker. There was no response," Thea said, almost to herself, as she continued in the flow of her story. "We waited a couple of minutes. Tal wanted to try so I lifted him up, and he gave it a good swing. Seconds later the front door swung open."

Pell sat silently, drinking in every word, looking for a clue they might have missed during their previous discussions about the odd events of that day.

"The door swung open. It didn't make a sound, didn't even seem to displace the air as it moved. A face appeared. The sweetest, nicest face. Like a super grandpa-archetype type of face."

" 'Beat it! You'll find no public bathrooms here,' the man roar-snarled, in such a menacing tone that Tal immediately broke into tears. As I turned to look down at Tal, I saw the man crank his arm back to shove the door closed. I leapt forward, throwing my right hand through the antique wood doorframe. 'Wait!' I yelled, as the solid three-inch thick mahogany-looking door slammed up against the small bone on the outside of my right wrist. I whimpered as I felt the bone split a little. 'I have something to show you!' "

" 'What?' the man asked as he continued to lean into the other side of the door. 'What, madam? What could you possibly have to show me?' "

"The door had scraped the skin off my forearm pretty good as it tried to close. There was blood—not a river, mind you, but enough to where it scared Tal even more, and his crying became caterwauling. Which combined with the events of the day, made me start crying too. 'I have a stupid blank business card. I found it lying on a library shelf out in the middle of Nowhere.' "

" 'A blank business card, you say?' the man said curtly. 'Well, who wouldn't want to take time out of their busy day to see such a unique thing?' The door began pressing harder against my wrist."

Thea leaned her head back into Pell's shoulder. "I put Tal down on the ground. I was done. That's all there was to it. Beat down. Years of worry, and looking. Finding nothing, and then only some crazy information that made no sense to anybody I had done the absolute best I could do, and that wasn't going to be good enough to protect Tal."

"At that moment, I snapped. 'Listen here, you jackass,' I screamed. 'We've had a really long day getting here to see you. Obviously the card wasn't always blank. It had the words

"M. Ryss," on one side and the address, "777 Shamb Hala Court" and words, "Royal Stationers & Cartographer," on the other side.' "

"There was no immediate verbal response but I felt the pressure on my throbbing wrist ease just a hair."

" 'What else?' came the softly spoken question."

"I was still raging, 'What else, what?' "

" 'What...else...did...the...card...say?' Still whispered, these words were spoken very slowly and distinctly."

"The pain shooting up my arm kept my anger well-fueled, I was making no attempt to be the least bit pleasant. 'It contained the Latin words for the phrase, "here be dragons".' "

"I heard the man inhale deeply, and then the door swung backward. The man stepped out, and gently pried my fingers open, taking the business card from my hand. As I flexed my fingers, trying to get the blood flow going, he stared at the card, flipping the blank card back and forth several times. He then looked down at Tal. 'Stop crying!' He said it gruffly, but less menacingly than his initial tone. Tal stopped. 'How old are you? he demanded.' "

" 'S-s-seven,' came the tremulous response."

"The man continued, his gaze focused totally on Tal. 'The Radiant Brow shall be accompanied by an unrelenting warrior brandishing a hidden truth,' he muttered *sotto voce*. 'Here be dragons.' The man then turned his attention to me. 'Does he play the lute?' "

"The what?"

"Are you daft, woman? The lute. A stringed instrument."

"Oh, right, that lute. No, but he plays the guitar."

" 'A stringed instrument,' the man said to himself. 'And he sings?' "

" 'Like an angel,' I replied proudly."

" 'Hold this,' he demanded, as he extended the card to Tal, who promptly took hold of it in his little hand. 'Lick it.' Tal did so. 'Both sides,' he demanded. 'Hurry, now, give it back to me.' Tal again did as he was told. The man repeated his earlier action of rapidly flipping the card back and forth. When he was done with that, he looked down his long, bony nose at Tal. 'What name go you by?' the man asked."

"Tal had finally stopped crying, and after a couple of left over sniffs, his manners training kicked in, and he stuck out his hand in introduction. 'Pleased to meet you, sir. My name is Taliesin Sm…' "

Thea again stepped out of her narrative for a moment. "I'm telling you, Pell, it was the damnedest thing. Before Tal could even finish saying his last name, that frail old geezer leapt half a dozen feet out of the doorway onto the stoop, grabbed Tal up with one arm, threw his other arm around my shoulders, and suddenly we were all three standing in the foyer with the front door closed and double-locked behind us. I was starting to ask for an explanation, when the guy flourished the business card at me—the words in purple ink now clearly visible on both sides."

" 'I am sorry to have been so abrupt earlier,' he said. 'The eight decades I have stood sentinel have been solitary, and I am afraid there was little call for courtesy.' "

" 'You're him?' I asked. 'You are M. Ryss?' "

"Oh no. The Emrys has not been here at the Court since before my father's father's time."

" 'What?' I asked stunned. 'I don't understand.' "

" 'What is there to understand?' he asked. 'Your son is the Radiant Brow. That is all the explanation necessary. If it is agreeable, I will call you Mother.' "

" 'Okay, I guess,' I replied, still absolutely lost, 'but my name is Th…' "

" 'Sshh!!' he demanded, placing his left index finger hard against my lips. 'Even though the Court has been warded by the Emrys himself, it is prudent to be cautious. There is much power that may be obtained from the knowledge of a true name, Mother. Knowledge of location is one such power. As I was saying, please accept my apologies. Mine is only one of many lifetimes spent keeping watch.' "

"Keeping watch for what?"

"For the smallest possibility you might choose to come."

" If you're not M. Ryss, who are you?' I asked."

"It is not 'M. Ryss,' Mother. It is the Emrys, and I am Keeper."

"Keeper. Is that a family name?"

"No, Mother. It is a title which is used as a name."

" 'Why?' I asked him. I noticed the man appeared confused by the question."

" 'Everyone knows a title provides no potential avenue of power for an adversary,' he replied."

"It was my turn to pause a moment, Pell," Thea said. "Finally I got it, like the answer to the last letter needed to finish a crossword puzzle. So I said, 'A title. You mean, like Mother?' "

" 'Yes. Like Mother,' Keeper affirmed. He then turned and began walking toward the far back left-hand corner of the sizeable foyer and we followed him. As we got closer, I saw there was a downward curving staircase. It, like all of the woodwork in the antechamber, was adorned with free-flowing symbols and glyphs. Without pausing, he turned back toward us. 'If you would learn that which you wish to know, please follow quickly. It is some ways to walk, and now that you have finally come, the Court's time on the Earth plane is limited.' "

"Stop!" Pell exclaimed.

"What is it?"

"You've never said that before—you've never told me Keeper said, 'the Court's time on the Earth plane is limited.' "

"I'm sure I have."

"No. We've talked about the foyer and the circular stairway. How beautiful the dark wood was, and how one symbol seemed to flow into the next in an unbroken pattern. You've even told me that you asked Keeper about one of them…"

"Right. I kept seeing the same glyph repeated all over. It looked exactly like a smiley face. When I pointed it out to Keeper, he told me it was the sigil that protected against internal magical attack, like from poison. I just blew it off at the time as crazy talk. You're sure I never told you the other part?"

"Absolutely."

"Seems strange I'd remember something now I haven't ever remembered before. Nothing's changed."

"Something has changed, Thea. It's been years since we've gone over this, and this time, Tal is about to turn eighteen. Go on with the story, maybe there's something else that will come up."

"Keeper picked up a large flashlight-lantern thingy from a table at the top of the staircase, and we began making our way down. We kept going down, and then down some more. Tal thought it was fun at first, he'd never been on a spiral staircase, then the novelty wore off and he faded on me. There weren't any floors, only the uninterrupted steps of the staircase. After about five minutes, the lights in the foyer had become a single pinpoint above us. Below, the blackness was Stygian. After another few minutes that seemed like hours, we reached a landing. Keeper put his lantern down, leaned over, and it looked like he talked to the wall."

"You mean, it looked like he was talking to himself and leaned over to flip a wall switch?" Pell asked.

"No, Pell, I'm pretty sure there wasn't any switch. It looked like he said something to the wall. Whatever he did, the entire chamber was lit by this diffused light purple glow. It was beautiful. The room was bigger than any room I've ever been in. There were dozens of pure white marble pillars that supported vaulted marble arches soaring all the way to the underside of the main floor. It was like the biggest cathedral you could possibly imagine, except underground. Everywhere I turned there were these long, tall tables; their tops were littered with papers, and scrolls, and oversized folios, and parchments. Dumbstruck. I think that's the best way to describe my reaction."

"Then Keeper said, 'We must hurry, Mother. The Court will soon return to its place in the Wheel.' "

" 'I don't have the faintest idea what you're talking about,' I said."

" 'And we don't have the time for me to explain it,' he replied. 'This way,' he said, motioning to his left. 'Quickly.' "

"I picked Tal up at that point, so we could move a little faster. We zigzagged through a number of aisles created by the tables until we finally came to one that had a long low glass case on it. The corners and seams were made of the same dark wood as the tables, again covered with carved symbols. The sides and top were glass. Inside was a piece of parchment—probably vellum. It was about the width of a letter-sized sheet of paper, but it had to be a foot and a half long. Like a scroll that had been unrolled, except it had no writing on it."

" 'Here,' Keeper said. 'Quickly, now.' "

" 'Here, what?' I asked. 'That paper is blank.' "

"He reached under his shirt and pulled out a leather thong that had a single key strung on it. He inserted the key into the keyhole in the case and the top gracefully swung upward until it was perpendicular. He looked at Tal and me and smiled, before gently closing the case until it clicked. Then Keeper took the thong from around his neck, and handed the key to Tal. He motioned that I should put him down, and I did. He made a turning motion with his wrist, directing Tal to try the key. Tal stepped forward shyly, looking at me for permission. I nodded. He put the key into the keyhole and turned the key. Again, the top swung silently toward the ceiling. I gasped when I looked back down at the parchment. It was now covered, its entire length and breadth, in symbols written in the same purplish ink as the business card."

" 'How?' I asked Keeper, as Tal looked up at me and smiled."

"His mouth barely moved as he faintly whispered, 'He is the Taliesin.' "

" 'He's not "the Taliesin," Keeper,' I replied, whispering because he had. 'That's his name.' "

"Both of our statements are correct, Mother. Your son is unique. In the entirety of Time, for all of the known Realms, he is the only Child of Dust who could choose to become an Avatar."

"I don't have any idea what you're talking about."

"There is no time. Hurry, you must replicate the Message."

"Wouldn't it be easier if you let me borrow it? I promise to take good…"

"The physical document is not here, Mother. It is home in Sandalwood Park."

" 'It's right there,' I replied. 'I'm looking at it.' "

" 'You're looking at a representation in this plane of the parchment which exists in Sandalwood Park in the Shamb Hala Realm,' he said, clearly trying to remain patient with me. 'Everything you see before you—everything except for me—is merely a representation of something on a different plane.' "

" 'I don't know how much more crazy I can handle,' I replied. 'My cellphone. I can take a picture of it with my cellphone?' "

"It would benefit you not. The image would fade when the parchment returns. You must create an independent replication of the Message."

"He so obviously believed in what he was saying, I gave up on arguing further. I reached into my purse, took out a pen and my grocery list notebook, and right below 'head of lettuce,' I started drawing the symbols. It took several hours to finish. Tal had long ago curled up on the musty floor, and Keeper had stood beside me motionless and silent the entire time. 'Done,' I announced."

" 'Good,' he replied. 'The Court began its return a few minutes ago.' "

"And you, Keeper. Do you 'return' as well?"

"He laughed a little. 'No, Mother, ample provisions were made long ago for the Keeper whose duties might end before his Kalachakra had completed its rotation. Amarantos willing, I shall now be able to travel and visit all of the wonderful places of which I have only read and dreamed.' "

"I finally realized what he'd meant by giving me his title when we'd walked through the front door. 'You've never left this building, have you?'"

"Never once in this existence."

"And the Keepers before you?"

"The same. Excepting the first, of course."

"What a terrible thing to do to someone."

"No one did anything to us, Mother. Being Keeper is a great privilege. It has been my honor to serve the UnFading Spirit."

"It was about that time I started feeling a little nauseated. 'I think I may throw up,' I said."

" 'It will pass, it is the merely the translation,' he replied. 'Listen to me, Mother. There are things you must know before we are no longer warded. Your son will not remember this trip. I will not remember meeting you, nor any of my time as Keeper. You, however, as the memories are needed shall ultimately remember all of today's events.' "

"I started to ask what kind of need he was talking about, and got shushed. 'There is no time. If you wish to protect your son, if you wish to protect all of us, he must never know anything about your journey here. You must never divulge to him any information you have obtained from the Message. His decisions must be his, unfettered by foreknowledge or prophesy.' "

"Tal apparently was feeling queasy as well, because he woke up then. 'Mommy, I don't feel so good.' "

"I bent down and picked him up. 'It's okay sweetie, we'll be going home in a few minutes.' I turned to Keeper. 'I'm dreading toting him all the way back up those stairs, but if the place is going to disappear around us I guess we'd better get started.' "

"Keeper leaned forward and placed one hand on my shoulder, and the other on Tal's. 'I can help with that,' he said. 'Both of you, close your eyes.' I watched to make sure Tal obeyed, before I did as well."

" 'Amarantos protect you,' Keeper said."

"I felt his hand lift from my shoulder, and I opened my eyes—to the blinding glare of the afternoon sun. To the sudden sound of taxis honking as they careened past us. To the back of a dignified, grandfatherly individual whistling a happy tune as he walked briskly into Morningside Park, to begin his new life."

"Wow! Just, wow!" was Pell's response.

"I know. Mental, right?"

"Would be a definite yes, if I hadn't seen what happens to Tal every year on his birthday. There were a couple of more things you've never mentioned before, babe."

"I would have bet a hundred dollars it was verbatim."

"I know," Pell replied. "I could see it in your eyes, and your hand movements. The way you told the story. I didn't interrupt you anymore because I thought it might be counterproductive."

"What was new?"

"You've always told me Tal must never know anything about all of this metaphysical whatever it is. But you've never been able to tell me why."

"Really?"

"Yes. You've never previously mentioned the word 'Amarantos,' and you've also never told me the building simply wasn't there anymore."

"I know that can't be true."

"Thea—we took a family trip to New York to try to find the place. You were as surprised as I was it simply wasn't there and didn't appear to ever have been there."

"But there's that ad on the side of the building in the 1899 Edison film."

"There was 'that ad.' Remember, we've checked out every version on the web since then and there's no sign of that ad on any of them. I'm merely telling you that you have remembered things less than a week cut from Tal's eighteenth birthday that you've never been able to remember before. Clearly, something has changed."

"Or is about to," Thea said, standing up to stretch.

"Okay, so back to it," he said, prodding her to continue. "After you got back home, you started looking for folks who could help you with the words and symbols?"

"Yes. It turned out three of the biggest names in symbology and dead languages taught at schools back in New York City. One each at Columbia, Berkley, and NYU. The first one I called asked me to generally describe some of the words and symbols I wanted her to translate. I did, and she hung up on me, right after she called me a 'time-wasting jackanape.' "

"You've been called worse," Pell observed.

Thea let the jibe slide. "I was able to make appointments with the other two, but I had to wait a few months to save enough money and to schedule my days off work. Which worked out okay. They both wanted me to scan my drawing and email it to them to study before meeting with me. Ellen, at Tal's daycare, had a five-year old too, and she was happy for him to have a sleepover. Which allowed me to make the trip by myself."

"I went to NYU, Dr. Guin Herald was the first of the two experts. She was more into wanting to know where the original was, what it was printed on, how it was preserved, how I found out about it, and when could she make an appointment to do some 'minimally' invasive testing on it, than she was about helping me out. I told her I was sorry my problem had been too complex for her, and that I wouldn't waste any more of her time. Her vanity kicked in at that point, which is what I had been hoping for. She told me the words were a mixture of Old and Middle English, with words from some language named Old Frisian."

"Old Frisian?" Pell asked. "Whoever heard of 'Old Frisian?' "

"Exactly," Thea replied. "Her best estimate without looking at the original was that the language indicated the document was written at least a thousand years ago."

Pell gave a low whistle through his front teeth. "What about the symbols?"

"She said she could identify symbols from at least ten different cultures, all of them from ancient cultures, some of them from proto-cultures of the ancient cultures. She wouldn't give me any more information unless I let her see the original."

"It got creepy. I left pretty quickly, and was glad I had used a fake name and a payphone to set up the meeting. I was so focused on trying to save Tal I hadn't even thought about how much the document might be worth, or what someone might do to us to get it, if they thought we knew where it was."

"Until you mentioned it Thea, it had never entered my mind either. I guess a properly authenticated document referencing a previously unknown language or culture would be huge, both from a research and a monetary perspective."

"I used a lot more caution going to see Dr. Flint at Columbia. I moved the car to a parking garage that was miles away from the campus. I left all of my identifying information in the car, and then I took the number one subway to the Columbia School exit."

"Which is pretty damn close to where the Court is located." Pell paused to correct himself, "Was located." And then again, "We think."

"The experts at the schools didn't seem to have any connection, so I decided that was merely a coincidence. Dr. Flint was a whole different experience than Dr. Herald."

"Did he know you'd consulted with her?"

"No, I figured that information was on a need to know basis. Dr. Flint had, however, come to the same conclusion as Dr. Herald about the words being a combination of Old and Middle English and Frisian."

"And about the approximate age of the source document?"

"Yes. I asked him about the repeated usage of the letter 'y,' it seemed to be everywhere in the document. He told me linguists weren't sure what caused it, but there was a sea change almost many hundreds of years ago. The frequency of 'y' usage decreased dramatically."

"Dr. Flint told me flat out he couldn't decipher most of the sigils. He called them that, the same word Keeper used. I looked it up later. It's a symbol having to do with magic."

"Dr. Flint is the one who gave you the information about the face-stealing spook that turns birthdays into nightmares?" Pell asked.

"Yes. He told me it was only an approximation in English of the actual words. It translated as some stalking demon or thing called a Crestfallyn. The longest sentence fragment he could piece together was, 'the Crestfallyn's greatest opportunity is on the Day of Choosing.' "

"Whatever that is," Pell replied.

"He said it was a common concept. Every culture has a turning point where a child or an adolescent is considered an adult member of the society."

"A rite of passage," Pell said nodding his head.

"Sometimes. Sometimes it's a time-related event. Like, the onset of menses for a young woman."

"And for our society? For Tal?" Pell noticed Thea was shaking a little now. "You think it's his eighteenth birthday, don't you? Next Friday."

"Yes," she replied. "I think the spook is going to do something awful to him next Friday."

Pell wrapped both his arms around her. "Honey, if I hadn't lived this with the both of you the last few years, I would say you needed to be committed. But I'm a believer."

"Thank you," she said, kissing him on the cheek.

"Here's the deal. You and I will protect him on his birthday. You let him take care of the school problem. We can monitor that situation, but he has to learn when he can find his way on his own, and when he needs to stop and ask for help."

"You are so wise, Pell Smith." She leaned into his arms as they enveloped her. "I think perhaps now might actually be a good time to cash in that rain check."

"I'm good with that," he said, picking her up to carry her upstairs.

CHAPTER TEN

"We've covered a good bit of material so far, and are a little ahead of schedule. We should finish the chapters on Ancient Greece tomorrow. On Wednesday, we will start the section on the Roman Empire. Your first test will be this Friday. Let's finish today with something fun. First person to answer this question correctly will get ten extra credit points on Friday's test. What was the very first Olympic sport?" Ms. Christie scanned the room until she saw an arm shoot up. "Yes, Mr. Sellars?"

"Go ahead and put those points in the Barton bank, Teach. It was the marathon. I set a new PR last month on the one in Memphis." Barton turned to the rest of the class, arms spread wide and grinning large, as he stood up and took a bow.

"Good guess Barton, but it's incorrect."

That look could be titled, 'angrily deflated,' Tal thought, as Barton slid back into his seat. This is not good.

"When the first few Olympics were held, there was only one contest, and it was not a marathon. Who else thinks they know the answer?" Ms. Christie started looking for someone to call on.

One quick glance around the room told Tal everyone else had come to the same conclusion. Barton was in high dungeon, and all of his classmates were smart enough to not even think about trying to get that extra credit. Ten points was not worth dying a slow death. Everyone was pulling a turtle into their shirt collars, and Tal started doing the same.

"C'mon, doesn't anyone else want to hazard a guess? I'll make it worth fifteen points. Anybody?"

Hazard is right. Call on anybody but me, Tal prayed silently, call on anybody but…

"How about you Mr. Smith? I understand Friday is your birthday. Wouldn't you like fifteen extra-credit points for your birthday?"

The event was called the stadion. A six hundred foot sprint. Legend says that Hercules marked the distance himself by walking two hundred strides. "Sorry Ms. Christie, I thought it was the marathon."

"Really?" She asked, clearly disappointed in Tal. "Oh well, that's okay. It was a hard question. That'll be all for today, we'll start on Chapter Seven tomorrow."

"Uhhh!"

"I thought we explained the rules the first day, Loser."

While Barton had gotten his attention, Gunnar had grabbed his arms so Fail could sucker punch him in his back—right in the middle of the half-healed Australian hematoma. "I said I didn't know the answer, Barton. What else was I supposed to do?"

"It's your job to figure out how to do a better job of looking stupid. It's our job to punish you when you don't." Barton nodded at Fail, who kidney-punched Tal again. The pain radiated all the way across Tal's lower back.

Don't cry, Tal told himself. Asshats don't get to win, they just don't. "That's not…"

"That's not what? Fair? Please don't tell me you were going to say, 'That's not fair'?' " He nodded at Fail, whose fist again became a pile driver right into the small of Tal's back. Tal felt his knees start to buckle.

"You're not half as smart as you're supposed to be Loser if you haven't learned the 'life ain't fair' lesson already."

Tal felt Fail pull his fist back again while Gunnar still held his arms.

Barton held his left hand up. "That's okay, boys. Loser's had enough schoolin' for today. Anyways, we got to go start planning his birthday party." He started to turn and walk off but turned back around to Tal. "In case you decide you want to run tattle to Mommy and Daddy, I got two words for you—Sellars Chemicals."

CHAPTER ELEVEN

"Got room for one more?"

Tal glanced up from his Calculus book, and somehow narrowly avoided a paroxysm of total teenage stupidity. It was the statuesque redhead from first-period Calculus. She looked to be every bit of six-feet tall, her long red hair cascading almost to the middle of her back. A healthy sprinkling of freckles accentuated her fair complexion, which provided an almost pointillist backdrop for a pair of opalescent green eyes. Which pulled his focus to her nose. Narrow with the slightest upturn at the end. Celestial, his information center told him. That's what that kind of nose is called. Celestial—fits perfectly in this instance.

As his gaze shifted lower it stopped abruptly at her mouth. Sonnet Red. If that's not the name of her lipstick then the person in charge of lipstick nomenclature conventions should be fired immediately and replaced with someone possessing a soul. Hokey, I know, he told himself, but damn it, that's the only way to describe what I'm looking at. Her lips are all fourteen lines of a full, moist sonnet that ensorcells you in line one of the first quatrain, posing the problem of how improbable it is they can be so vibrant, so inviting. Then they taunt-rhyme you crazy for the next eight lines. Seesawing promises, first of sophisticated gentility, then licentious ribaldry, then back again. But the clincher is the volta—the turn. The final couplet composed of the two lines framing that beautiful mouth, irresistibly tugging you upward with them into that perfect smile. Yep, Tal thought to himself, that there is one fine pair of lips. Without caveat or exception—perfect. Looking at her lips, Tal just wanted to, they were compelling his whole body to want to…"

"You might want to close your mouth, dude," she said. "Mouthbreather really isn't a good look for you."

Tal barely had the presence to close his mouth, because even her voice was full…and rich…and…moist…and—oh hell, Tal thought, did I drool on myself? He hurriedly placed his hand over his chin just in case.

"In case you missed my rhetorical question which was intended as an icebreaker, I'll repeat it for you. I was wondering if you have room for one more?"

Tal's brain attempted—with limited success—to divert some processing power from the worshipful staring area to the area controlling tongue motor function. "Uh, uh, ye…, uh, uh, no…, uh it's j-j-j…"

"I'm going to take that somewhat random assortment of syllables as a yes." She stuck her hand out across the table as she sat. "My name is Elle."

He reached out and shook her hand. When did a girl's firm handshake become hot, he wondered. "T-Tal, and it's nice to meet you too. Please don't take this the wrong way, but you might not want to sit down here."

"Why? Are you allergic to women?"

He shook his head. "That's not it."

She looked around. There were six eight-top library tables, all empty. "Is it because you have an unusually specific neurosis that prevents you from sitting at a large empty rectangular table with another person?"

"It's not that…"

She smiled at him again, this smile a couple of thousand watts brighter than the last one. "Is it because you refuse to be seen in public with women who think you're cute?"

Tal finally composed himself sufficiently to make a coherent reply. "The less said, the better, Elle. It was nice to meet you," he replied, dismissing her.

"I see," she said remaining seated. She sat there motionless for a full minute, motionless except for slowly tapping a finger to the tip of her chin.

Wow, Tal thought. Instead of being offended and stomping off, she's working her way through the problem.

"I get one more guess," she finally said. "Is it because there is a monumental jackass at this school named Barton Sellars?"

Tal gave her the tiniest nod.

"And that douche and his two sycophants have made you their science project for this semester?"

Tal smiled and nodded, a little bigger this time.

"I'd a thought a Brainiac like you could outsmart some third-rate bullies." She again paused, tapping her slender left index finger against her lips this time. "There has to be," she said to herself. "This equation doesn't solve unless there's another variable." She leaned toward him across the table. "Are you afraid of him?"

Tal thought about it for a moment. "No. For the record, however, I am opposed in principle to the incursion of unnecessary pain. Particularly if I'm the incuree."

Elle leaned back and laughed. "Nothing wrong with that, I think we all are. Here's the deal. I've been trying to stalk you in the lunchroom. Then I realized you would be smart enough to discover the library is the only place that's sanctuary from my twin brother."

"Well, I can study here, and…"

"I understand, Tal. Anyway, I upped my game today stalking-wise because I heard Friday is your birthday."

"It is."

"Your eighteenth birthday?"

"Yes."

"We all know eighteenth birthdays are special. You're new here, don't know too many folks, so I'm taking it upon myself to make sure you have a memorable birthday. Lunch, in the cafeteria. I'm baking you a birthday cake."

"Well, I guess…"

"Look at that. Three coherent words linked together. Keep it up and you'll be making complete sentences in no time. So, it's a date. Friday, first lunch period. Please be on time, I'm a strong believer in punctuality."

"Bedtime, Tal. Lights out."

"Yes, ma'am." Elle's image had occupied all of his brain functions every moment since meeting her in the library. The information-processing portion was only just now coming back online for other purposes, and was having an internal dialogue with itself about what occurred.

What did she say?

She said she thought I was cute.

Really?

Yes.

She said that?

I already said yes.

What other wonderful things did she say?

She said you had a lunch date with her on your birthday, and that she was baking you a cake.

She did say that didn't she?

Yes, and she also said she believes in being punctual.

That's all wonderful, Tal, what else? Did she say anything else that might be the least bit important?

Let me think, Tal. Seems like there was one other thing…what was it? Oh, yeah—she said Barton Sellars is her twin brother.

"OH, SHIT!"

CHAPTER TWELVE

Tal was pissed. He'd never been called to the Principal's office for discipline—ever. Any little hiccup could jack him up on early admit. Particularly when it was something crazy like the present ridiculousness. Principal Davis had informed him a formal complaint had been made concerning his mental stability, and pursuant to the school district's threat assessment policy, Tal was being ordered to go to an evaluative session with the school psychiatrist. The secretary gave him a note with directions to the shrink's office and sent him on his way. Tal knew exactly who was behind the whole imbroglio. He repeated his new mantra—"One of these days the Bartons of this world will get what they've got coming"—a dozen times as he stomped through the school's hallways.

He made all of the turns as directed in the note. He was looking for Room 724, and found it—at the butt-end of a dead-end leg of the farthest hallway past the cafeteria. When he got there, he saw a piece of masking tape stuck on the office door. Someone had used a Sharpie to write, "Dr. Mertin Wilt, Substitute Counselor," on the tape. Great, Tal thought, on top of everything else I have to deal with a second rate quack. He knocked on the door.

"Come in," a wobbly high-tenor voice warbled in response.

Was that a British accent, Tal wondered, as he opened the door. When he entered, the only person in the room was a kid, who looked like he should be in the fifth grade. Sixth grade tops. The large room was completely devoid of furniture. The youth was holding a slender six-foot long dowel rod with an oblong funky wooden golf putter type end on it. He was using the stick to arrange various colored sands in an intricate pattern within a circle that covered nearly the entire floor of the office. He was slight of build, with sandy blonde hair topped off with three world-class cowlicks. His getup added an extra dimension to the already surreal situation. From head to toe, he was wearing various shades of purple. His topsiders were eggplant—Tal's mom had taught him the fancy name for that specific hue was aubergine. His knee-high violet socks just met the bottom of his mauve-colored chino shorts. He wore a heliotrope polo shirt that was covered by a deep magenta prep school jacket. The glass in his rimless round spectacles was a light lavender.

The kid looked up at Tal. "It's about Time."

What the hell? The kid really was either British, or faked a pretty good accent. "I came straight here from Principal Davis's office."

"That wasn't my intended meaning, Mr. Smith."

Okay, that's a little off, Tal thought. Not that this whole scene isn't a little off. "I was sent here to see an adult."

"No, you were sent here to see Dr. Wilt."

I'm getting attitude from someone who doesn't even wear long pants yet. "Correct. So that would be an adult. Where is he?"

"I'm Dr. Wilt."

How did Barton get Principal Davis to go along with this whole thing, Tal wondered. And where'd he find a prepubescent British student to play the part? "Real funny. I'm out of here." Tal turned around to leave.

"Look at me." Tal turned back around. The kid used his right pinkie finger to hook his glasses and slide them down his nose.

Tal was so shocked he involuntarily took a half step backward. The kid's eyes were a dark red-purple color. Not just the iris, there was no white in the kid's eyes. None. The eyes were solid red-purple. But it wasn't just the freaky color, the eyes looking at him were an old person's eyes. Not barely old, Tal decided. Really, really old. Like gnarly giant Redwood tree kind of old.

The kid pushed his glasses back up his nose with his left index finger. "Thought that might help you a little. I once wrote, 'The eyes indicate the antiquity of the soul.' "

"No, you didn't."

"Pardon?"

"I got an A-plus in tenth grade poetry." Where I learned about sonnets...which led to describing those perfect lips, and...focus you idiot. "You didn't write that. Ralph Waldo Emerson did."

"That's what I said."

"No, it isn't. You said you wrote it."

"So I did."

Great, Tal thought, I've been sent to talk with some acid-dropping Benjamin Button plagiarist. Lord, please don't let him be armed. "You look busy with your sand pile, I'll come back..."

"Hang tight, I'll be done here in a...well, I'll be done when it's Time to be done." As Tal watched, the kid began walking around the circle, picking up and putting down a series of short carved hollow wooden funnels that were about a half-inch in diameter on the larger end, and teeny tiny on the smaller end. He'd pick a funnel up, and rub a small ribbed wooden stick up and down the side of the funnel, making a grating sound, and a small amount of colored sand would come out. Then he'd put that funnel down and repeat the action with a funnel containing different colored sand. It looked to Tal like the sand was sometimes coming out as little as one grain at a time. It must have taken him forever to make that design, Tal thought.

Tal's curiosity about the ongoing weirdness was quickly supplanted by his residual anger at being sent here in the first place. Plus he was starting to get mad for a completely different reason, as the freak ignored him and played with the sand for about fifteen minutes.

Finally, the whoever-he-was took a three hundred sixty degree tour of the floor pattern, walking around and behind Tal, before returning to his starting point. Then he looked up and smiled. "Done. See? I told you—it's about Time." He pointed at the sand design with the blue sand funnel. "You do know what that is, don't you, Mr. Smith?"

"No."

"You should. It might be important. It's a mandala."

"Huh?" Okay fine, Tal thought. Mad has to give way to learning. For the moment, at least.

"My composition is a mandala."

"I might have heard the word before."

"Mandala is a Tibetan word. Do you know what the English translation is?"

"Umm, no."

"You should. It might be important. It means 'center and that which surrounds it.' "

I don't want to be playing Jeopardy against this guy, Tal decided. "Good to know."

"What you see before you is a specific type of mandala— a Kalachakra. Do you know what that is?"

Tal was pretty much fed up with the boy's guessing game. "Since I didn't even know what a mandala was fifteen seconds ago, I'm going to go with 'no.' "

"You should. It might be important."

Did he just "tsk" me, Tal asked himself. I think I just got tsked for the first time ever.

The kid continued on. "A Kalachakra mandala is a Wheel of Time." The kid started walking and kept going until he was one hundred eighty degrees opposite from Tal. He leaned over the sand, and without touching it used his long stick to point to a small circle limned in black in the very center of the mandala. "There," he said gesturing with the stick. "What's that?"

"Let me take a wild stab. The center?"

"An unimaginative response, Mr. Smith."

He did, Tal thought. He tsked me. That kid tsked me. Again.

"Do you know the word, 'utopia'?"

I didn't know I was going to need my dictionary, Tal thought. "Yes, that's kind of like a perfect place."

"That is how it has come to be defined in common parlance. Do you know the literal translation of the Greek words Sir Thomas More combined when he coined the word utopia?"

Okay, Tal thought, I've had Latin, as he searched for an answer. Nope, not going to get this one either, he quickly decided. "I guess not."

"Utopia literally means 'no place.' You should remember that. It might be important."

Tal looked around the room trying to ascertain if there was anything he could use to defend himself. Just in case the pleasant-crazy morphed into ugly-crazy.

"How many cardinal directions are there, Mr. Smith?"

Random, Tal thought, but at least I definitely know the answer. Before the guy could shut him down he responded. "Four, definitely four. North, South, East and West."

"Wrong. You should know the answer. It might be important. The four you named are recognized in modern Western cultures, but humans knew even before they drew pictures on cave walls that there is a fifth cardinal direction. Center."

"Oh, really." Tal started tensing his legs in case he needed to make a run for the door.

"How many cardinal directions are there in my Kalachakra, Mr. Smith?"

Tal looked down at the intricate floor design, then back to Dr. Wilt. "Look Dr. Wilt—if that's what you want me to call you—I really need to be getting back to class…" Tal caught a brief movement in his far right peripheral vision. No, he told himself, there's no way. It looked like the sand design turned clockwise a couple of degrees around the stationary black outlined center.

"Do you know why I asked that you be sent to my office?"

So it wasn't Barton, Tal realized, as he shook his head. This guy is the one messing with my future.

The escapee from fifth grade naptime a/k/a Dr. Wilt removed several sheets of paper from the inside pocket of his jacket. "I have all of your grades beginning with your first year of formal education, as well as your standardized test scores." He looked through the sheets, one at a time. "This report says you have a well-documented photographic memory. Which is incorrect. Technically, you have an eidetic memory. This one, that your deductive reasoning skills are in the top tenth of the top one percent in the entire world." He picked up another sheet. "And this summary indicates you have always been an involved student, even to the point of volunteering to help tutor other students." The kid put all of the papers back in his jacket pocket. "That is you were an involved student until you came to Nemeton High last week. Your teachers have all reported that except for answering a couple of questions the first day, you have ceased any verbal interaction during classes. Is there something you'd like to talk to me about?"

"No."

"Mr. Smith, you need to realize everyone's universe is populated by its own Barton Sellars—or worse. Every person, in every lifetime, has a choice: concede to the darkness or fight for the light. Sometimes they win, sometimes they don't."

"Like one of me is going to be able to take down all three of them," Tal snapped.

"I wasn't referring to pugilism or some form of physical altercation. The fight I mean begins when you finally choose to begin 'Seeking the Center'."

'Seeking the Center?' What the hell does that mean? Tal felt goose pimples run up the back of his neck. This weird little British Doogie Howser dude was starting to creep him out big-time. "What are you a doctor of anyway?"

"Many things, actually. Our Time is short, however, so why don't we address your problem."

"I didn't know I had a problem."

"Exactly. You are directionless, and your Day of Choosing is upon you."

"What?"

"You would throw away every day of your now to be then. And once you were then, you would promptly find a new then to throw away your then now."

"You don't happen to have any Tylenol, do you?"

"Sorry, no. If I asked you right now if you could fast forward your entire senior year—you would simply lose that year of your finite existence—and find yourself on scholarship in the college of your choosing anywhere in the world, what would you say?"

Tal paused for a second. Not because he didn't know the answer, he wasn't sure he wanted to say it out loud. To a stranger. To himself.

"Well, Mr. Smith?"

"I'd say, 'make it happen,'" Tal replied.

"Hold fast to your honesty. It can be formidable armor."

"Do you work for Hallmark?"

"A destination is only an ending. You will never find the destination you desire until you learn to 'Seek the Center,' to embrace the journey—both the pain and the joy."

"Thank you, Sensei. Aren't we supposed to burn some incense now, and hold hands and chant 'Kumbaya,' or something?"

The kid chuckled. "Remember your gift of humor. You're going to need it on your Journey."

"Unless you're with Publishers Clearing House, and know something I don't, I'm not going anywhere anytime soon."

"That is a choice only you can make. I will see you soon, Tal Smith. Actually, it will be soon for you, it may be quite a long time for me. Remember, one of my more famous sayings, 'Appearances can be deceiving.' "

"You didn't write that. People have been using that aphorism for hundreds of years."

"Nevertheless, I wrote it. You now have only thirty-nine seconds to memorize the Kalachakra."

Odd, Tal thought. "Why?"

The teen looked at his watch, "34, 33, 32..." Then back at Tal. "It might be important."

Tal shifted focus to the floor. He looked at every segment, how they interlocked and flowed, how all of the pieces connected in some manner except for the center. The black circle circumscribing the middle was unbroken. His brain sorted the individual component pieces, and then reassembled them. Got it, he said to himself.

"3, 2, 1." Suddenly, the door to the room blew open from the hallway, the resulting draft swirled all of the detail and nuance of the time wheel into an indiscrete multicolored mélange of sand.

"You are dismissed." The kid pointed at the open doorway and Tal turned and walked out into the hall.

It took him ten minutes to work his way back to his locker. His Mom would be worried because he was late. As Tal was hurriedly getting his books out, he sensed them walk up behind him. Then he felt Barton's moist, fetid breath on the back of his neck.

"Nice work, Loser. You've only been here a week and a half, and I hear you've already been sent to the shrink because you're losing it. Wish I'd thought of that. Next time, maybe. Because of your progress, I'm giving you tomorrow off. We'll see you on Friday. We're planning a fun birthday party. Fun for us, anyway."

CHAPTER THIRTEEN

While opening his locker Thursday morning, Tal realized he was happy. For the first time since he'd been at Nemeton High, he didn't have to look over his shoulder. He'd been given a one-day reprieve and it felt good. As he was getting his books out for the morning classes, a pink envelope fell out. He picked it up, and opened it.

> Tal –
>
> Looking forward to celebrating your birthday at lunch tomorrow. First-period lunch, fourth table from the left when you come in from the "B" corridor. Don't be late. Most girls don't like that kind of thing. I hate it.
>
> Elle

Finally, an intelligent, smokin' hot chick who thinks I'm cute. Maybe freaky Wilt wasn't wrong about that whole enjoying the journey thing. Then he remembered one specific fact that doused his good humor—that little thing about her being Barton's twin sister.

"How was school today?"

"Best day so far, Mom," Tal replied smiling.

"Great. Right in time for your big day. Ready to be an adult?" Pell asked, as he walked up behind Tal and put his hand on his shoulder.

"You know, I think maybe I am."

"That's good to hear, Sweetie," Thea said as she started clearing the plates. "Will it be okay if we wait until dinner tomorrow evening to celebrate? I have to get the twins to school early for a class project."

"Sure, Mom." Tal stood up to help clear dinner's detritus. "Let me get the dishes for you."

"I'll get them. Why don't you go check on your brothers. They should be through destroying the bathtub by now."

"Okay."

"Tomorrow is going to be extraordinary, Tal," his Mom said. "I just know it."

CHAPTER FOURTEEN

"Dad!" Elle exclaimed, slapping her father's fingers away from the mixing bowl.

"What?"

"What do you mean, what? You haven't even washed your hands."

"You didn't used to care."

"She didn't used to have a boyfriend, Dad," Barton said as he walked into the kitchen, at which point he immediately changed course heading toward Elle's cooking project.

"Don't even think about it," Elle growled as she clenched her left fist before cocking it back.

At that moment, Portia Elizabeth Sellars—the Sellars family matriarch—walked into the kitchen on her way to the laundry room. "Elle, please put your fist down. There is no possible social situation in which raising a fist is acceptable behavior for a lady. In some situations, emptying your semi-automatic into some lowlife may be ladylike. Fisticuffs? Never." Portia stopped and placed the laundry hamper full of whites on the top of the red granite countertop so she could waggle her finger at the men of the family. "As for you two—Fourth, I'm sure you have some homework that needs doing. You'd think a young man of your standing in the community would be more than a little embarrassed to be getting academically thrashed by a girl. Even if the girl is your sister. Third—I've asked half a dozen times this week for the azalea bushes on the west side of the house to be trimmed. They're blocking my view of the roses."

"We have gardeners to take care of those things," Barton Sellars, III replied.

"Yes we do, and they have failed to meet my expectations. I'm tired of waiting. As the man of the house, I expect you to take care of it." When he didn't jump to it she continued, "Now would be a good time. For the both of you."

As the guys turned on their heels to head off to perform their assigned chores, Mrs. Sellars turned her attention back to Elle. "Who is this boy?"

Elle was immediately defensive. "Don't start on me, Mom. I thought you would be happy I was showing some interest in the opposite sex."

"Ellyse Holly Sellars, every rutting animal shows interest in the opposite sex at some time. What's his name?"

"Tal Smith."

"I haven't ever heard of him."

"He's new to town."

"Who are his people?"

"I don't know Mom. Probably Mr. and Mrs. Smith."

"There's no need to be snide."

"I haven't had a chance to ask him to email me a genealogical chart." Elle knew what was coming. "I know, I know. Sarcastic is not ladylike either."

"Never."

"Tell you what, Mom. If you help me make this cake, I promise to ask him a few probing questions about his family history at lunch tomorrow."

Mrs. Sellars smiled as she picked up the hamper, before placing it on the floor to make more room for the cooking project. "I'll be delighted to help you. It's been a long time since you've asked me to help with anything."

CHAPTER QUINDECIM

The gong sounded again. "That's the ten-minute warning," Borras advised. The jam-packed central hallway emptied quickly as its occupants scattered down the myriad feeder arteries. "We need to hurry. Hunts classes are at the far end of the school." Borras took off at a good clip, without looking back to see if Tal was following.

Keeping up with Borras didn't leave Tal much of a chance to sightsee. Lockers lined both sides of the main hall, the walls of which seemed to stretch forever. In the Greek portion, the flat ceiling was about five stories above them, and every inch of the ceiling was covered with frescoed murals. There were wonderfully intricate battles with thunderbolts and tridents. Clouds, chariots, and snakes seemed quite popular as well. There were even a few halos scattered here and there. In staggered alcoves there were statues. Oversized sculptures, each of them breathtaking in their detail— nostrils flared, biceps flexed, some mouths agape in laughter, others convulsed in anger. Tal recognized many of the subjects, they made up a marble Greek pantheon. If both Myron and Phidias had a dozen hands each, they still wouldn't have had time to sculpt all of these treasures. As he walked past hundreds of sculptures, he saw Zeus,

Aphrodite, Poseidon, and Medusa. He was pretty sure he also recognized Helen, Achilles, Hercules, and Pandora.

"Pick it up, Quint. Tardies count against team points for Hunts ranking," Borras said, as he took a hard right into the cathedral area, and began navigating his way through the morass of students still trying to get to classes.

"I'm trying," Tal said, as the various colored marble finishes of the Greek temple transitioned to the mammoth wooden arches and the stained glass of the Gothic cathedral. The ceiling was so high above them now that the stained mahogany of the arches disappeared into the dark wood of the ceiling.

"In here," Borras said, as he turned left into the next opening.

They stepped out of the hallway and into an oversized classroom with a sloping roof. In keeping with the Gothic theme, the outer wall had leaded glass windows, and two massive flying buttresses arched upward over their heads from the outside wall of the classroom to support the main wall of the cathedral building. As Tal quickly canvassed the room, he counted approximately forty students. The seating was unusual for a classroom. There were nine narrow rectangular tables, each of the tables absolutely as far away from each other as possible. Looked to be about ten to fifteen feet between each of the tables. All of the tables, except one all the way across the room had either four or five students sitting together around the table. Each group had a mix of guys and girls, with the ratio varying from group to group.

"Hey Hippocampus, you know you can't bring pets to class."

Tal turned to his left and saw some squint-eyed guy—who apparently ran out of shampoo last month, or maybe the month before that—pointing at him and laughing.

"Nord of the Släkt," Borras whispered to Tal. "They're in first place, and the odds-makers have them favored to win. Be wary of him, Quint. Stupid jerks are of small moment, it is the extremely intelligent ones who are of consequence."

Tal was about to engage in a philosophical discussion with Borras about the fact that a punch in the nose from a moron hurt every bit as bad as one from a genius, when he saw an arm waving at Borras from the three-person table across the room.

"The Omada table is over there," Borras said to Tal. "Fasten your baldric, it's going to be a bumpy ride."

Tal watched his new friend as they walked across the room. Borras licked his lips a couple of times, and his pace slowed. It was almost as if he was nervous about something. After reaching the group, Borras began the introductions. "This is Dysi."

"Charmed," Dysi said in response. She was short with close shorn auburn hair, and plenty of freckles. Dressed in a black t-shirt and a pair of jeans, Tal could tell from her shoulders and arms that she was ripped. The gymnast kind of all muscled up.

"And this is Notos."

Notos was more scarecrow than teenager. Tall and gaunt, he didn't so much wear his clothes as provide them with a human wire hanger. And pale, man was the boy pale. If there was such a cosmetic color as cadaver white, Notos was the poster boy.

"Not sure why you're here, or why I'm having to spend time being introduced to you, but fine, nice to meet you. I guess."

Okay, Tal thought, so far the team includes a giant, an Olympic gymnast, and vampire Eeyore.

"And this is Anatolia," Borras said pointing at the final member of the Omada.

Anatolia was dressed like she was attending a fancy garden tea party. She had on a cornflower blue sundress, its color looking intentionally faded. Her ebon hair was so coal black it appeared to have shimmering blue highlights. Or maybe it has blue highlights, Tal thought. It was cut shoulder length in the back, and fell perfectly across her shoulders. She was the only one of the group wearing any jewelry, a gold necklace strung with smooth cabochon style gems of various sizes, with matching earrings. As she turned toward Tal her gems caught the light streaming in from the windows, refracting it a dozen different directions. She's wearing fire opals, Tal realized. Fire opals, in every color imaginable, the stones splitting the natural light into every possible hue of red, blue, yellow, and green. Especially the blues, which picked up her eyes, her dress, and the highlights in her hair.

"It's nice to meet you," Anatolia replied.

"I like your fire, um, I see you're wearing some fire, um..." was the best response Tal could muster.

"I see you've brought us a gifted orator, Borras," she said smiling.

Borras took a deep breath, then hurriedly said, "OmadaletmeintroduceyoutoQuint."

All three Omada leapt out of their chairs, screaming at once.

"What the hell?"

"No, absolutely not!"

"You had no right!"

Tal noticed the rest of the class was now completely still. Not a word. Eerily—not even any sound of breathing—quiet.

Notos stood up and took a step around the table toward Borras. "Our team contracts were bound years ago. This, this thing, is a stranger. We know nothing about him," Notos said to the rest of his team. Turning to Tal, "We're not binding you. Get out."

Tal watched as Borras squared his shoulders and bowed up. This must have been what Krakatoa looked like the split second before it shook the entire world, Tal thought.

"Under the Hunts Rules, I am now the Omada Prime Direction..."

Impending explosion or not, Notos wasn't backing off. "We made it to the Hunts Finals with our present squad, Borras. We don't need this guy screwing things up."

Borras wasn't letting up either. "You know as well as I do that it has been many Tyrnings since a four-person team won. After what happened to Kentro last year..."

Dysi interrupted him, "Borras, there's no need to talk about that now, with everyone else listening."

"He's gone, Dysi," Borras said softly. "It wasn't anyone's fault."

"That's not true. It was someone's fault." Dysi wheeled on her left heel and pointed to the far end of the room, at the only girl sitting with Squinty's group. "Hers! It was that whore's fault!" she screamed.

Tal took a good look at the object of Dysi's anger, a petite, attractive dishwater blonde. When she saw Tal was looking, she made eye contact with him, and smiled. Tal smiled in return and then tried to turn his head back toward the Omada. And couldn't. He couldn't not look at her eyes, which he decided must actually be ocular tractor beams. Blue. Her ocular tractor beam eyes were blue. Wrong. Her eyes were flawless cerulean blue. Wrong. They were flawless—insert here every ridiculous over the top poetic descriptor ever used to describe blue eyes— blue. She was quite simply, a honey-butter-blonde-gleaming-white-teeth-undoubtedly-preferred-by-ten-out-of-ten-dentists-small-rounded-breasts-that-strained-against-her-polo-shirt-as-they-stood-up-proudly-to-say-no-thank-you-we-can-support-ourselves walking dreamfest. Come to life.

"You!" Tal didn't realize Notos was talking to him until he poked him in the shoulder. "What can you do?" Notos asked.

Tal turned back around to address the question. "I don't understand," he replied.

"What power do you have that will be useful in helping us to win the Hunts?"

"Are all y'all crazy?" Tal asked the entire group. "I'm a freakin' teenager, I don't have any power."

"Just as I thought," Notos replied. "No major magyk. Probably only some low-grade lucky charm crap," Notos said. "We already lost Kentro. This idiot will get one or more of the rest of us killed too."

"Stop it!" Dysi yelled, putting her hands over her ears. "Stop it! All of you—stop it!"

Anatolia took a couple of steps to her right, and put her arm around Dysi. As she helped her sit back down, she turned to Borras and Notos. "What is the matter with you two? We are in public. Stop this discussion. Now!"

Tal was totally lost. "Who's Kentro? What happened to Kentro?" he asked.

At that moment the door opened and everyone else in the class stood and faced the doorway.

CHAPTER SEDECIM

She who opened the door was talking before she even entered the room. "This is Hunts Orientation. I am Lilith Empousa, this Tyrning's HuntsMistress. You will refer to me as HuntsMistress or HuntsMistress Empousa. I know everything of any importance there is to know about each of you. You are collectively a most unimpressive group of Hunts Finalists."

She stopped to scan the room, stopping when her review got to Tal. "This class is limited exclusively to team members of the nine Hunts Finalists. If you are not a team member of one of the nine teams you are not supposed to be in Hunts Orientation, and you need to leave immediately." She paused again, clearly giving Tal the opportunity to leave.

Tal thought about taking the opportunity to hightail it home, but decided to stick it out. To be honest, one of the reasons was Ms. Empousa. It had taken all of the guys in the room only a split-second to refocus from the Omada drama to HuntsMistress Empousa. She looked like she'd stepped out of a Wonder Woman comic. Amazonian stature—check. Voluptuous—check. There was the untamed mane of raven hair, the simply-had-to-be-collagen-injected-because-they-were-so-plump pouty lips, the hourglass waist, and the unblemished, almost translucent alabaster skin. And there was the ass. Wow!

When she turned her back to the class, her all-black skintight spandex bodysuit left nothing, and therefore everything, to his teenage guy imagination. On top of everything else she had what appeared to be a brace of shuriken on the front of her belt, and she carried a holstered knife on each hip. She's a badass live action Laura Croft, Tal decided.

"As dictated by the Hunts Rules for countless millennia, two centuries following the last Tyrning, each of your Folk sent their permitted number of contestants to Hunts School."

Centuries? What the hell, Tal wondered.

"Thousands of contestants were eliminated after the ninety-eighth year, narrowing the field down to three hundred sixty teams for the Snype Hunt. At the conclusion of the Snype Hunt—this Tyrning's qualifier Hunt—the scores were tallied, and the nine Finalist teams were determined. They are the teams in this room. One of the teams in this room will win the Hunts, and be installed as the new Tyrning's Ruling Council."

The only part of what the teacher was saying that registered with Tal were the numbers. Tal noticed that while the class had been checking out the teacher, the teacher had also been taking stock of her students. He also noticed that every time she got to his corner of the room, her gaze lingered on him. He made eye contact with her, then quickly looked away. Apparently all parts of his body thought she was hot. He had an immediate and profound involuntary physical reaction to her, which if it didn't subside prior to the end of class was going to prove very embarrassing.

Ms. Empousa turned her back to the students, walked over to the chalkboard and started writing as she continued her lecture about the Hunts.

Tal found it difficult to concentrate. Her suit was a second skin, with apparently only the real skin underneath. Even the smallest movement translated into something erotic. Her shoulder muscles moved as she wrote on the chalkboard, which caused her upper back muscles to contract, which cause her lower back muscles to ripple, which caused her ass to... . Yeah, this is going to be tough when it comes time to go, he admitted to himself.

"There will be one Hunt per term. The first Hunt term begins today, and the results will be announced on Samhain. As HuntsMistress, I have the sole privilege to select this Tyrning's Hunts. I have selected a Scavengyr Hunt for this term. All nine teams will compete in the Scavengyr Hunt. Based upon the Scavengyr Hunt results, I will narrow the field to five teams. The Rules provide that if there is a ranking challenge following the first term Hunt, there will be a Combat Challenge between all challenging teams."

Tal wondered again if maybe he had actually been knocked out when he was pushed out of the truck and whether this was all some coma-level dream. Or nightmare.

"The second term will begin the day after Samhain, and end on Imbolc. The second Hunt will be announced later. If there are three teams with sufficient members alive after the second Hunt, the final Hunt field will consist of the top three teams."

The phrase "sufficient members alive" caught Tal's ear. These people are insane, he thought.

"The term for the last Hunt will start the day after Imbolc, and finish on Beltane. The Ruling Council will announce the Hunts winner at the Tyrning Ceremony."

Tal knew about Samhain, Imbolc, and Beltane. They'd studied them one summer in a college prep European History class. All three were feast days in agrarian cultures that marked the start of Winter, Spring, and Summer.

"Any questions so far?"

Tal thought about raising his hand to ask about the part where some of them might not still be alive, but saw Borras giving him the stink eye so he didn't move. Tal saw a hand go up at the far front corner of the room.

"Introduce yourself."

"Kita, Second Prime of the Shuzoku."

"You have a question?"

"Yes."

Ms. Empousa turned to her desk and dipped a quill into an inkpot, and wrote in a cracked-leather bound tome that must have been at least a foot thick. "The Shuzoku will leave last on the First Journey as penalty for the stupidity of their Second Prime."

Kita looked like she had been pole-axed. One of the other Shuzoku members smacked her flat-handed in the back of her head.

"Does anyone else have a question?" She quickly surveyed the room. There were no additional hands raised. "Good." She turned back to the blackboard and began writing again. "Hunts Rule 1.14. Team Complement. A team may continue to compete with four members on its active roster. A team is automatically disqualified if it falls below four members. Regardless of whether the reduction is due to death or dismemberment."

"Holy shit," Tal muttered. His involuntary outburst resulted in a swift under the table shin-bruiser from Borras.

The HuntsMistress apparently didn't hear him. She slowly turned clockwise back toward the class. As she turned, Tal saw her outfit stretch and bend around her right breast…and nipple. Damn, he thought, I gotta get a grip on this. I can't walk out of here sporting wood.

"For any team not presently at the maximum, you have six weeks, until you leave on the first Journey, to bind the contract with an additional member. After that, there will be no substitutions allowed." She glanced toward the clock on the wall. "Your next class is Creatures. Before you go, please take notice of the top left corner of the blackboard. Principal Chiron has not only required me to place that warning on the board, he has ordered me to specifically mention it to you during the first Orientation class. Even though I consider it an interference with my position as HuntsMistress, I have decided to comply with his order. What you do with the information is entirely up to you."

Tal looked at the top-left of the blackboard. There was a rectangle drawn in red chalk with the words <u>NEVER ERASE</u> immediately above the rectangle. The contents of the rectangle, also written in carnelian, read:

FOREST FELL IS NOT PART OF HUNTS SCHOOL. IT IS UNWARDED. TRESPASSING MAY RESULT IN DEATH [OR WORSE.]

"Death [Or Worse.]" The same phrase from back at Sol's Gas Station, Tal thought.

"In addition to serving as HuntsMistress, I am also the instructor for both Orientation and for your last class each day—Combat. During Combat you will each be symbiotized with a Puca." She motioned to her outfit. As she did she ran her hand down from her breast to the side of her waist, then leaned over to run her hand down the side of her thigh before standing erect once more. Baseball, baseball, baseball, Tal repeated in his head.

"The Puca will instinctively learn every muscle of your body and will augment your physical prowess. Maximum implementation of the Puca's functions however depends upon your cooperation. Train hard, it may mean the difference between life and death."

I've never heard of Puca athletic gear, Tal thought. With the way it fits her, it's probably illegal in at least half the United States.

"You will have an hour break before Creatures to discuss team administrative matters. Your Prime knows where your assigned secure team room is located. If there are no questions," Ms. Empousa paused and looked around the entire room, before ending with her focus on Tal.

Why does she keep staring at me, Tal wondered. And why is my body reacting like this to her? He had absolutely nothing to use to hide his physical state. This was going to be embarrassing.

"You are dismissed."

CHAPTER SEPTENDECIM

The Omada team room was in the minaret section, which Tal learned was all the way across the rear portion of the main building. As the team marched wordlessly to their destination, the leaded glass, dark stained woods, and granite floors of the cathedral changed to vibrant tiled floor mosaics, and intricate filigreed wood window coverings. At ten-foot spaced intervals, sculpted heads of mythological beasts were placed head high on the walls with water spilling from eyes, mouths, fangs, tails, and claws. The heads were placed above small floor fountains, that contained water lilies exploding with every variation of reds, blues, and yellows.

Music echoed through the halls in all sections. It looked to Tal like every student not in the Hunts must be required to take music class. They passed numerous groups of students practicing. As the building changed, so did the music. In the gothic portion, Tal heard baroque tunes underpinned with organs and woodwinds, and saw students plinking away on dulcimers and harps. There was *a cappella* Gregorian chanting, as well as a choir of dozens of students singing harmonies in Latin. Both the music itself, as well as its variety, was…well…ethereal. The music and the instruments changed again as they entered the Eastern quadrant. Tal recognized a small tambourine, it was called a riq. There was also a bent-neck guitary thing, an oud, he thought. It didn't have frets and had more strings than his guitar, but he figured with a little practice he could wail away on that one. Other than those instruments, he had no idea what all of the drums, and cymbals, and fiddles were called. In the minaret portion, the harmonies from the man-made music melded with the murmuring of the falling water to create a relaxed, happy environment. Now that he thought about it, except for all of the Hunts related activities, the entire building and everyone in it seemed to generate a positive vibe.

There was, however, nothing relaxed or happy about the Omada as they transversed the school. Shoulders were hunched, faces screwed up into every category of scowl imaginable, and absolute silence—until the Omada room door sealed shut behind them.

"WHAT WERE YOU THINKING, BORRAS?" Notos was yelling as loudly as he could, and looked like he was pissed off he couldn't yell even louder.

"I was thinking no four-person team has won in millennia, and that if I didn't grab him some other team might get him if someone else gets injured." Borras was speaking slowly and distinctly, enunciating every syllable clearly. Tal understood what he was doing, he had decided the best way to resolve the issue was not to assert his authority but to try to defuse the situation.

"We understand that Borras, but an improvident addition could not only lose us the Hunts but our lives as well. Do you even know anything about him?" Anatolia asked.

"Hello, I'm standing right here," Tal said.

"Shut it," the other four said in unison.

"No, I don't," Borras admitted. "Except I know he was admitted during a Tyrning year, and that his enrollment is a singular event in the entire history of the Moiety."

Tal watched as the apparent significance of that fact sunk in with the other three.

"That may be so, but the rules are clear—he's not in Omada unless we unanimously vote him in," Dysi's voice was calm, but Tal could tell from the way her voice trembled that she was still experiencing emotional aftershock from the events in the classroom.

"There's no need to argue," Tal interjected. "I have no intention of staying where I'm not wanted. I'm not hanging around here to play Dungeons and Dragons, or whatever it is you do at this freak show school."

"Problem solved," Notos smirked.

No wonder he doesn't smile much, Tal thought. It's not a good look for him.

"No, it isn't," Borras said to Notos. Looking back at Tal he said, "You can't leave, Quint."

"Why? Why can't he leave, Borras?"

So much for Notos's rictus smile, Tal thought. He must really be angry. His face is even getting some color.

"I have already bound him to Omada."

A few minutes later, as the Omada again walked silently and in single file—this time on the way to Creatures—Tal realized they must have all felt the vibrations of the ten-minute gong. They definitely hadn't heard it over the jet plane engine decibel level screams and insults that were being thrown around the Omada team room.

CHAPTER DUODEVIGINTI

"Lilith, I have already given you the exact same answer to that exact same question three times. So, for the last time, here is my exact same answer. I checked The Book as soon as the Keepers alerted me a new student passed through the front doors."

"And?"

"For the fourth time now, his name is in The Book."

"That's impossible," the HuntsMistress replied.

Principal Chiron paused, looking over his wire-rimmed spectacles before using his finger to trace a line down his cheek. "Saying something is impossible over and over again does not render the thing impossible. Under the Hunts Rules, it is not in fact impossible."

"In the entire recorded history of Hunts School a new student has never entered during a Tyrning Year, much less become a team member of one of the Hunts Finalists."

"Again HuntsMistress, there is a substantial difference between the concept of impossible and that of improbable."

"Save your semantics lessons for the students, Chiron."

"Lilith, what would you have me do? His name is in The Book."

"Someone forged his name in The Book."

"Now that is a perfect example of an impossibility. Names are placed in The Book only by Amarantos herself."

"Then someone has perpetrated a fraud. All of the Folk sent their maximum representation when the new term started, almost a hundred years ago. You and I confirmed the tally together."

"We did," Principal Chiron agreed.

"Then you checked all of their names to make sure they were in The Book."

"I did."

"That means one of the Folk is over-represented. Which is a violation of the Rules, and the new student must be expelled."

Chiron walked back over to his desk and started counting names written in red ink on a four-foot long scroll. It took him several minutes to complete his counting. When he finished, he said, "As the HuntsMistress, you used your authority to schedule the Snype Hunt as the Qualifying Hunt."

"Your point?"

"My point, Lilith," he said, his voice raised for the first time during their conversation, "is the Snype Hunt hasn't been utilized for tens of thousands of years because it is so damn bloody."

"So?" she asked with her arms folded across her chest.

"So?" he asked in disbelief. "So, many hundreds of students at this school were killed or maimed last year."

"The Snype Hunt hasn't been deauthorized."

"Well, it should be."

"Well, it hasn't, and as the HuntsMistress it is within my authority to choose the Hunts I think will produce the best Ruling Council for the next Tyrning." She walked over to the front side of his desk and pointed her finger at the scroll. "Are you saying one of the Folk has sent a replacement candidate? In a Tyrning year?"

"I am neither confirming nor denying his status. I am merely pointing out that last year the school sustained an unprecedented student loss and there are hundreds of Realms below their maximum number of permitted students."

"I am entitled to know what Folk sent a replacement candidate."

"You know that information is forbidden."

"Fine. What magyks does this new student wield?"

"That information is forbidden."

"I am in charge of Finalists' access to the Prime Omphalos chamber. He did not come through there. How did he gain access to the school property?"

"That information is forbidden."

"Do I need to remind you Chiron that I am the HuntsMistress?" she asked, pounding her fist on his desk.

Chiron stood, drawing himself up to his full height. When he spoke it was as if his words were made of steel, not air. "No, you don't, HuntsMistress. Do I need to remind you that while you occupy your position for a single Tyrning, that for the past thousand years, I have been the Principal of Hunts School and Chief Archivist of the Moiety?"

"No," Ms. Empousa replied angrily, as she retreated backward from his desk. "So you're not going to tell me anything else about the new candidate?"

"My answer remains the same. That information is forbidden to you. It is forbidden to all."

"Not to you, it's not," she replied angrily. "Fine. I may not have the authority to decide who participates in the Hunts, but it won't be my fault if he dies before Samhain."

"His name is in The Book. Which means, if bound, he is entitled to participate on a team. As HuntsMistress it is within your authority to discharge your duties in any manner that is in accordance with the Hunts Rules. The morality or immorality of your decisions is within your discretion." As he sat back down in his chair he added, "I have important school business to address Lilith, so please close the door on your way out."

Ms. Empousa slammed the door so hard, the entire doorframe shuddered. Twice.

CHAPTER UNDEVIGINTI

"Good morning, I'm Professor Sprite Elphinstone. Congratulations on making the cut as Hunts Finalists. It is my privilege to teach Creatures to you this term. There should be a textbook for each of you on your team tables. We have a lot of material to cover, so each of you please take a book, and open to Chapter One concerning Water Creatures. We will spend all of today's class reviewing some basic information concerning aquatic beings.

Tal knew every one of the instructor's words were important, but he still couldn't stop his mind from wandering. It was trying, without experiencing catastrophic system failure, to process the prodigious amount of data thrown at it in the last few hours. When he got up this morning he was in his own bed, it was his eighteenth birthday, and he was headed to a lunch date with a hot chick. Since then the world had gone bat shit crazy.

"Please turn to page five," Professor Elphinstone paused a moment to allow the class to catch up. "On this page you'll find a drawing of an 'each uisge'—a water horse found only in the Scots Realm. And, of course, prior to the imposition of Alberich's Bane, in the mirrored Scottish highlands of the Earth

Realm. They are not to be confused with the Bäckahästen, which are white water horses that entice Folk to ride on them in order to drown them. The each uisge's powers are..."

Tal's brain stepped away from the lecture again. He'd learned much by eavesdropping on other students as the Omada had made the lengthy walk from the Omada team room to Creatures. The Omada may not have been talking, but everyone else was talking—about them.

There was actually something called a Snype Hunt last year. It was the Hunt chosen by the HuntsMistress as the qualifying Hunt to reduce the three hundred sixty semi-finalist teams to the nine squads qualifying for the Hunts Finals. Something had gone terribly wrong, he didn't know exactly what. Apparently, there had been a singularly large calamity, which resulted in the deaths of hundreds of students. As a result, dozens of the teams were eliminated because they fell below the four-person minimum. Several teams were totally obliterated. He'd heard the name Kentro and the word "hero" mentioned in close proximity to each other several times. What am I doing here, he asked himself. Hazing by Barton and his two goons wasn't looking so bad right now.

"The next water creature is the Hydra. It is the only nine-headed animal..."

I have to get a handle on this, Tal thought. It's like I've entered some kind of alternate universe. An alternate universe with a school that has field trips where students are killed. What's the purpose? What's with all these odd names? Why am I number five in Latin? What did I do when I agreed to bind the contract? Can it be unbound? The class bell roused Tal out of his ruminations.

"Take your books with you and study them this weekend please," Professor Elphinstone said. "On Monday we will jump right into the discussion about draugrs and wights."

CHAPTER VIGNITI

Finally, it's lunchtime. Tal wasn't sure if he was more thankful for some comestibles or for the tension timeout, the Omada having gone their separate ways after Creatures. Borras had grabbed hold of him and taken him on what was obviously the long way around to get to the cafeteria. Tal got it, Borras was giving the team a few extra minutes to maybe, just maybe, cool down a little. He hoped it worked. As they walked, Tal reached into his right back pocket. It was the one that had been torn when Barton and his crew threw him out of the truck bed. "Damn!"

"What's the problem?" Borras asked.

"My wallet's gone. I must have lost it when Barton and his boys tossed me."

"Wallet?"

"Yeah, wallet. You know the leather accessory where you keep your money?"

"Oh, right. Your money purse. Your Folk call it a 'wallet?' Odd word, that. Might not be a bad idea for you to work on minimizing the strangeness with the rest of the team for now."

Tal quit paying attention to Borras as he realized for the first time he didn't have any of his stuff other than his clothes. No cellphone. No house key. No wallet with money and driver's license. None of it.

"Quint, did you hear me? Reduce the odd."

"Got it. Borras, I have no money to pay for lunch."

"None needed. Since we all come from different planes with different forms of commerce, it is a requirement that the Folk fully sponsor each of their Hunts School contestants. Surely you knew that?"

Tal started laughing.

"What's so funny?"

"One of my lifelong wishes finally came true—I'm on full ride scholarship. It's at a school in the bizarro universe, but I'm on scholarship. Clearly I need to be more specific with my prayers."

"Odd, Quint, reduce the odd."

"Got it, buddy. C'mon let's go eat. I'm starving," Tal replied.

When they finally got to the cafeteria, Borras and Tal found themselves at the back of a lengthy line that snaked all the way to the other end of the hangar-sized room. Looking at the thousands of students in the cafeteria, Tal realized Hunts School was an immense enterprise. As they approached the buffet itself, Tal got the chance to scope out the food selection. It looked like every kind of known fruit was present, together with quite a few he didn't recognize. There were various meats as well, none that looked totally familiar, although there were chunks of flesh that looked like ribs. Right next to the pseudo-ribs was some other type of meat, sliced into long, narrow strips.

"What's that?" Tal asked, pointing at the strips with his fork.

"Ouroboros Snake. Big delicacy, we only have it on the first day of each school year so grab a plateful. You know what they say, it tastes like…"

"Chicken," Tal finished.

"No, It tastes like gryphon. Who in the history of the million planes ever said snake tastes like chicken? I asked you to lay off the crazy, Quint."

"Sorry." There were other unidentifiable meats, and finally a whole pig. On a spit. Not a slice of pepperoni pizza in sight, Tal thought, but I can get a whole pig on a stick. The last item in the dessert section was a massive cut-glass bowl containing a sparkling gelatinous material. Every student in front of him took a plateful, and the bowl looked as full afterward as before. Borras loaded up when it was his turn.

"Jell-O?" Tal asked.

"Ambrosia," Borras replied, ladling a third large helping on the food foothill atop his platter.

"Ambrosia. The food of the gods," Tal replied. "Right. So, I guess the drink in the pitchers on the tables is…"

"Nectar."

"Why of course it is."

"What else would it be," Borras asked. "Load up Tal. You're going to need the energy."

Tal followed Borras's suggestion, and they headed over toward the Omada table.

CHAPTER TWENTY-ONE

Elle looked at her watch. Again. Only twenty minutes left in the lunch period. He's past late, she finally admitted. He's officially into having stiffed me. I baked him an awesome cappuccino-chocolate cake complete with candles, bought him a really funny card, and put myself out there. Sorry Tal Smith, but there will most definitely be punishment levied for your actions. An assload of punishment.

Why am I chasing after him anyway? You've already had this conversation with yourself, she reminded herself. Because I could tell he was different than any other guy the first time I saw him. Not sappy true love at first sight type of different. Really? Hello, it's the twenty-first century. Everyone knows it's more about pheromones than some Jane Austen metaphysical soul mate connection. But I digress, with myself. Shit, now I'm digressing with myself. Get a grip on it, Elle! Oh yeah, he's got to pay big time.

Another glance at her watch. Eighteen minutes. He could still show, I guess. What are you going to do about it if he does? That's right, girl, you'd better get the form and manner of your expression of displeasure planned.

Her mind quickly changed course back to the first day of school. She had noticed the difference as he walked in the front door. She happened to be standing at the far end of the long entry hallway. He was no big shakes physically—not ripped, not scrawny, somewhere in between. He was roughly her height, so close to six foot. She had to admit that overall the physical package was nice, but it was the first thing he'd done when he walked in the front door that sparked her interest. He had walked through the threshold of the school, his backpack slung over his shoulder, then he took a slow three sixty, before stopping in place and smiling. Not a grin, mind you. An honest to goodness beamer, a smile that kept growing until it involved his entire face. It was a smile that declared no matter how much he might have enjoyed the summer, and his trip to the beach, and hanging out with his friends, and getting into all kinds of halcyon summer trouble-fun—no matter all of that, he was ridiculously happy to be back at school, giddy at the chance to learn.

That smile was smoking ass hot. Then he'd known his stuff in Calculus on the first day. Not preening showing off trying to impress knowing his stuff. Quiet confidence in his own brain knowing his stuff. Smoking ass hot.

She'd kept an eye out for him every day after that, noticing as soon as her brother and his two sycophants had predictably started harassing him. She'd listened as the other girls talked the "new guy" down for being a geek. Wrong, they had it all wrong.

Elle realized now that he wasn't the only one at least a little nervous when she introduced herself in the library. His difference wobbled her a little when she actually met him face to face. "Difference" isn't quite the best word to describe him, she decided. "Otherness," maybe. Yes, she decided, otherness is more accurate. He is really cute—not rock-jawed handsome, mind you—but cute. His clothes are sensible, not trendy. Which is also kind of hot. When did sensible become hot, she wondered. Tal clearly didn't want to mix it up with her brother, but he was being truthful when he said he wasn't afraid of him.

"Unnecessary pain." He's funny too. She could tell from their conversation that Tal wasn't one of the kind of guys who thought he was all that, but he actually sorta was.

I do it for him too, she thought. I know I do. He was nervous too when I introduced myself. It wasn't because I'm a Sellars either, he clearly didn't know that until I told him. It was just me. Pretty crazy, I guess. I had my life planned out. Finish this year strong, and then book it to school someplace far away, where no one knows, or cares, about the Sellars millions. Where I can make it on my own merit—or not at all. A place where I don't have to constantly worry about whether people like me or merely like my family's money. And in the schematic of my future, boys had only been penciled in as disposable accessories.

Then some new kid walks in my senior year. I barely catch a glimpse of him all the way across a crowded hallway, and I'm rethinking my well-organized game plan. What's going on here? I've had guys chasing me for years, and now I'm the one obsessing. I've been practically stalking him. And I've been thinking about him nonstop since the library, and wondering what it would be like to kiss him, softly at first, and then to part my lips, and…"

"That's a pretty fancy cake you got there, Sis."

"Get lost, Barton."

"Hey! That wouldn't be a birthday cake, would it? It sure looks like a birthday cake to me." Barton turned to look at his henchmen. "Guys, who do we know who's having a birthday, today?" Elle noticed Fail actually raised his hand to answer.

"I said, beat it, Barton," she said.

"Sure, sure." He looked at the clock on the wall. "Lunch is almost over. Looks like somebody is late for a date." Barton leaned over and put his arm around his sister's shoulder. "Do I need to teach someone a lesson for you?"

"Yes, you do," she replied, shaking his arm off her. "Please teach your two monkeys about the concept of deodorant."

"Just looking out for the family name, Sis." Barton smirked, signaling to his cohorts to follow as he walked off.

Elle sat at the lunch table. By herself. With a really funny card, and an awesome cappuccino-chocolate cake complete with candles, and a single tear that despite her best efforts welled over as the final lunch bell rang. Maybe you're not so different after all, Tal Smith, she decided.

CHAPTER VIGNITI DUO

"I don't know who you think you are, or how you even got into Hunts School."

Tal could see Notos hadn't cooled off even a little from the argument in the team room.

"We've put everything on the line to get to this point. We've risked our lives," he said motioning at the rest of the Omada. "Our Folk have trusted us with the future of their Realms, and you waltz in here just in time to screw it all up."

"Enough, Notos," Borras ordered, as he stepped in front of Tal to slide onto the bench first. Tal could see he did it to put himself physically between Tal and Notos. "We don't discuss team business in public, and we still have a long second half of the day in front of us."

"We're going to have to finish this discussion soon, Borras," Dysi added calmly.

"Fine," Borras replied nodding his head in agreement. "Not in the lunchroom, where everyone can hear Omada business."

Anatolia took a sip of nectar from her goblet. "I agree with you both. Borras, we acknowledge you are our Prime now, but it is in the best interests of the Omada we resolve this disagreement at the first available private opportunity."

"Okay, but until then we all need to be one happy Omada. No evidence of weaknesses to exploit." Borras looked over at Notos. "That's all of us, Notos."

Tal saw Notos attempt his version of a fake smile, which made him look kind of like an animal that had been sideswiped by a speeding car. We definitely do not need to be encouraging Notos to smile, Tal thought, as he finally got to try the ambrosia. "Hey, this stuff is delicious." He took another bite, and could feel a surge of energy. "It's better than a Red Bull."

CHAPTER VIGNITI TRES

"Women to the locker room on the left, men to the right." Ms. Empousa pointed the Hunts contestants in the appropriate direction as they arrived in the antechamber to the gymnasium. "Each of you has a locker with your name on it. The locks have been secured so no one but the assigned individual can open them. Place your right index finger on the lock, then speak your name. The lock will open. Leave all of the weapons in your lockers. Any weapons you need for today's exercises are already in the gym. Initialize your relationship with your Puca, and be back here in ten minutes." Ms. Empousa was wearing the same outfit as earlier, but now had a quiver with arrows on her back and she held a bow in her right hand.

I'm going to have to get this under control, Tal thought, as he turned right and headed into the guy's locker room. I can't be sporting wood every time I see Ms. Empousa. There's no way I can put one of those skin-tight suits on right now. After they'd eaten lunch, the other two afternoon classes—Structures and Cultural Mores—had flown by. There had been no additional break for team business, so no further headway had been made on the "that idiot Quint problem," as Notos was now referring to him. Tal had counted during their afternoon classes, and there were six teams with five players and three teams with only four.

Twenty-five guys and seventeen girls. Girls were the Prime Direction for several of the nine teams.

Once in the locker room, all the guys immediately started shucking their clothing. No modesty, Tal thought, but if I was built like most of them I wouldn't be shy either. Even Borras, who must weigh four hundred pounds, was shredded. Ambrosia must be Paleo, he decided. He watched everyone else walk up to their locker, place their right index finger on the lock, and say their name. The locks popped right open. Inside their refrigerator-sized lockers, he could see an array of weaponry hanging on the walls and from the inside ceilings.

One by one he watched as all of the other competitors took out their spandex outfits. Each team had apparently been assigned a team color. Omada was wearing candy apple red. Oh damn, he thought, this outfit is what the HuntsMistress is wearing. If all of the girls are wearing these things too, Combat is going to kill me.

The uniforms were some type of high-tech outfits. The contestants didn't put them on like they would a wetsuit. They placed them on top of their head, mumbled some words he couldn't make out, and in a flash—except for shoes—the students were fully dressed.

Notos was the last member of the Omada to head back into the gym. "Hurry up Quint! We don't want you anyway, and we certainly don't want you getting Omada docked points for being late."

Tal sat down on the bench and started untying his tennis shoes. He'd been so busy all day his body hadn't even had a chance to catalog its complaints. His knees were seriously banged up. The place on his elbow had congealed, but it cracked and started oozing every time he bent his arm. It was going to be a few days before his hands didn't ache. His Mom was going to start crying when she saw his torn jeans, and his shoes weren't in much better shape.

Suck it up and get this over with, Tal told himself. It's not like you haven't been embarrassed in gym class before. He followed the pattern everyone else had used. He touched his lock with his right index finger, and said his name, "Quint of Omada." It opened. Voice-activated locks, or magyk—which was the funky way it was spelled in their textbooks. Whatever they wanted to call it, the technology was pretty sweet, even for some high-dollar freaky private high school. In addition to a host of knives, and maces, and swords in his locker Tal saw the folded up red outfit. He picked it up.

'Munedan!' A voice screamed in his head.

Tal screamed himself and jumped backward, dropping the garment, and falling over the bench. Add a sprained ass to my injury list, he thought. As he gently stood up, he told himself it was okay, there really had not been a voice screaming in his head. You talk to yourself in your head all the time. But there's no one else talking to you from inside your head, he replied. It's only your hyperactive imagination, Tal. He stepped back over the bench and picked up the red suit.

'You are a Dust Child?'

Tal didn't fall out this time. "It's not my fault, damn it. I was thrown out of the back of a moving truck. Am I speaking with my gym clothes?"

'I am not clothing. I am The Piras.'

"Nice to meet you. I'm T…,uh, Quint. I've never met a Piras."

'Not a Piras, The Piras. I am the Piras of the Puca.'

"Still lost."

'We will pair symbiotically more effectively if you will learn to think-speak in your head, Quint of Omada.'

Tal tried forming the words as if he were silently talking to himself. 'Okay. Still lost.'

'The Puca are shapeshifting Creatures. From the establishment of the Moiety, the Puca have furthered the Lex Immortalis by voluntarily serving the Folk races by assisting Hunts Finalists.'

Tal translated the Latin in his head: "forever law." That's what they've been saying all day. The Lex Immortalis. I need to find out more about "the Moiety," Tal thought. "You've done this before?"

'Think-speak, Quint of Omada. Yes, many times, although never before have the Puca been asked to serve a Munedan.'

"Okay, I'll try." 'Like this?'

'Yes.'

'Munedan. That's the third time today I've heard that word. What do you mean?'

'The Munedan are the youngest children of the UnFading One. The Munedan alone possess the Divine Spark.'

'You're kidding, right? I just saw all the other guys naked, and they're clearly human. Well-endowed humans, but humans nonetheless.'

'Can you truly know so little?'

'I haven't been in that many locker rooms, but they looked pretty well-endow...'

'The Hunt contestants are representatives of every kind of Folk that exist. Prior to being admitted to Hunts School, each student was magyked to have a human appearance, voice, and mannerisms.'

Tal's brain was beginning to function again. 'You're saying that before me there has never been an honest to goodness human at this school?'

'Correct.'

'And these Folk—they are the Moiety?'

'Yes.'

'The Folk come in all shapes and sizes and colors?'

'Yes.'

'I get it. They were all made to look human so that none of the other contestants will know exactly who they are, what they are, or what they can do.'

'This is so.'

"So this magic they keep talking about?"

'I can see how you frame the words, Quint. It is magyk. You must learn to think in Folk language. "Y"s carry much power.'

'Magyk.'

'*Correct. There are innumerable types of magyk among the Folk, some greater, others lesser.*'

'I haven't seen anybody whipping out any Harry Potter wands or spells or nothing.'

'*Hunts School exists on the Earth plane. There is no magyk on campus except that of the Ruling Council which runs Hunts School. With the sole exception of last year's Snype Hunt, the Folk students have lived without their magyk for almost a century.*'

'Are you one of these Folk?'

'*No. I told you, I am Creature.*'

'And what about the teachers?'

'*They are Folk who have also been magyked to human form, lest old friendships and rivalries influence the outcome of the Hunts. They have also submitted to a geas which prevents them from disclosing secrets they should not disclose.*'

I'm the only person here who looks like he actually looks, Tal realized. No wonder they don't care about being naked, they aren't showing any real skin. It also means none of the rest of my team really look like they do now. What if Notos is a girl, he wondered. Worse, what if the super hot chick with the Släkt actually looks like Notos. Yikes!

'*Your teammates do not know you are human?*'

The totality of Borras's comments to him about humans now made sense. 'No, they don't.'

'*They will need to know soon but it is best that no one else know, at this time.*'

'Piras, do you not want to work with a Munedan?'

'*Service to a human is not the issue.*'

Tal was about to ask what the issue was when Borras's voice came echoing down the hallway. "Quint, we need you out here. Now!"

Omada is counting on me, Tal thought. 'Let's do it, Piras.'

'*Place any part of me on the top of your head, and think-say the following—"I consent. Do you"?*'

Tal placed the shimmering red fabric on the top of his head and mentally said the words, 'I consent…'

'Hopefully I will not kill you…'

'Do you? Huh??'

'Quint, Son of the Dust.'

"Wait. Did you say kill me?"

'Yes,' Piras said answering both of Tal's questions. As the word echoed through his head, Tal felt liquid strength pour down through him, and spread through his neck, down over his shoulders, and continuing until the red fabric covered every bit of him except his hands, his feet and above his neck. Even his banged up elbow and knees felt solid. "Wow," he said out loud. "Why are certain areas exposed?"

Puca are vampyric creatures. If we completely cover one of the Folk, we assimilate them into ourselves. We serve Hunts contestants as penance for past misdeeds. Remember Quint, you must think-speak so that others will not know, and so that we may move better together.'

Tal looked across the room to the mirror over the sinks. He looked pretty ripped in the red getup. Damn, I look good, he thought.

We look good,' Piras chimed in.

"Quint, now!" Tal could tell from the strain in Borras's voice that things were tight in the gym.

"On our way," Tal yelled back, as he headed toward the gym.

The gymnasium was a color-coded nine-ring circus, with Ms. Empousa being the Letters-to-Penthouse-esque Ringmaster. All of the other teams were hard at their assigned physical activities. Omada was standing in the middle of the gym. Doing nothing. Waiting. On Tal.

"Because their Fifth was late, Omada will be penalized one hour during the First Journey."

"Good work, Quint," Notos snarled.

"Teams rotate, Omada to Skill One."

"I'm sorry, Borras," Tal whispered as he stepped close to the giant.

"It's okay, Quint, but neither you nor our team can afford any more self-inflicted damage."

"I know. It won't happen again."

"Just kill it in practice, and it'll get Notos off both our backs for a while."

"I'll try," Tal replied as they both started walking to the area set aside for Skill One. 'Piras—help me. Please.'

It will be okay. You have to learn to trust me, as I learn to trust you,' Piras replied.

'Stage One looks like it's gymnastic tumbling. I can't even do a somersault.'

'You can't, but together we can.'

The other four had apparently warmed up before Tal showed up in the gym. He pretended to be stretching, while he watched them. Which started creating a different kind of problem. Every girl in the gym had on a skintight Puca in their team color. There were dozens of comely thighs, and well-shaped calves, and ripped shoulders and biceps, and oh hell, the gym was cold. So there were…nipples. Lots and lots of nipples. 'I'm screwed Piras.'

'Actually, from what the Puca know of Munedan slang vernacular, you're not. Which is contributing to the present dilemma. I am helping redirect your blood flow toward your brain and larger muscle groups, and away from a certain anatomical region. But you have to work with me and focus, because there's only so much I can do alone.'

'Right. Baseball. Baseball. Baseball.'

'It is an irritating repetition, Quint, but it does seem to be working.'

Borras started lining Omada up, for their formal practice runs. "Okay, we'll do the basic movement series to make sure we're properly warmed up. Anatolia?"

Tal watched amazed as Anatolia did back flips to the far end of the exercise station. 'I'm done for,' Tal thought.

'You have to trust me and let go, Quint.'

Notos went next. He was good, really good actually, Tal thought. Then Dysi, and she was better. Finally Borras, looking like some type of bright red leviathan. And he was the best of all of them. The boy weighs a good portion of a ton, Tal thought, and he just nailed more than a dozen back flips in a row.

"It's your turn, Quint," Borras said.

Tal turned with his back to the mats.

"Quint, if we don't get this done we're going to lose points," Borras said urgently.

'I can't do it, Piras.'

'Visualize the action from something you've seen or experienced, and then let your muscles go. You must learn to trust me.'

Tal bent his knees, and thought about all of the studly Olympic gymnasts he had watched on television over the years, and then he threw himself backward as hard as he could.

Several minutes later, when Tal was finally able to stop and think about what had happened, his mind's eye replayed it for him in slow-motion. It had been like gravity was no longer relevant. He'd left the mat, and as he turned upside down almost fifteen feet in the air, he could see everyone in the gym stopping to stare at him. His body completed its slow lazy arc, as Tal stuck a solid landing at the far end of the tumbling mat. It had taken Borras twelve flips to travel that distance. Tal had done it in one move. In one back flip. He looked back to his teammates. Even Notos was visibly impressed.

Piras was the first to comment this time. *'That was unexpected.'*

'Piras, how did we do that?'

'I'm not sure, Quint. We know from data the Puca have obtained from thousands of years of symbiotic interaction that each of the Folk species react differently with us. Some Puca are better symbiotically than others. I am the most proficient, it is one of the reasons I am the Piras. But the magnitude of the energy produced from our partnering is unprecedented. It is exponentially beyond any known previous relationship. I will have to conclave with the Puca about this matter.'

'What now?'

'Now we see what else the two of us may accomplish together.'

Omada moved through seven other stations in the next hour. Rock-wall climbing, balance beam, martial arts, archery, rowing, knife throwing, and sprinting. Tal and Puca ran the fastest time of the day on the sprint.

'What's up with that?' he asked Piras.

'It is something at which you are naturally proficient. So we are stronger together.'

Ms. Empousa strode back into the middle of the gym. "All teams to Skill Nine."

As Omada headed that way, Tal communicated with Piras. 'What's the last skill?'

'Dueling.'

'You mean like Three Musketeers type of dueling?'

'Oui,' Piras replied lightly.

'Merde!'

The other eight teams had been waiting for Omada to catch up. Ms. Empousa assigned opponents. Omada was picked to duel Släkt. Of course, Tal thought. Each team member was assigned an opponent. Tal ended up facing Väst. She was wearing royal purple, the Släkt team color. And Tal wasn't sure if it even counted as a second skin, it was that tight, and that revealing, and... 'A girl, Piras, I can't fight a girl.'

"You must. She is your counterpart Direction."

"What?"

At that exact moment Väst leapt about two feet into the air, and took a hard cut with her sword right at Tal's face. Even though he was momentarily stunned by her clearly murderous intent, Tal felt himself crumple to the floor as the blade cut some hairs off the crown of his head. 'Holy crap!'

'Quint, you must concentrate. We are a team, mind and body. We cannot function without you.'

'But you just did.'

'No, I simply relaxed all of your muscles and it worked. We will not trick she and her Puca like that again.'

'They're trying to kill us.'

They battled back and forth for about five minutes, with neither Tal nor Väst gaining a significant advantage.

"Time," Ms. Empousa ordered. All of the students stopped in their tracks. As Tal turned his back on Väst to walk over to his teammates, he heard the whisper of feet moving. Instinctively he leapt high while think-yelling, 'Jump, Piras!' Next thing Tal knew, his head was twenty feet in the air, as his body slowly turned clockwise. As he turned in mid-air he could see Väst finishing the sword swing that had been meant to cut him in half.

Ms. Empousa was across the room in a heartbeat. "Is there a problem?"

Tal and Piras landed softly in a crouch. As Tal stood up Piras said, *'She did not hurt us Quint, let it go.'*

'That's not the point, Piras. Everyone on that team is a low-life bully.'

'You assume too much Dust Child, and the only proper way to teach Folk like her a lesson is by "Seeking the Center." Let it go.'

"Omada. Släkt. I asked if there was a problem. Answer me, now!"

Tal scowled at Väst. "No, HuntsMistress, we're all good."

As Väst walked away, Tal thought-spoke to Piras. 'Wow, seems like the girls may be even more dangerous than the guys.'

There was a brief silence before Piras replied. *'I am sorry that I have failed you, Quint of Omada.'*

Tal thought he could detect a difference in Piras' voice, the Puca sounded distressed. 'What are you talking about? We were awesome, we could totally own the NBA.'

'You are bleeding.'

Tal looked down to the top of his right foot. Väst must have nicked him on his way up. 'It's just a scratch. Doesn't even need a band-aid.'

"RED BLOOD!" The scream came from one of the Bùluò.

"RED BLOOD. He has red blood!" Merkez of the Aile exclaimed.

"He is a mortal!"

"Munedan!" Someone else screamed. After the word finished echoing off the gym walls, there was an eerie silence. A split-second later, eight Second Primes had some type of sharp weapon to Tal's throat. He looked to his teammates for help. All of them, even Borras, were looking at him as if he were the lowest species of ratfink in the entire world.

"Stop! None of you are to touch him," Ms. Empousa ordered. She had her bow drawn, and arrow nocked, and pointed at the Second Primes. "This is a matter for the Ruling Council"

CHAPTER VIGNITI QUATTUOR

They'd been stuck in the gym for at least two hours, everyone but the Omada having left long ago. Ms. Empousa had advised all of the other teams that if any of them mentioned a word about Tal, their entire team would be disqualified. She'd ordered Omada to change back into their street clothes, and then they were ordered to sit silently and wait. On what, Tal wasn't sure, but he'd noticed she's written a note and handed it to one of the Allyu to take somewhere. If nonverbal communication could kill, Notos would now be a serial murderer. For killing Tal about a thousand times.

The note-toting student finally stuck his head back in the doorway. "HuntsMistress—Principal Chiron says they're ready for you now."

"All of you, come with me," she demanded as she stalked out of the gym. All of Tal's teammates, excepting Borras, walked ahead of him. Tal felt terrible about letting Borras down, and kind of wished he would yell at him, but he simply trudged along at Tal's side looking glumly down at the floor. The group made their way out the back of the building, and into a throng of students and faculty. The other Hunts School attendees shrank away from them, as if they were untouchables. They don't know exactly what's up, Tal thought, but they know they don't want to get too close to us right now.

Tal could see their trajectory had them heading toward the ziggurat. On the north side of the pyramid, the side closest to them, there were three sets of stairs cut into the pyramid wall. Each set of stairs was wide enough for five people to walk abreast. At the stairs' terminus, halfway up the structure, were giant arched doorways. The two outside stairways were packed from top to bottom, the center one was completely empty. It was to the center stairs that Ms. Empousa led them. They walked up the stairs unimpeded and entered the rounded stone portal.

A cacophony of sound assaulted Tal well before his eyes had the opportunity to adjust from the sunlight's glare to the comparative darkness of torch lighting. He closed his eyes to speed the adjustment process, trying unsuccessfully to identify the individual sounds in the din. After a few seconds, he opened his eyes.

Holy crap, Tal thought, as he subconsciously took a step closer to Borras. The place was either Halloween on steroids or Mr. Potato-Head meets Wild Kingdom. Take your pick. He was surrounded by every combination of animal, vegetable, and mineral you could imagine. Humanoid, human head with lion body, lion body with serpent tail, serpent tail with wings and human head. Zebra legs, eagle talons, dragon wings. Scales, fur, leather, and horns. Name any imaginable combination of colors and body parts, and there was such a creature.

As his eyes adapted, it enabled Tal to sync the individual sounds with their points of origin. There were scales slithering over stone, creatures cawing, as well as lots of honking, beeping, and shrieking. Everywhere Tal looked there was some new configuration of body parts, a creature of some odd color or size. There must have been thousands of beings packed onto the main floor of the pyramid. The only apparent humans were the students and the faculty from the school. "What the hell is all of…"

Borras finally broke his silence. "We have been summoned to a special convocation of the Areopagus. All appear in their true form here, excepting only those associated with Hunts School."

"Where did all of these creatures come from?"

"For the most part, these are Folk, not Creatures. The Prime Omphalos is located in the basement of the ziggurat." Borras saw Tal remained confused. "I'm sorry, I keep forgetting you are human and you know nothing of the Folk Realms. Omphalos are located on all of the planes. Omphalos passage is limited to that plane. On each plane one of the Omphalos is located at the world navel of that Realm and connects directly with the Prime Omphalos."

"Which is here at Hunts School?" Tal asked.

"Yes, it is why Hunts School is located on the Earth plane."

"And from this Prime Omphalos, Folk can travel to and from any of the other Omphalos on any of the other planes?"

"Correct. The Folk present here have all traveled using the Prime Omphalos for this Areopagus."

"Who are they?" Tal asked.

"They are the leaders of the Folk from every Realm. Most of them were students here at Hunts School. Over there, those are the Merrow, they're sea-spirits. Standing by them are their cousins, the representatives of the Naiads and the Nixies. The swans and cranes are the Yosei from the Japan plane. Over there are the Yumboes of an African Realm. The tall, kind of regal looking Folk over there…"

"With the white feathered wings?"

"Yes. Those are Sylphs, they're air elementals who reside on many planes. They're loners, and are seen only infrequently, but they always send representatives to the Areopagus."

"What is the Areopagus?"

"It is composed of the elected representatives of all Folk in the Moiety."

"Over there," Tal said, hooking his thumb back over his right shoulder. "Who are those shorter bearded guys?"

The Electors of the White, Brown and Black dwarves of Rugen Realm. They are standing between the Peries and the Deevs of Persia plane. That group over there is the house-spirit faction: Brownies from the Scots world, Duende of the Spanish plane, and the Esprit Follet of Le Monde France." Pointing to several individuals standing head and shoulders above the rest, Borras said, "Surely even as a human you can guess who those Folk are?"

"Uh, giants?"

"Correct. On the far side of the giants are the wood and mountain Folk, the Shinseen and the Rusalki, of Chinese and Russian planes respectively."

"And all of these creatures…"

"Folk."

"Folk. They all get along?"

"Not necessarily," Borras answered, "but in the Ziggurat, at the Areopagus, the Lex Immortalis governs."

"And is at least one of every kind of non-human being here right now?"

"Of the known Folk, yes," Borras replied. "Not the Creatures though, nowhere close. Many are bound to certain places, but Creatures don't count anyway."

"What do you mean?" Tal asked.

"Creatures are lesser beings, and are not part of the Moiety. They don't get to vote in the Areopagus or participate in the Hunts."

"Why not?"

"Long story. It has been that way since the Tyrning first began. Some Creatures are even the property of Folk."

"It doesn't seem right for the Folk to own other intelligent creatures."

"Are dolphins not kept in aquariums, and treated as property for human amusement in your world?" Borras asked.

"Yes."

"What is the difference?"

There was simply too much going on for Tal to focus on whether there was a good answer to that question. He promised himself he would give it some serious thought when he had more time. Looking toward the southern end of the structure he saw a series of cascading stair-stepped balconies, the highest dais being in the middle of the southern wall. There were five occupants on the uppermost level. The person in the middle was tall and wore verdant silk robes together with a filigreed circlet of gold on top of his flowing ice-blonde hair. His skin seemed to change color, depending upon how the light hit him: emerald hued, then ruby, next sapphire, followed by citrine, all of the colors of the gemstones of the earth. As Tal watched, the man slowly seemed to become transparent, then solid once more, but only long enough for the cycle to begin anew. He's beautiful, Tal thought to himself. Beautiful in a manly way, his teenage guy brain quickly corrected. "Who is that?" he whispered.

"The Alberich, King of the Tuatha dé Danaan, Lord of all the Feadh-Ree," Borras replied in a hushed voice. "All of the Fey Folk of the Hollow Hills Realm bend their knee to him. He has been Archon since the last Tyrning."

"Who are the Fey folk?" Tal asked.

"The Fey are one type of Folk—the Sidhe. Fairies you call them."

"But I thought fairies were little tiny creatures with wings."

"Who spread pixie dust, I suppose," Borras replied. "Quint, our worlds are not all Disney, some parts are very Grimm."

Ms. Empousa motioned for the Omada to follow her. They complied and shuffled toward the middle of the pyramid floor.

"That's Queen Aine over there with her court. First platform down on the right," Borras said pointing to the specified platform.

Tal turned to look, and was immediately bewitched. Alberich, who had seemed impossibly beautiful only moments before, paled in comparison to his Queen. She was dressed in a diaphanous silver gown with a cape trimmed with silver fox fur. Both the gown and the cape glittered. Tal's initial thought was that the fabric itself shimmered, but he quickly realized the light was ricocheting off hundreds of faceted diamonds sewn into her raiment. Her hair was night black, and crowned with a thin circlet crafted from a single hollowed out ruby. She was the morning star descended to earth, slowly strobing—twinkling—solid then translucent, and back to solid again.

Somehow over all of the other sounds, Tal heard a loud rhythmic pounding. He looked back to the high balcony and saw someone banging a long carved staff on the floor of the dais. The creature was humanoid in appearance except that he was ten feet tall, a deep reddish orange, smoke was rising from his skin, and he looked like he was—well, he looked like he was smoldering.

"Order. The Areopagus will please come to order," the stick-wielding individual demanded, his voice carrying to the four corners of the pyramid.

"That is the Marid, Suleyman of the Djinn, Seneschal of the Council. He is second only to Alberich," Borras whispered as the entire building became silent. "The other three members of the High Council are Raja Jinn Peri of the Malay Folk, the Márku—who is Princess of the Finfolk, and the Proteus."

"I thought Proteus was a Greek god," Tal said.

"Many of your Munedan legends and stories are a result of interaction with the Folk. There have been many Tyrnings in which the victors believed that humans should be subjugated. During those periods, the Archon allowed members of his or her Folk to freely traverse the Earth plane, and to use their magyk."

"Ergo, myths of Roman and Greek gods and goddesses," Tal replied.

"And many, many more cultures," Borras continued.

"What changed?"

"The last four Archons have decreed the Folk may not wander the Earth plane, and magyk is limited to an almost imperceptible level by Alberich's Bane."

At that moment Alberich stepped forward to the front of his dais to speak. "Thank you for convening on such short notice. There is a grave matter that needs attending."

He's just talking, but his words are like a song, Tal thought.

"Something has happened, which is unprecedented in the history of the Moiety. A Son of Dust has entered Hunts School."

The floor of the pyramid frenzied, like they were all army ants and a size fifteen steel-toe boot had kicked over their anthill. Twice.

Questions and exclamations rang from all corners of the crowd. "How did he cross the wards?" "Where is he?" "He is not supposed to be here." "The penalty for trespass is death." "His life is forfeit."

"Silence!" Marid ordered, reducing the room to a simmer. "HuntsMistress Empousa, please bring the mortal forward."

And I thought getting thrown out the back of a moving truck had to be the low point of my birthday, Tal thought, as the HuntsMistress grabbed his arm and pulled him with her as she walked forward. The crowd around them melted away, leaving Empousa, Tal and the other members of Omada alone in a circle about fifteen feet in diameter.

Alberich looked down at Tal from on high. "How is it mortal that you have entered Hunts School?"

It was all Tal could do to speak, much less think. "Well, your Highness, my step-father, Pell, he got a job offer and we moved to Nemeton, and I started school at Nemeton High, and…"

"Bow before you address the Archon, Munedan," Marid commanded.

"Marid," Alberich said, "I will handle this.' Where Marid's voice was coarse and crackled like logs on a bonfire, Alberich's voice seemed to harmonize with itself. "When Hunts School was created, the strongest magyk from all of the Folk in the Moiety was used to set the protective wards. Many attempts have been made to breach those wards, to compromise the Tyrnings. No one—no one—singularly or in concert has ever had sufficient magyk to breach the school's defenses. Who gave you the magyk to avoid the wards protecting the school's boundaries?"

"No one s-sir," Tal stuttered. "I came in through the Ladies' Room at the Gas Station."

A wave of muttering rippled from end to end of the convocation, and back again.

As the echoes of Tal's voice receded, a voice rang out from the floor. "The Släkt claim default by Omada."

Tal looked to his right, and saw it was Mitt, the Släkt's Prime Direction.

A turbaned individual, the color of cocoa, sitting immediately to the left of the Archon's chair, spoke next. "State the nature of the claimed default."

Borras leaned over and whispered in Tal's ear, "Raja Jinn Peri is Parliamentarian for the Ruling Council."

Mitt stood up straight, and spoke loudly so all could hear. "Omada is one of the nine Hunts Finalists. Omada has allowed a mortal to participate in Hunts activities. It is impossible for a Munedan to bind the contract. Rule 4.3(B) specifically prohibits any team from practicing with a non-bound contestant. Omada must be disqualified." Mitt paused and looked directly at Tal. "As reward for exposing the Rules violation, and pursuant to Rule 12.4, Släkt claim the mortal as their chattel property."

I got to get me a copy of those damn Rules, Tal thought.

The Raja turned his attention to the Omada. "A breach of a material Hunts Rule has been alleged. Omada Prime, is the allegation well-founded?"

"It is not," Borras promptly replied. "The mortal has accepted the binding. I exercised my emergency authority under Rule 1.8 to bind the contract with him. He is properly Quint of Omada."

The Raja turned to his seatmates and whispered for a few minutes, before turning back to the group on the pyramid floor. "The remaining members were not allowed to vote on the issue?"

"No, sir," Borras replied.

"Proper challenge has been made," Raja Peri stated. "Does anyone else have information relevant to the challenge before the Council confers to make its decision?"

Tal looked around him. No one was doing anything. "Borras, what's going on here?" Tal asked.

"They're trying to disqualify Omada. Well, that and also make you their slave for the rest of your life."

"Really? Is that all?" Tal asked, his voice shaking.

A voice reverberated from a shadow-covered corner of the floor. "I have relevant evidence to present to the Council." A figure limped to the front of the crowd. Tal saw the man was bent over almost in half. He was wearing some type of full-length hooded parka or robe. Threadbare, it looked like it might have originally been a light purple color. He did have a pretty awesome cane to lean on. It was much taller than its owner, made of carved mahogany, and at the top it had a baseball-sized faceted amethyst. As the guy hobbled toward the center of the pyramid, an undercurrent of murmuring grew from the crowd.

"You are not of the Moiety, Traveler, and are not welcome here," Marid said.

"Seneschal, the convocation is Sanctuary, open to address by all," Lord Alberich said, rebuking his second in command. "Welcome, Myrddin Wyllt. It has been two Tyrnings past since your last appearance before the Areopagus."

Did he just say Wilt? Two Tyrnings? That's six hundred years. What the hell? Tal wondered.

The man threw his hood back from his face, and straightened his crooked back until he was perfectly erect. Tal saw that there were no whites in the man's eyes—they were totally purple. It's him, Tal realized. The school counselor. It's Dr. Mertin Wilt. How is he here? And how come he no longer looks like he's in the fifth grade?

The man continued moving forward, finally stopping in front of Mitt. Mitt involuntarily took a half step back before regaining his composure. The stranger held his cane in his right arm, and then slowly described an arc over the Släkt leader. A

135

brilliant purple nimbus surrounded Mitt. It's the same royal purple as their team's Pucas, Tal realized. He then stepped in front of the remaining members of Släkt and performed the same action. A purple cloud appeared over each of their heads. Wilt then stepped over to Borras and the other members of Omada. He swept his staff over each of their heads, and without exception they all glowed the vivid crimson of Omada.

Turning to face Tal, he performed the gesture yet again. Tal felt soothing warmth surround him as he saw a halo encompass him, a halo exactly the same red hue as that of the other four members of Omada. Everyone in the assembly saw it too. Tal heard snatches of response.

"Impossible!" "More trickery from the madman." "He has the Aura." "But he is Munedan."

Using his left hand this time, the Traveler gestured again with his cane, and the colors surrounding the students faded.

"Strange doings indeed," Alberich stated. "Principal Chiron?"

Chiron stepped forward from a large group of teachers. "Yes, Lord?"

Alberich pointed at Tal. "His name?" Alberich asked.

"It is in The Book, Lord Alberich." There was a collective gasp from the crowd.

"Most passing strange," Alberich stated, clearly at a loss. He leaned over and spoke with the others on his dais.

Raja Jinn Peri stood again. "The Släkt claim is denied," he intoned. "As it was never foreseen that the Munedan might participate in the Hunts, it is not expressly forbidden by the Rules."

"Sire, this should not be allowed," Marid protested.

"His name is in The Book. It is the law," Alberich responded.

Raja Jinn Peri continued. "The human is adjudicated Omada's Fifth, with all of the privileges and responsibilities appurtenant thereto. HuntsMistress?"

Ms. Empousa stepped forward. "Yes, your Lordship?"

"As we are all aware, the Rules require assessment of a material penalty for an unsubstantiated roster challenge."

Ms. Empousa turned to face Mitt, and the rest of Släkt. "Släkt forfeits one of their three Journeys for this term's Hunt."

"NO! You can't do that!" Nord screamed.

"Silence," Marid commanded, slamming his staff on the floor.

Raja Jinn Peri turned back to Alberich, "Your word is Law, Archon, subject only to the Lex Immortalis. You realize by allowing a Munedan to participate in the Hunts, that it creates the possibility of a blood price?"

Tal saw Alberich's shoulders lower a little before he responded. "We will address that matter if and when it becomes necessary," Alberich responded sadly. He then leaned over and whispered in Marid's ear.

When Alberich was finished, Marid addressed the congregation. "All remaining matters are for only the High Council to discuss. This Areopagus is concluded. You are all dismissed."

With that statement Tal saw the Archon wink from sight.

The crowd quickly began dispersing. Mitt and the rest of the Släkt stormed past the Omada. Mitt detoured toward Tal and came close enough to whisper in his ear. "You're dead, human. I am going to kill you myself."

Borras stepped in between Mitt and Tal, and with his fist clenched looked directly into Mitt's eyes. "Take care, Prime. I would hate for Släkt to suffer another penalty."

"Take care of your own team, behemoth," Mitt replied. "We will win this competition."

"Come along," Borras said to his team. "We have much to discuss."

Tal followed the rest of Omada, but as he walked he scanned the throng looking for Dr. Wilt. Or Myrddin Wyllt, if that was his name. Why did they call him Traveler? And how was Wilt only in elementary school last week, and now he's old as Methuselah?

CHAPTER QUINQUE

Heck of an eighteenth birthday, Tal thought, as he walked through the open front doors, and past the six silent sentries. Bone-weary, and facing a long-ass walk home, he still couldn't help but notice the beauty of the Hunts School campus. The fountain, with its thousand jets prisming the light, was surrounded by countless partial rainbows that appeared and disappeared as the summer breeze shifted the mist. He'd never seen a lawn so lush, every blade giving a superlative effort on behalf of the entire team. The school landscape crew should work for the NFL, he thought. During one of the trips between classes he'd heard several members of the Allyu refer to the fountain as Fountain Flow, and the front lawn as Grass Grow.

The school was built with the front doors facing true north. The cotton fields were kind of off to his front left, which meant they were to the northwest. The Gas Station Crossing, which he knew was there even though he couldn't see it, was between the cotton fields and the lawn. Straight ahead at the far end of the lawn was the creek. His eavesdropping had paid off there as well, it was named River Run. It meandered along the far end of the manicured grass, and circled the campus. From what Tal could see, the water in some parts was only skin deep, while in other stretches it appeared to be waist high, or better. He'd heard one of the students say no matter how low the water level got, the river always had an unbroken ribbon of water.

As the river ran to the northeast it was the divider between the campus and Forest Fell. The riverbank dipped four feet down one side, before rising a like elevation up the other side, a landscape sorbet between the grass and the trees. Immediately on the far side of the embankment, the hardwood wall of Forest Fell seemed to rise to the clouds. Borras had said it was old growth forest, having never suffered Folk nor human manicure. He'd also told Tal that even though the forest was not on the human plane, it was permanently magykly anchored to Hunts School to help guard the Prime Omphalos. Tal hadn't obtained any more details on that subject so he was unclear as to how it provided protection.

As Tal walked down the steps and past Fountain Flow, he studied the forest. Surely nobody in their right mind would voluntarily go in there. The forest had a light-sucking demeanor that made even Notos seem cheerful in comparison. As he walked across the lawn, Tal thought about the warning on Ms. Empousa's blackboard. "Death [Or Worse.]" He'd have to ask one of the Omada what that meant. He certainly wasn't costing the Omada points by asking the HuntsMistress.

He'd been so busy musing about Forest Fell, he hadn't noticed he had made it to the far end of the lawn. He took one step over its well-manicured edge, and...

"Son of a biscuit-eater!"

In the total blackness, he'd barked his right shin on something hard before promptly falling over whatever it was. When he tried to catch himself, his right hand went down into some water before hitting bottom. He felt around with his left hand and realized it was a toilet bowl. I'm in the girl's bathroom, he realized. He stood up and walked slowly toward where he thought the door would be, his hands extended out in front of him. When he finally touched the wall he ran his hand up and down until he found the light switch, and flipped it. Sure enough, he was in the Ladies' Room. Although he had no prior experience hanging out in Ladies' Rooms, this one seemed quite swanky. There was a double sink with linen hand towels embroidered with the Hunts School crest, a little sitting area in the far right corner with two chairs and several back issues of a travel magazine called *The Omphalos Quarterly*, a couple of stalls made out of dark wood that might be hickory, and yes, even a bowl of seasonally appropriate potpourri. His best guess was apple cinnamon. Tal noticed a nicely lettered sign on the inside of the door:

> Enjoy your weekend, Tal Smith. I'll see you on Monday.
> You will find your Munedan belongings—other than your garments—immediately outside the door.
> You won't be allowed to mention today's activities to any other humans. Please don't try. There is an escalating furball magyk spell involved.
> Wash your hands, and please turn the light off on your way out.
>
> Thank you,
>
> The Ladies' Room

Got to be the politest Ladies' Room ever, Tal thought, as he rinsed his hands in the sink. He turned off the light as he stepped out of the bathroom, found his personal belongings nicely stacked on the sidewalk, and started the long walk back in the direction of Nemeton—and home.

CHAPTER TWENTY-SIX

Yep, that was every bit of ten miles, Tal thought as he drag-assed up his driveway. The books in his backpack—from both schools—felt like they were made out of lead the last half mile. Or maybe bismuth, that's an even heavier element. Only by one proton though and it's much more brittle than lead. So on a scale, they would probably evidence the same mass. But the purpose of this internal discussion, he reminded himself, is to convey the heaviness of the books, not the durability. So, definitely bismuth then, he resolved. Damn, first thing I do when I get to my room is check my scalp above the hairline. There had to be at least one physiologically significant blow to my head sometime today. Had to be.

He'd flip-flopped a half-dozen times about what story to tell his parents. He'd ultimately decided to come clean with Mom and Pell about the day's events—most of them anyway. He wasn't going to tell them about Barton's participation. He didn't want to say anything that might cost Pell his job. Don't know who that Ladies' Room thinks she is, anyway. Telling me what I can and can't say. Apparently Ladies' Rooms don't believe in the First Amendment.

Rem and Rom were in the driveway shooting hoops with Pell. "Tal's home. Happy birthday, Tal!" Rem yelled. "I get Tal on my team," Rom said quickly.

"Give him a break guys, he just got home," Pell interjected. "Besides, I think Tal and your Mom and me need to have a conversation." He walked up and put his arm around Tal as they started toward the house. "You could have at least called us. Your Mom has been beside herself."

"My battery ran down, Pell." First thing he'd done when he'd picked his stuff up was to check his phone. Deader than a doorknob even though he knew it had been at a hundred percent when he left his house. The Gas Station—or Hunts School—must have sucked the charge out of it. Which he'd decided made sense, at least compared to the rest of his day. He'd noticed there were no electrical appliances on the Hunts School campus. Guess if you have magyk to run things you don't need electricity.

Tal had barely opened the screen door when his Mom came running out and grabbed him, hugging him hard. "Tal Smith, where have you been? It's almost eight o'clock. I've been going crazy."

"I know. I'm sorry. I can explain."

"We waited after school, and you never appeared. I went to the Principal's office and they said you never showed up for first period..."

"I can explain."

"Tal, if you're doing drugs, tell us. We can help you, but you have to be honest with us. Are you doing marijuana?"

"No, Mom. Give me a minute, and I can explain."

"If it wasn't your birthday, I would turn you over my knee, and..."

"I'm sorry, Mom."

"I cooked a special dinner for you. And your favorite dessert. Tal, you missed your birthday dinner, and we have all your presents..."

"I'm really sorry, but I can explain."

"And, and,...oh, Tal. Your new clothes. They're ruined."

"I can explain."

"Today of all days, Tal. Today…"

Pell reached over about that time, and gently put his arm around his wife. "Take a deep breath, Thea." She did as instructed. "Now lower your shoulders." She complied, and relaxed a little into Pell. "Tal says he can explain, so give him a chance."

"You dropped me off at school, and I decided to take a walk out to this abandoned gas station out in the middle of nowhere, and while I was there the service bay—ach!" His throat closed on him, and he felt parched, like he hadn't had any water for days. "Then the service bay and the air hose they—ach." Tal grabbed his throat, as he unexpectedly gagged for the second time. "I went into the Ladies' Room and saw—ach—ach—ach…" He couldn't finish the sentence. It was like he had some huge disgusting wad of nastiness in his throat, it felt like a, well actually it felt like a giant slimy ball of hair must feel. Damn that Ladies' Room. Somebody needs to teach it about the Bill of Rights.

"That's it? That's your explanation?" his Mom demanded.

"I was at a different kind of—ach!" Now his entire throat was clamping down.

"You left school to go play hooky, and you've been hanging out in a girl's bathroom at a gas station?" She turned her head to Pell. "He's doing the dope, Pell. He's on the dope."

"Mom, please believe me I—ach!"

"I'm really disappointed in you son," Pell added.

Thea recovered enough to continue. "Tal, I know it's your eighteenth birthday, and you know I love you…"

"I know, Mom."

"But you're grounded. Go to your room."

Forty-five minutes, and a hot shower later, Tal felt better. Physically anyway. Emotionally, he was still knotted up. Even though his mom was still high-pissed, she apparently believed all prisoners deserved at least bread and water. Or in the case of a prisoner's eighteenth birthday, some reheated lasagna, and a fat slice of double-chocolate birthday cake—with eighteen candles. Tal wolfed it all down as soon as she'd left. Her eyes were red and swollen, he knew she'd been crying. Heck of an eighteenth birthday. He didn't blame his folks for being mad. It had to look bad from their perspective. He'd lived it, and his brain was still refusing to believe some of the day's events could have actually occurred. He wanted to sit there with his eyes closed, and process the entire day, but he couldn't. He was too tired, and his bed's warm embrace too welcoming.

Downstairs, Thea had been pacing around the kitchen table nonstop since she had taken Tal's dinner up to him. "Something big happened today."

"I agree, but what?" Pell was sitting at the table nursing his third cup of coffee since dinner. Caffeinated coffee.

"I don't know, but Tal wasn't telling us everything. Actually, he didn't tell us anything. He would never leave school to go for a walk. Never. Certainly not to walk out to some gas station in the middle of nowhere. He had no way to know that gas station even existed. If he went there, someone took him. Who? Why? On his eighteenth birthday. Why? It's a miracle he made it home alive."

"Okay, sweetheart, calm down. It might have been some new kid hazing. He's home and he's safe."

"He's not safe, Pell. This is no coincidence. Today is the day. Well, tonight is the night. If those experts interpreted any of that Frisian mumbo-jumbo correctly, tonight is the night that Crestfallyn, or demon or whatever it is, makes its move. I thought we could protect him, that it would be better if he didn't know. Never knew. I wanted him to have a normal birthday today, like every other kid gets. I thought you and I could take care of that thing this evening, and all of his problems would be solved."

In response Pell held up his coffee cup for a refill. "Hello? I've had a half a pot since dinner. There's nothing on earth—except a caffeine-induced heart attack—that will stop me from keeping Tal safe tonight."

Thea finally stopped pacing and sat down at the table by her husband. "Maybe we lost it when we moved."

"Maybe. Regardless, we have our game plan and we'll be ready." Pell stood up and took Thea's hand pulling her to her feet, "Why don't you go make sure the twins are out, and then go to bed. I'll wake you around two for the second shift." As she looked at him, her fear evident in her eyes, he picked up his chair "And why don't I go ahead and move my chair outside his bedroom door right now."

'It is almost time, Tal Smith. After hundreds of years, tonight, as midnight tolls, I will take your face, and be returned to my former self. Wake up, Tal Smith. Wake up to die.'

"Uhhh." Tal raised his head a couple of inches, a tendril of drool stretching from his chin to the pillow. Man, was I out, he thought. That was some freaky dream about a gas station, and a place called Hunts School, and a skintight outfit that pretty much made me Kal-El. Kind of, sort of. Then that creepy faceless spook showed up to ruin things.

'Aaaah, you are awake, good. You have only minutes left, human.'

"Holy shit, it's back," Tal yelled leaping to his feet on his bed. "Mom! Pell! Help! Help!" he screamed, his voice cracking with fear. "Pell!" he yelled, even more frantically this time.

'Stupid Munedan. They thought they could stop me. Even in my present state, I have sufficient magyk to send them to Morpheus. After I am restored, I will have enough power to insure your parents never wake again. Your little brothers I shall give to those like me.'

"No!" Tal yelled.

'More,' the apparition said gleefully. *'Your fear makes me stronger.'*

Tal heard something smack his window. The faceless thing whipped around. As it did Tal could see the ghost was as thin as a sheet of paper.

From outside his window Tal heard, "Psst! Quint Hey! Wake up! Let us in!"

'No. It's cannot be,' the thing said as it oozed toward the window to look out. 'His kind cannot be here. On the Earth plane. Nor the rest of them, with their full magyk. It is impossible.'

The window got smacked again. "C'mon, Quint. We don't have all night."

'No, just ten more minutes. I am so close.'

The spook is whimpering, Tal thought. He's afraid of the Omada for some reason. Actually, it's Borras that's hollering. He must be afraid of him. Nothing scary about Notos—except everything, I guess. Get it together, he told himself. Get off of this bed and walk over to the window, and open it. But that thing will be close enough to touch me. C'mon, Tal, it told you it couldn't make a move on you right now. He slowly stepped off the bed, seemed like it took him forever to put the first foot, and then the second, on the hardwood floor. Then, just as slowly he took baby steps toward the window. For each step Tal took, the faceless thing took a step toward him. As he finally reached the window, the apparition flowed into him. Tal threw his hands up in front of his face. As he did, he felt air move into him, and through him. Cold air. He'd played a game in the seventh grade with some friends. They each took turns sticking their hand in a bucket of ice water to see who could leave theirs in the longest. First it was really cold, then your fingers went numb, and after they went numb, they started to burn because they were so cold. That's what his face felt like as the thing stopped in his chest.

Not knowing what else to do, he reached out to the window latch and flipped it. Immediately the coldness left his body, and the wraith moved toward the closet door where it stopped. 'This is not over Dust Child. Your face is promised to me.' With that it slid between his neatly spaced dress shirts and was gone.

Tal's entire body felt like it was burning, exactly like his hand had in the ice bucket. He pushed the latch, and the window swung wide open. Borras, and the rest of the Omada, were positioned on branches in the white oak outside his window. That is one stout tree not to call it quits with Borras perched in it, Tal thought. "Man am I glad to see you, but why are you here?"

"We're checking in on our new teammate," Borras said, as he somehow manipulated his massive frame to make it fit through the window opening.

"I didn't think students were able to leave the campus."

"They're not," Borras replied. "Except for the one sanctioned field trip during second term of the Tyrning year. Unless of course one of their members happens to be human."

"I don't get it."

"Our boy Notos came up with the idea. Rule 7.7 says no matter where one teammate is located, the others may follow. Excepting only one place, of course. We decided to test the Rule. We walked to the edge of the campus, and the wards allowed us to walk right through the Gate Crossing. In the entire history of Hunts School, Omada is the only team that may set foot on the Earth plane. And our magyk is at full-strength." Borras started laughing.

"Five-Hells Realm is the one place, in case you were wondering," Notos said as he inchwormed one bony leg into the room, and then the other. Immediately upon crossing the sill he stopped short, his eyes shifting first to the left, then to the right and back again. "Something is not right," he said grimly.

"Hey, move it," Dysi said from her place on the tree.

Borras saw Notos had stopped dead in his tracks, and wasn't moving. "What's up?" he asked.

"This room reeks of deathmagyk," Notos replied, sniffing repeatedly as he crawled out of the window and walked the four corners of the room. Dysi and Anatolia wiggled their way into the now extremely cramped bedroom. "What's up?" Anatolia asked.

"Notos says he smells deathmagyk," Borras responded.

"That's impossible," Ana replied. "Alberich's Bane, remember? We're the only Folk allowed on the Earth plane."

"You can say what you want," Notos said, as he walked to the bedroom closet, and smelled the shirts hanging inside. "This room is stained with magyk. It came and left through this closet." He turned to face Tal. "What are you keeping from us human?"

"It's kind of a long-story," Tal replied. "Bottom line is I have my own personal boogeyman." Tal stopped cold as he remembered what the spook had said about Thea, Pell and the twins. "He was going to kill my family, said he had enough power now to 'send them to Morpheus' and after he took my face he would have enough power to kill them and give the twins to some other spooks."

"That's what he said?" Notos asked sternly. "Quint, the specific words are extremely important. He said he was going to 'take your face?'"

"Yep. The same thing he's said to me almost every year, on my birthday."

"What?" Borras asked Notos, who'd suddenly sat down in Tal's desk chair.

"Don't you understand, Prime?" Notos asked bleakly. "It's one of the Crestfallyn."

"Stercus!" Dysi exclaimed. "Stercus! Stercus!"

"It's okay, Dysi," Notos said calmly. "The Crestfallyn are only semi-corporeal. That's what allows them to sneak onto the Earth plane. It also substantially limits their magyk. It only had power sufficient to place Quint's parents in a coma. I have now amended their physical state to REM sleep. They sleep soundly and will do so until morning breaks."

"How do you know all of that?" Tal asked skeptically. "How can you be certain they're okay?"

Notos looked perplexed. "How can you walk around with your eyes wide open and see so little, mortal?" Notos asked with a sneer.

"Enough, Notos," Borras interjected.

Notos turned his attention to Borras. "We need to follow the Crestfallyn immediately, Prime. While I can track it."

"We don't have the time now," Borras replied.

"I don't want to sound ungrateful," Tal said, "but really, why are you all here?"

"We came to ascertain your intentions, Quint," Anatolia said.

"About what?"

"About the Hunts."

"My intentions are the same now as they have been for the last four years. Graduate from high school, and get a full ride scholarship at a college far, far away."

"Quint, you are bound to Omada. If you don't participate, we forfeit the competition," Dysi explained.

"I'm not sure that's my problem," Tal replied.

"Forfeiting is worse than losing. We will not even be allowed to remain at Hunts School. We will be sent home immediately, and our Folk will be censured," Anatolia said. "Quint, it's not simply a matter of embarrassment, it would set our Folk back for generations."

"So? I'm only a Munedan, remember?" Tal asked sourly.

"If the Omada do not compete and win, all of our worlds, as well as yours, will be ruled by one of the other eight teams for the next three hundred years," Borras said.

That information gave Tal pause. "You mean Squinty and his crew could…"

"Exactly," Notos answered.

"I guess I could multi-task this year. Skip classes at Hunts School, go to Nemeton High during the day, and y'all could catch me up in study group each evening."

"That won't work," Borras said. "In addition to completion of the Hunts, Hunts School has strict attendance requirements, tests, and weekly combat sessions."

"Is there no way to get me removed from the Omada roster?"

"Sure. Two different ways," Notos answered. "First is if you die, which I will be happy to take care of right now, if necessary. Leaves us where we should have been anyway, so not a bad option."

Anatolia walked over and put her hand on Tal's arm. "You have to make a choice, Quint."

"He already chose. He chose to be bound to Omada," Notos replied.

"He is Munedan, Notos," Borras interjected. "He had no idea what I was asking when I asked him to bind the contract."

"I'd like to help," Tal said, "but there is no way I can go to both schools at the same time. There's only one of me."

A supersized grin started rolling across Borras's oversized face, "You're a genius, Quint."

"Huh?"

"Man's got the gift of gab," Notos said dourly.

"One can't be in two different places at the same time, but two can be in one different place at the same time," Borras said, pointedly looking over at Anatolia.

"No, Borras…I can't," Anatolia said desperately.

"You have to try, Ana. It's the only solution."

"What is?" Tal asked.

"A golem," Borras replied.

Tal was totally lost. "What's a golem?"

"I can't," Anatolia continued. "Borras, even at home I've never tried anything even close to that level of making, and I can't use anyone else's lyfeforce to help me with creationmagyk."

"It's your call, Ana" Dysi added. "We all saw what you did last year on the Hunt. You know your magyk is off the rails."

"One of the Hunts purposes is to help us learn our limits." Borras was pleading with her.

"Borras, this isn't a classroom exercise. If I pull that much of my lyfeforce and the golem doesn't make, the draw—combined with the rebound from the negative discharge—will kill me." She paused a moment, Tal could tell she was calculating in her mind. "Borras, it may take enough of me that it kills me even if it does make."

"What's a golem?" Tal was angry about being ignored, and he knew from the heat he was feeling that his face was actually turning red.

"How does that solve our problem, anyway?" Anatolia asked. "Even if I can do it, you know golems can't speak."

"So the Nemeton High Quint will be extremely shy and retiring," Borras added.

"Okay," Tal said, interrupting their discussion. "I'm tired of being ignored."

"We're sorry, Quint. We forget this is all new to you," Dysi said.

"I'm a fast learner, but y'all are going to have to take a little time to teach me. What's a golem?"

Anatolia answered him. "A golem is a Creature made out of genesis clay. In this case, Borras wants me to make a simulacrum golem."

"How does it work?" Tal asked.

"In almost every respect, the golem would be your duplicate," Anatolia told him. "It would have shared knowledge of everything you know at the time of its creation, but not afterward. It would exist until it's deactivated, or until…"

"Or until what?" Tal prodded.

"Or until you die, Quint," Anatolia said. "Simulacrum golems die when their original dies."

"You said it would be like me 'in almost every respect.'"

"Right. Physically, it will be an exact replica. Every mannerism and reaction will be yours. It will, however, be a magykal Creature, and therefore won't have the same physical limitations. It won't feel pain, and it will be wholly without emotion. As a Creature, your Creature, it will have to obey you in all respects."

"Why won't it be able to speak?"

"Golems are Creatures made by Folk magyk," Dysi answered.

"So?"

"The Folk do not have the power of True Creation," Borras replied. "That power belongs to Amarantos alone." Seeing the explanation didn't help Tal, he continued, "Any Creature made using Folk magyk has no psuche name—no soul."

"Folk can't create an equal, only a lesser. In the case of golems, the magykal physical limitation is muteness," Dysi added.

"How do you know golems, or any other magyked Creatures, don't have a soul?" Tal asked.

They all looked at him as if he was simple.

"Is that part of this Lex Immortalis that you got from Amarantos? Whoever that is."

The other three looked at each other for a moment before Anatolia answered. "Well, no. The Lex doesn't actually say that Creatures don't have souls."

"Lots of humans can't talk," Tal said. "Are you saying they're soulless or inferior?"

"Of course not. That's a ridiculous comparison," Notos said. "A square is always a rectangle, but a rectangle is not always a square."

"Sorry, Notos, but you lost me on the geometrical aspects of having a soul," Tal replied.

Dysi tried to explain it to him. "No one is perfect, Quint. Limitations, mental or physical, may be dramatic or subtle, but all of the Folk as well as the Munedan are True Creations of the All-Spirit, and she has endowed each of her children with a soul capable of 'Seeking the Center'."

"As far as answers go, that one is inferior and soulless, Tal replied. "So the golem will go to Nemeton High while I go to Hunts School?" he asked.

"That's the plan," Borras confirmed.

"And during the evenings, he and I will exchange information so no one, including my folks, will catch on."

"Correct," Borras said.

"And it's going to look exactly like me?"

"Exactly as you look at the time of its creation," Anatolia said. "Except the lyfeword which animates it must appear on its body somewhere. It's usually the forehead, but that obviously won't work in this situation."

"So the golem gets body art?"

"Yes."

"And it's going to wear my clothes?"

"It will have to in order to carry out the plan," Borras said.

"When you create it, will it be wearing what I'm wearing?"

"No, it will be naked," Dysi replied. "Why?"

"I'm not comfortable with the thought of you and Anatolia seeing me naked."

Dysi laughed, "Modesty is just so…so…Munedan of you."

"We're running out of time." Borras said. "Anatolia, get your clay out."

"Borras, I don't…"

"I know you have some in your bag. Even at Hunts School where he have no juice, you're always playing with it."

She reached into her purse, and removed a softball-sized wad of reddish clay. "I need some hair," she said to Tal. Before he could even think about moving, Notos leaned over and pulled out a small fistful.

"Ouch!"

Ana took the hair from Notos, pressed it into the clay ball, and shook her head at Notos. "You know I only needed one or two strands."

"Really?" Tal said looking at Notos. "Really?"

Ana began kneading the clay. "Now I need some blood." As Notos reached into his pocket for a knife, she continued. "I got this, Notos." She reached up into the back of her hair, and unclasped the barrette holding her hair back. "Hold out your finger," she told Tal. As he complied, she lightly pricked the end of his left index finger, and then squeezed it until a drop welled up. She ran the clay across the blood, and then continued working it as she handed the barrette to Dysi.

"Now," Ana said, extending the ball toward Tal once again. "Spit."

"You want me to spit on that?" Tal asked.

"For a supposed genius, you really are slow sometimes," she replied. "Yes, spit please."

Tal commenced clearing his throat to comply.

"Gross," Dysi said. "She said spit, not summon forth the contents of your sinuses. What do you want, some kind of slimy snot double?"

"Cut me a little slack will ya? I've never been cloned before." Tal swallowed his first effort, and then simply spit on the ball of clay.

"Finally," Anastasia said, "I need some of your essence."

My essence, Tal thought. I have deodorant, conditioner, and some cologne, but no essence. "Sorry, fresh out of essence," he replied. "I guess I need to whip up another batch, huh?" At that Borras, Ana, and Dysi actually guffawed. Tal saw that Notos even smiled. Barely, but he smiled.

"Essence is the Folk word for male ejaculate, Quint. Semen." Anastasia said, still smiling.

"Yeah, so why don't you whip up another batch, since you're fresh out," Notos said. "We'll all stand here and watch."

It's probably just as well he doesn't smile much, Tal thought. He kind of looks like Freddy Krueger when he does.

"It's required," Dysi said. "If the golem is going to be fully functional. I'm sure there is a cup around here somewhere." She started looking around the room.

"Whooaaa," Tal interjected.

"If there's a problem, I can help you Quint," Dysi added.

"There's no problem," Tal said emphatically. "Let's be sure we're clear on that, there's no problem. There's also no need for fully functional. If I'm not getting any, neither is the golem." He stopped and looked at his teammates. "Right, I know. TMI."

"Then I have everything I need," Anatolia said. She looked once more at Borras, pleading with her eyes.

"Ana, you know I wouldn't ask you to risk if it wasn't absolutely necessary," Borras said.

Anatolia walked over to Tal's bed, first pulling the bedspread back all the way to the foot of the bed, and then pulling the top sheet back the same way. She then knelt beside the bed, placing the clay on to the top of the bed. After that she began rolling and pressing it. After a few minutes Ana started humming softly to herself, then she began singing an odd, lilting singsong tune. The rest of the group circled Anatolia, and watched for the next half-hour while she continued working the clay and singing. Before their eyes, the clay began to elongate, and to gain definition. First a torso, and then a head, followed by arms and legs, hands and feet. Next came its facial features, followed by a skin covering and then hair began to sprout all over. Finally, they were looking at Tal—naked—laying on top of the bed sheets.

"Okay, that part's done." Anatolia said. As she tried to stand she started to fall over sideways, clearly exhausted. Dysi quickly stepped closer to help her, and in so doing got an up-close look at the replicate. "Oh, my," she said as she ogled the naked golem's midsection.

"Impressive isn't it?" Anatolia whispered, before smiling wanly at Tal.

"Hey! Stop it! The both of you," Tal said from behind them. "Haven't you any sense of decency? Cover me up, I mean cover it up."

As Borras moved over to support Anatolia, Dysi let go of her, and then she pulled both the bedspread and the sheet over the golem until it was covered up to its neck.

"Why is he not moving?" Notos asked.

"The lyfeword must be placed upon him," Anatolia replied.

"Do it," Notos urged.

"That task is not mine to do," Anatolia said. Her right arm shaking, she motioned for Borras to hand her bag to her. When he did she reached in and took out a scrap of parchment and a quill. As Borras helped her she stepped back over to Tal, "You cannot be reproduced absent your voluntary agreement. Do you consent?"

"I consent."

Anatolia made a quick, small jab of the quill into the largest vein in Tal's arm. The hollow portion of the quill immediately filled all the way to the top with bright red.

"Sonofabitch," Tal said grabbing his bleeding arm. "What is this, a game of 'let's see if we can hurt Quint a lot'?"

Borras looked at Tal as Dysi helped Anatolia wobble back over to Tal's desk. "Quint—do you understand that while you complain about a pinprick, Ana has put her life on the line for Omada?" Tal's pique vanished immediately. "And that even if the making is successful, she may have expended too much of herself, and still die?"

I guess I missed that part, Tal thought to himself. She's risking her life for me. Well, not for me, for the team. Ana chose everyone else's well being over her own.

"Borras," Anatolia said, "I think…, I think I'm going to need you to hold me…"

Despite Dysi's help, Anatolia began to crumple slowly to the floor. Borras was across the bedroom to catch her in two of his Brobdingnagian steps. Tal saw the color was completely gone from Ana's face and arms, and that her lips were starting to turn blue.

Anatolia seemed to draw a little strength from Borras's arm around her waist. She gripped the quill, and although she was only able to write one letter for each labored breath she took, she wrote a single word in Tal's blood on the parchment. Ana then folded it twice, leaned forward, and touched it to her lips as she mumbled something Tal couldn't make out. Exhausted from the additional magyk gone out of her, she passed out and sagged into Borras's titanic arms.

"Can't you help her?" Tal asked Borras.

"Anatolia is the only one of us who possesses healmagyk, Quint. She knew that before she started." He turned to Dysi. "Notos and I have to finish this here, else Ana's effort will have been wasted."

"You want me to let the physicks know you're bringing her?" Dysi asked gravely. Borras nodded, "Tell them they need to distill some fresh moribund serum." Dysi didn't move. "Dysi, I promise you I will get Ana there in time. Now go, it will take some time for them to prepare the serum."

"I vote yes," was Dysi's somewhat cryptic reply, and then Dysi was no longer there. In her place there was a silent explosion of multi-colored motes of dust. From floor to ceiling every color in nature's palette flashed, then faded away.

It was clear to Tal there was no time to waste for his Munedan questions. Anatolia didn't even look like she was breathing. Teleportation was obviously one of Dysi's magykal gifts. Since she didn't take Anatolia, he was guessing she must not be able to move anyone but herself.

"Okay, let's stick the name on the thing, make a golem, and get her back to campus," Notos said.

"Ana told you that's not how it works with a simulacrum," Borras said. "The golem has to be invigorated by the original. It has to be Quint's choice."

"I don't know if leaving it up to him is a good idea," Notos said.

"It is how it should be, if we are all truly 'Seeking the Center'," Borras replied. "Which brings us to the other thing we need to do before we leave," Borras said, as he laid Anatolia gently on the floor for a moment.

"No, we don't. Problem solved," Notos said hurriedly. "We're in a hurry, remember? There is nothing else to do, except power up the golem, and get Ana back to school."

"What are you talking about now?" Tal asked.

"The second way you can be released from the Omada," Borras replied. "By unanimous vote."

"Have you lost your mind, Borras?" Notos screamed. "Whoever wins the Hunts will rule until the next Tyrning. It's not only important to us—it's important to every being on every plane that we win. It was important enough for Ana that she put her life on the line."

"It is important to every living being that we win by 'Seeking the Center'," Borras replied.

"We can't win if that's how he leaves the team," Notos hissed through clenched teeth. "We would forfeit one scavengyr piece for voting him out."

"I put it to a vote of Omada," Borras replied. "Dysi cast her vote before leaving."

So that's what she was voting for, Tal realized.

"Do we release Quint from his binding?" Borras asked. "I vote yes as well. As Prime I have the right to vote for Anatolia while she is…well, in case she…well, I have the right. She votes yes. Notos?"

"I can stop this madness right now," Notos said. "We have worked so hard…"

"Yes, we have," Borras said quietly.

"We made it through the Snype Hunt, and Kentro died trying…"

"Yes, he did," Borras said, putting a hand on Notos's shoulder.

"I told you we'd be sorry we ever met him, didn't I?" Tal could see that Notos was trembling. From anger, and loss, and desire. But he didn't shake Borras's hand off his shoulder. "Yes. Damn him to the Five-Hells, I vote yes." He turned to Tal. "I hope you're worth it Dust Child. Anatolia may be dead because of you."

Borras turned to Tal. "It's not done yet. It takes a unanimous vote of Omada. There are five members, and only four votes have been cast." He stepped over to Tal, and pressed the folded parchment into his left hand. "We must go. You have until dawn's break to make your decision. After that, the golem will revert to a ball of clay."

Borras picked Anatolia up, cradling her in his massive paws, and he and Notos made their way over to the window. Notos exited first, and Borras handed Anatolia's limp body to him through the window. Once Borras got situated in the tree he turned back to Tal. "Whatever you decide is okay, Quint. Really. This whole thing is my fault, not yours. If we don't see you at homeroom on Monday, I hope you get that college scholarship. Oh, and happy birthday." With that the giant dropped from sight.

CHAPTER TWENTY-SEVEN

Loud noise.

    Loud noise.

        Loud noise.

More specifically a shrill claxon, in a repeating pattern. It's familiar, he thought, but different familiar. One-second of noise, one-second of silence. He knew that noise. Giving up on sleep, he opened one eye, then rolled over on his back, and looked sideways at the nightstand. Stupid much? It's the alarm clock, he realized.

Why does it sound different?

Alarm clock means time to get out of bed, so I won't be late for school. Get your head in the game, it's Saturday. Saturday means no school. Saturday means you turn off the alarm, roll back over, and catch a little more shuteye before family breakfast. Saturday is the day you can lay here just a little longer and relax. And last night was an unusually late night.

Late night! The entire sequence of events exploded into clarity in a heartbeat. First the faceless spook showed up to take his face. Funny, the creep didn't seem so scary this morning. Actually, he didn't feel the least bit scared of the thing. That's a first. Then the Omada had showed up in his bedroom. There had been the loud discussion about his continued Omada participation, and the consequences for the universe if he didn't. Anatolia had taken what looked like a chunk of modeling clay, added his blood, spit and hair, and made something that looked exactly like him. And then she'd passed out.

After that Dysi vanished, a vote was taken, and Borras and Notos split in a hurry saying Anatolia might die and they had to get her back to Hunts School. Leaving him alone. Alone.

Thinking. About everything.

Thinking. About who he was, who he wanted to become, about high school, and college, and Mom and Pell, and the twins.

Thinking. About the Omada, and about Borras and friendship, and obligations, and promises to be kept.

Thinking. About the Släkt, and Ms. Empousa, and Piras.

Thinking. About what the Gas Station fixtures told him. That's right, he told himself, he'd factored in the wise words of a couple of gas pumps.

Thinking. About the piece of paper folded in his hand that supposedly would animate his doppelganger.

Thinking. That Anatolia might have actually given her life because she believed the Omada were fit to rule the universe.

Thinking. About all of these things until he could no longer keep his eyes open, and all of the thinking had conflated into exhaustion.

Next thing he remembered was some smartass mockingbird right outside his window getting a running head start on dawn. Which was odd. They normally didn't start their verbal impersonations until the sun came up, but this one beat the sunrise by a few minutes. Which was lucky—his alarm was set for 7:30 a.m., which would have been too late.

He'd fallen asleep with the scrap tightly gripped in his right hand. He remembered when he woke that first time thinking the time for thinking was over—it was decision time. He had unfolded the paper, finding one word written in his dried blood. Emet. Then he'd pulled the covers off the golem, and decided the most inconspicuous place for the tattoo was high on the side of its left upper thigh, vertically oriented. That way his boxer shorts would hide the tattoo. He'd rolled the creature over on its stomach, placed the parchment face down on its leg, and said "Emet" out loud. Then he'd covered it up so it wouldn't be cold. That was the last thing he remembered until the alarm woke him up.

Time to see what happened, he decided. He sat up enough to lean over the side of the bed, and look down. Yep, there he is. On the floor, snoring. Wearing the same clothes as I had on last night. Man, is he going to be all jacked up from sleeping on the floor.

Hold on. That's not right. How did I end up in the bed, and the golem on the floor. When did that happen? Why am I naked, and it's wearing my clothes? When did it put my clothes on?

He threw himself upright in the bed, and ripped the sheet off his body. Sure enough, there it was on his left upper thigh, vertical letters. A tattoo that said—Emet.

I am golem.

CHAPTER TWENTY-EIGHT

The bedroom door flew open. Remy and Romy came barreling in, blackberry jam smeared every which way on their faces…and hands…and shirts. "Tal! Tal, come on down. Mom is making…" Dumbfounded, Remy pulled up short causing Romy to fall over him, adding blackberry jam to the back of Remy's shirt.

"Tal's asleep on the floor," Remy said, puzzled.

"Tal's standing up naked," Romy noted, "and he has a tattoo."

Remy compiled the two thoughts. "Tal is asleep on the floor, and Tal's standing up naked with a tattoo."

"Mom! Dad!" They yelled in unison, their purple stained hands flailing the air as they ran out the door.

Emet realized he had only moments before one of the adults came upstairs. He started yelling—'Tal, you have to wake up. Tal—wake up!' But there was no sound, not even any grunting. I can't speak, he remembered. He bent down to grab Tal to shake him, and before he knew it he'd thrown Tal all the way to the ceiling. Emet was so startled, he almost forgot to catch Tal on the way down. Anatolia said the golem would be strong, he thought. That I would be strong, he quickly amended. She wasn't kidding.

"What's going on?" Tal asked groggily. "My entire body is sore." Must be from sleeping on the floor. But I'm not on the floor, Tal realized. I'm three feet up in the air. Three feet up in the air, and being held by a naked me.

"Wauuggh!" Tal screamed, startling Emet who promptly dropped him on the floor. The parts that weren't sore before are now officially sore, Tal thought. "Emet? That you?"

The golem nodded.

"Anatolia did it, she really did it."

Another nod.

Okay, this is freaky, Tal thought. It's like looking in the mirror except it would have to be a three-dimensional mirror. Actually, it's more like Superman looking at Bizarro Superman, except Bizarro Superman didn't look exactly the same as Superman. And Emet looks exactly like me. So, it's not at all like Superman and Bizarro Superman. Definitely more like looking in the mirror, except, again it would have to be a three-dimensional mirror. Or maybe like looking at a hologram. Except it would have to be a hologram made of flesh and blood. Which wouldn't be a hologram. Man, this is really freaky.

Through the open door, he heard Romy yelling from the top of the stairs, "Mommy, Daddy, Tal's just like us now."

"What's going on?" Tal asked.

Emet motioned to his mouth.

"Right, I forgot. We'll have to figure out how to get around that later. Did the twins come in my room?"

Emet nodded.

"So they saw us together?"

Emet nodded twice for emphasis.

Tal quickly collated the available information. "You need to hide out while I defuse the situation. It's Saturday morning which means Mom will insist on a family trip to the Farmer's Market. After we get back, you and I can make a plan."

Emet looked around the room for some place that wouldn't be searched.

Tal realized the problem. "Out the window, then after we leave you can get something to eat, and hide out in the attic."

From a flat-footed standstill the golem leapt twelve feet over the bed, across the bedroom, through the open window, and grabbed hold of the oak tree, with one hand.

"Wow," Tal said. "Really, wow. But you're going to have to use your brain, Emet. Clothes. Next time remember, you really have to put on some clothes."

Even though the door was open, Pell knocked on the doorframe.

"Yes?" Tal asked.

"May I come in?"

"Absolutely," Tal replied.

"I'm not sure what's going on, but the boys swear there are two of you up here."

"Really?" Tal asked. He didn't want to lie to Pell, or to his Mom for that matter. "You can look around if you want, but I'm the only Tal in this room. My bet is that they've already been hitting the gummi bears too hard this morning."

Pell laughed. "You may be right." He walked over and sat down on the edge of Tal's bed. "There's something else, Tal."

"What?"

"They also say they saw a tattoo on your leg."

"That's crazy talk."

"Your Mom's afraid that maybe you went a little loco for your eighteenth birthday yesterday. She thinks maybe you skipped school and came up with that crazy story so you could get inked."

"You're kidding, right?"

Pell turned very serious on him. "You weren't very forthcoming about where you were yesterday, Tal. She asked me to come up here, and take a look. To save us both a lot of trouble, would you mind offering to show me?"

Pell is a genuinely good guy, Tal thought. He's always stepped up to the plate for me, even though I'm not his kid. "I'll be happy to show you, Pell. But you'll have to tell me where the tat is supposed to be."

"On your upper leg."

Tal peeled his jeans down, and lifted his boxers high, first on the left side, and then on the right.

"Thank you. Get dressed. Your Mom is cooking celebration pancakes this morning."

"Great, but what are we celebrating?" Tal asked.

"Uh, oh just life in general," Pell replied, as he headed into the hallway. "I'll tell her you're on your way down."

Well, he dodged the answer to that question. I guess I can place that conversation into the "odd" column for today, Tal thought, as he walked into the hall bathroom to wash his face.

CHAPTER TWENTY-NINE

Emet waited in the uppermost part of the oak's expansive canopy. He watched as his step-father opened the front door, stepping through the threshold, followed closely by the rest of his family. That's not right, he told himself. That's Tal's stepfather and Tal's family, not mine. This whole golem self-awareness thing isn't as simple as it sounds. As soon as they'd turned the corner in the car, he climbed back down, and jumped into his bedroom. Strike that, he thought, it's Tal's bedroom. Surreal, he thought, that's the perfect word. I am Tal, but I'm not. I know in my head I should have felt embarrassed to be naked in a tree, but I wasn't. No emotion. None whatsoever. I felt my body physically react with goose bumps to the chill morning breeze, but I had no sensation of feeling cold. My brain recognizes all of the tactile physical stimuli, but there is a complete void of an accompanying emotional response.

Knowledge, with no emotion. Tal's knowledge—my knowledge—tells me that there should be emotions. I'm Spock, Emet finally decided. Without pointy ears. And I can't mind-meld. At least I don't think I can mind-meld. There will be no pon farr either. But I'm not Spock because there's no human half. So that means I'm more like the Terminator. Except I'm not an android because no part of me is machine.

Emet walked around the room picking up his keepsakes. Tal's keepsakes, rather. The signed major league baseball Tal caught a few seasons ago, the framed photo of Mom and Pell's wedding, Tal's first place ribbon in the hundred-yard dash from Camp Five Points, the summer after eighth grade. Sprinting. The only physical activity in which Tal excelled. Emet knew Tal had a memory about each of these things with a specific emotion attached, but to Emet they were only historical objects. Like something he'd read about in a book, or seen in a documentary. He picked up Tal's most treasured belonging, his guitar, and strummed it a few times before placing it back in its rack. It appeared the muscle memory had transferred as well, so he'd be able to play it.

He wandered over to the dresser and got a black t-shirt and some underwear, and put them on before picking up the dirty pair of jeans Tal had tossed on the floor. He realized he needed to take a whiz only because he felt the sensation of pressure on his bladder. It's going to be the same with all of my body functions, and with things like sleeping and eating. He didn't feel hungry, but his whole body felt kind of shaky. Interesting. Even though his body ran on magyk, not electricity, it still required food for fuel.

Emet walked barefoot down the stairs, his toes experiencing first the lightly grained texture of the oak hardwoods and then the polished smoothness of the kitchen's marble flooring. When he took the smoked turkey out of the refrigerator, he knew from Tal's memory it was something Tal thought smelled wonderful, but it didn't make Emet salivate. After he finished his sandwich he peeled an orange. He knew Tal loved the crisp smell of freshly peeled citrus, but his brain simply catalogued it as the smell of an orange.

I am golem.

CHAPTER THIRTY

"Tal, is there some reason you're looking at that tree like you're expecting it to attack us?" Pell asked laughing.

"Don't worry, Tal," Remy said striking his best martial arts pose. "The tree's going down. We got your back."

"Yeah, both of them," Romy agreed.

"Give it a rest you two," Thea said. "It wasn't that funny this morning when you made it up. Surely you don't want your mouths washed out with soap for storytelling."

"But Mom, it's true…" Remy started.

Tal decided he had to do something to change the topic. "Tell you what guys, after we get changed and have lunch, I'll beat you both. Two on one."

"Yay!" came the two-part chorus.

I'm going to have to be more careful, Tal decided. Pell was right, I was looking in the tree to see if Emet was still there. Of course he wasn't. Emet knows everything I know. At least up through last night. He'd been thinking while they cruised the Farmer's Market and on the drive home, about the logistics of making the two-Tal system function. He didn't have all the details worked out yet, but had enough of a plan to bounce some things off Emet. He was still at a loss though about the single biggest problem—that Emet wouldn't be able to utter a word.

After a few moments of silence, his Mom began again. "I'm calling bygones about yesterday's unpleasantness, son." His Mom had been unusually happy all morning. Tal wasn't sure what was up but as long as it got him out of the doghouse he was good with it.

It seemed to Tal like lunch took forever. Finally, it was over. Knowing Emet would need something to eat, he asked to take his slice of day old birthday cake up to his room. His Mom and Pell had really outdone themselves for his birthday. He got a new pair of jeans, a couple of shirts, and a laptop. It wasn't an expensive model, but he knew his folks had paid cash for it. No debit or credit cards, nothing that would leave an electronic trail. Finances were always tight because they moved so often, and because his Mom always insisted they take nothing with them when they moved. Not a stitch of clothing, nor a stick of furniture. He'd decided it was some strange kind of anti-hoarder compulsive disorder. Whatever it was, Pell indulged her and participated in the program wholeheartedly. The only exception had always been Tal's guitar. His Mom had never taken that away from him. Tal got up to leave the table to head to his room.

"Tal, you promised to play basketball," his Mom reminded him, as she started running the hot water in the sink.

"And I intend to give them both a proper whipping.," Tal replied. Turning to the twins he said, "Give me about half an hour to try out my new laptop and digest my lunch, and I'll come down and skunk you both."

Remy and Romy both squealed with delight, "Nuh-uhh, old man, you're going down," Remy said. "C'mon, Rem, let's go get warmed up," Romy added, as they ran out the screen door to the driveway.

After locking his bedroom door, Tal searched his bedroom, even reluctantly looking under the bed, and in the closet. Get a grip Tal—you're eighteen years old for heaven's sake, he told himself. He even gave the floor a careful once-over, in case the golem had dissolved or melted. "Emet," he whispered. "You still alive?"

He heard the smallest sound of a floorboard creaking in the attic, then saw the oak shiver a little, and Emet bounced in through his window. "The dormer window?" Tal asked.

Emet nodded.

"Perfect. The stairway is in the hallway, so it's no good. With the attic window being right above my window, you'll be able to sleep up there, and then come and go through my window without being seen. It's a great solution, exactly what I would…" Tal stopped talking when he saw Emet smiling at him. Of course, it's exactly what I would have done, he realized.

"We have a whole lot of things we need to talk about, but I promised the twins I'd play basketball with them. While I'm doing that, why don't you have some cake, and get the new laptop set up. I have an idea how to improve our communication."

After totaling smoking their trash-talking butts the first two games, Tal had already decided he was going to let the twins win the third game when his cell phone dinged, signaling he had a new email. He called time, stepped off the driveway, and then clicked on the email.

It was from emet@golemmail.com—'Ready when you are.'

'Good work,' Tal texted back.

'Figured this is what you had in mind. Since I can't talk, and electronic devices apparently don't work at Hunts School, I'll take the laptop, and you can keep the cell phone while we're separated during the day.'

Tal returned to the game and let the boys win. At which point the trash talking immediately resumed. "That's enough for me guys, you've worn me out," Tal said to the twins as he walked back to the house. That was exactly how I was going to solve the problem, Tal thought Then the realization hit him—again This is kind of cool and creepy at the same time.

CHAPTER TRIGINTA UNUS

Kentro closed his eyes as he lightly touched the tip of his knife to the beginning of the scar. Diagonally transversing his face, it started a few millimeters above the hairline over his left temple, and continued its journey as a razor-thin white vein, juxtaposed against the jet black of his eyebrow. The knife continued its tracing as the scar wallowed through puckered flesh that had been exposed when his left eye was ripped in it's entirety from the socket. The offending sword had then hewn a valley that desecrated the cartilage of his nose. Below that it became a finger-wide crinkled gash through his once full lips. His dagger finally arrived at its conclusion—where the flourish marking the end of the sword stroke had carved a lopsided divot of meat from under the right side of his chin.

The tracing was a focusing ritual he'd used for well over a thousand years now. She'd made him learn it as one of her conditions for healing him. He had once been the handsomest, most physically perfect male in many generations of his Folk's royal blood. Then, as now, She had the magyk to completely restore him, to make him whole again. That, however, didn't suit Her purpose.

She'd never hidden the fact She'd saved him only to further her goals. Her requirement that he repeat the knife tracing multiple times every day, for centuries, was designed to continually stoke the furnace of his hearthate. He hadn't looked in a mirror for centuries—he didn't need to. He remembered every detail of what he'd looked like, and of the beautiful women who had once obsequiously fawned over him, begging to give him pleasure. They would gag at the unglamoured sight of him now. His face—once chiseled marble—was now a freak show caricature. It didn't matter that She'd glamoured him so no one but him could see his true appearance. The disguise was for Her purposes, so he could do Her bidding unknown. She'd left him able to see his true appearance, to constantly see the carnage that had been wreaked upon him.

Hell, his defeat that day may also have been part of Her plan. He didn't think so, he had always believed even She had been caught unprepared by what happened. She'd laid the sole blame for Her plan's failure upon him, though.

Throughout the history of the Moiety there had been many attempts to fix the Hunts, none had ever succeeded. The school's wardings were too strong, with redundant levels created using magyks from a multitude of planes. Kentro didn't know how She'd gotten hold of the magyk necessary to guarantee his win in the Hunts. When she'd first come to him and told him She could insure his victory, he hadn't asked. Nor did he ask why She needed it to be him that became Archon. It was enough that She did, and that he would be. For ninety-nine years, eleven months, and thirty days everything had gone perfectly. She had known in advance which Hunts would be chosen, and he and his team had been prepared. It was a runaway victory—until that last day.

Something happened. Something well beyond simply unexpected or unforeseen. Those contingencies had been addressed. No, someone, somehow, did something that could not, should not, have been possible. At the last minute, that fucking Pendragon had shown up with the Sword of Many Names and ruined all of their plans—as well as his face.

She had hovered above him, as he lay drowning in his own blood on the battlefield that final day of the Hunts. Unseen except to him She had whispered to him. She would use her magyk to keep him alive, but She intended to use his vanity to make him her slave forever. So She left him physically mutilated, his manhood impugned. Every day his vanity would rip the scab off of any mental healing that might otherwise occur.

She told him many things that day as she floated motionless above him, the Kiss of Lyfe on her lips, mere inches above his face. She told him She intended he should be disfigured inside every bit as much as his outward physical deformities. She told him that even though She had the magyk to keep him alive, he would have to provide the power for the spell.

As his body wracked itself in its death throes, he'd told Her he would do anything She asked. Anything, just please let him live. She'd smiled sweetly, brought her lips even closer, and quietly demanded the unthinkable—that he break his vow as Prime, and betray his teammates. That he use their bindings to steal their lyfeforce.

He had agreed, damn Her to the Five-Hells. Only then had She pressed Her blood-soaked lips to his, and given him the Kiss of Lyfe, after which She'd magyked him and his team to a distant plane. After the others fell asleep that night, trusting him to watch over them as their Prime, he'd fulfilled his pact. He became the only Prime in school history to pervert the binding contract. He woke them one by one and forced his will upon them. All four of them had fought for their lives, Dysi had even died in the struggle. They never had a chance, their binding required obedience, and they'd had to submit. The other three had been only specters since that day. She'd allowed him to leave them each the thinnest sliver of magyk necessary for them to continue existing. As additional leverage she'd allowed them to become the Crestfallyn.

It had never crossed his mind that a Munedan had cost him the win. Folk were of course prohibited by the Hunts Rules from interfering. Creatures were suspect, but they rarely intervened in what they considered Folk business. Munedans were only chattel, pawns to be moved around the battlefield chessboard. In all of the ensuing centuries, the official historical accounts of the Battle Hunt attributed the result solely to the Pendragon's heroism. The truth had remained a closely guarded secret, a secret which She'd somehow recently unearthed.

The Dust Child whose face She'd given to him for payment to Borras had something to do with it. Kentro wasn't sure how this Munedan fit in with the human from a thousand years ago, but it didn't matter. Kentro had gleaned enough from Her comments to understand it was critical to all of their plans that the mortal not survive his Day of Choosing.

So today was a day for rejoicing. The first Munedan ever in Hunts School history had had an exceptionally short run. He had been as surprised as anyone else when he saw his name was actually in The Book. Yesterday was the mortal's Day of Choosing though, and Borras had gone to take his face. There would be two of the Crestfallyn corporeal for the first time since Kentro had betrayed his teammates. Borras's restoration will give the last two hope, and tie them even closer to me. They would have killed me for what I did to them, except for the contract. He still held their binding, and they knew they retained the faint breath of their existence only so long as he allowed it.

Borras's restoration was the reason for them all meeting for the first time in five centuries. She had promised that once Borras had taken the human's face, she would be able to engineer Kentro becoming Archon. Not for only one Tyrning, but Archon for life. Once he was established, She had also promised to restore him to his original unblemished physical form, and to grant him the magyk to restore his other two remaining teammates.

Kentro pulled himself from his brooding back to the business at hand. He'd set the meeting in this boiler room. It was the only functioning portion of an abandoned sub-basement of the school. He had arrived early and unmagyked all of the glow lamps except one, the one in the corner of the room closest to the door. The last conspirator to leave would renew them all, so there would be no evidence anyone had been here. Steam vapor filled the room, spewing intermittently from a byzantine maze of valves, and pipes, and junctions. Its sibilant voice provided protective white noise from any eavesdropping security spells or any of the campus sentries who might have been magyked with extraordinary hearing.

He felt Notos and Anatolia as their essences drifted into the room, then saw them backlit as they moved past the lamp. Interesting that they had come together. The steam jets blew them asunder, rendering them featureless silhouettes. Without any greeting, they all silently waited on Borras, who would be material for the first time in a millennia. Finally, another draft of air and the steam was momentarily displaced over by the doorway. Something's not right, Kentro realized. In fact something is terribly wrong. "Borras?"

'Yes, Prime,' he heard the formal reply in his head, and his heart sank.

"Speak aloud, Borras. Use your new voice, and let us hear you speak for the first time in many, many years."

'I cannot.'

Notos's and Anatolia's voices were babel inside Kentro's head. 'No! 'What?' 'Why not'?'

Kentro's anger, always near the breaking point, was fanned to eruption by Borras's failure and the disruption to their plans. "You, fool! It was a simple task."

'I was magyk-barred!' Borras exclaimed.

'What do you mean?' Anatolia inquired. 'You mean the Munedan had magyk?'

'No,' Borras replied. 'His Hunts School teammates were present.'

'That's impossible,' Notos exclaimed.

'Are you calling me a liar, Notos?' Borras asked tautly.

'Even if they were there it wouldn't matter," Kentro replied, "You had the magyk She gave to us to take his face. No one else on the Earth plane has magyk. Alberich's Bane remains in place.'

'They were not limited,' Borras said.

In his mind, Kentro heard a gasp from the others. "That cannot be," he said slowly.

'Well, it was,' Borras said defiantly. 'And one of them wields deathmagyk at a royal level.'

'There has never been one from that plane allowed in the Hunts,' Anatolia hissed. 'You are sure?'

'Yes,' Borras confirmed. 'I had no choice but to bow to his authority, and leave immediately.'

Kentro suddenly heard Her in his mind. He immediately knew the others had been excluded. He knew this new failure would come at a price. "No," he replied vehemently.

'No, what,' Anatolia asked.

"No, this cannot stand," Kentro covered.

'I blame you,' Borras said. 'I'm Second Prime, and you promised me the human's face. You also promised to restore Notos and Anatolia shortly afterwards. Was that also a lie?'

She was immediately in his mind again, Her voice much louder than the others. 'Borras's time has passed. He cannot take the Munedan's face now. If the Dust Child lives you cannot be Archon. Do not fear, I can give you the magyk you need to kill the Munedan, and restore the other two.'

'No,' Kentro whispered in his mind, making sure he said nothing further to her out loud.

She continued. 'Borras is at fault. He has failed you, he has failed your teammates. For the magyk necessary to kill the Dust Child I need his blood's last breath on your blade.'

'No,' Kentro repeated. 'They are my team. I betrayed them one time. I will not betray them again.'

'I thought you wanted to be made whole. To take your rightful place as Archon,' She urged.

'I do.'

'Then you will do as I command,' She replied.

'What you ask is impossible. He remains only spirit.'

'I will give you the magyk to restore him.'

'And then?'

'In the moment he is restored, when he takes his first breath in a thousand years, when he experiences the joy of a physical form that has been denied him for centuries, in that moment, you will take your blade and stab him through his heart. Five times.'

'No,' Kentro pleaded.

'With his last words he will curse you, and I will be able to meld that hatemagyk into your blade.'

"No,' Kentro pleaded yet again, knowing he would do it. That he would do anything She asked of him. Anything.

'Yes?' came the question.

'Yes.' Seemingly of its own volition his knifepoint went to the scar at his hairline and began working its way downward.

'Well?' Borras demanded stridently. 'We're waiting? How are you going to fix this, Prime?'

'Tell them you have talked to me,' She whispered.

"I-I-I have been in communication with Her." After an initial stumble, Kentro found his rhythm. "She is happy with our service, and wants to reward us."

'It's about time,' Anatolia said. 'What's our reward?'

'You've been given the magyk to restore Borras. You know what you have to do. Tell them now.'

"Even though things didn't work out as planned, She had an alternate plan. She has imbued me with the magyk necessary to restore Borras without the Munedan sacrifice."

'We all know there is no magyk on Hunts Campus. Her power would have to be greater than that of the Archon,' Anatolia replied.

There was a pause before Borras answered Kentro. 'If this is a joke, Kentro, somehow the three of us will find a way to put you down, even if it means our deaths.' The other two grunted in agreement.

'Tell them all to come to you in a circle. Tell Borras the other two shall also receive a reward this evening.'

"It's not a joke, Borras. Our time has finally come. Even Notos and Anatolia will receive a reward this evening for their loyalty. Now come close to me in a circle."

He felt them move toward him through the steam until they were all within arm's length. 'Remember, five times in the heart,' She said. 'Now touch him on the shoulder with the dagger.'

Kentro reached out to touch Borras on his right shoulder. As he made contact he said, "By magyk taken, by magyk restored." Borras's wraith-form went rigid, like a sheet of paper that had been starched and ironed flat. Then, beginning at the soles of his feet and slowly, slowly creeping up his feet and to his ankles he gained color and his body parts became three-dimensional. The other three watched awe-struck as the process proceeded, quickening as it went. To his thighs, past his waist and his torso, up to his shoulders, and then back down his arms as the restoration worked its way up his neck. As it passed his lips, they rose into a smile.

When it finally enervated the individual hairs on his head, Borras screamed at the top of his voice, "Free! I'm free! After a millennia I am restored to myself. It feels…it feels…glorious."

'Now,' Kentro heard in his head, 'it must be right now.' Instinctively obeying Her voice, he swung his knife through Anatolia's and Notos's specters and plunged it to the hilt in Borras's chest. A plume of blue blood leapt outwards as Borras's mouth curved from unbridled joy to consternation to agony.

In the background Kentro heard Notos and Anatolia asking him what was going on, but She was much louder than either of them. 'Four more times,' she urged. With droplets of blood flying from the blade he swung through the others four more times, each time sinking his knife deep into the blossoming hole in Borras's chest.

As Kentro pulled the knife out following the fifth blow, Borras sank to the floor, "Why? Why?" he asked with the voice that had been denied him for centuries.

"You failed me, Borras. You failed all of us."

Borras had only enough strength left to raise his head for a moment to make eye contact with his murderer. He spat first, his spittle more blood then saliva. "I curse you, Kentro, Prime Direction of the Symmoria, Twice-Betrayer. I curse you to burn forever in the Five-Hells."

What happened next—everything that happened next—was a stop motion blur to Kentro. As Borras's head slumped to the floor, his words became visible, at first hanging motionless in the air. Then, as if shot from a bow, they flew first into Anatolia, and then into Notos. After that both of them began to solidify. As they did, their repeated screaming of the word 'TRAITOR' inside his head, became verbal. As they finished their transition to human form, his hand brought the knife back to his chest. No, his hand didn't do it. It was the knife, on its own, that cocked his hand back to a striking position.

'Finish them,' he heard Her whisper in his head while Notos and Anatolia screamed at him out loud.

"Why?" he asked Her.

'You have to finish them.'

"No, please, let it be enough," he cried.

'Even after all I've done for you, you remain weak,' was Her reply.

At that moment the knife threw itself forward, first plunging into Anatolia's chest, then jumping sideways to slash Notos.

'Now. Finish them now,' She demanded.

As he thrust four more times into each of his teammates, he realized the knife was no longer in charge, he was. He dropped the knife and collapsed to his knees, his bloody hands covering his face.

'Wonderful,' he heard Her laugh in his head. 'The knife has now been thrice-blooded. It will serve me well. Now, get on your feet. I will magyk the blood away, but you must throw the bodies into the boilers.'

"Why," he asked her anemically. "Why don't you simply magyk them away as well?"

'Because throwing their bodies into a boiler to be burnt as if they'd never existed is the final and most disrespectful thing you can do to them now. So you'll do it. Be sure and take the knife with you when you leave.'

After he was through, while he was still gagging from the smell of burning flesh, he remembered to use the cuff of his shirtsleeve to wipe the blood from his face. He'd have to be careful, and avoid being seen on campus until he could take a shower in his quarters. He knew from prior experience, blood spatter always got caught in his scar.

CHAPTER THIRTY-TWO

Tal and Emet had spent most of the evening working out the details of their subterfuge. They'd both quickly acknowledged there was going to be a learning curve to this whole thing. Any mistake, no matter how insignificant, might bring their hastily constructed Potemkin Village crashing to the ground. They'd discussed everything they could think of, even down to little details like which Nemeton High schoolbooks would be left lying around the bedroom on which days.

Apparel was high on their Daily Details List. "Clothing continuity," they called it. They couldn't be seen wearing different clothing without a reasonable time interval between Tal sightings. Once they had time to scrape together enough cash to purchase duplicate pieces, it would get much easier.

Personal hygiene was a little easier, except for the fact Tal would have to be prepared to explain why he was all of a sudden taking a minimum of two showers a day. Since Tal would need to leave first to get to Hunts School, and Emet would often be riding to school with either Thea or Pell, they decided Tal would shower at night, and Emet in the morning. That way Emet's hair would still be wet when he got in the car.

The logistics of Tal getting back and forth to Hunts School was a bigger problem. Tal couldn't take the bike. Someone in the family would notice it was gone when Emet still hadn't left for school. They decided Tal would tell the adults he would be late getting home each day because he was going to run intramural track. He and Emet would address the problem of why the folks couldn't come watch him at track meets later. Participating in a sport also provided cover for Tal showering twice a day, as well as his dramatic increase in food consumption.

They'd snuck out the window after dark for a few minutes to test some of Emet's physical capabilities. Although Emet appeared in all respects to be flesh, he definitely wasn't human. He was a magykal construct. Best they could tell, as long as he was well fueled, Emet could run all day at about thirty to thirty-five miles per hour. He could probably go faster, but they were both worried about the wear and tear on shoes and clothing. Emet's strength seemed to be situational—he was as strong as he needed to be to accomplish a designated task.

There simply was no foolproof way for Emet to help Tal get to the Gas Station in the mornings. The best strategy they could come up with was for Tal to start making really early appearances—while still wearing the t-shirt and gym shorts he normally wore to sleep in—to say hi to the family. Tal would then head back upstairs, ostensibly to shower, get dressed, and finish his homework but would actually immediately head out the window. The master bedroom was at the back of the house so they should escape notice from the parents. Emet would shower, dress, and appear downstairs in time to get to school with whomever he was riding with that day. As soon as Emet got out of class, he would sprint to the Gas Station, and wait for Tal. Based on their testing, Emet should be able to carry Tal piggyback back to town at his full speed, drop Tal off a couple of blocks from home, and they would make their way separately to Tal's bedroom. Barring complication, this would put them back to the house well before dinner time each day. They could then start debriefing each other on the day's events, and preparing for the next day's schoolwork.

They knew the single biggest impediments to their charade were the problems presented by Emet's muteness. That got put on the back burner while they worked out smaller details, hoping their collective subconscious would come up with a workable solution. A scheme finally emerged which they felt had a better than even chance of succeeding. It was going to be a tough sell, but it was the only plan they could cobble together. Tal realized that in their particular case, two heads weren't automatically better than one.

Tal looked at the clock, it was almost midnight. Mom and Dad were still downstairs, he could hear them talking, but they'd be turning in soon. "Guess there's no need delaying implementation," Tal said, standing up from the bed.

Emet mouthed the words, 'Good luck.'

When Tal got to the bottom of the stairs he saw that Thea and Pell were sitting around the kitchen table. Based on the papers spread out in front of them, they'd been discussing bills. "Got a minute?" he asked.

"Sure thing," Pell replied. He pushed the papers into a pile in the middle of the table. "We need a break anyway."

"I know money is tight, and I'll have to get a full ride scholarship to be able to go to college."

"That's a pretty good opener for a conversation starting at midnight," Pell said. "Son, you know we'll help the best we can." Pell looked down at all of the bills. "It should be pretty obvious to all of us that we aren't millionaires."

Thea smiled and reached across the table to grasp Pell's hand. "Which makes us the same as almost every other working class family."

Here goes nothing, Tal thought. "Every school is besieged with scholarship applications from students with perfect grade points and off the chart standardized test scores. To get a full scholarship I'm going to have to differentiate myself from the herd."

"We're with you so far," Pell said.

Keep it rolling, Tal told himself. "I've spent substantial time researching different opportunities and possibilities to accomplish that goal."

"I'm guessing you've come up with an idea?" his Mom asked.

Mission accomplished, they're both interested. "Yes, I have. I think it's a winner. Not only for the short-term goal. It's something that might have the legs for a master's thesis, or even a doctoral dissertation."

Pell smiled. "It sounds like you've put a lot of thought into it."

"I have. And one of the best parts about it is that I won't need a lot of expensive equipment to perform the research to prove or disprove the thesis."

"Okay, Tal, we're intrigued," his Mom said. "Give us the details."

"I have designed an experiment to either prove or disprove a specific sociological thesis. The experiment will consist of two separate phases. In phase one, I will acquire statistical data from an analysis of communication by and between members of my peer group to determine what percent of our communication is verbal and what percent is nonverbal. Once I have quantified those results, the second phase of the study will be to compare the results of my study to any published reports concerning verbal/nonverbal ratios of prior generations."

Pell got up to go pick up the brownie plate off the counter, and brought it back to the table. In response to Thea's raised eyebrows, he said, "What? This discussion requires some serious thinking, which of course expends serious amounts of calories. Which of course means multiple brownies." He ate one whole, and after finishing it turned back to Tal. "What's the theorem you're attempting to prove or disprove?"

"I believe the explosion in the utilization of social media in the last decade has substantially altered the percentage of verbal versus nonverbal communication that existed for hundreds of years preceding the electronic revolution."

"You're positing that nonverbal communication has increased?" Thea asked.

"Exponentially, I believe. My specific theory is that as a result of this paradigm shift, daily verbal communication by and between members of a society may actually now be unnecessary."

"By social media, you mean Facebook?" Pell asked.

"That, and texting, Twitter, Instagram, Tumblr, and a number of other social media platforms. After completing both phases, my plan is to write a paper setting forth my study protocol and my findings and conclusions." Man, me and Emet make quite the team, Tal thought. Which I guess means I make quite the team. Focus, Tal, focus.

Pell had finished his second brownie, and was leaning over to pick up another one until he got a disapproving glance from Thea. "Who are you going to use as your control subjects to obtain the data?" he asked.

Here comes the critical part, Tal thought to himself. "I have an extremely short event horizon to complete this project and write a paper. Then there's the additional complication that if I involve anyone else the experiment technically qualifies as human testing. There are all kinds of research protocols and regulations governing any research involving human testing. Since most of my peers are minors, involving them would also require obtaining parental permission. To answer your question, Pell, I would be the guinea pig." Now, he told himself, give them the opportunity to buy in. "As a minor, I would need y'all's permission."

Tal watched as his Mom took a knife, cut one of the brownies in half, and gave a half to Pell. "That's the last one for you," she told him. "You're not having to cogitate that hard." Shifting focus back to Tal she said, "I don't understand, son. How are you going to obtain information?"

"He's going to quit talking, Thea," Pell said, as he picked up his brownie half.

"Oh," she replied. "When?"

"Immediately," Tal replied. "Early admittance decisions are made during the first semester. Most all of the good scholarships are spoken for shortly after that. Here's what I'm thinking." Keep them actively involved, he reminded himself. "If you see any opportunity to fine tune my plan, I'm open to your suggestions. Every day, beginning immediately after I go upstairs after breakfast each day, and continuing until the beginning of dinner each evening, I will only engage in nonverbal communication."

"Why after breakfast?" Pell asked.

"I didn't think you'd even consider letting me try the experiment if I didn't provide you with a daily window for us to communicate about my plans for the day, as well as any afterschool activities."

"You're probably right," his Mom confirmed.

"So, the same procedure then for after school, but before dinner?" Pell continued.

"Yes," Tal replied. Uh-oh, Tal thought, Mom's frown lines just went deep into her face.

"What about during school?" she asked.

"The experiment isn't viable without including school, Mom. That's when I have the majority of my verbal interaction. And it has to be the entire school day. Every day, no exceptions. Intramural track so that will be included as well."

This wasn't sitting well with her. "For how long?"

He and Emet had talked about how long they could possibly make their scheme last. They'd figured they could keep it up until maybe February at the latest. They'd have to deal with the rest of the school year later. No need to push it right now. Omada might not still be in the competition by then. "I'm thinking the whole first semester. I can knock out the research paper over the holidays, and get it to some schools before they make their final scholarship offers."

His Mom still wasn't buying in. "You're going to tell your teachers about this, right?"

"I can't, Mom. It has to be on a need to know basis. Every single person who knows presents another possibility for contamination of my results." Tal could see she didn't understand. "If someone knows about my research they might not try to engage me verbally which would mean I wouldn't have to find an alternate nonverbal response, which would skew my findings. I'm not telling the teachers, the students, anybody. I'm going to conduct a totally blind study."

"I don't know Tal," Pell added. "The whole purpose of this exercise is to make you a more attractive scholarship candidate. If this project hurts your grades, then you've defeated the reason for the study."

"I can text and email during school hours, and of course, talk every evening from dinner on. The only possible day-to-day classroom impact is that I won't be answering any questions during class. Lots of students who don't answer questions in class make straight "A"s. Let's face it, we all know that only one or two students in each group actually do most of the question answering."

"Gonna make it kind of hard to get acquainted with the opposite sex, isn't it?" Pell asked him.

Shit! We completely forgot Elle, Tal realized. This is going to be tougher than we imagined. Stay focused, dude "I'll have evenings to get caught up talking on my phone," he replied. "And if my hypothesis is correct, the lack of verbal communication won't present much of an impediment." I have to reel them in, he thought. "So, what do you think?"

Tal saw Pell look at the dozen or so bills scattered across the kitchen table, before he looked over to Thea. Some type of married person telepathic communication passed back and forth between them. "We support you, Tal," his Mom said. "We appreciate that you're always willing to try to help out around here. It is a really well thought out plan." As she saw him start beaming, she added, "You will be giving us regular updates on your grades and if they start falling, we're pulling the plug."

"That's a deal, Mom."

"The twins will have to be told something," she added.

"We talked about that…" Tal started to say.

"Who's we?" his Mom asked.

Way to go genius! You've already almost busted yourself out and you haven't even started. "Sorry. I meant I've already had that conversation with myself in trying to work out the details. I agree. Since they're not in my social peer network, any disruption to the data would be minimal."

"When will you start?" Pell asked.

"Tomorrow morning, right after breakfast," Tal replied.

"Sounds fine to us, Tal," Pell said. "We'll try to remember, and help any way we can."

Because of the possibility the downstairs conversation might wake one or both of the twins, Emet had taken the safe course and remained in the attic. As soon as he heard Tal close and lock his bedroom door he was through the bedroom window to get updated. Tal filled him in. Tal was so wound up, he couldn't even think about sleep, so he decided to take a look at his Hunts School textbooks. Emet headed back out the window and up to the attic.

This book is awesome, Tal decided. He was reading the *Creatures* textbook. Emet had messaged down that apparently sleepiness contained an emotional component, so he didn't feel sleepy. They both assumed Emet would need sleep to function properly although that was an open question given that his brain ran on magyk as opposed to nerve synapses. It made sense for Emet to adopt the same sleep pattern as Tal, so that's what they decided he should do. Emet started working on his homework in AP Biology. His pallet in the attic was right beside an air conditioner vent over Tal's bed. Tal could speak softly, and Emet, with his extraordinary hearing, was able to hear. Per their arrangement, Emet had the laptop, and Tal had the cell phone. They were going to switch occasionally at night so that Tal's parents could see Tal using the laptop, and it would reassure them he was keeping up with his schoolwork. They both thought it would be a good idea for Tal's family to hear him talking on the phone at night in addition to the post-dinner face-to-face oral communications. As soon as Tal could make time to get to the store, he was going to pick up a drop phone, so they both could text on a phone.

Tal couldn't seem to put the *Creatures* textbook down. He'd read Tolkien religiously when he was in his early teens. Over and over, he'd read *The Hobbit* as well as the trilogy. So he was familiar with the term "wight," or at least "barrow-wight," and how Tolkien had used the word. He had no idea that part of Tolkien's fiction was based on Norse and German mythology. Of course, Tolkien hadn't known the human mythology was based on real live—sort of—creatures that existed in the worlds of the Moiety. As Tal read further, he was even more surprised to learn the Middle English word "wight," was based on an even older Norse word—draugr.

"Emet, listen to this." He read him part of the draugr entry.

Emet's typed response appeared on Tal's phone, 'Draugrs were the original zombies.'

"I hadn't thought about it like that. They were, weren't they? They were Viking zombies." The information in the book totally absorbed Tal for the next couple of hours. He vaguely remembered his Mom sticking her head in the door, and reminding him that even though it was the weekend, it was way past time for bed.

Draugrs were undead. Some lived in graves, others lived in barrows, which could apparently be pretty fancy underground digs. Draugrs stunk badly, were incredibly strong, and could increase themselves in physical size. They weren't ghosts, although they had the ability to move through dirt and stone. The book described their underground movement as "swimming." Some draugrs could apparently see into the future, others could create fog or mist to hide themselves.

One of the signs of a draugr's presence was a dead zone surrounding the draugr's lair, sometimes called a "howe." The dead zone was pretty creepy actually, plants couldn't live there, and animals were afraid to go near it. Draugrs were described as being either drained-of-blood white, or by a Norse term—hel-blár—that could be interpreted as death-black. Like many of the Folk and Creatures, they had a strong aversion to iron objects. Tal read that sometimes relatives put iron scissors on the chest of the deceased, to keep them from turning draugr. Occasionally needles were driven through the soles of the dead's feet, or their big toes were tied together, to keep them from moving through the earth if they became a draugr.

The textbook info was skimpy on information about how to kill something that was already dead. The only sure fire way appeared to be using a sword to decapitate the draugr, and then burning all of the severed draugr parts.

When Tal couldn't keep his eyes open any longer he finally put the book down. His last thought before he drifted off to sleep was if zombies were real, what other nightmares might actually exist in the Folk planes. Nightmares like his faceless ghoul. He had told himself since he could first remember seeing the ghost that he wasn't crazy, he knew he'd seen something under his bed, coming and going from his closet. Always out of the corner of his eye. When he'd looked directly, there was never anything there. When Thea and Pell had searched under the bed or in the closet for him, they'd always reported there was no danger, nothing to worry about. Still, they had indulged him, and to this day his Mom never made his bed so that the bedspread went all the way to the floor, and everyone in the house knew to leave Tal's closet door open at all times. Tal had known though. He wasn't crazy, the danger presented by that thing was real.

Upstairs, Emet had finished his homework as well, and felt like he knew everything necessary to get a perfect score on Monday's biology quiz on mitochondria. Before he let himself fall asleep, he too thought of draugrs. His thoughts, however, were about how he was more like those creatures than he was like anyone else in the house.

CHAPTER THIRTY-THREE

Sunday had been uneventful. Tal and the family went to church, and afterward out to Morley's Diner for family lunch. During lunch Thea and Pell explained to Remy and Romy that as part of Tal's schoolwork there would be times he would not be talking. As they were eight and it didn't involve video games, or transformers, or toy versions of weapons of mass destruction, they could have cared less. After lunch Tal begged off going to the afternoon movie, citing a stomach ache. As soon as everyone else left for the show, he and Emet went downstairs. They knocked out some laundry, and found Emet some cold cuts in the refrigerator that Tal didn't think would be missed. The rest of the afternoon was spent "talking." Tal would have called it some "getting to know each other better" time, except that really wasn't possible. They had fine-tuned a few details for school, and communicated about Tal's worries for Anatolia. He'd prayed for her—silently of course—in church, and she'd been on his mind since the Omada left Friday night. She'd risked her life for him, for Omada. To 'Seek the Center,' whatever that was. Emet understood the gravitas of the situation, but explained analytically how worrying wasn't going to help Anatolia one bit, and they should be using their time to insure her sacrifice, at whatever level it ended up being, was worth her effort. When they heard Pell's car in the driveway, Emet headed up to the attic for the rest of the day. When dinnertime rolled around Tal started speaking again, which seemed to give the adults some comfort level with his project.

He and Emet put their plan in action first thing Monday morning. Actually, the night before, when Tal took his shower. Tal set his alarm an hour and a half earlier than his usual time. In the morning, he first went downstairs in his t-shirt and gym shorts, making sure he greeted both parents. After reminding them he would be playing the quiet game until dinner, he grabbed a plate of food to share with Emet, and raced back up the stairs. They both inhaled their food. After that Tal shaved, put on deodorant, brushed his teeth, threw on some clothes, and grabbed his backpack. After making sure the coast was clear, Tal was out the window. It took him longer to get down the tree than it did Emet, but he knew he'd get better at it. He glanced backward and saw Emet standing at the window. Tal waved, put his backpack straps squarely over his shoulders, and took off at a slow jog. He knew even with the books in his backpack that he could do ten-minute miles, so it was going to take him a little over an hour and a half each day to get to the Gas Station.

As Emet showered and dressed, he noticed each toiletry item was exactly where he expected it to be when he reached for it. Of course they are, he thought, I do everything in the same order as Tal. When he was through dressing, Emet gave himself the once over in the mirror. No use delaying it, time to go meet the folks.

He'd barely made it to the base of the stairs before the boys were all over him, demanding that he come outside and play with them a few minutes.

"Tal, do you know what time you'll be home from track practice?" his Mom asked.

Emet made the zipper motion across his mouth with his left hand.

"Oh, right. Sorry, I forgot. Boys, leave Tal alone, he's conducting an experiment. We all need to get going anyway, we're going to be late." They all grabbed their backpacks and lunches and headed to the minivan. The twins were, as normal, practically jumping out of their seats. Emet rode in silence in Tal's customary place—the front passenger seat. They drove to the high school first.

"Good luck with school, Tal, and with your project."

Emet started to open his car door.

"What, no kiss for your Mom today?"

Wow, almost messed that up, Emet thought. I had no emotion to remind me. He leaned over and kissed Thea on her right cheek. He got out of the car, closed the door, and turned toward the front entrance for his first day of school.

Right at an hour later, Tal finally huffed up to Sol's Station. He'd pushed himself as hard as he could, and stopped for a moment about half a block away to catch his breath and to stow his wallet, cellphone, keys, and all of his Munedan personal effects underneath a thorny holly bush. He and Emet had talked about hiding his stuff before he got to the Gas Station so the phone would keep its charge, and the rest of his stuff wouldn't be laying around outside the Ladies' Room door.

The first thing he heard when he arrived at the gas station was the air hose hissing at him. "Hurry, Tal S-S-Smith." Gas Pump No. Duo started dinging. Tal looked over to see a message, it was scrolling down this time. 'Have a good day at school. Oh by the way—your life is in danger.'

Right about then Gas Pump No. Unus also started dinging. As Tal looked, he saw one word scroll by, repeating over and over. And over.

'BEWARE!'

At least the Gas Station is looking out for me, Tal thought, as he opened the Ladies' Room door, and stepped into blackness.

CHAPTER TRIGINTA QUATTUOR

Tal hoofed it full speed ahead across Grass Grow. The morning run from home is going to be a problem he thought, particularly when the weather turns bad. He saw the last of the students walking past the door guardians. The bell must have already rung, and I don't even know where I'm supposed to go first. He picked up his pace as he passed the fountain, and took the steps two at a time. He looked past the sentries when he got to the top of the steps, and there he was. Waiting on him.

I can't imagine there is any smile on earth as wide as that boy's, Tal thought as Borras walked over to him. A genuine smile that's so big it has a Doppler effect as it rolls across his face. How could you not smile in return?

"I knew it. I told them you wouldn't let us down. That you wouldn't let yourself down." Borras hugged him so exuberantly, Tal thought he heard a rib groan a little under the stress. "The golem?"

"Emet is alive and kicking, and on his way to Nemeton High. Anatolia?"

If Tal thought the grin was big before, it was several sizes larger now. "She's fine, Quint. We got her back in time. Barely. Thank Amarantos, Dysi's magyk is teleportation. They had everything set up for Ana by the time I got her to the infirmary. They kept her all weekend for observation, but she was supposed to be released this morning in time for class. The HuntsMistress and a couple of the physicks gave us the third-degree interrogation trying to find out what happened to her. Notos and I talked about it on the way back and decided no one outside the team should know we can cross the wards because you're on our team. Even more importantly, they can't know the Bane doesn't apply to us when we're off campus. You should have seen Notos. He was stone cold perfect. He looked them straight in the face and said, 'The primitive Earth plane's electrical and magnetic fields must have had an unexpected and delayed adverse allergic interaction with her base magyk. You should probably issue a warning to all Hunt's participants before this year's field trip.' I mean, she's been at Hunts School almost a hundred years, and they bought it. Totally."

Borras was so excited he barely took time to draw breath. "She's unbelievable, Quint. Anatolia is unbelievable. It's been generations since there has been so strong a Maker. C'mon, the team is going to want to hear all about the golem," Borras stopped, a crease of concern appearing between his eyes. "Crap. I sent the rest ahead to take care of things, in case, well, you know…in case…"

"In case I was running a little late," Tal said, letting Borras off the hook.

"Exactly," Borras said, smiling once more. "Come on, we can't be late by even a second for Orientation this morning." Without waiting, Borras turned and took off down the hall, each of his strides equaling three of Tal's, who although still winded tried to keep up with his Prime.

CHAPTER THIRTY-FIVE

As he walked to Tal's locker, Emet was thinking about possible complications with their operation. He and Tal had talked through the ones they could think of, and had a response plan for those issues. Not speaking with other students wasn't going to be a problem. It's not like Tal had had a chance to make a lot of friends his first two weeks. They'd decided the other kids would decide he was weird, or stuck-up, or simply fell into the category of general-asshole-for-undisclosed-reasons. In any event they would end up steering clear.

After Thea had expressed her concern about Tal's grades falling, the two had decided it was a legitimate issue that needed to be addressed proactively. The consensus solution was to get Principal Davis to provide cover for them. Emet typed up a note for the Principal saying that Tal was attempting to get a full-ride President's Scholarship at Hendrix College. Hendrix was a small, highly regarded liberal arts school in Conway, over towards the middle of the state. The letter stated that in an effort to secure the scholarship, Tal was attempting to distinguish himself from other candidates by conducting an independent study sociological research project. They made sure the letter stated Tal had not coordinated the project with any adult—other than his parents.

This included any person at Hendrix. The letter also stated that to secure the integrity of the project and the data to be collected, Principal Davis was the only person other than Tal's parents who knew about the experiment. The letter concluded with a thank you, and a request for any assistance Principal Davis could give Tal with his teachers.

Tal and Emet hoped the letter would flip the Principal from being a potential liability, into an asset. If Tal's folks ultimately decided they needed to talk to the Principal, it was essentially the same story Tal had told them. He and Tal had decided it was better to ask for forgiveness instead of permission. Hopefully, Principal Davis would backstop the deal with Tal's teachers. There was no reason for him to call Hendrix to confirm since they weren't in the loop. Nicely played, Emet thought.

Emet realized Tal would have been smiling with satisfaction at this point, so he made the appropriate muscle adjustments to make himself smile. For practice. So far everything was proceeding exactly according to plan. He picked up the books from his locker for Tal's morning classes, checked his watch as he was closing the locker door, and when he looked up…there she was.

CHAPTER TRIGINTA SEX

Ms. Empousa was in full lecture mode and every member of the class was writing notes at warp speed, trying not to miss a word. He and Borras had gotten to class right before the final bell so Tal hadn't even had a chance to say hello to his teammates. He saw Anatolia first. She was white as a ghost and was wearing an extra sweater, but she was there. He saw her mouth the word, "Yes?" and when he nodded she grinned wanly. Dysi caught his eye, and nodded her approval of his presence. Notos had given him his usual, "I've just eaten a sour green apple" stare. Of course.

    "Since you first enrolled at Hunts School a hundred years ago," before looking over at Tal, "well, all of you, excepting the single most pathetic replacement Fifth in the history of this school, your curriculum has encompassed the known Folk universe. You have learned histories and current events of the hundred most populated planes, with a special emphasis on the histories, cultures and languages of the Earth plane. You have also studied the biographies of every Hunts' Finalists in every Tyrning. Team names, direction names, avatar names, which Folk they represented, and what primary and secondary magykal abilities. You have learned the fundamental tenets underlying the philosophies of the Prime Directions who became Archon, and you have learned all of the different categories and combinations of the Hunts themselves." Tal was scribbling faster than everyone else in the class. He knew Notos would be on his ass if he missed a syllable of this recap.

"Last year was your penultimate year here at Hunts School. As you know, the Hunts Rules require that in the year immediately preceding the Tyrning there be a winnowing Hunt to cull the three hundred sixty semi-finalist teams down to the nine finalist squads." She paused, to walk slowly, angrily, back and forth in front of the class, before beginning again. "Unfortunately last year's Snype Hunt produced more deaths and maimings than any Hunt in the history of the school. More Folk deaths in any event. In the good old days when we were allowed to schedule Battle Hunts, there were tens of thousands of Munedan deaths but the Folk mortality rate was very low. Unfortunately, Battle Hunts have been banned from the curriculum. I quite frankly never understood what the objection was."

I don't care how tight her outfit is, Tal thought to himself. There will be no more wood associated with her hotness. That is one granite-hearted bitch. Oh shit, when she bent over just then, and there was that crease right there...in the middle of her...focus, you idiot. Focus.

"There has been some administrative finger-pointing alleging that the unusually large number of casualties occurred because I chose a Snype Hunt, and also perhaps because you were not provided adequate preparation for all of the variables presented by a Snype Hunt. I prefer to believe it was more a reflection of this class's abysmally low caliber of competitors I have had to deal with during this Tyrning. It's simply not that hard to kill a dragon, even a dragon prince."

Wait, what? Dragon? Dragon prince? Tal wondered, as he quickly shook a cramp out of his left hand. Who said anything about killing dragons?

Ms. Empousa resumed her pacing. It was like when Tal was little, going to watch the big cats at the zoo. They silently walked back and forth in front of the bars, waiting, just waiting for that day when maybe a cage door was left open, or some unfortunate climbed up and stuck a hand or a leg into the cage. "There are three Hunts each Tyrning year. To prevent collusion or advance planning, the types of Hunts are selected at the sole discretion of the HuntsMaster or HuntsMistress. There will be three Journeys in the Scavengyr Hunt, and four categories of artifacts eligible for points. Your goal is to collect at least one scavengyr piece each Journey. You are allowed to collect one piece in as many categories as you can. In the event a team obtains a piece in each category, there will be no more Journeys for that team."

Tal took a quick look around. He didn't think he'd ever been in a classroom where every student paid such close attention to the lecture. Of course he'd never been in a classroom before where the curriculum included death and/or loss of multiple body parts.

"Team strategy plays a critical role in the Hunts. Each team will decide what category of piece they wish to acquire on a Journey. These are directed Journeys. The Prime Omphalos will accept the Journey information only from your Prime Direction. Unless you choose to disclose that information for strategy reasons, the other teams won't know where you Journeyed. If one team travels to the same plane at the same time you may wound or maim—but not kill—members of the other team to secure a piece." She stopped walking to emphasize her last statement. "Your team will be eliminated and one of your teammates terminated if you kill another Finalist. This rule has only one exception—you may kill in self-defense."

Tal had no idea why he chose that moment to look over at Nord, maybe he'd felt old Squinty glaring at him. Which he was. Nord slowly drew his finger across his throat. That boy needs to feel better about himself, Tal thought. Maybe a high colonic or something, because being a total and complete douche is not fulfilling him. Tal held his left hand in front of his chest, so Ms. Empousa couldn't tell what was going on, and gave Squinty the finger. Apparently the students had learned their Earth plane cultures well because Squinty came halfway up out of his chair before Mitt saw what was going on, and pulled him back down.

"Your teachers will explain the various categories and what artifacts will qualify for which categories. You may not, for defensive purposes, acquire more than one piece in each category. If your team obtains more than one piece in any category, your team forfeits the competition. If your team fails to maintain the minimum number of non-maimed team members, your team is out of the competition. If your team fails at any time to comply with all major Hunts Rules, your team may forfeit the competition."

"After the three Journeys, I will rank the strength of the scavengyr pieces, add that to your other points, and the top five teams will move to the second Hunt. Artifact strength ranking is a discretionary decision on my part. My decision is not appealable, with the sole exception of a Combat Challenge. The Hunts Rules provide the first runner-up team may seek to be advanced in rank by declaring a Combat Challenge. If challenge is issued, all teams lower in ranking may join in if they so desire. The Challenge Combat continues until at least one member of all participating teams—except that of the victor—is dead."

Dead, Tal wrote. How many times already this morning has she said the word "dead?" Or "maimed?" Or "wounded?" Who in their right mind would call for a Combat Challenge knowing that at a minimum one of their team members would die if they lost?

"I expect strict adherence to the rules." Ms. Empousa paused and looked around the entire room. "Any questions?" There were none forthcoming. "Good. By the way, I fully expect several of you will be dead within the next few weeks." She then pointedly turned, and looked at Tal, and smiled.

Tal realized it didn't matter now if Ms. Empousa's Puca elongated, flowed, protruded, or rippled—he no longer needed to think about baseball, or golf when he looked at her. Not even a little bit. The woman was a bone-chilling freak.

CHAPTER THIRTY-SEVEN

She'd seen Tal the minute he walked in the front door. During the weekend she had diagrammed, rediagrammed, and re-rediagrammed her game plan. Operation ONoUDidn't changed radically each time, depending upon her rage quotient at that particular moment. The exercise had required her to conduct a pretty frank assessment of herself. Academically she was killing it. She was first in the senior class with Barton second. Angie Alison was running only a fraction of a point behind Barton, and had the potential to leapfrog over him and be a dark horse winner for valedictorian. No, she doesn't, because I'm giving that valedictorian speech. Sorry Angie, you can beat Barton's ass if you you're able, but you won't be taking me out.

Taking the full three hundred and sixty degree look around herself also meant performing both a physical and metaphysical critique. There was always room for improvement, but good nutrition, competing on the volleyball team, and hitting the Crossfit box at least three times a week had yielded excellent results. Her height might be a problem for some insecure bantam roosters but that wasn't her type anyway.

She volunteered at every opportunity. Not solely because it looked good on her college applications—she genuinely enjoyed helping others, giving to others. Whether it was extracurricular activities like the school paper, or answering the phone down at the county hospital, she made an effort to use the assets she'd been given to improve the lives of other folks in her community. She tried to avoid gossiping, and she'd always made an effort to pay attention in church. Admittedly sometimes with more success than others. But in her defense, Pastor Hayes could be more than a little dry sometimes. Way, way more than a little.

Like anybody else she had her faults, but her conclusion was that she was intelligent, pretty, fun, and nice. The point being? The point being, I don't know who that Tal Smith boy thinks he is, but he had no call to stiff me on our lunch date. Sure, he had been entitled to a fair allowance for the Barton interference factor, but he didn't even attempt to get my phone number, or my email to apologize. He had an entire weekend to make some effort. Any effort.

He'd left her no choice but to let him have it with Operation ONoUDidn't. Both barrels. Phase One was the cold shoulder—the subzero cold shoulder, the give his ass some frostbite if he even looked at her from all the way across the hall cold shoulder. For a few days anyway. Until he understood he should be attracted to her, until he wanted to get to know her as much as she wanted to get to know him. More, actually. Then there would need to be profuse abject apologies. Many iterations of profuse abject apologies. All of which she intended to reject. Repeatedly. After that he would have to perform some labors of devotion. She'd spent a few hours reacquainting herself with the Twelve Labors of Hercules. The twenty-first century version of several of those should do nicely.

So she had nonchalantly walked up to a locker that was only a couple down from his and waited. He had his head down when he came in, focused on something. He went straight to his locker, opened it, and got some books out. Excellent, she thought. I have the element of surprise. When he closes the locker he'll see me. She watched as he closed the locker, and looked up and saw her standing there. Wait for it, she told herself. He'll be falling all over himself, stuttering. Like in the library.

Cue closing the locker door. And he sees me now. He's nodding his head at me. Good, good…and now he's going to beg my forgiveness. For the first time. Get ready Tal Smith, it's about to get decidedly chilly up in here.

What? What? Are you kidding me? He turned his back on me, and is walking down the hallway toward homeroom.

Oh no, he didn't!

CHAPTER TRIGINTA OCTO

Tal was in the Omada room with his entire squad. They were all seated, well except for Notos, who had been pacing since the moment they secured the door. The first order of business had been for Tal to bring everyone up to speed about Emet and all of the details of their plan to disguise Tal's absence. Anatolia was getting stronger by the minute, and Tal's report about Emet seemed to energize her. Based upon her smiles and the many congratulations from Dysi and Borras, the creation of a simulacrum golem was an exceptionally rare feat.

After that the discussion turned to an analysis of the strengths and weaknesses of the other teams, not only for defensive purposes, but also to discuss possible strategic alliances for the Scavengyr Hunt. While they were doing that, and despite Notos's near constant interruptions, Dysi was giving Tal a quick overview of Hunts' nomenclature.

"You have to remember Quint, Principal Chiron is the Chief Archivist and even he doesn't know exactly how many millennia have passed since the Moiety was agreed, and the first Tyrning happened. No one even knows how many type of Folk presently exist. Folk languages have come, and gone. There are some types of Folk who apparently no longer exist, their entire race having been gathered to the UnFading Spirit."

"UnFading Spirit?"

"Oh, Quint," she said, momentarily daunted. "I don't know how we can teach you everything you need to know in such a short time. We'll save Amarantos—the UnFading Spirit—for later. There are other things you must know now. It may save your life…and ours." She got out a piece of paper and drew a diagram of a compass, with an odd diagonal line transecting the center. "Regardless of whether a Folk have a written language, or communicate by signing, verbally, or only telepathically, in every plane created by Amarantos there has been a single common reference. The five cardinal directions."

"Actually," Tal interrupted, "I've had this same discussion recently with the Traveler or whatever you want to call him."

"You've had an audience with the Traveler?" Borras asked, his mouth wide in astonishment.

"Well, technically it was a psych eval with some punk ass know it all kid who said his name was Mertin Wilt. But I'll go with 'audience.' "

"We don't have time for this right now, Borras," Dysi gently chided.

"Right," Borras agreed. "Later then."

"Anyway," Tal continued, "you're all wrong. There are only four cardinal directions."

Notos interrupted. "See, he doesn't even know first year information." Turning back to Tal, he said, "Shut your yack and listen up Munedan, She created five cardinal directions…"

Dysi continued. "The UnFading Spirit created five cardinal directions. North, South, East, West…"

"That would be four," Tal said.

"And the Prime Cardinal Direction—Center."

"Really?" Notos yelled. "Are we really spending our time on information any Folk infant learns almost before they even learn to walk?"

"Notos, sit down, you're driving us all crazy," Borras said. After Notos complied, Borras turned his attention back to Tal. "Quint, you are simply going to have to accept that everything you know has been seen through the filter of human knowledge. What may be a certainty in your world, may only be a possibility—maybe even fantasy—in all the others."

Anatolia stepped in to help explain. "Even some human cultures have known about the fifth direction. Think about it. How could you possibly know which way you were going on one plane, much less multiple planes, if you didn't have a center to always guide you home from your journey?"

"Where did you think all of our squad names came from, human?" Notos asked.

Dysi stepped in quickly. "Lay off, Notos. Quint, when the Hunts teams are announced, all of the team members caucus and pick a name for the team. The Hunts Rules require that in some Folk language the team name must mean family, group, tribe, or a similar concept. Omada is the Greek Realm word for 'Team'."

"And some of the Folk languages are reflected in their Earth plane counterparts," Tal noted.

"Some," Dysi agreed.

"Kentro, Borras, Notos, Anatolia…" Tal mused out loud. "Those are Latin. Your names are the names of the directions in Latin."

"Yes," Borras confirmed, "and when a replacement is added, the name corresponds to a number to show the individual was not an original member."

"Why are we wasting precious time trying to teach him this?" Notos demanded. "He doesn't even know the team names and members. We don't have time to spoon-feed him. Everyone else is spending their team time strategizing for the first Journey"

"Always with the negative waves, Moriarty," Tal said.

"What's that supposed to mean?" Notos growled, as he took a half step toward Tal.

Tal realized Notos was ready to have a throw down with him. "Nothing," Tal replied. "I was just trying to be funny. Look

Notos, I can learn. I've got this thing with my memory. If somebody will write all of the names down and let me look at them, I'll learn them pronto. I'll still need help with the pronunciations but I'll know all the names."

"I'll do it," Anatolia said. She walked over to the blackboard, and in about five minutes she had written down all of the individual and group names. "Okay, these are the other eight finalist teams. Actually," she said as she looked around at her teammates, "since he needs to know as much as possible about our opponents, this is a complete list of the finalist teams before the Snype Hunt. Except for our squad, of course."

Tal saw Dysi take a moment to compose herself. Because Kentro isn't on the list, he realized. "Take however long you need to look at the board," Dysi said.

Tal slowly scanned the names left to right. One line at a time. He looked at the information for about two minutes. "Got it."

"Sure you do," Notos laughed. "Don't be ridiculous. It would take any of us at least a whole day of studying to even get most of that information memorized."

"Try me," Tal said, crossing his arms.

"Fine," Notos replied as he walked over to the blackboard, and quickly erased all of the information. "Okay, genius, let's hear it."

Tal closed his eyes, and started visualizing the list.

"In cardinal direction order," Notos added.

"Fine. The Släkt have a Northern European Realm name, and are currently the points leader in the competition. Mitt is their Prime. Squinty…er…Nord is their Second Prime. Then its Söder, Ost, and Väst. Next in points is the Bùluò. It's one of the two teams remaining whose names derive from Far Eastern planes, Shuzoku is the other one."

"Perfect, so far," Dysi commented.

"Zhong is the Prime Direction of the Bùluò, Bei is Second Prime, then Nán, Dong, and Xí. In the Shuzoku, the Prime is Chuushin, Second is Kita. The other three are Minami,

Higashi, and Nishi. The Allyu take their name from a South American Realm. There's Yaxkin, Xaman, Nohol, Lik'in, and Chik'in. Pleme's team name is taken from an Eastern European plane. The team members are Sredina, Sever, Istok, Jug and Zapad. Next are the Hak'éí, with a North American Indian Realm team name—Ulh-Ne-Ih, Nahookos, Shádi'Ááh, Ha'A'Aah, and E'E'Aah.

"You need to work on the glottal stops a little, but not too bad for your first try," Borras said.

"Thanks. Kabila is the only team remaining in the Hunt whose name is derived from an African Realm. It's members are Kati, Kaskazini, Kusini, Mashariki, and Magharibi. The last team, other than us, is the Aile who chose their team name from an Eastern Asian Realm. Merkez, Kuzey, Güney, Dogü, and Bat_."

"Great, so he can name them," Notos said sourly. "He has no idea what each of them can do to us, or for us."

"It's not like the rest of us know that much more," Borras said. "We only know what we learned from watching the other teams during the Snype Hunt. It's a start."

The ten-minute bell rang for the next class. "Let's go, Omada," Borras said, as he unsealed their door.

CHAPTER THIRTY-NINE

Screw the plan, Elle decided as she sprinted after Tal. When she caught up, she grabbed his shoulder, spinning him around, and then let him have it. "Really? Really? Do you have nothing to say for yourself?"

He just stared at her with an infuriating blank look on his face before finally shaking his head, no. That was it. Period. She'd only thought she was mad before. "Listen here, Buster!" Damn I must really be mad, she thought. Did I really call a guy "Buster?"

"You could at least apologize for not showing up last Friday for our lunch date." What is he doing now, she wondered. He has his mouth wide open, and now he's motioning like he can't speak. Oh hell, no. "That's it? Really? That's all you got? You're going to fake laryngitis? Unbelievable!"

Again, Tal just shook his head at her. Which kicked Elle up several more levels on the infuriation scale. "I'm not some tragic-low-self-esteem-searching-for-validation-by-engaging-in-serial-relationships-teenage-girl out of some novel, you know."

Not a word. He said nothing. Nothing. The five-minute bell rang. Still he stood there staring at her, then motioned to the watch on his wrist.

Apoplectic, her face feeling like it was about to explode, she couldn't stop herself from yelling. "I know it's almost time for class, you jackass!" She spun around and started marching down the hallway toward her homeroom. Then, after she'd taken a couple of extremely strident steps, his hands—his really strong hands—were on both her shoulders, gently turning her back toward him. Nope, I'm not looking at him, she told herself. Then there was his left hand gently touching her chin, and lifting it upwards, until...until she was looking into a pair of huge, warm brown eyes—brown flashed with golden flecks. He's finally going to say something, she realized. Well no, he's not, but he's mouthing some words—'I'm sorry, Elle. Please forgive me.' And now, he's thoughtfully turning me back toward where I need to go. And now—he's gone.

Oh, hell, she thought. Breathy, silent apologies are fucking hot.

CHAPTER QUADRAGINTA

"This morning we will begin our discussion about the first of the four Scavengyr categories—Weapons. We will be studying weapons in this class for the next two weeks. There are those among the Folk who would argue that in a Scavengyr Hunt it is the most important piece. I believe that to be a myopic viewpoint. It is true no team has ever won a Scavengyr Hunt without obtaining a significant weapon. However, if you're trying to win the competition, or maybe just survive this school year, you and every one of your teammates must always remember how critically important each scavengyr piece may be."

Professor Daedalus Hardcastle had been half-sitting on the front of his desk during his opening remarks to the class. He got up at this point and walked over to a large chart that took up pretty much an entire wall of his classroom. "As you can see, it is almost impossible to identify all of the types of weapons existing in the Folk Realms."

Tal took a quick glance across the rows and rows of illustrations and descriptions. What the hell? Is that a feather?

"In past Scavengyr Hunts, the weapons category has included a broad panoply of qualifying artifacts. Swords, maces, sickles, tridents, bows, or any other item, which could arguably be utilized as an offensive weapon. HuntsMistress Empousa has elected to increase the difficulty factor this year, and has limited the universe of qualifying weapons to blades. Not just any blade either, only certain enumerated blades will count for points."

Tal could have sworn he heard somebody say, "Yes!" in response to Professor Hardcastle's announcement. He looked back over his shoulder and saw Squinty smiling. He thinks they have a leg up for some reason, Tal thought. How could they possibly have an inside track on something that was only just announced? Of course he's probably only being a dick and trying to intimidate everyone else.

"There are nine finalist teams. The HuntsMistress has named only twelve blades—eleven swords and one kris—that will qualify as a weapon piece for the Scavengyr Hunt."

Tal leaned ever so slightly toward Borras. "Kris?"

"Long wavy knife. More like a long dagger than a sword. Sshh! We don't need any demerits."

Professor Hardcastle continued. "You'll find copies of the weapons list on your tables. Please pick them up now and give them a quick lookover." The professor paused about a minute as the Primes handed out the lists, and the students scanned them. Then he continued. "Actually, the whole twelve qualifying blades is a little bit of an inside joke by the HuntsMistress. One of the swords is unavailable at this time. Who can tell me which sword that is?"

Tal saw a hand go up from Ulh-Ne-Ih, Prime of the Hak'éí. "Yes?"

"Excalibur."

"That is correct," Professor Hardcastle replied before leaning over to make a notation in his grade book. "And what was its name before it became Excalibur?"

This time is was Nohol of the Ayllu trying to get the points for his team. "The Sword of Many Names."

"Points for the Ayllu. Why is it unavailable?" The hand which shot up the fastest belonged to Güney of the Aile. "Yes?"

"It was retired because it was scavengyd and used by the Prime Direction of the Hunts winner four Tyrnings past."

"Right. In keeping with Hunts School tradition, Excalibur became his personal weapon until such time as he is gathered to the UnFading Spirit. At that time it shall again become the Sword of Many Names and be available once more."

Wow, Tal thought. Excalibur was King Arthur's sword. So Arthur was Folk, not human, and if he's still alive he would have to be over a thousand years old.

"By limiting the number of qualifying weapons, the HuntsMistress has also increased the importance of team strategy for this Hunt. There are significantly more qualifying pieces in each of the other three categories. In all probability, any team that fails to acquire a weapon won't advance to the remaining Hunts. Additionally, the probability that all team members will survive the Hunts is dramatically decreased if a team fails to obtain a weapon. Bottom line? Get a weapon, but don't forget to grab pieces in the other categories. Your lives depend on it."

That's about as clear as you can make it, Tal thought. Find a weapon, secure the weapon, hold on to the weapon.

Professor Hardcastle walked over to the blackboard. "We will now go over the remaining eleven qualifying weapons. I am not listing them in rank order. That determination has been made in secret by the HuntsMistress, and tendered to the Principal. The list is stored in a safe in the Principal's office. Before any of you even start thinking about cheating, you should know there are walleye wards in place to protect the list."

I'm not even asking Borras what a walleye ward is, Tal thought. And cheating? He wondered why he hadn't even thought that might be something to worry about. Apparently some things are common across all planes of existence.

"You will find in-depth descriptions and information concerning each blade, beginning on page fifty-six of your *Weapons* textbook. You will notice fairly quickly that more than one of these weapons are reputed to be "unbeatable." Please remember that all of the blades normally reside on different planes. They are brought together only for the Hunts, so their supremacy is a relative thing. In other words unbeatable might be beatable by a more unbeatable unbeatable."

Professor Hardcastle walked over and picked up a piece of paper from his desk. "As you leave you will each be required to initial the written disclosure that you have been advised no other instruments qualify as a "weapon" for the Hunt. Do not forget to initial the disclosure on your way out. Your team will be docked points for any omission." He placed the paper back on his desk before walking over to the blackboard to begin writing.

"Heaven's Will is a sword originally from a Far East Realm. It gives the holder the ability to grow to giant size, and gives him or her the strength of a thousand." As he mentioned the name of each weapon, Professor Hardcastle wrote it on the board as well as the page number of the textbook where a longer description could be found. "Caladbolg is a two-handed sword. It holds within itself sufficient force to slice the tops off of hills. The Sword of Peleus insures its bearer will be victorious in battle. Taming Sari is another Eastern plane weapon, the sole kris in the approved weapons. The exact nature of its magyk is unknown. Fragarach is also known as 'The Answerer.' There is no armor which can withstand it, and it gives its holder power over the winds. Also, no one can lie when Fragarach is placed to their throat. Any wound inflicted by Fragarach is fatal. One hundred percent of the time, no matter how minor the wound. Gram is said to be so sharp it can cleave an anvil in half. Kladenets is a sword from a Russian plane. It cannot be slowed or affected by water or fire, and is sometimes called 'Asp the Serpent.' "

"Mistilteinn, has an interesting history. At one time it was owned by the infamous draugr Prainn. During the time he owned the sword, he transferred some of his Creature magyk into the blade. In one single battle, Prainn used Mistilteinn to kill over four hundred Folk. He was, of course, ultimately defeated, his head cut off, all four limbs severed from his torso, and all of his body parts first burned and then separately buried with large bodies of water situated between the parts. Can't be too careful with draugrs you know. It was the largest slaughter of Folk by a Creature in the history of the Moiety. Skofnung was forged by the legendary Norse Realm dwarf, Brokkr. Who knows what other famous weapon Brokkr and his two brothers made?"

Istok of the Pleme's hand went up. "Mjolnir. From the Norse plane."

"Thor's magyk hammer," Professor Hardcastle confirmed. "The dwarf blacksmiths also created Gungnir, one of the Spears of Power. When they forged Skofnung they placed within its steel the life essence of twelve berserkers. Its weakness is that although sunlight may touch the blade, it may never touch the sword's hilt."

Tal quickly flipped to the description of berserkers on page one thousand, seven hundred and seven. Looked like they were pretty much super-warriors who volunteered to forego Valhalla so their souls could be placed inside Skofnung.

Professor Hardcastle had moved on to the next blade. "You will know Tyrfing by its golden hilt. When Tyrfing is drawn from its sheath, it never—ever—misses its intended target. It can cut through rock, stone, iron, anything in order to reach its goal." He then drew a question mark on the chalkboard. "That's for the final weapon. It hasn't ever been given a name of its own, and is known only as the Flaming Sword of Surtr, the fire giant." Tal heard a low "ooohhh" wash through the students.

Professor Hardcastle looked at the clock on the wall. "There's fifteen minutes until the bell for your next class. You may use the rest of your class time to begin reading the chapters concerning the relative strengths and weaknesses of each of the weapons."

Gotta be the damnedest scavenger hunt ever, Tal decided. Ever.

CHAPTER FORTY-ONE

Tal and Emet learned a few things on their first after school trip home. To prevent any wardrobe continuity errors, they'd decided the first thing each afternoon would be a clothing exchange at the gas station. That way when Tal walked up the driveway, he would be wearing what Emet wore to school that morning. As far as the actual trip home, Emet's enhanced hearing provided an early warning system if a car was coming on the highway. When that happened, Tal hopped off, and they were merely two teenagers walking along a two-lane country road. Emet was going to put a couple of ball caps in his backpack, which should help in disguising their twinship. There was still plenty of after school daylight this time of year so when they got near town, they split up with Tal taking the lead. That way neighbors might see them individually, but not together. Once winter rolled around, there would be less chance of getting busted as it would be getting on dark by the time they got home. On the days Emet took the bicycle to school, he took Tal there so Tal could ride it home.

Emet had no problem maintaining a good pace. Tal's weight didn't seem to slow him even a little. Tal asked Emet to put him down a couple of blocks early, to make it a little easier to talk before they had to split up. He was quickly getting the hang of asking Emet yes or no questions. If there was a topic Emet thought needed to be covered, he used the notes app on the phone to type the issue. Tal realized there was at least one area where two minds that were actually one mind were actually better than one mind that was actually only one mind—processing ability. Since Emet had known nothing about the day's events at Hunts School, he'd been able to focus on Nemeton High schoolwork and thinking about the Elle situation. A good thing, since Tal had more than he could digest at Hunts School. After a few minutes of stream of consciousness discussion, a decision was made that one would disseminate all of his new info, they would completely discuss all of those matters, and then the other one would provide his update.

It made sense for Emet to disgorge his info first. That way Tal would be fully apprised of the Nemeton school activities before dinner. Emet typed about his run-in with Elle, his delivery of the note as planned to the Principal's office, that he hadn't been called on in class, and that the two times he'd seen Barton and his group, he'd been able to move along before being spotted. Except for Elle, Tal thought, it had been an uneventful first day at Nemeton. Which is what they'd wanted. Except for Elle. It was time to split up when Emet got finished, so they decided to discuss Elle, and Tal's day later.

"How did the project go today?" his Mom asked at dinner.

"Not a peep all day from any of my teachers."

Pell reached over and grabbed the bowl of fried okra, and spooned another helping onto his plate. "So, you're going to stick with the experiment?"

"Absolutely."

"How was track practice, Tal?" Remy asked.

"It was fun," Tal replied.

Rom was not to be out questioned by his twin. "When do we get to come watch you smoke all the other losers?"

"It's intramural track, Rom. I'm pretty sure we won't have a meet or anything until the end of the season."

"Well, maybe we can bring the twins by some day to watch you practice," Pell suggested.

"Sure. Not a problem," Tal replied. "Let me get better though. Most of the other guys have been running for years. If y'all don't mind, I'd like to eat my dinner up in my room so I can get started on my homework."

"As long as the dirty plates get back down here and into the dishwasher," his Mom replied. She watched him load another whole layer of food on his plate. "I'm going to have to start cooking more if you're going to eat three chicken breasts at a time."

"I guess it's all the exercise, Mom. I feel like I'm eating for two these days."

Later, after he and Emet had eaten, and Tal had taken his shower, and returned the dishes downstairs, they were both in their respective beds reading, and conversing. Tal whispered his part of the conversation, the typed response came back from Emet with only a few seconds delay. Tal had finished debriefing Emet about the day at Hunts School and their focus had come back around to Elle.

"Do you not feel anything, even for her?" Tal asked.

'That's a difficult question for me to answer. My golem brain acknowledges your feelings for her. For me they register as factual statements stripped of any emotion.'

"I don't get it."

'Tell me something you feel about her,' Emet typed.

Tal thought for a moment. "Well, she's smoking hot."

'I need for you to be a little more specific please, Tal.'

"I feel like she might be the perfect woman for me."

'Not much better, but I will attempt to translate. Her eyes are green, her hair is a shade in the orange-red spectrum, her skin appears to be well-hydrated, she is appropriately curvilinear, she smiles frequently, and she laughs truthfully.'

"She's 'appropriately curvilinear?' Come on Mr. Spock, you're killing me."

'I have limitations as a Creature, Tal. There's nothing I can do about those parameters.'

"How am I—strike that—how are we going to get her to go out with us?"

'There would have to be several substantial logistical problems resolved for that to occur,' Emet typed back. 'First, my muteness. Second, maintaining the integrity of our research project alibi. And third, we have the same brain but I don't have a heart. Emotionally speaking. I, of course, have the functioning organ. Or at least the magykal equivalent.'

"I think we should tell her the truth," Tal whispered very softly.

"You think we should tell her I'm really a very well-developed semenless hairball?

"Not that truth."

"I see. You think we should tell her the truth about our lie?"

"Yes, that one."

"Interesting. That would of course mean you would be entrusting your entire future to someone you really don't know very well."

"I guess you're right. It's just I feel she's important, Emet. Really important. And that I should trust her."

"'I will ponder the matter while you sleep. Good night.'

CHAPTER QUADRAGINTA DUO

Tal finished writing his answer to the last question on the test, before sagging backward into the slats of the wood chair. He was completely spent. System failure had been coming since late last week, and he had ignored it for as long as possible. The last three weeks for Hunts Finalists had been brutal. Every day there was a prodigious amount of new information shoveled at all of them. He could tell everyone else in the class was struggling, and unlike him, they weren't playing catch-up. Added to that were the physical demands of the Hunts School curriculum. Even with Piras's help, he was taken to the brink of collapse each day in Combat. Finally, there was the mental wear and tear of maintaining his and Emet's ongoing deception every minute when he was home. And there was Elle...

It wasn't only the Hunts Finalists who'd been getting hammered. He could tell from talking with other students that the level of intensity had intensified for the entire student body as the Finalists began their preparations for the first of the Journeys. At lunch today, Principal Chiron had announced a school-wide event for this afternoon. As soon as lunch was over, the entire school was shutting down for a sports festival. All of the students were told to head over to the stadium on the south end of the campus. There would be athletic competitions and serious socializing. Tal was looking forward to simply being a teenager for a while, and maybe hanging out and jamming with some of his non-Hunts classmates.

Then Ms. Empousa walked in and ordered all members of the nine Finalist teams back to the Orientation classroom for a pop quiz. Gotta be a better word than "quiz," Tal thought, for a two-hour timed examination covering everything from the first day of school to the present date, in three of their core subjects.

"Time," Ms. Empousa called, about two minutes after Tal had finished.

Judging by the snail's pace at which everyone collected their books, they all felt as beat down as he did. Like the constituents of a chain gang, they put their heads down, and shuffled out of the classroom following Kati of the Kabila, simply because she was first out the door. She turned left heading toward the back of the building, the quickest way to the stadium.

"Yo K. Where do you think you're going?" Kaskazini asked his teammate.

"Figured we could probably still go catch some of the fun," she replied.

"I heard the teachers talking in the cafeteria. Since everyone was supposed to be at the fun out back, Principal Chiron ordered all of the school doors locked up for the rest of the day. Only the front doors are still open." The pack line paused while Kati turned one hundred eighty degrees, resumed her place at the head of the Kabila, and lead the group toward the front doors. The hallways were empty of other students, as the group snaked its way through the cathedral section to the temple area, finally reaching the front doors, where the Keepers kept their silent sentry. As soon as the last of their entourage stepped through the doorway, the Keepers leaned into the doors, inch tall blue veins jumping up out of boulder-sized deltoids. Slowly and in total silence, the doors began inexorably swinging closed.

Tal and the Omada were at the tail end of the exodus. He had just stepped onto the sidewalk at the bottom of the steps when the shrieking started. It sent every student to their knees, hands clasped over ears The noise ululated—like an air raid siren on steroids, rising both in volume and pitch, before retreating, then climbing again. Over and over. Tal quickly surveyed his fellow students. Everyone, including himself, had been forced to their knees by the aural assault, several had blood oozing out of their ears and noses.

Suddenly the screeching stopped. As abruptly as it was, it wasn't. Tal saw Anatolia and Borras stagger to their feet, some of the other students appeared to be too dazed to even stand without assistance. Others were kind of wobbling in place, drool dribbling from their slack lips. The area around the near side of the fountain was littered with textbooks, and other scholastic debris from abandoned backpacks.

"What was that?" Nahookos asked.

"I've never heard anything like it," Uh-Ne-Ih, his Prime replied.

"Maybe it was a banshee," Higashi of Shuzoku interjected.

"Banshee screams don't cycle up and down," Minami said, her voice strained from the aftermath of pain.

"Guys," Bati said raising her hand timidly. Even though she was on an enemy team, Tal had some sympathy for her. Like him, she was the least important on her team, and the smallest physically of all of the contestants. Not that she wouldn't bust a cap in my ass if she got the chance, Tal thought. "I checked a book out a few days ago about dark Creatures."

"And?" Merkez prodded. Tal had noticed Merkez's style as Prime was completely different than Borras's. He was much more impatient and dictatorial.

She swallowed. "I think…I think that was a CryHavoc."

"Couldn't be." Merkez responded sharply. "CryHavoc would mean Furies."

"What are they talking about?" Tal asked.

"Furies, idiot human. Death demons," Notos replied, the tremble in his voice and his drawn face evidence he was still suffering from the screeching. So that's what a whiter shade of pale looks like, Tal thought.

"Even though they're Creatures, the Keres are warded against interference with Hunts contestants," Yaksin said.

"Besides that, they've been bound to the protection of the school for the last ten Tyrnings," Zapad of Pleme offered.

"Somebody's messed with the school's wards. They were designed to stop mortals, too," Nord said.

"What are you saying? That this is Quint's fault?" Väst asked.

"It's a fact that nothing like this ever happened before a mortal was admitted," Mashariki of Kabila replied.

"Why do the Furies scream?" Tal asked.

"Two reasons," Borras answered. "First, to herald death in battle,"

Dong of Bùlùo interrupted Borras's explanation. "We need to go back. Now! Everyone who can help us is at the stadium."

Tal turned back toward the school, in time to see the doors finish closing, with the Keepers inside.

"The Keepers won't open the front doors again until the morning," Sever of Pleme said. "Around the side, let's go."

Tal jumped as he heard a sharp cracking. He had a friend in eighth grade whose leg had gotten broken on the field during a junior varsity football game. The sound of his friend's leg bone as it first splintered, and then snapped, was the cracking sound Tal was hearing now. The sharp retorts were followed by groaning noises, as if someone had some serious gastrointestinal issues. The same sound sequence started repeating, sometimes it sounded as if it were almost right on top of them, and sometimes it seemed farther away.

"What is it?" Nishi of Shuzoku asked.

The noise repeated again, this time it sounded to Tal like it was coming from over his left shoulder. He looked to the roofline of the school. "That gargoyle is moving." All eyes followed Tal's outstretched arm. Sure enough one of the figures was moving, and when it stretched, it made the cracking sound. Inside the ruptured exterior, Tal could see the deep red stone pulsing. A breeze blew from south to north over the school and through the students. As it passed them, the wind stank of rancid milk and stale vomit.

"The second reason for the CryHavoc is for the Furies to release their Keres," Borras finished, looking out of the corner of his eye at Notos. He's looking for information, was Tal's immediate thought.

Tal thought he saw Notos shake his head almost imperceptibly. "Are you talking about the gargoyles?"

"Those are not gargoyles, Quint—they are Hell-hounds," Borras said. Seeing his friend didn't understand he continued, "Keres. The Furies' favorite weapons."

"We have to get back indoors as fast as possible," Anatolia said. "The sidewalk to the girls' dorm. It's the closest," she said pointing back over their shoulders.

"We'll never make it to the dorms," Notos replied. "The Keres are spaced around the entire building."

"The Gas Station Crossing?" Borras asked.

"Everyone else can't pass," Dysi replied.

"That's not our problem," Notos said.

"Where then?" Anatolia asked, ignoring Notos.

Now Tal heard growling. He looked to see the two Keres flanking the main doors shaking themselves free from the roof. His brain tumbled all the options, like turning a Rubik's cube. There was only one choice—screw what the blackboard said. "Forest Fell," he screamed, as he took off running. "Run! Everyone, Run! To the forest!" Tal heard Borras echo his call, telling everyone to run to the trees.

The sounds and the images of the next few minutes slammed all up and over and into each other. It was about two football field's distance from Fountain Flow to River Run. Sprinting, Tal was sucking air after only twenty steps, and he could already hear something slavering closely behind him. There was a keening, like a high-pitched long-play version of fingernails on a chalkboard. Tal heard someone scream in agony, and started to slow to look.

"No, Quint!" Notos said, grabbing Tal by the elbow, as he passed him. "You cannot help them. Run!" Some of the others had passed he and Notos, but others lagged behind. Only half a football field left now. Tal's lungs were raw, and every gasping breath felt like sandpaper inside his chest. With every mouthful of air now came also the taste of burning tar, like when buildings are reroofed. On the far periphery of his vision he saw several Keres from the east side of the school trying to flank them. They're pack hunting us, Tal realized. They know we're trying to beat them to the woods. One of the beasts looked over at him, gray cancerous-looking tumors covering its misshapen body, red froth dripping from its yellow-stained foot-long canines. The red foam smoked whenever it landed on the ground.

The beast's bloodshot eyes made contact with Tal, and it smiled cruelly before running faster toward him. Thoughts were flying so fast through Tal's mind he couldn't even finish them. They were only disjointed words. Never—death—woods—can't—run. Ten feet more, then down the near embankment, a shaky leap over the trickle of water, and up the far side. Tal took a deep breath preparing to throw himself into the brambles to find a tree to climb.

Borras stopped him. "No need, Quint. They either won't—or can't—come across the water."

Then Tal heard a girl scream in terror. Whipping his head back toward the school, he saw someone prostrate on the turf. It was Väst, she had tripped and fallen only fifteen feet from the hill right before the creek. One of the Keres was only forty feet behind her, and closing fast. She looked across the creek to Tal, her grass-stained face blurred by tears. She saw him looking at her, "Quint. Help, me. Please, help me."

For some reason Tal couldn't stop himself—he had to cross the creek to help her.

He heard Notos screaming at him, "Stop! Your duty is to Omada." Ignoring Notos, he leapt up and out of the brush, hurdled the creek bed, and ran toward Väst. While he was running Tal began screaming and flailing his arms. It worked, the Keres were momentarily distracted. He could hear Anatolia behind him yelling, "Quint, come back—they'll kill both of you."

Ost had ended up downstream about a hundred feet, and was too far away. Tal could hear him screaming at Mitt and Nord, "Go help Quint!" Tal glanced quickly backward to see if he could expect any help. Neither was moving, they were fear-frozen on the safe side of the creek.

Tal reached Väst, and stood straddling her, gulping the tar-soured air. The closest Kere stopped for a moment, waiting on its brethren. If size or ugliness mattered in the hellhound hierarchy, the one facing Tal was their leader. It stared balefully at Tal. That is the one that was chasing me, he realized.

He felt Väst try to pull herself up using his belt loops, but she fell back to the ground, moaning loudly. Her left ankle's either sprained or broken, Tal realized, as he continued turning, constantly turning. As he turned he could see several of the creatures fighting each other as they ripped chunks of flesh and viscera out of the fallen student about another fifty yards back toward the fountain. There wasn't enough left of whoever it'd been for Tal to identify the student. All of the rest of the Keres, more than a dozen, were pacing up and down the creek bed looking for a break in the water. Finding none they abandoned the effort, and joined the one facing Tal. Reacting to some unseen sign from their leader they began circling Tal and Väst in a well-rehearsed hunting dance. Counterclockwise they went, the circle spiraling smaller, ever smaller. Tal stood his ground, fists balled as tightly as he could make them. He could feel the Keres' hatred, he could see their blood throbbing, liquid crimson pulsing in their distended neck veins.

There was nothing the Omada could do, the Keres would kill them if they crossed the creek to help Tal and Väst. Tal could tell from the look on Borras's face that he was seriously thinking about trying anyway. It doesn't matter what he wants to do, Tal realized. He is the Omada leader. The team could compete with four players, but Omada was out of the competition with only three. Notos was right, Tal realized. He had a duty to his teammates. He should have stayed put, but for some reason when Väst called, he had no choice but to help. And what about 'Seeking the Center'? Tal looked directly at Borras and emphatically shook his head no. Maybe someone from the school heard the Furies, he thought, as he continued to circle, keeping the leader where he could look him directly in the eyes. They can't get here in time to help me, he realized as the animals closed their circle even more, but maybe I can keep them off Väst until help comes.

Apparently the Keres' leader had the honor of the kill. Tal watched in horror as the creature leapt ten feet in the air, arcing downward toward Tal's throat. Tal stepped backwards to cover Väst, then closed his eyes…as the beast screeched in agony. Agony…and surprise?

As Tal opened his eyes, his other senses acknowledged something had passed immediately over his left shoulder. As he watched, he saw a large silver shape had collided with the Kere, and the two animals had landed in a tangled heap on the ground. The intervenor, which looked like an oversized silver wolf—but not a wolf—stood up and engaged the lead Kere, clearly in a battle from which only one was walking away. The snarling creatures circled each other looking for an opening to take out the other's throat. Tal heard baying, this sound much different than the Keres' howling. These sounds, though also feral, were unlike the discordance of the Keres' voices. The new noises were in harmony with each other. As Tal watched, several dozen of the wolves—but not wolves—materialized from the underbrush, each leaping over the crouching students, then the creek, and finally attacking the Keres.

After his initial shock, Tal made the most of his second chance. He put his left shoulder under Väst's right arm, helped her to her feet and half-dragged, half-toted her down the bank, and to the creek bed where the others were waiting to help.

"Good work, Quint," Borras said, picking Väst up, and cradling her in his sapling-sized forearms. "They can't cross River Run." Borras walked over to Mitt to give the hysterically sobbing girl to her Prime.

Tal turned back to look at the ongoing battle on the north end of the lawn. It was vicious but short lived. As the fighting ebbed, Tal saw several of the Keres lying on the grass with their throats ripped out, a viscous red-black fluid pumping onto the ground. As each Kere died, the corpse spontaneously combusted. Oily black smoke billowed until the flames went out, leaving a small pile of black gummy ash on the previously pristine lawn. The remaining Keres turned and raced back to the school, clambering straightways up the school walls to the eaves. As Tal watched them return to their gargoyle positions they froze into red marble once more. To the casual observer there would be no proof they had ever moved. Tal, however, could identify newly created gaps in their formation.

Several of the wolves—but not wolves—were also severely injured. They stayed on the battlefield with the uninjured members of their pack until after the remaining Keres became inanimate. No sooner was the last Kere back in place, than the leader of the wolves—but not wolves—headed back across River Run. The others followed him, the injured whimpering as they hobbled across. After apparently making sure that all of his pack was safely into Forest Fell, the leader turned, and dissolved into the latticework of thornery.

Tal looked back across the lawn at the bloody fragments of flesh and bone that were all that remained of the unlucky student. Blue, he thought. Folk blood is blue, was the thought that kept repeating in his mind. You're going into shock Tal, he told himself, focus on something else. The Keres' attack helped Omada because one of our opponents is no longer at full strength. That thought was immediately succeeded by—how can I even think that? Someone died, someone in my class is actually dead. One of the other teams has lost a friend, a teammate. Tal quickly scanned the team groupings. The person missing was Bati of the Aile. The one that had been smart enough to warn them all, perhaps saving all of their lives, had been too slow to outrun death herself. The Aile were all huddled together, away from the others. Tal left the Omada, and walked over to them. "Merkez, Prime Direction of the Aile, I am sorry for your loss." He paused, and bowed to the Aile, "Bati's wisdom saved us all this day. The Hunts will be less for her death." He bowed again, then turned and began walking away to leave them to their grief.

As Tal approached the other team groups, he was surprised to see mouths wide open. He heard nothing, there was only stunned silence. A few seconds later, he felt a hand on his shoulder. It was Merkez. "To acknowledge an honorable adversary, Quint of Omada, is to 'Seek the Center'. Our lessons evidence such an act of sportsmanship has not happened in many Tyrnings. You have earned Aile's respect, Munedan." He snapped his closed fist on his right breast in salute, nodded to Tal, then he and the surviving members of the Aile began walking towards Bati's remains.

As Tal neared the Omada, he noticed Väst and the Släkt were immediately to his right. She was gingerly standing up on her own. "Are you all right?" he asked her.

"I think it's just a sprain," she replied. "If you hadn't come back for me," she paused, as her breath caught in her throat, "if you hadn't come back for me Quint, the Keres would have, they would have…," she could go no further. Tal heard her saying something that sounded like, "I'm sorry I had no choice but to make you," over and over before the syllables dissolved completely into tears.

Suddenly Squinty was there, stepping up into Tal's face. "We don't need your fucking help, human. We can take care of our own."

Tal had half a dozen barbed retorts on the edge of his tongue, but he let it go. There had been enough tragedy for one day. He simply shook his head at Squinty, and kept walking toward Omada.

"The doors are opening," Mashariki said.

They all looked up to see the front doors swinging wide, and Principal Chiron running down the stairs, followed closely by the HuntsMistress, Professor Elphinstone, and several of the other teachers. Half of the group stopped where Bati had died, the remainder continued on to meet the students at the forest's edge. Principal Chiron was with the second group, stopping right in front of the Omada. After taking several deep breaths, he was able to wheeze out a question. "Can somebody please tell me what in the Five-Hells happened here?"

CHAPTER FORTY-THREE

The impetus of life held sway at both schools the next few weeks, with one school day running smack up into its successor. At Hunts School, the horror of Bati's death—while not forgotten—immediately receded under the pressures of preparation for the Journeys. At Nemeton High, each day presented its own challenges to their scheme.

Tal and Emet quickly learned the calculus of solving an equation containing two equals involved an almost infinite number of variables. The adjustments to everyday life, broad stroke and flourish alike, necessary to maintain their gambit were endless. They had been lucky on several occasions, and had—so far—not run afoul of the one single unbreakable rule. Only one Tal could be seen by family or friends, at any given time. Tunnel vision helped out with all other issues. Everyone sees what they want to see, and what they expect to see. Therefore, any plausible explanation that Tal and Emet could devise for their minor missteps had been accepted. So far.

They'd developed a rudimentary sign language for simple issues such as showering, eating, and sleeping. Raking and mowing yards one weekend, when added to Tal's birthday cash, had provided the necessary funds for Tal to get a drop phone, and for him to go to Wal-Mart and get two pairs of the same jeans, and five duplicate sets of cheap t-shirts.

In an effort to keep the laundry to a below suspicious level, they'd tried wearing their clothes two days instead of one. Even with their minimization efforts, Thea made several comments about the volume of laundry Tal was generating. Tal thought he could have knocked her over with a pin when her teenage son suggested she teach him how to do his own laundry. After feeling his forehead to make sure he wasn't feverish, she gladly showed him. After that the clothing issue was entirely manageable.

Meals were another problem. Although Emet was an emotionless replicate powered by magyk, he seemed to require the same amount of fuel as Tal. The first few nights, Tal's folks cut him some slack and let him take his meals up to his room, but that practice got shut down. Family time at meals was a longstanding Smith family tradition and attendance was mandatory. The boys' adaptation to that was an increase in "substantial snacking." Thea and Pell had numerous conversations with Tal about the increase in the grocery bills occasioned by his quantum increase in between-meals consumption. Since Tal was cleaning his plate at family meals and didn't seem to be putting on any weight, they appeared to have accepted his explanation that the change in his eating habits was attributable to either a growth spurt and/or teenage metabolic fluctuations.

Hair was the next issue. It was only little more than a week before Pell made a comment to Emet about how shaggy he was getting. They realized it was a potential recurring problem they hadn't previously addressed. Tal had always shaved every day so facial hair hadn't been on their list. Tal couldn't go to a barber, his and Emet's hair would never look the same if he did. So one evening, Emet and Tal cut each other's hair. It was easy for them to use the same number of cuts in precisely the same locations. Tal went downstairs and announced he had done it as a cost-saving measure. The adults were appreciative, and since his

Mom agreed that it didn't look horrible, they figured he could keep doing it.

Emet reported his teachers were initially perturbed at his lack of vocal involvement during class. However, since he kept knocking the top off the grading curve, they elected to treat him as an intellectual eccentric, and let him do his own thing. Or maybe the Principal had told them to lay off. Emet had only had several brief encounters with Barton and his goons. Since football season was in full swing, they were apparently on bully sabbatical. The boys had decided since Emet couldn't feel any pain that it was simpler, at this point, to let them go ahead and push him around. Some.

In return, Tal filled Emet in about his different classes at Hunts School, and about how Combat was going, how he and Piras excelled as a team, which in turn helped the Omada out in points standings. Which helped keep Notos off his back. A little.

Depending upon his class rotation, Tal had at least one hour a day on his own. He'd had a chance to meet quite a few of the non-finalist students and had been generally well received. He told Emet he realized that different societies had varying standards of propriety but that it sure seemed like a lot of the girls were hitting on him. A couple of the suggestions could probably have been described as pornographic. While he wasn't adverse to the propositions, it all seemed a little…well, a little inexplicable. He told Emet as crazy as it sounded, there were several instances when it seemed even Väst had made overtures. She'd deliberately gone out of her way in the lunchroom, and in the halls, to speak to him. Tal had noticed it was always when no other member of either of their respective teams was around.

He'd found several large groups of musicians and singers who met during his lunch hour who were open to him sitting in and jamming with them. He hadn't had to learn how to play the oud after all. The earliest six-string guitars had been invented not too long before the last Tyrning, and someone found a cache of them in a music history classroom. They played different than Tal's modern acoustic guitar, but he quickly adapted. The Hunts

School pluckers enjoyed Tal teaching them the guitar chords for unplugged versions of some rock classics. Bon Jovi rock ballads went over huge with the Folk. One day he'd played "Don't Worry, Baby" by the Beach Boys. The Folk chicks went crazy over that one. If the gong hadn't sounded for class on the last chords of that number, it appeared he might have been about to lose his virginity on the spot. Several times. Again, not that he was necessarily adverse to that situation, but something did seem to be holding him back. Not something—someone. Someones, actually. Väst and Elle. How can I feel so strongly about two different women?

That discussion segued nicely into his and Emet's last topic on this particular evening—the last topic they discussed every evening. Elle. Every night, Tal required Emet to tell him what she wore to school, whether she was happy or sad that day, what questions she answered in class, had he seen her reading in the library,…and did it look like she had found a boyfriend? This evening was no different. 'Yes,' Emet typed, he had in fact seen her on the far side of the room in English and Calculus, but nowhere else. When Tal asked where Emet thought she was all day. 'Every place other than where I am,' he typed back.

CHAPTER QUADRAGINTA QUATTUOR

Alberich gently kneaded his wife's shoulders. After all of their centuries together, he knew from the tension in her neck muscles she'd gone spectral. Aine's awaymagyk was one of the principal reasons he'd been able to accomplish so much as Archon. She'd been her team's Prime, and they'd come in a close second in the Hunts. By herself she was better than an entire network of lesser magyked spies. Knowing she had the power to protect him, he'd been able to focus all of his own substantial magyk, together with the additional power bestowed on him as Archon, to create a protective shield over the entire Earth plane. Alberich's Bane, the Folk called it. It prevented both any physical presence by the Folk on the Earth plane proper, as well as any significant magyk. Following Arthrys's policy, his two immediate predecessors had also issued decrees prohibiting such things. They hadn't been as strong as he was, so there had been a large number of incidents during their reigns. Even as strong as he was, it had been an almost unsupportable drain on Alberich's magykal power to maintain but it had been worth every minute of the lyfeforce it had cost him. Earth Realm had been totally protected during his tenure, more so ever than when Arthrys ruled. Except for the thrice-damned Crestfallyn. There wasn't enough left of their bodies to which his magyk could adhere. They hadn't been heard from in centuries though and Alberich had learned long ago he shouldn't worry about the things he couldn't control. He simply had to trust Amarantos and continually 'Seek the Center'.

He couldn't, of course, stop non-physical magykal incursions—dreams, visions, nightmares. Even if he'd had the strength, he wouldn't have stopped those activities. If mortals were ever to have a chance to be true partners in the Moiety, they needed to know about the Folk. Since his Ascension, Alberich had acted consistently with his belief that 'Seeking the Center' required the Munedan to exist unfettered, in order to discover their proper place as the UnFading Spirit's youngest children. That had been Arthrys's philosophy too, although they were in the minority. In fairness, the Munedan were infants when the Moiety was established, and perhaps the mortals had needed shepherding eons ago. That time was long past, and Alberich believed humans should be allowed to exercise the free will given to them by Amarantos.

It had been difficult to hold the reins, even members of his own Council—Marid, for one—vehemently disagreed with him. That faction believed humans needed to be subjugated. For their own good, of course. Alberich's time was almost done. The end of this school year would mark another Tyrning, another Ascension. Alberich would pass the crown to the new Archon, and he and Aine could return home for the rest of their days.

Alberich was proud of his team's accomplishments, directly and indirectly. Over the last several hundred years, the majority of human literature had begun to fictionalize and make light of magyk—and of the supernatural. Fairies were now usually described as well-meaning pixies, such as Tinker Bell, or tiny invisible winged philanthropic creatures that brought children money when they lost a tooth. Because of his team, the Dust Children no longer knew that most fairies were seven-foot tall, vicious assassins. Humans didn't know—didn't need to know— that if Alberich's wards weren't in place the Folk they called "tooth fairies" would return to feasting nightly upon the blood and marrow of the teeth they had physically ripped out of the mouths of sleeping young mortals. Even the stories involving Folk predators like zombyes, vampyres, and wyrewolves had evolved. Most of those stories now made them anti-heroes, gave them consciences. Modern day fairy tales inevitably had happy endings. Superheroes now almost invariably bested super-villains.

There were still Munedan scholars who continued to unearth relics evidencing the truth. These scholars didn't know why fairy tales had undergone a dramatic transformation in the last several hundred years, only that they had. Those who dug deep found scraps of the original stories—rife with darkness and malevolence—the stories which ended up more often with children being eaten or sacrificed, as opposed to being saved at the last minute. Those humans sensed maybe the original stories weren't fiction, but were historical recountings of true events from Tyrnings long forgotten. A select few had pieced together enough facts to know Rumpelstiltskin was a gremlin who also happened to engage in serial infanticide. The same Munedan suspicioned Red Riding Hood's wolf in the forest was actually Fenris himself running amok, slaughtering entire villages.

He could feel through his hands that Aine's spirit had returned to her body. Her shoulders lowered, and then he felt her whole body shudder. "What did you see this time, beloved?"

"Malice. Black hatred. Envy. Alberich, someone seeks to undo the fabric of the Lex, to usurp Amarantos herself. Who could want that? Who could possibly be so selfish?"

"Were there no clues to his identity?"

"I looked in every way I know. I followed trails of spectral mist as it wandered through many Realms, weaving in and out of halls of power. Whoever it is has protection, some type of ancient magyk beyond my ken. I can feel the evil, it hides in the veil just beyond my Sight. I am scared, Alberich. It is stronger than me. Beloved, it is even stronger than you." As she finished she turned and slid her arms under his, pressing herself close for comfort.

Alberich wrapped his arms around her, and kissed her forehead. "I have felt the disruption, Aine. Fell magyk it is if the Queen of the Green Children cannot skry its source. I know only that it has something to do with the presence of the Dust Child."

"How did he come through the Crossing?" she asked him. "It is impossible for anyone—Folk or Munedan—to get by the School's wards."

"Chiron swears his name is in The Book." Alberich stood and walked to the far side of the room, gazing out the floor to ceiling window of their bedroom. "At my request Chiron has investigated the Keres incident. Someone used powerful magyk on campus. Between the school's wards, which he maintains, and my magyk it should have been impossible."

"And?"

"Nothing, Aine. Whoever did whatever they did with no residue left behind."

"I didn't think that was even possible," she replied.

"Neither did I," Alberich confirmed. "Marid has reminded me—several times—that the Ruling Council's duty is to protect the entire student body. He counsels we take the safe course with the human," he whispered.

"We are not murderers," Aine said crossing the room to be near him. "Marid often forgets we are called by Amarantos to 'Seek the Center'."

"He argues—correctly—such action might foil the unknown evil's plan."

"The Lex Immortalis forbids murder. Folk and Munedan, we are all her children."

"And the Creatures, Aine? There is unrest there as well."

"Your heart answered that question long ago, Alberich," she said as she wrapped her arms around his waist. "They too are children of the UnFading Spirit."

He turned into her. "And what of our daughter? Did you discern the path that lies before her?"

"I sense the evil has somehow ensnared her. Her fate is tied to that of the Dust Child."

CHAPTER QUADRAGINTA QUINQUE

Professor Hardcastle had already filled up about two-thirds of the chalkboard with information, and he was just getting cranked up. "Your first Journey will take place next week. Before that trip we will have covered all four categories of scavengyr pieces. We have previously discussed Weapons, today we're going to discuss the different types of pieces that will fulfill a second category— Defense.

"Most any item that can be used for defense, can also be used for offense. To qualify in this Hunt, the object's use must be primarily defensive. A stave, for example, would of course qualify as a Defense piece but a pole-arm or a spear wouldn't. There are certain types of items that automatically qualify. If you pick something unusual or questionable, you will be at the mercy of the HuntsMistress's discretion."

"Death [or worse]," Tal mumbled.

"I'm sorry was that a question, Quint of Omada?"

"No, Professor Hardcastle. Just clearing my throat."

"Very good." The professor turned back to the chalkboard. "Armor is an easy qualifier, but has no secondary offensive capability. There are many armor sets that qualify. The armor of Achilles, Thor, and Beowulf, are good examples bearing high point values. There are a couple of famous 'skins,' that will also earn Hunts points. The Hide of Leviathan, and the Hide of the Nemean Lion."

"I know that one," Tal whispered to Borras. "Hercules killed the lion."

"The Hercules," Borras corrected.

"What?"

"It's the Hercules. Sshh, I'll explain later."

"A piece that provides its wearer with invisibility counts as a defensive weapon. These include the Tarnhelm helmet, the dagger Carnwennan, and the Ring of Gyges. There are two cloaks of invisibility—the Tarnkappe and the Cornwall Mantle. The latter is one of the Thirteen Treasures of Britain. The invisibility piece worth the most points is the Helm of Darkness. It's described on page seven hundred thirty of your textbook.

"Shields are for the most part low-point defense pieces. You must be careful as there are a large number of counterfeit shields that resemble shields of power. You will of, course, be awarded zero points for a non-qualifying shield. Pictures of the qualifying shields are found on page three twenty-four of your textbook. Qualifying shields are those of Achilles, Ajax, Galahad, and El Cid, which bears a golden dragon. The highest-point target for shields is the Aegis."

"The shield of Zeus," Borras whispered.

"The shield of Zeus," Professor Hardcastle said, as he continued. "It has a hundred woven tassels of pure gold…and the head of the Medusa."

The bell rang, summoning them to Combat.

CHAPTER QUADRAGINTA SEX

Tal liked Professor SilverTongue. Unlike most of the Hunts School staff, she seemed to have a sense of humor. The Hunts' Finalists didn't get to see her too often, as most of her assignments were in non-Finalists' courses. She'd been called in today to pinch hit for Professor Elphinstone as she was the acknowledged expert on today's scavengyr category—Transportation.

"Today we will be talking about Transportation," she said to begin her hour-long lecture. "In the Scavengyr Hunt, Transportation is the second most varied category, with Wyld Thing being first. Transportation pieces fall within several subcategories: flying devices, flying Creatures, and teleporation or teleportation equivalents."

Okay, Tal thought, cars, trains and planes may have some of those things beat hands down, but teleportation? That's beam-me-up-Scotty type of stuff. Very cool.

Professor SilverTongue rapped her pointer on her desk to focus everyone's attention "Please turn first to page two-hundred twenty-two, Chapter Eighteen, of your *Movement* textbook. This chapter discusses a few of the qualifying transportation devices. The complete listing of all the eligible pieces is found in

Appendix Twenty-Four at the back. Although there are several exceptions, generally the transportation point total is determined by three factors: difficulty in piece acquisition, number of team members that may be simultaneously moved, and distance capability. The first device discussed in the textbook is the Flying Throne of Kai Kavus. As you can see, it contains the fifth highest scoring point value. The Flying Throne will transport all five of your team members at one time. That's a huge advantage. However, the throne's propulsion is provided by four of the most ill tempered eagles you will ever meet. So, not only must your team find the piece, but you must also convince the eagles that it is in their best interest to operate the Flying Throne for you. They are Creatures, therefore not barred by the Hunts Rules from assisting, but they will require some form of compensation."

Food, Tal thought, they will want food. He made himself a note to research eagles' top ten food items.

"Flip over two pages and you'll see an example of a flying vimana. The points allocated for a vimana vary as they come in all shapes and sizes. Some might hold only one team member at a time, others would easily move the entire team. Chapter Nineteen contains an enumeration of all known existing flying carpets. Flying carpets are a dime a dozen. The overwhelming majority will only sputter along for a few hundred yards before exhausting their magyk, and maybe not that far depending on how much weight is placed on it. Some carpets go much farther, much faster. The highest points for a flying carpet are awarded for Solomon's Carpet. It is number three on the transportation list, as it is unquestionably the fastest, most powerful flying carpet on any plane. It is also unique in that it gives its rider the power to control the wind within an approximately five-mile radius."

"Chapter Twenty-One provides information about a number of the magykal chariots that may be acquired for transportation. You'll need the maximum SPF sunscreen if you try to pick up Helios's Chariot of the Sun." Professor SilverTongue guffawed to herself. "That joke makes me laugh every time. Chariot of the Sun, sunscreen—that's a real corker. But really, you should wear asbestos gloves if you're gonna joy ride in that one." She stopped for a moment to laugh at her own joke. Again.

"Anyway, all of the chariots are pulled by Creatures so you will have to negotiate compensation with them to utilize a chariot. Let me repeat, the Creatures are under no obligation or compulsion to assist you on your Journeys. If you run into something extremely contrary, it is prohibited from killing you, but it can make you wish you'd never been born, hatched, fissioned, fragmented, or agamogenesized. Whichever fits in your particular case."

Agamogenesized, there's something else I have to look up, Tal thought. Magyk's great, I guess, but I'd give my left nut for some Google to help me out.

"There are two goats that pull Thor's Chariot of Thunder. The sea horses that pull Poseidon's Chariot of the Sea can go for days, but they are limited to water travel. The last chariot listed is the Chariot of Morgan the Wealthy. It's one of the Thirteen Treasures of the British plane. It is number two on the transportation points list because it is one of the very few devices that teleports, and the only magykal transportation piece that can transport an entire team simultaneously.

"You will see the number one ranked Transportation artifact—the Taleria—has a chapter all to itself. It is a most fascinating object. If you have the time you may want to read the chapter for the sake of knowledge. The piece has never been located for use in any Hunt. Ever. It hasn't even been seen in centuries, and is presumed dead."

Dead is kind of an odd reference for an inanimate object, Tal thought.

"On more than one occasion teams have lost the Hunts competition solely because they became obsessed with trying to find the Taleria. You might call it the Holy Grail of Transportation pieces." With that, Professor SilverTorgue actually guffawed. "Oh, I crack myself up sometimes, I really do.

Mixing myth metaphors like that. Ooh, that's a really good sequence. Mixing myth metaphors. Say it five times really fast, I'm going to."

While the teacher was repeating the phrase, Tal quickly flipped to Chapter Twenty-Three. Wow. No one may have seen the Taleria for centuries but it was on the Earth plane many times during ancient times. References to it were all over centuries of Earth history, scattered throughout many different cultures and mythologies. Most commonly, the Taleria had been referred to as Herme's winged sandals.

Professor SilverTongue had finally stopped giggling and returned to teaching. "The Taleria is not a magykal object, it is a unique Creature. Singular in all of the known Realms, it is made of filaments of woven gold."

Okay, that's pretty cool, Tal thought. Something living made out of a precious metal. And it's a Creature, which means the Rules wouldn't prohibit it from helping a Hunts contestant.

Tal continued to read, while listening to the Professor. "The Taleria is a shapeshifter. Its most common form is that of winged sandals, but it can appear as almost anything. Almost anything—with wings. Even though it can only be used to transport one person at a time, it is the number one Transportation piece because, unlike any other object or Creature, it has the ability to transport to any location it has previously visited, on any plane."

Tal heard a collective "ooohhh," go around the classroom. He realized this was clearly big jujube in the Folk worlds. Although they all used Omphalos to travel across their home planes, only the Prime Omphalos could move the Folk between planes. Only the Prime Omphalos and the Taleria.

The gong sounded signaling the end of the class period.

CHAPTER FORTY-SEVEN

'Tal, it's Elle.'

Emet had been sitting motionless for the last ten minutes, staring at that email on his laptop. He was spending his free hour in the library going back over the two questions he'd missed on yesterday's calculus test. Trying to figure out which variables had led him astray. Then the email had arrived. And now, a second one.

Tal, I know you've seen my email. You started doing a pretty good impersonation of an inanimate object right about the time I sent it. (I'm three tables over and yes I'm stalking you.)

Emet looked to his left. No Elle. Then to his right. Yep, there she was. She smiled and waved. He gave the barest vestige of a return wave. It's okay, Emet told himself. Tal and I discussed the possibility this might happen. Actually, we discussed the possibility that either he or I would attempt to institute nonverbal communication with her. Now she's done it. What would Tal do? Panic, probably. Or flee. Since I don't have to worry about an elevated heart rate, or the "flight for survival" instinct kicking in, what would Tal do if he was able to engage in an unemotional sit-rep. Stall for time, Emet told himself. *'Uh, hi?'* he typed.

There was a brief pause. She's simply taking her time typing, Emet thought. *Really? That's your best shot? I think I deserve answers to some questions. Don't you?'*

'I don't know if it was my best shot but it seemed at a minimum to be a socially acceptable response.'

'Oh no you don't, you don't get to pull that Mister Spock shit on me. Answers. To questions.'

Seems logical, Emet thought. Answers normally follow questions. I, however, need Tal's emotional input to improve the quality of my responses. *'I think perhaps it might be best if Tal called you this evening to discuss the matter.'*

This time the response was immediate. *'I'm sorry? Did you text-refer to yourself in the third person?'*

Well damn, that was an unforced error, Emet thought. *'Sorry, I had something in my throat. What I meant was I will call you later on tonight. If that is an acceptable resolution to this conversation.'*

'Fine, Mr. Polysyllabic,' Elle replied. *'As long as I get answers to some questions. Here's my number.'*

Emet wrote the seven digits down on his notepad, before he sat back to reflect on what had happened.

'I had something in my throat?' What kind of response was that?

CHAPTER QUADRAGINTA OCTO

'With the sole exception of the Snype Hunt last year, you've each used the Prime Omphalos only to travel from the Axis Mundi on your home plane to Hunts School."

That statement in Professor Elphinstone's lecture caught Tal's attention. They're all stuck here, away from their families for a hundred years. Sure, they may live longer than me but it's still a long time to put your entire life on hold. Plus they've all had to live at Hunts School without their magyk. Basically like humans, Tal thought. Actually worse. They're denied the use of their powers which is a major part of who they are.

"For you Hunts Finalists that changes with your first Journey next week. From this point forward, all of your team meeting time should be utilized deciding which scavengyr pieces you wish to acquire and developing a check down contingency plan to utilize in deciding the order and method for obtaining each of those pieces."

There's a whole lot more strategy to this competition than I first thought, Tal realized.

"Each Journey will last exactly three hours EPT."

Borras must have seen Tal's raised eyebrows, because he leaned forward and wrote, "Earth Plane Time," in large letters on his notepad.

"You need to factor into your plans that time itself moves at different speeds in each of the Realms. Depending upon which plane you choose, the three hours may take only a few minutes on that plane. While in other Realms, it may take two to three days. The Recall automatically occurs exactly three hours EPT after your departure.

"In the early Tyrnings, contestants had to make their way back to their point of origin Omphalos to be Recalled. This led to too many instances of whole teams never returning, or being heard from ever again. The Prime Omphalos has now been magyked so each student sent on a Journey has a mystic thread which adheres to them throughout their Journey. When the Journey time has expired, the thread will pull-teleport each contestant back to the arrival Omphalos for Recall to the Prime Omphalos here at Hunts School."

Professor Elphinstone wiped his forehead with his handkerchief. "Which brings us to two final matters. The HuntsMistress has made two material changes to the customary Hunt protocol. Normally one team doesn't Journey until after the previous team has returned. This prevents any possible confrontations between teams. This year the teams will be leaving in thirty-minute staggered departures according to their team ranking at the time of the Journey."

Tal felt the ripple of tension that went all the way across the classroom. That modification was clearly a big deal. That's why the HuntsMistress made those comments about killing a few weeks ago, he realized. She knew she was going to do this to the teams.

"There are thousands of known Realms, so even with the staggered start times there would normally be an almost infinitesimal chance of simultaneous-plane Journeying."

However, Tal thought to himself.

"However, there are nine teams and only eleven eligible weapons. The Prime Omphalos will send you to a Realm where there is a possibility you can secure an object in the category selected by your Prime Direction within the three-hour Journey window. This means…," Professor Elphinstone paused again to wipe the sweat running down the side of his face, "this means the odds have been exponentially increased that more than one team may be on the same plane at the same time."

Tal heard Squinty say, "Yes!" with no attempt to disguise he was the person speaking.

"Quiet," Professor Elphinstone said sternly. "That change is no reason to cheer. This Hunts cycle has seen the death of more students than any other Tyrning in the history of the Moiety. Each team needs to review Chapter Thirteen of the Hunts Rules. The entire chapter concerns dueling, self-defense, and permitted physical confrontation between students. I expect you to strictly adhere to the limitations set forth in the Rules. I will personally see any team disqualified and its members expelled from school if there is a material violation of the Chapter Thirteen rules."

"Which brings up the second change that has been implemented."

This can't be good either, Tal thought watching Professor Elphinstone wear out his forehead. That handkerchief is sopping wet.

"Your assigned Pucas will not be making the trip with you."

Tal heard a collective groan from almost every other student, and was pretty sure he heard someone mutter, "That's bullshit."

"As you may remember from the year thirty-eight Hunts School History course, from almost the inception of the Hunts, the Puca have volunteered to assist contestants in their Hunts and on their Journeys."

"Volunteer, my ass," Tal heard Xi of the Búluó whisper to one of his teammates. "It was either that or species extinction for crimes against the Moiety."

I'll have to ask Piras what that's all about, Tal thought, as Professor Elphinstone continued.

"It was discovered shortly after the Moiety was formed, that it is hazardous to use the Prime Omphalos multiple times in a short period of time. There has never been an issue with the initial use, but there is the possibility for disabling pain both at Departure and during Recall on all subsequent Journeys. It is an individual-specific reaction, and bears no causal relationship to your plane of origin. Some barely feel a tingle. During the early Hunts, however, some contestants died or were rendered permanently insane from the pain. It is not a condition that healmagyk can repair. The Puca, because of their unique physical abilities, are able to prevent any material adverse physical consequences to a Folk host."

I'd certainly categorize death as a "material adverse physical consequence," Tal thought. It's almost as if Empousa is trying to kill all of us. Or maybe just one of us, he decided.

"Upon arriving in the Journey chamber your team will take its place around the stone in the identified positions for each Direction. The Prime will stand in the stone's center. The Prime will announce the target category and the difficulty level of the scavengyr piece the team is seeking and the Prime Omphalos will automatically send the team to the world navel physically closest to that place in the target Realm where a scavengyr piece of that category may be found. Remember, you are not guaranteed availability of a specific piece, only that there are one or more Hunts-qualifying pieces within time range of your landing site.

"The number one team starts its first Journey next Monday morning at dawn. The other teams leave in staggered order based on team ranking. Except for the Shuzoku, who have been penalized and will leave last. The Omada have also been penalized, their Journey has been shortened by one hour EPT."

Tal didn't even bother to look at Notos, he knew he was sitting in his chair about to spontaneously combust.

The gong sounded. "Thank you. You are discharged for lunch, followed by your free activity hour, the team meeting class period, and then Combat lessons to conclude your school day."

CHAPTER QUADRAGINTA NOVEM

Ever since he could remember, Tal had loved music. His Mom always had the radio on in their house. He never knew from day to day what her selection would be. Some days it was classical, on others it might be the Carpenters, or Billy Idol. She'd encouraged him musically at every opportunity. She always made sure he had a ride to and from every regional concert—as long as she was off work and could scrape ticket money together for him—and they'd both attended every free public concert in the park in whatever town they lived in at the time. He'd been enrolled in band class from first grade on, and had always sung in the choir, as well as the shower. Learning to read music had come easily, as well as learning how to play any number of instruments. The guitar was his first love, however, and had held him in thrall since he was a toddler.

Thea had always been honest with him about their finances, and Tal understood there wouldn't ever be money for the private lessons most of his bandmates received. It was always enough for him that he got to play. Some of his favorite childhood memories were listening to his schoolmates and acquaintances strum, blow, bang and of course, sing.

It had been no surprise to his conscious mind then when

he realized whenever he'd had Hunts School free time the last few weeks, he'd subconsciously sought out and hooked up with various groups of non-finalist students who were playing music.

Every group had let him join in, and they all seemed genuinely glad to meet him and talk to him. At first he assumed it was because he was a novelty—his fellow students certainly took the time to ask him a billion different questions about the Earth plane. He was okay with answering all of their questions though, particularly since his *quid pro quo* was info about Folk civilizations, and about Hunts School. He taught his new friends quite a few songs; from early rock and roll, to punk, lots of rock ballads, as well as some of his country favorites. Friends. Tal had already made more real friends in the short time he'd been attending Hunts School than he'd previously made in his entire life. It didn't matter what type of instruments his new pals played, they all had good ears and were able to quickly adapt their movements to play the Earth songs. As far as the singing went, whether backup vocals or singing the lead, they could do some wailing.

Tal learned each of the known Folk planes was given a quota of contestants they could send to Hunts School. The student population continued to grow each Tyrning as new Realms became known, their inhabitants joined the Moiety, and then started sending contestants. As each student journeyed through the Prime Omphalos, they were magyked to change their physical appearance and a binding geas was applied, preventing them from disclosing their psuche name, what Folk they were, and what magyks they possessed.

The course of study at Hunts School took a full century. The school term was the last hundred years of each three hundred year Tyrning cycle. The curriculum was designed to prepare all of the students for the task of returning home to leadership roles and to educate their Folk on what had happened throughout the Moiety since the last Tyrning. The Hunts School agenda of course included substantial time spent learning everything there was to know about the Earth plane since that was where the Prime Omphalos was located.

Every one of the approximately thirteen thousand Hunts School students was initially eligible for the Hunts. When they arrived on campus each student was assigned an identification number. That number became their name. There was only one reference source that contained the information of who they were, what they were, and what they could do magyk-wise—The Book. The Book had some type of major funky magyk from Amarantos herself so that it appeared blank to everyone except the Principal of Hunts School, and even then only the information deemed necessary for that individual to perform their duties was disclosed to them by The Book.

During the first nine decades the top eighteen hundred students were winnowed from the total student crop using a formula including grades, athletic competitions, and social skills quantification testing. That selection process had occurred nine years ago. At that time the Hunts School student population was divided into two divergent subsets: eighteen hundred Hunts competitors, and everyone else.

The Principal then consulted The Book, which now contained pages dividing the Hunts competitors into five-person teams. The highest ranking student on each team was designated the Prime Direction. Once teams were assigned, they were allowed to pick their own team name, that decision then dictated the language of their competition names, which replaced their numbers. From that point forward the teammates took all of their classes together, studied together, ate together and physically trained together. The non-competitors—still known by their numbers—found that they had a much more enjoyable and social final decade at Hunts School than did the competitors.

At the end of the penultimate school year, after nine years of studying and training together, the three hundred sixty Hunts teams competed in a Qualifying Hunt. This Tyrning, HuntsMistress Empousa had selected a Snype Hunt. The more Tal heard about last year's Snype Hunt, the more he realized how much carnage and destruction had been inflicted on members of the Hunts teams. The overwhelming majority of teams had a member either die, or suffer an incapacitating injury. Like the Omada, he realized.

His mind was pulled back from wandering by a quiet harumph. "Sorry," he said as he picked up his early guitar prototype, before thumbing each string in turn. E-A-D-G-B-E, stopping as he went to adjust the "D" and "B" strings before strumming them all together several times. Satisfied, he said, "Okay, here's one that seems to fit. It's called 'The Wood Song,' by a duo called the Indigo Girls, and it's all about experiencing the journey, and not skipping ahead to the ending."

He taught the intro chords to several of the guys playing the same guitar version he was using. The intro was easy: Asus4 twice, then C, a D, then D to F flat-G C twice. There were three girls with wind instruments and a guy and a girl knocking on some odd looking percussion. Obviously gifted, they all transposed the sounds to their respective instruments. He then spent a couple of minutes going over the chords for the chorus and taught them the words. They decided that given their limited time he would take the verses solo this go round.

Then he started, "The thin horizon of a plan is almost clear…." When he'd finished the first two verses, the other ten in the group joined him on the second chorus in flawless harmony that sounded like they had the entire Mormon Tabernacle choir on site. Tal was moving his fingers in place to make the last few chords for the final chorus when he looked up and saw Väst had taken a seat where she could hear and watch the singing. She was wearing her royal purple Puca, glistening with sweat, and whenever she took a deep breath there was all kinds of wet motion. Tal twanged a wrong note, and stopped on the spot.

"I would talk with you Quint of Omada," she said matter of factly.

"Let 'er rip," Tal replied.

"In private, if you don't mind. Come with me." She stood up, turned and started walking away, obviously assuming he would comply with her directive. Tal didn't move. When she turned and saw he hadn't, she added, "Please."

The rear view of Väst's assets brought Tal up short. She's doing that on purpose, he thought. There's swaying, and then there's…. His train of thought totally derailed, he shook his head, blinked a couple of times, then picked up his instrument, and told the group he'd catch up with them later. As he hurried down the hall he heard from behind him the opening notes of a mash-up of Joe Jackson's, "Is She Really Going Out With Him," and Bon Jovi's "Bad Medicine." Asshats, he thought to himself, as he smiled. Bandies apparently have the same sense of humor everywhere in the universe. He'd taught them both of those songs a couple of weeks ago, and they'd had the skills to figure out how to hook the tunes together. It would have been a blast to go to this school—if it weren't for the possibility of maiming—and death.

They had been in the minaret portion of the school. Väst led them across the transition into the Greek temple section, took a left into an alcove, and Tal watched as she turned a bust of Callisto clockwise about fifteen degrees. A section of the frescoed wall slid back revealing a small sitting room. The room was sparsely but nicely furnished with a low table, a half-dozen intricately patterned floor rugs and many different sized throw pillows scattered across the floor. Väst crossed to the table, slid the vase sitting on it to the side, and the wall closed behind them.

All the hot chick warm fuzzy thoughts suffusing Tal's young male brain dissipated in an instant as Tal realized he had legit reasons to be afraid.

"You are probably wondering why I asked you here, Quint of Omada," Väst said as she patted her face dry with a small towel from the table before sitting down cross-legged on one of the pillows.

"You might as well call me Quint. All of the rest of the people who try to assassinate me do." Don't know what her game is but I'm not going to let her know I'm afraid of her.

Without acknowledging his smartassery, Väst continued. "It occurred to me I haven't properly thanked you for saving my life."

"It occurred to me you haven't properly—or in any other manner—apologized to me for trying to decapitate me in Combat," Tal snapped back.

"You are on an opposing Hunts team," she replied matter of factly.

"Not an apology," Tal said.

She hesitated for a moment. "We didn't know each other very well back then."

"Still not an apology," he said firmly.

She hesitated for several moments this time before continuing. "It was my time of the lunar cycle."

It was Tal's turn to take a moment before the corners of his mouth crinkled upward. "I don't know enough about the Folk to call bullshit on you, so instead I'll just say well-played. Your non-apology is accepted."

"My death would have been in Omada's best interests. Why did you save me?"

"I remember feeling at the time like I had no choice," he replied. "Now that I think back, that was only part of it. I did it, I think, because it was the right thing to do."

Tal thought her voice seemed to catch in her throat a little before she continued. "I had hoped that might be the case," she stated.

"Why? What difference does it make why I did it?"

"It doesn't," she said, this time refusing to make eye contact with him. When she finally looked up at him she gestured at his instrument. "Play me a song, Munedan."

Tal was nonplussed. It was an odd conversation. From death to music, with no small talk in between. "Fine. How about the one I just played with the group?" he asked, taking a seat on a pillow about a foot away from hers.

"No," she replied. "Play something for me you haven't played for anyone else."

"Here at Hunts School?" he asked.

"No. Ever," she replied.

"Okay," he said. He ran through a favorites set list in his

mind's eye, making several tentative selections, before discarding them. He finally thought of the perfect song, one that would sound nice with his almost guitar and his high tenor range. "I think you'll like this one. It's called 'Collide,' by a singer named Howie Day." He made sure of the notes first, placing his fingers in position for what he thought would be a G major chord, before hitting a D, an E minor, and finally a C. Then he began. Lost in the harmony between the complex beauty of the lyrics, and the simple beauty of the guitar chords, he sang the remainder of the song with his eyes closed. As he sang the last line, "I somehow find, you and I collide," he opened his eyes, and saw Väst had closed her eyes as well. There was a single tear that had made its way halfway down the almost translucent skin of her cheek.

A few seconds after the music ceased she opened her eyes. "Students cannot perform magyk at Hunts School," she said softly.

"I know this," Tal replied, a little confused by her abrupt change of subject.

"We have always been taught Dust Children are without magyk," she said, still speaking softly.

"We are," Tal confirmed.

"It is a falsehood," she replied, slowly shaking her head. "It is clear you have royal level musemagyk."

"Nope, just lots of practice."

Shaking herself free of the song's enchantment she sat up straight on her pillow. "That will be our song, Quint of Omada. You will play that song only for me. Forever."

Without even thinking, Tal nodded.

"No, you must speak the words of binding. Do you consent?"

What could possibly be the harm, he asked himself. "I consent."

"It is done," she said solemnly. "Only for me. Forever."

"Sure. Tell you what, why don't you tell me what this whole little get to know each other session is all about."

Väst scooted over to the pillow immediately opposite his. "I want to thank you with a kiss."

Tal was stunned. The conversation had now gone from death to music to making out. "I'm pretty sure that's got to be against the Hunts Rules," he replied.

"It isn't," she whispered, leaning closer so that he was looking straight in her eyes. Yep, those flawless—insert here every ridiculous over the top poetic descriptor ever used to describe blue eyes—blue eyes.

"Hold up there," he said holding his hand in front of her face. "I don't want you thinking I'm easy."

"I could always magyk you," she countered.

"Hello? We just went over that whole Alberich's Bane thing," Tal replied. He couldn't take his eyes off of her. She was mesmerizing. No, he told himself, that's not an overstatement. He really couldn't look away. "Actually, out of everyone I've met here, you might have the chops to beat the Bane. Of course, I would then have to report it as a rules violation to Lily..."

"Sshh!" She said putting her finger to her lips. "Are you crazy? Even use names can summon their owners."

At that moment he couldn't imagine anything more sensuous than the simple act of her placing her finger on her own lips. Message from Earth plane Tal to Hunts School Tal—if you remember, someone else has a pair of lips you're somewhat partial to as well. Quiet, about that, you Jiminy Cricket you, I'm focusing on the pair here in front of me. "You don't really believe that, do you?" he asked. "Let's find out. Alberi..."

"Quit it," she said, amping up the coquette factor. "You know we don't have much time." And then she laid that gigawatt smile on him.

Careful, Tal, he told himself. If I had to guess, that's the self-same smile with which Helen smote Paris. That's right, he told himself, I'm history. "Fine, but it's going to take more than a kiss."

"You realize while wearing my Puca, I could rip your throat out in an instant," she replied angrily.

Oh hell, Tal thought, she thinks I'm talking about…well, she thinks I'm talking about what I'm thinking about. "No, no. You got me wrong. I would never…"

"Never?" Her eyebrows gathered quickly, like a summer thunderstorm. "So I'm not pretty enough for you to lay with. Is that it?" she spat at him.

Damned if I do, damned if I don't, he thought. "No, of course, you are. Look, a kiss would be tremendous, but I badly need some information, as well as a kiss."

"What?" she asked, the storm's energy dissipating a little.

"I need for you to tell me the Origin Story."

"What?" she repeated, but this time more puzzled than angry.

"My team is already having to play catch-up since there's so much I don't know. I've been afraid to use any more of the team's time to ask for an explanation."

She gave a little laugh. "That's all you want as compensation for saving my life?"

"Well, that…and the kiss you promised me," Tal replied.

Väst smiled, then closed her eyes for a moment, took a deep breath, and began. "Before even the breath of a beginning, the UnFading Spirit is."

Tal interrupted. "What the hell does that even mean?"

"Hush, Munedan," Väst said sternly. "If you want to understand, it is important that you learn it as all Folk children in the Moiety are taught. Every Realm, every child." She took a breath, and began again in the same cadence. "Before even the breath of a beginning, the UnFading Spirit is. She first created her Seneschal—When."

"When?"

"Really Quint, you must not interrupt," Väst chided. "It is impossible to learn when your mouth is open, not your ears. When—like the UnFading Spirit—has many names. Tempus, Quando, Chronos, Otav. Most commonly on the Earth plane, she is called Time. When is the first-born of the Elder Children—the Principes. All of the UnFading Spirit's other children, even the Elder Children, bend their knee to When's authority. The four Principes are When, followed by the twins—Sol and Luna—and their youngest sister Aurora."

"I get it," Tal said. "It's a group of five, with the UnFading Spirit being the Prime."

"Yes," Väst confirmed. "See what happens when you truly listen? After a great period of time, She made her Middle Children."

"Middle Children?"

"The Folk."

"Just how many of the Folk are there?" Tal asked.

"I'm not sure we will ever know. There are multitudes of different Folk across the known planes."

"The known planes? You're saying after all these thousands of years you still don't know?"

"We don't. The Prime Omphalos is the only connection to the individual planes…"

"And you can't tell it to send you to someplace you don't know exists and have never seen," Tal said finishing for her.

"Right."

"How did any of the Folk initially find the Prime Omphalos?"

"There comes a point in the maturity of each Folk where they choose to 'Seek the Center.' At that time the Axis Mundi on their plane will translate one of their leaders to the Prime Omphalos here on Earth."

"The reason Hunts School is on the Earth plane is because the UnFading Spirit placed the Prime Omphalos here?" Tal asked.

"Yes."

"So, all of Earth's mythemes, the common stories of our myths and legends from every human culture—they all came from the Folk being on the Earth plane?"

"Yes, Quint."

"And where do humans fit in this whole creation story?"

"The Munedan are the Last Born."

"So this UnFading Spirit made different types of children because she made mistakes?"

"No. She created different children because we are all necessary layers in the complex fabric of her Creation. Infinite worlds, countless Realms. Everything and everyone is different, and yet we are all important parts of the UnFading Spirit's plan. Material must have immaterial, light must be countered by dark."

"UnFading Spirit? That's her name?"

"That is what the Folk have always called her. The Principe know her as Amarantos. She has been known by thousands of names through countless centuries. Many of her names are lost, given to her in languages now covered by the dust of millennia. Some male, others female. Aeon, Arche, but the Elder-Born have always called her Amarantos."

"I still don't understand the relationship of the Realms to each other," he said.

"Think of the entirety of Amarantos's creation as a gemstone with millions of facets, rotating suspended in the brilliance of a noontime sun. Each face of the gem catches the sun's light uniquely, yet they each have connection points with other facets."

"The Axis Mundi?"

"Not quite. In each of the Realms there are many world navels which allow passage between physical locations on that one plane. Earth Realm has many world navels as well. Earth Realm however, is the only plane that connects to every other plane. Through the Prime Omphalos, here at Hunts School."

"Hunts School is the Axis Mundi of the entire universe?"

"Right," she confirmed.

"But why Earth?"

"You really don't know anything, do you?" Väst paused, apparently to give him a fair chance to admit ignorance.

"I guess not," he replied.

"Earth is the home of the Last Born."

"Got that. You also call us Dust Children and Munedan," Tal added.

"Yes," Väst confirmed.

"Right. The youngest. The most short-lived. As you've pointed out to me, the only ones with no magyk."

"You really don't understand, Quint. The Last Born received Amarantos's greatest blessing. They are the Children of the Divine Spark."

"Haven't heard that one."

"Earth Realm is different. Every other plane has magyk. Every other plane uses magyk as its source of energy. Earth plane is the only Realm with electricity."

"Get out!" Tal said loudly.

"Sshh! she said quietly. "We don't want to be discovered. "But, why? Why must I get out?" She asked looking around the room. "Did I say something offensive?"

"No, sorry. It's a colloquialism."

"I see," Väst said, before laughing a little.

"What's so funny," Tal asked.

"You really don't know the reason all of the girls in Hunts School have been trying to lay with you, do you?"

Wow, he thought, they were really hitting on me. Tal shrugged, "I figured it was my brilliant wit and rakish good looks."

Väst smiled. "They want to kiss you for one of the reasons I want to kiss you, Quint. Because of the Bane, it has been fifteen hundred years since Folk and humans intermingled. They want to feel the spark of legend for themselves."

"The spark of legend," Tal thought. I certainly like the sound of that. I could totally get behind being the "spark of legend." It's go time, he decided. "Close your eyes," he whispered to her. After she did, he did as well, before leaning into her. The moment before their lips touched, a spark of static electricity leapt the gap between them. She gasped as it surprised her, took her breath, then smiled as their tongues each took turns enticing, and encouraging. I could stay here with her forever, Tal thought, when their lips finally disengaged.

Väst smiled languidly at him. "We shall have to do that

again," she said. "Soon. I must go, I have stayed overlong tutoring you. Mitt will be very displeased if he finds out I have been educating the enemy."

"Is that the only reason he would be displeased?" Tal asked.

Väst laughed lightly. "Maybe, maybe not. It is sufficient reason. You are Omada. You are the enemy."

"Maybe by kissing me, you were 'Seeking the Center'," Tal replied.

"Perhaps there is truth in your jest," she said casually as she unfolded her legs to stand.

"Wait. You said the spark was only one of the reasons you wanted to kiss me. What are the others?" he asked.

She smiled, the smile being followed by another short laugh, before Väst leaned forward to brush her lips against his again. As she almost touched him, the static spark leapt between them causing her to moan into his mouth, "I see that I was wrong, Quint of Omada."

Tal pulled back, thinking he had done something to offend her.

Just before she again pressed her mouth insistently against his, she whispered, "You can in fact learn with your mouth open."

CHAPTER FIFTY

Elle was finishing the third revision of her English essay. After this version she would set it aside and reread it tomorrow for typos. It wasn't due until the day after tomorrow but there was no need taking a chance on committing an unforced error this late in the game and giving Angie Alison a chance to snake her position as valedictorian. That honor is an integral part of my ticket out of here. A ticket to a fresh start. Totally and completely.

She hadn't been able to stop her mind from wandering—to him. It'd been a hard call swallowing her pride and emailing Tal. She'd finally decided she wasn't a child anymore and wasn't going to play juvenile games. There was a possibility he might be worth the effort, and she wanted to know definitively. One way or the other.

Right when she finished, her phone rang. The number wasn't in her contact list but he promised he'd call tonight so she answered. "Hello."

"Hi, um, it's Tal. I told you today I'd call you. Um, tonight."

"Actually, what Tal told me today was that Tal would have Tal call me tonight," she replied glibly.

Elle didn't know it but Tal had spent the early evening game-planning the phone call so he didn't come across looking like a total idiot. Years ago, he and Pell had stayed up all night watching a John Wayne movie marathon. One of the movies was *Hellfighters*, which was about lunatics who capped off oil well fires for a living. He'd read up on the subject afterwards. The movie was based on the life of Red Adair, one of the pioneers of using nitroglycerin to use up all of an oil well fire's oxygen, thereby extinguishing the fire. Mr. Adair had once capped an oil well fire seven hundred feet tall, nicknamed the "Devil's Cigarette Lighter." Tal had known he was going to have a hard time talking to Elle tonight so he'd decided to take the offensive. "Elle—I know I sound ridiculous when we talk and I apologize for the instances past and those undoubtedly that will occur in the future. The simple truth of the matter is that you are so absolutely fucking drop dead gorgeous I can't even think straight—much less string two words together—when I talk to you."

Elle couldn't even respond, it was like he'd sucked all of the oxygen right out of her room.

"Elle? Are you there? Hello?"

"Um, yeah…so, hey, I'm a little tired tonight, can we talk tomorrow?"

"No problem," Tal replied. "I'll call again tomorrow night."

"I'm in trouble," was what Elle gasped to herself when she finally caught her breath after hanging up. Big, big trouble, she thought as she got into bed. What she didn't know was that a few blocks away, Tal's sole thought was the exact same as hers.

CHAPTER QUINQUAGINTA UNUS

"Today's lesson concerns the parameters of your final scavengyr category," Professor Elphinstone said, as he turned to write on the blackboard—'Wyld Thing.' He then turned back to address the class. "There is no dedicated textbook for this category. The winner of the Wyld Thing category will be the team that does the best job of creatively synthesizing everything you have learned during your century here at Hunts School."

I can only imagine what Notos is thinking at this moment, Tal thought. He copped a quick peek sideways. Yep, he was getting the stink eye. Nailed that one.

"The good news about Wyld Thing? Any magykal artifact counts. The bad news? Any magykal artifact counts. The possibilities are limitless. For example, the cornucopia in the lunchroom is an eligible piece. I wouldn't however suggest you take what might seem to be an easy path to scoring a major piece. Chef Hestia's standing punishment for even attempting to steal the cornucopia is that during the Beltane Feast, in the cafeteria, in front of the entire student body and faculty, she strips one member of the offending team and then strings that contestant up by two of their appendages." Professor Elphinstone took a moment to glance meaningfully around the entire classroom.

That's any two appendages she chooses, each tied to ropes run through pulleys at diagonal corners of the cafeteria, and then the offender is hoisted thirty feet into the air. Any…two...appendages. Her choice." Tal saw every one of the guys in the class shiver a little at the image.

"It would take weeks of class time to even scratch the surface of all of the different high-value pieces that have been utilized in past Hunts. As you are aware, we do not normally discuss strategy during class. That is part of the contest. However, Principal Chiron has mandated that I raise an issue during our discussion today. Team strategy is more important with respect to this category than any other piece in your Scavengyr Hunt. Each team will be tempted to garner whatever Wyld Thing points it can in an attempt to make the cut for the next Hunt. It is critical you remember, the pieces you acquire this Hunt are the resources you will have to survive not only this Hunt, but the final two Hunts as well."

"Any magykal piece on any plane qualifies. The Tablets of Destiny, the Cintamani Stone, the Mani jewel, the Cup of Jamshid, the Seal of Solomon, the Pelian spear, and the Caduceus, are a few examples of high value targets. Choose wisely. It may mean the difference between your life and death."

CHAPTER QUINQUAGINTA DUO

'I got to tell you Piras, I'm so excited I'm about to pee in my pants.'

'I'd prefer you not do that, Quint, as I'm now basically functioning as your pants.'

'Oh yeah, sorry.'

'Now that you've alerted me to a potential problem, I can assist in its resolution.'

Almost immediately Tal felt every bit of the pressure he'd been feeling removed from his bladder. 'Good work on that Piras.'

'You're welcome.'

Tal had some time left after his most recent tryst with Väst before the team meeting, so he'd gone to the gym and put Piras on. Even though the Puca weren't going to be making the first Journey, Tal knew he and Piras needed all the practice together they could get.

Väst, Tal thought. She's pretty much perfect. Actually, no need to use the qualifier "pretty much." And wearing that royal purple Puca.... Tal felt different pressure building, and then it went away.

'Piras?'

'You're welcome. Again.'

"Are we boring you, Quint?" Borras asked.

"No. I'm sorry, Prime."

"Okay, Omada, it's decision time. The first Journey is tomorrow morning, and this is our last team session before Quint heads home for the day. What are we shooting for?" True to form, Tal thought. Borras was asking for everyone's input rather than using his authority as Prime to dictate their strategy.

Notos answered first. "That's a no-brainer. We need a sword. There's nothing more important than that."

"I agree, Notos, but we can't even think about it on the first Journey," Anatolia added.

"Why not?"

"We're down an hour," Dysi replied. "There's a real possibility the scavengyr piece could be within a three-hour capture window but outside of a two hour Journey."

"That's right. Thanks for that, human," Notos said turning to scowl at Tal.

Is Notos, right, Tal wondered. I know Borras said a four-person squad hadn't won in forever, but they're a strong group. Have I cost them the competition? Or maybe put their lives in danger?

"The hour loss is unfortunate but penalties happen," Borras said. "Penalty or no, my recommendation was going to be that we not look for a weapon first."

"You're trying to cover his ass," Notos said quickly.

"No, he's not," Anatolia interjected. "The hour-penalty hurt us, Quint," she said looking first at Tal, then at Notos. "But we don't get our Pucas this first trip, we don't know about the other two Journeys."

"Probably not then either," Dysi added. "The HuntsMistress likes the smell of student blood."

"That's true," Anatolia continued, "but I'm with Borras on this. We know a couple of the teams would have no problem bending the Hunts Rules if two teams land in the same Realm looking for the same object. Let's face it, if the object is a sword, it's going to get used by the finding team, if possible, before the Recall."

Borras took the conversation back over. "Eleven weapons, nine teams. We can all see what the HuntsMistress is doing."

"So we piss away any chance of getting a sword?" Notos asked brusquely.

"No, Notos," Borras responded quietly. "You know, we all know, it takes brains—and luck—to win the Hunts. Let's use our brains, and go for something else we need."

"Here's the deal, folks," Borras continued. "Every one of the eligible swords is at the highest point level. They are the eleven most significant magykal swords in all the known planes. You know what that means." There was no response from the others. "Come on," Borras continued. "The price a team must be prepared to pay to acquire a scavengyr piece is in direct proportion to the piece's value. I wish no ill on any of the other squads but I sense something terrible is going to happen this first Journey."

He's right, Tal thought. That's exactly what Empousa intended to happen when she restricted the weapons category, dictated no Pucas on the first trip, and gave us staggered start times. She's a stone cold bitch, he told himself. But why? Why do this? What's she got to gain from it?

"Okay, I'm good with it," Notos finally conceded. "Given our one-hour penalty." Tal noticed he got the look of death yet again. "What do we go for?" Notos asked.

Tal saw everyone was getting ready to voice their opinion simultaneously when Borras stepped in. "We need to hear everyone's perspective. We'll go clockwise around the room. Ana?"

"If our basic premise is correct and most everyone else is going for a weapon, we should be able to go big on any specific piece we want from any of the other categories without much chance of running into one of the other teams. That way the only price we may have to suffer is the piece price itself."

"It's good logic," Borras said. "Remember though, the higher the point value, the more likely it is we will strike out going for it."

It's like swinging for a home run instead of taking an infield bunt, Tal thought.

"My vote is that we try for a medium to upper range Transportation piece," Anatolia said.

"It's your turn," Borras said, as he turned to address Notos.

"I think we should try to secure a high value defensive piece first," Notos said. "Maybe one of the invisibility pieces."

"And if we strike out?" Borras asked.

"We can try again after we get a weapon on one of our other two trips," Notos replied. "And put the failure in the Munedan's column."

"Making progress, I guess," Borras responded. "At least the first part of your suggestion was constructive. Dysi?"

"I'm basically with Ana on this one. Absent additional penalties—against us or any other team—the next level of culling depends primarily on our total points awarded from all three Journeys. I think we should try for a lower to medium Transportation piece. I can't see us wanting to spend another Journey on a better Transportation piece but if we do and we nab something we can relegate the first piece to Wyld Thing and the new piece to Transportation."

Brilliant, Tal thought. She's playing Yahtzee strategy to try to make sure we stay in the game.

"Your turn, Quint," Borras said. Tal watched as eight eyes lasered in on him. What's the right move here, he wondered. Every choice has pluses and minuses. I've already cost us an hour. If I suggest something that's accepted and we get nothing it may irreparably tear Omada apart. I need to follow Borras's example.

"Quint?" Borras prompted.

Then it came to him, exactly what he needed to do. "I think we should have given our opinions in directional rank order. As Borras and I are the only ones who haven't stated their ideas yet, I believe the Prime should go next and so I pass until our Prime has spoken." Now Borras, Tal thought to himself, now I need you to be as good a leader as I think you are.

Tal could tell from Borras's expression he was about to be knee-jerk humble and tell Tal to proceed. Then Tal saw Borras's eye narrow momentarily before returning to normal. He got it, Tal told himself, he got it.

"You're right Quint. From now on we will go in rank order, except that as your Prime I will be going last to allow free and unfettered discussion by the entire team. I second Notos's suggestion." When Borras finished, Tal saw him look right at him with his eyes narrowed again just a bit before returning to normal.

He's telling me it's my turn to be smart. If I cop out and say Wyld Thing, it's a tie situation with all of the resulting friction. If I go with the girls, Notos will become further entrenched in his hostility. "That's my vote as well—to go with our Second Prime's idea."

Borras smiled. Notos attempted to smile but obviously had used up his smile quota for the week. The two others were apparently content they'd been heard.

Deftly handled, Dust Child,' Piras said in Tal's mind.

'Thank you,' Tal replied. 'I wish you were making the trip.'

"It's settled," Borras announced. "I will announce to the Omphalos we wish to Journey to a Realm where we might obtain a medium to high value defensive piece." The gong sounded three times. "Time for Combat."

CHAPTER QUINQUAGINTA TRES

No question about it—he and Piras were easily the best duo in Combat today. They now moved as one. The electrical nature of Tal's synapses seemed to give Piras an advantage over all of the other Puca. Wearing Piras for the extra couple of hours during non-physical stress time today had allowed the Puca to learn more of Tal's body's natural reaction motions. With the temporary truce between them—and it being First Journey's Eve—Tal didn't rub it in Notos's face that he was a big points asset to the Omada in Combat. Just as well, Tal decided. The points from all other activities combined were insignificant compared to the points available from the three Journeys. They would only become important in case of a tie—which was extremely unlikely—or in the event several teams were unsuccessful on most of their Journeys—which was apparently not an uncommon event.

His pillow was going to feel good tonight. After a couple of Advil. Even though Piras bore the brunt of all contact, Tal was still sore as hell after Combat. He gave the Keepers his customary greeting as he walked out the front doors. "Hey, guys!" No response. Of course.

He went down the steps two at a time to the fountain. Just as he was getting ready to veer left toward the Gas Station Crossing he saw movement at the edge of Forest Fell. When he looked back a second time he saw nothing and was getting ready to blow the whole thing off when he saw it again. It looked like Väst was standing right inside the forest, urgently motioning for him to come. That's odd, he thought. None of us go anywhere near the forest, and she and I always meet in our little room. Then, abruptly, she was gone. It looked like she was jerked back into the woods. Something's wrong and she needs me. Tal immediately changed direction and ran toward the woods.

Väst's motion had come from almost exactly the same spot where he'd crossed the creek the month before. He knew he should listen to the part of his brain telling him being curious could result in death. Or worse. But Väst was in trouble. As he sprinted up the far embankment Tal noticed a well-defined path leading into the forest. Funny, you'd think one of us would have seen that path last time. Guess we were all too busy trying not to die. He followed the path, the underbrush solid on both sides but when he turned to look behind, he saw no evidence of the trail, only impenetrable brush.

"Hello? Väst?" No response. "Väst? Where are you?" He'd gone several hundred feet when the path opened into a small glade. Tal stopped and looked around. "What was I thinking?" he muttered to himself. "She wouldn't have been so stupid as to come in here." As he turned to leave he found the path had disappeared completely, leaving only a solid wall of shrubbery. I came in this way, he thought. No, that can't be right, this looks like it over here. Tal felt panic beginning to bubble. What was I thinking coming in here? This is a trap. We were told never to enter Forest Fell.

"Move, and thou wilt surely perish." The stentorian male voice seemed to emanate from the air in the glade.

'Move and thou wilt surely perish?' Who talks like that, Tal wondered. Still better safe than sorry so he stood still. A small band of men, faces painted in camouflage, stepped effortlessly through the brambles and into the glade. Men—but not men. Camouflage—but upon closer examination—not camouflage. They looked like men except for their perfect posture. Uniformly tall, their lean muscles rippled beneath close-fitting shimmering gray hooded tunics and green leggings. As Tal looked at the faces under the hoods he realized they weren't painted—their dappled skin mirrored Forest Fell. Each face was a distinct tapestry containing the golden rays of the sun, the various greens of the forest canopy, and the dark earthy brown of its fecund floor. All had gleaming swords drawn, and were holding them motionless scant inches from Tal's chest.

"Trespasser, art thou from Hunts School?" their leader asked. He was the one squarely in front of Tal. The badge of his leadership was worn in the body language of his men. The leader's sword was a burnished work of art, a glowing silver blade with fiery runic lettering running all up and down the blade. Its black hilt was inlaid with gossamer-thin threads of what appeared to be rubies, which sparkled in the mottled light of the forest.

"Uh…yes," Tal finally responded, his voice cracking. He hadn't realized how scared he really was. Now that he knew, it occurred to him there was a distinct possibility he might wet his pants.

"Does Hunts School no longer warn its students that trespassers are subject to death for entering these woods?"

"Well, yes sir, it's on the bla…the bla…the blackboard. Actually it s-s-says death…or, er…worse," Tal replied honestly, his voice cracking even more. He realized the "or worse" part might be death immediately following the public wetting of your pants.

The speaker looked at his cohorts, then back to Tal. "If it were my decision, I would let…" He paused before continuing. "My personal feelings are irrelevant. It matters not your age or what manner of Folk you be. It is our charge to keep this forest inviolate. Having been properly forewarned, your life is now forfeit." With that he raised his sword over his head.

A fireball of teenage anger quickly supplanted Tal's fear. "You know, I'm getting pretty sick and tired of all the adults around here saying my life is forfeit. Every time I turn around it's, 'You're a dead man.' 'Your life is forfeit, Dust Child,' is popular as well. Well, it's chicken tender night back at the old Smith household and they go pretty fast. So if you don't mind, I'll just be on my way now." Tal started to make a move to his left, but the swords remained motionless, so he was forced to stop as he felt several press through his shirt.

The leader motioned for his men to lower their swords. "Dust Child? Art thou mortal?"

"Yeah, pretty much. Sorry to disappoint you. No superpowers, no channeling, just me. I am however a National Merit Finalist if that counts for anything."

The commander finally sheathed his sword, and lowered his hood as he took a step towards Tal. "It cannot be you. It has been more than a thousand years, yet you say you are mortal."

Totally lost, Tal came up with the most intelligent thing he could say. "Huh?"

"Your name, human. What is your name?"

"Quint."

"It is he," the leader announced to his company. Tal saw several of the soldiers step backward, almost as if they were afraid. Another couple looked bewildered. The commander took a half-step toward Tal. "In exchange for the greatest gyft ever given me, you asked for only one boon."

"Umm,…I did? Well, um, hail fellow well met. Again," Tal said stupefied. "What exactly was that boon, again?"

"Please do not kill me the first time we meet," their leader replied. The man still seemed stunned, Tal thought.

"I am Arthrys," he continued.

"Great," Tal replied. "Nice to remeet you." He started to turn to walk back the way he thought he had come.

"Stop," Arthrys demanded. "My name, does it mean nothing to you?"

"Nope."

"How long have you been at Hunts School?"

"This is my first—and apparently one way or the other—last year."

At Tal's response, Arthrys pursed his lips. "Stranger and stranger, indeed. The same mortal whom I met more than a millennium ago has been admitted to Hunts School. Admitted during a Tyrning Year, at that."

"If you don't mind my asking, what kind of Folk are y'all?"

"We are Alfar. Mortals call us elves, although there are as many different of our kind as there are trees in the forest. Some light-walkers, others tread the darkness."

At that moment, the Alfar immediately to Arthrys's left leaned over and whispered in his ear. Tal heard Arthrys ask him if he was sure. The elf nodded in response.

"I was away on Lailoken's business that day, but G'wain says my company has seen you before."

"I'm pretty sure I've never met any of y'all," Tal replied.

"They bore personal witness to your valor in battle with the hell-spawn," Arthrys replied.

"I haven't done anything valiant..." Tal started saying, before Arthrys's words sunk in. When he finally understood them, he responded angrily, "What do you mean they were witnesses? Do you mean y'all let those things chase us down? They were trying to kill Väst, me, all of us."

"Child of the Dust, if you are a competitor you should know the Hunts Rules by now. It is forbidden for any of the Folk to interfere with Hunt contestants."

"That's crazy," Tal responded. "The Rules couldn't possibly have been written to allow murder." When no answer was forthcoming he continued, "We didn't need your help anyway. There were some funky silver wolves that came and saved our lives. If you want to talk about heroes, they're it. Well, they're not really wolves, I forgot what Borras called them."

"Cooshies," Arthrys responded.

"That's right, Cooshies." Something clicked. "Hey! Borras said Cooshies are elf-hounds."

"'Tis so."

"If the Rules wouldn't let you interfere, how come you sent your pets to save our lives?"

Again the short laugh. "You misunderstand. Cooshies are with the Alfar of their own choosing and we are bound only by mutual respect. The Hunts Rules forbid Folk from helping or hindering Hunts contestants. The Cooshies are Creatures, not part of the Moiety, so the Rules do not apply to them. For as long as any can remember, all Creatures—other than the Puca—have chosen not to help nor hinder Hunts contestants. The Cooshies came of their own volition that day, Quint. They were summoned to battle by a hero's self-sacrifice. It was of the Center, and called to them."

Tal shook his head, trying to sift the frenzy of events of that day. "I must have missed something in all the fighting. When did the hero show up?"

"The hero that day was you, human," Arthrys replied. "The Cooshie chose to enter the fray in response to your act of selflessness."

"You mean helping Väst."

"Just so," Arthrys confirmed. He waved a hand over his head in invitation, and several dozen Cooshie stepped through the undergrowth into the glade.

Tal recognized the one to Arthrys' right, its silver mane shot through with ribbons of white. "It was him. He saved our lives."

"Yes, it was Perun who intervened on your behalf. He is Chieftain of the Cooshie, as I am Pendragon, by the will of the Alfar."

Tal was at a loss for words standing before the regal creature that had undoubtedly saved both he and Väst. Not knowing what else to do, he instinctively dropped to one knee and bowed his head in homage to the great beast, acknowledging his debt to Perun and his kin for saving their lives.

Tal's action created a buzz of excitement in the Alfar. Tal thought he heard one of the elves gasping about a human kneeling to a Cooshie, even if it was the leader of the elf-hounds. For his part, Perun stared—without blinking—straight at Tal, and when Tal finally raised his head, Perun remained motionless, staring. Through his eyes, into him, searching, searching...searching.

Arthrys had been watching the proceedings with interest, and turned to Perun, "Aye Perun, strange proceedings indeed. A Munedan at Hunts School, a mortal who somehow lives a life span worthy of the Alfar, and who acknowledges a blood-debt to a Creature. Mayhaps you know something about this human you have not shared?" A grin was the only response Perun tendered.

Tal stood back up and turned to Arthrys. "For what it's worth, as far as I'm concerned, I don't qualify as a trespasser. I was invited into this forest," Tal said defensively.

The members of the band looked questioningly at each other. "There is only one who may invite you into Forest Fell," Arthrys said.

Tal told Arthrys about the events of the afternoon, the summoning arm, and about how the forest had opened before him and closed behind him until he reached the clearing.

"We wondered how you were able to find Council Glade. It was the woodwose who summoned you this day into the wood, they that cleared your path. They are not evil creatures, but their minds are small. They fear those greater, ones whose bidding they would obey. Today, something powerful summoned you to your death."

Or to worse, Tal thought, as a cold chill came upon him. The Gas Station tried to warn me. The blackboard is right, Forest Fell is a very dangerous part of the world. "You said the Hunts Rules forbid any of the Folk from helping or hindering Hunts contestants."

"Just so," Arthrys affirmed. "Questions without answers. For now. It is lucky for you our patrol brought us so close to Council Glade, otherwise the woodwose would have completed their assigned task, and delivered you to their master. They fled because they sensed our presence."

"Who would be the woodwose's master?" Tal asked.

Arthrys stiffened, becoming again the guerilla commander. He turned to his left while whispering his order, "G'wain take three, scout the perimeter and meet us at the western point." Four of the elves and a like number of Cooshie dissolved into the wood.

"Woodwose?" Tal asked again.

"This is not class, mortal. Now is the time for silence. Come!" Arthrys commanded.

"Not until you tell me where we're going," Tal stood his ground, not moving an inch.

Several hands went to scabbards, but at a nod from Arthrys they relaxed. "He needs to hear these things from your mouth. He can answer all your questions—and perhaps mine as well—if he will."

"He?"

"We are taking you to Lailoken."

"Who is Lailoken?" Tal asked.

Arthrys laughed quietly. "The Hunts School education must not be what it was during my schooling four Tyrnings past. Lailoken is the Myrddin."

That just answers everything, doesn't it, Tal thought.

"Come, time is short. We have a ways to go, and the forest has become a very dangerous place—even for the Alfar— once night holds sway."

"Okay, but this better be good if I'm gonna miss chicken finger night," Tal replied. They walked for what seemed to Tal like hours, but it couldn't have been because the forest still retained a measure of dusky sunlight. He still didn't understand how the elves and the Cooshies moved through the close-knit underpinnings of the forest. It seemed as if wherever they were and were going to be for the next few steps, the forest wasn't. But as soon as they passed that place, the forest was again. Several times Perun growled, a bass rumble deep within his throat. Each time the troupe froze, with Arthrys smelling the close air of the surrounding wood.

"Trow," he announced to his men one time, "Dusith's clan, almost a hundred warriors. There are several of the woodwose with them. They're just over Caer Melin, by Slaughter Bridge." Turning back to Tal he said, "Trow are the darkest of elves. They are named trolls by the Children of Dust. Dusith has many while we are only patrol number. Hurry, we are almost to Myrddin's Star."

CHAPTER QUINQUAGINTA QUATTUOR

He was never going to be able to describe this to Emet—or the Omada. Of course, he wouldn't get the chance if death [or worse] happened first. Arthrys and crew had brought him to a shimmering curtain of rainbow light. Tal had often cruised the National Geographic magazines in whatever library he was in at the time, and the only way to describe what he was looking at now was by reference to some pictures from a National Geographic photo contest about the Aurora Borealis, the Northern Lights. Right here in the middle of Forest Fell, it was like somebody had taken the Aurora Borealis out of the sky, and turned it vertically so that it went from the ground to the heavens. Tal reached out his hand to touch the multi-hued surface.

"DO NOT!" Arthrys yelled, grabbing Tal's hand. "Aurora is not a glamour, Munedan. She is a Principe, one of the First-Born. She zealously protects the boundaries of the Pentacle of Lailoken. Whether human or Folk, it is always a good rule to keep your hands to yourself."

Funny, Tal thought, that exact same statement is stenciled in the limestone arch over the entrance to the Hunts School cafeteria. I thought it was only a reminder not to grab someone else's ambrosia. I didn't know it was a warning to keep me from being rainbow-fried.

Arthrys resumed walking along the rainbow's edge, looking carefully at the ground, searching for something. As Tal followed he noticed the constantly morphing wall of light had facets to it. If the rest of the structure's pattern mirrored what they had already walked around, it was shaped like a five-pointed star.

Arthrys looked up to see Tal staring at the curtain. "The entrance to the Pentacle is never twice the same, the protecting magyks constantly change to stop those who might seek to usurp the Myrddin's power." Turning his attention back to the ground, Arthrys walked a few more steps before stopping and signaling his company. They immediately stopped but remained in formation. "It is here," Arthrys said.

Tal looked at the spot on the forest floor that held Arthrys's gaze. There was a rock about the size of a large anvil, which bisected the curtain—part within and part without. Unsheathing his sword, and gripping the haft with both hands Arthrys extended his arms vertically, raising the hilt high over his head, chanting, "Sword of Justice, known by many names— Caliburnus, Cut-Steel, Excalibur—grant us safe passage." Arthrys then drove the blade downward toward the rock with all his might.

Tal gasped, sure the blade would shatter upon contact with the raw granite. It didn't. The stone welcomed the steel, with the sword sliding in more than half its length. As they watched, the curtain melted away around the rock, leaving a portal a few inches wider and taller than the biggest of the Alfar. Arthrys motioned to his men and ducking their heads, careful not to touch the rainbow wall, they passed through into the Star of Myrddin. Arthrys nodded to Tal that it was his turn, and Tal entered as directed, with Arthrys following close on his heels. After he passed through Arthrys turned around, grasped the sword hilt with both hands and said, "Avalon." The sword withdrew easily from the stone and as it did the opening in Aurora grew smaller and smaller until the rainbow curtain was intact once more.

"Come, he awaits."

CHAPTER QUINQUAGINTA QUINQUE

It looks like the inside of a sawed in half geode, Tal thought. Crystals of every size, from the length of his fingertip to bigger than a house. Amethyst, violet, and lavender, they were every shade and hue of purple you could possibly imagine.

In the middle of it all the granddaddy of crystals extended like a redwood hundreds of feet into the air. As big around as a missile silo, it had smaller crystal branches protruding at seemingly random intervals. Tal could see thin streams of purplish vapor emanating from the tip of each of the branches.

"Wow!"

"I see thou hast the gift of eloquence, mortal," Arthrys said with the barest hint of an upturn at the corners of his mouth.

"Sorry, Arthrys. But I mean…wow!"

"This space is a singularity protected by Aurora. There is no other like the Myrddin, nor like this place. It is our charge from Amarantos to keep his sanctuary safe while he is about Her business."

A door materialized at the base of the center crystal, then swung open on crystal hinges. Tal squinted as rays of white and yellow light shot forth from the opening, out of which strode a handsome young man, arrayed in a purple shirt, and trousers, with a full-length traveling cloak of the same hue. He quickly scanned their group, his purple eyes as sharp as his cheekbones. He looks like a purple-ized version of Prince Charming, Tal thought. The man gestured behind his shoulder, and the door disappeared. As he walked toward them, each of the Alfar took a knee.

"It can't be," Tal whispered. "You're in your twenties. A couple of months ago you were barely a teenager and last month you were older than dirt. Older than really old dirt, actually. Who are you?"

The man laughed. "Do you remember our conversation about the Kalachakra?"

"Vaguely."

"I seem to recall I told you that you should remember it, that it might be important."

He did, Tal thought. I halfway blew Kid Know-It-All off, but he did. "So, you were Mertin Wilt the first time. Then you were the Traveler. And these guys call you Lailoken?"

"That is the name which the Alfar have always used."

"Why," Tal asked.

"Because I am Time's Fool in the service of the UnFading One," he replied.

"What should I call you?" Tal asked.

"It might make things simpler if you call me by my function—Myrddin."

"I don't understand."

"I am the avatar of the Myrddin for this age."

"Still lost," Tal said.

Arthrys interrupted, "Mage, my scouts have sent word the dark elves have begun a major skirmish. Caliburnus has much work to do this day if I am to keep the Pentacle safe."

"You have my leave to go, Arthrys. I will see this one safely home." Myrddin took a purple crystal wand from under his robes and pointed it at Aurora, who opened a portal in response. With a nod to the Myrddin, Arthrys and his men carefully stepped through the doorway, which promptly disappeared after their exit.

"Now Taliesin, tell me everything that has happened since I saw you last," Myrddin requested. Tal proceeded to give him the CliffsNotes version of everything he could remember.

"Your story is both wonderful and frightening. It has been many Tyrnings since someone had sufficient creationmagyk to make a simulacrum golem. But there is also the reappearance of the Crestfallyn, after centuries of quietude," Lailoken said, when Tal had finished. "Someone is violating the Hunts Rules, and more importantly, they're violating the Lex Immortalis for reasons obscured to me now. I will ask Amarantos about sending me othertyme to look into the matter."

"Myrddin," Tal said, "I really don't get it. This place. You being young, then old. What's the deal?"

"As the Myrddin, it is my privilege and responsibility to go where and when She sends me. It is why the Alfar call me Lailoken. I am Time's Fool—Time's Exception—until my Wheel has completed its turn."

"So how old are you?"

Myrddin paused a long moment. "I do not know how to truthfully answer that question, Taliesin. The Myrddin is singularly released from the strictures of time—to effectuate Her purpose." He cocked his head toward the morphing kaleidoscope, and tilted his head as if listening to someone whispering in his ear. "Aurora has asked if you enjoyed meeting her brother's emanation?"

"I'm sorry, who?"

"Tal, you must let go of your predetermined notions. Surely you know Aurora has a brother and a sister."

Think, Tal told himself. What Väst told him that first time they made out. Aurora is from Greek mythology. Aurora was the Greek goddess of the dawn, and she had two siblings. Luna, goddess of the moon, and Sol, god of the sun. There are four Principes: Chronos, Aurora, Luna and Sol. "Wait a minute.

You're saying that dilapidated old gas station is actually…that the junkyard is…that's ridic…"

"Since the time Hunts School was founded Sol has agreed to act as guardian of the passageway between Hunts School and the mortal realm."

"The sun is actually a boarded up gas station?"

"Open your mind, Tal."

"And the junkyard is really Luna, the Moon?"

"Sshh! It is not wise to call upon that Principe. I do not think you would enjoy her attention." Myrddin stopped to listen again. "Aurora has something to give you."

"A gift, but…"

"Tal, you really need to read the Rules. Aurora is a Principe…"

"Not part of the Moiety."

"Exactly."

As Tal watched, a small part of the curtain folded in on itself and began extending toward him in a Mobius band that continued to shrink as it rotated in midair. It grew smaller and smaller, taking the shape of a ring, as it moved toward Tal.

Tal looked at Myrddin, who nodded his approval. He reached up and took the ring. As he turned it in his hand he could see every color of the rain's bow deep within it. He placed the ring on his right ring finger. As he did, the ring became a solid silver.

"Strange and worrisome happenings, indeed," Myrddin muttered, running his hand back and forth across his forehead. "It has been many Tyrnings since Creatures took any interest in the Hunts and never have the Principes concerned themselves with the Moiety. Clear your mind Tal, Aurora wishes to speak to you."

'Greetings, Taliesin Smith.'

Wow. This wasn't like Piras talking to him telepathically. Tal could feel the energy behind her voice. Maybe if you took the energy in the entire ocean and put it all in a cup of water, and the cup of water was poured over you. That was kind of what it felt like, except more. He bowed to the shimmering curtain of light. "Lady Aurora."

Never before has a Child of Dust been allowed into the Pentacle of the Myrddin.

"Thank you," Tal replied.

'My ring is for you. The rain's bow has been completed in this perfect circle. It is a gyft, freely given.'

"Thank you."

'You may not thank me by your Journey's end, Youngest Brother. Someone has paid the pryce for every gyft ever given. It is you who shall have to bear the gyftpryce this time. Four times before the Tyrning shall you have need of my ring, but only thrice may help it bring. Choose well Taliesin, and only when your need is clear, for by your choices you doom someone dear.'

Tal felt the link terminate, and the feeling of restrained boundlessness removed from his mind. He bowed his head again in respect.

Myrddin stepped up to him and placed his hand on his shoulder. "I will not ask you what she said, for that is between the two of you. You need to remember every word though, as if more than only your life depended on it. Because it does." He turned and walked toward Aurora, and as he did a portal as tall as Tal opened. He motioned for Tal to walk through. "You should hurry. I understand chicken finger night is an important occasion at the Smith household."

Tal took a deep breath, stepped through Aurora, and found himself squarely behind the massive bough of the hoary white oak in his front yard.

CHAPTER FIFTY-SIX

A couple of hours, and approximately twenty-six chicken fingers later—in all fairness some of them had been small and that was the total tally for both he and Emet—Tal felt human again. "Felt human." Funny how that reference had taken on a completely different meaning in the last few months. His Mom thought she'd cooked enough to pack for sack lunches pretty much all week. She was going to be unpleasantly surprised in the morning, but it couldn't be helped. He and Emet were going flat out ninety to nothing every day and their fuel burn rate was astronomical.

It wasn't until they'd finally gotten the time to do detailed catch-up that they realized the speed of events had outstripped their ability to effectively communicate real time. Tal hadn't gotten to keep Emet up to speed about he and Väst's amorous activities. Emet had had to make decisions about Elle that he'd implemented without first clearing them with Tal. Tal's initial reaction was to get pretty severely bent out of shape. Almost immediately he realized Emet was doing exactly what he would have done in like circumstances. And it wasn't as if Emet's actions were ever going to be a problem, so no harm no foul.

There was no way in hell that Elle and Väst would ever meet. Ever.

It was an important turning point for the both of them though, as it resulted in Tal's epiphany that he'd been harboring a latent bigotry with respect to Emet. He had been treating him as a Creature, as less of a sentient being because Tal was the original and Emet was the copy. It was a version of the same Folk-Creatures issue he'd questioned Borras about when they'd first met. Sure, Tal had emotions and Emet didn't, but in certain respects Emet was superior to Tal. They were equals though. Emet was himself, not a second-rate Tal.

I'm not mad at Tal because being mad isn't possible for me. Frustrated? Uneasy? Nope, same problem—they're all just dictionary words to me for certain emotional responses. I'm incapable of emotional response. Still, when Tal yelled at me tonight, when he'd expressed his displeasure toward me for taking the initiative, it almost seemed for a moment as if something colored my logical response. For a moment, but then it was gone.

They simply hadn't had time to sequence out their decision-tree the last few days. Battlefield command decisions sometimes had to be made without reporting in to HQ, that was completely logical. He'd listened carefully to Tal and Elle's conversation last evening. He could tell from Tal's responses to her that she'd been hurt, and that a failure to properly communicate during school today was going to exacerbate that situation. On the way to Nemeton High, he'd written out an explanatory note for her. To be prepared. On the outside chance she'd catch him before he could vanish down the hallway after one of their joint classes.

He'd thought the band room was safe. Other than a library, that's where Tal went to find peace for himself. Emet was proficient at playing the guitar and never seemed to have time to play at the house. There was no way he could have been prepared for what happened. As far as his actions, and reactions, he would have said they were a coincidence. Except he and Tal were one and the same.

It had been a really good day, Elle thought, as she sat brushing her hair. That had been the penultimate step in her evening ritual for as long as she could remember. Up until recently the final step was reading herself to sleep. If she had any input in the decision, it would now be talking with Tal until one of them couldn't keep their eyes open any longer. First, there was accidentally running into him in the band room today. And then there was that note, that absolutely lovely note.

She hadn't been looking for him. In fact, the opposite. She'd seen him cut out after Calculus and their other advanced classes. He could have hung back to try to dialogue with her. He didn't. He was gone likkity-split. Since the library was the Fortress of Solitude for both of them she'd gone to her backup hiding place—the band room.

Right before she pulled on the door handles she heard the guitar. Someone was in there tuning their strings. Looking in through the glass panel she'd seen it was Tal. She remained outside while he quickly ran through a couple of tunes. He didn't sing—which fit with his "Silent Running" persona as she'd nicknamed him—but his instrumental versions of the songs were breathtaking. She realized she wanted to feel his fingers move across her face, across her body with the same skill as they summoned sound from the guitar strings.

Finally, she couldn't stand it anymore. She had to be a part of that. Even if he rejected her, even if he might not want her in the same way she wanted him The look on his face when she came in through the swinging door was priceless. He was trapped and would have to deal with her. Elle wasn't really sure what had come over her. She didn't greet him. She didn't try to make him talk when it was obvious he didn't feel like it She desperately wanted to be part of him, of what he was doing. So she asked him to play her a song. Any song she told him, that he thought she might know the lyrics. Because he might not want to speak to her but she desperately wanted to communicate with him, even if it was only by singing along.

He'd paused, thinking. Then he started and stopped several times, not quite long enough for her to figure out what he was playing. Finally he began to pick a few notes, not fumbling this time but with assurance. About five notes in she realized what he had picked for her. It was one of her favs, by a wonderful singer-songwriter. It was almost as if he'd read her mind.

After he went through the first verse, he paused to see if it was acceptable to her. She had nodded and he began again. First a G major chord, then a D, an E minor, and finally a C. And she began to sing along, "The dawn is breaking, a light shining through."

"Collide," by Howie Day. It was almost as if he'd reached inside her to pull out the perfect song for them to perform together. She sang the whole song and she knew she sang it well, even through the tears rolling down her face. It was the most intimate thing she'd ever done in her life. Exposing herself like that, opening herself up to the joy that coursed through her body as he made love to the guitar and by extension to her. When it was over she was exhausted, the two of them had done something flawless and beautiful. Together. Then she saw him get up and she realized with a cold chill the heartless bastard was actually going to walk out of the room without saying a word, leaving her raw...and vulnerable. As he walked by her he looked at her with those gorgeous damn eyes of his. He said nothing but merely held out his hand. As she took it he pressed a folded up piece of paper into her palm and continued on out the door. Without a word. Without exhibiting a shred of emotion. Cruel, heartless bastard.

The first thought through her mind was where Barton might be at that moment. She had never stooped so low as to enlist her brother's aid but Tal's actions were extraordinary. The cruelty he'd exhibited was nonpareil, beyond anything she'd ever seen Barton and his pair of idiots do. He had to be taught a lesson and she obviously didn't have the skill set necessary to do it.

She picked up her phone, but right before she dialed Barton she thought about the piece of paper pressed in her hand. It was wrapped tight, the corners neatly tucked to form a perfect square. It took her a minute or so to unwrap it. She did so and then she read it. And read it again. And read it again.

Damn him. Damn that beautiful, intelligent asshat of a man. Why hadn't he told her what he was doing? Didn't he know that she of all people would understand? That what she wanted was exactly what he wanted. He was doing anything and everything he could possibly think to do to try to reach the same goal she was trying to attain. To get to a place where she could learn, and grow, and be her own person.

Thanks to Emet's bold move, we're in it now, Tal thought, as he picked up his phone to call Elle.

We have to communicate better, Emet thought, as he leapt out the window heading for his attic roost. And I need to figure out what logic function is it that's making me feel solitary. Because it can't be an emotional response. That's impossible.

Elle's phone rang, pulling her back to the present. She smiled as she answered it, "Tal…"

"I hope you have a few minutes, I'm thinking we need to have a pretty long chat."

CHAPTER QUINQUAGINTA SEPTEM

The HuntsMistress led the Omada out one of the main building's intricately carved rear porticoes and down a macadam walkway. The campus was landscaped with flowers of every imaginable hue, their blooms so thick it was as if some giant impressionist had troweled great daubs of oil paint reds, oranges, blues, and greens onto the campus. The walkway led past the dormitories, the boys' Viking longhouse to their right, the girls' Taj Mahal on the left, before taking a slight zig to the left around the stadium. The path's terminus was the plaza in front of the ziggurat.

There were several differences between this trip and Tal's initial visit to the pyramid. This time they went down, into the ziggurat's bowels. The staircase was about twenty feet wide. At the bottom they were met by an honor guard of twelve immense torch-toting dudes who looked exactly like each other. Tal thought he was experiencing déjà vu until he realized they not only looked like each other, they looked exactly like—and were dressed exactly the same as—the six sentinels who guarded the front door twenty-four seven.

The basement they entered turned out to be only the first level of a basement complex undergirding the entire pyramid. Their group kept heading down, this time on a long winding ramp that in size and curvature felt like the ramp of a large parking garage. They walked briskly downward for almost ten minutes, finally reaching the antechamber of the Prime Omphalos. Tal started trying to calculate how far they'd descended and how many hundreds of tons of rough-hewn but elegant quarried marble there were in the ziggurat.

"Hold here," Ms. Empousa announced. "The Släkt are being Recalled from their Journey." With that she walked briskly across the room, before opening the door and stepping into the next room. Tal and his teammates looked at each other. Remembering Borras's admonition in the team room, rather than making chit-chat, they elected not to say anything at all.

The door to the Prime Omphalos chamber flew open and the Släkt erupted like a swarm of ants. Okay, Tal thought, it takes more than five to make a swarm of ants. Anyway it's bees that swarm. Actually, he told himself, there was that magazine article he'd read a couple of months ago on ant swarm intelligence. Focus, Tal, he told himself. In any event the Släkt sure seemed like they were many multiples of five as they blew into the antechamber. Upon seeing the Omada, Mitt held his closed right fist over his head and his team went silent and formed a line. Nord was carrying a large narrow object shrouded with a gray blanket.

Shit, Tal exclaimed in his mind. Shit! Shit! SHIT! They got a sword. He must have made some noise because Borras looked back over his shoulder and gave him the "shut it down immediately" look. Damn it! Their first trip out, they got a sword. Notos is going to be on my ass even more.

Nord gave Tal a sallow smile as he walked by, intentionally bumping Tal with his shoulder hard enough to knock him sidewise a step. Väst was last in line for the Släkt, as Tal was for the Omada. With no one else on either of their teams being able to see her, she gave him a huge smile as she walked by and mouthed the words, "See you in our room later."

Tal felt his face flush with the heat of his response. Hot, hot, hot! Damn, that girl is hot! She's Galatea carved out of the wood of my every fantasy. She's also the enemy, he reminded himself. Tal watched her swish out of the antechamber as the guard led the Släkt out and closed the door behind them.

"Omada, it's now time for your first Journey," Ms. Empousa announced.

CHAPTER QUINQUAGINTA OCTO

Okay this is pretty freaking cool, Tal thought, after quickly scoping the place out. Of course he'd expected something unexpected. I mean come on, the Prime "O" was the gateway to the entire universe. His guessings had included numerous permutations, one being the Prime Omphalos would be a humongous diamond as big as an SUV—like something out of Scrooge McDuck's vault. It wasn't. A diamond anyway. It was, however, an enormous irregularly shaped boulder, maybe about two stories in height and about forty feet in circumference at its widest point. Just your regular run of the mill, plain vanilla, immense black and gray mottled ginormous boulder. There were only two unusual things about it. First, it had a doughnut hole void in the middle roughly ten feet in circumference. Second, it was—

Hanging—as in suspended. With—no visible sign of support. In—a cavern bigger than the Dallas Cowboys' football stadium. Like I just said to myself, Tal thought, pretty freaking cool. The majority of the cavern, what Tal could see in the flickering magykal torchlight, remained in its natural state. Stalagmites as big as Sequoyahs thrust upward, continuing centuries of efforting to reach their smaller sibling stalactites, whose tips dripped down to meet them.

Encompassing the PO was a spider web of Folk-made catwalks crisscrossing each other at every possible angle, horizontally and diagonally. They never once touched or supported the PO, their purpose being to provide access to every square inch of it. Pretty freaking cool.

Clearly, the Prime Omphalos had been located here forever, maybe even since the Earth cooled. The Folk had constructed their ziggurat, in fact the entire Hunts School campus, over and around the Prime Omphalos cavern. As Tal watched, Ms. Empousa wordlessly directed Borras to a walkway leading to the center hole. Notos was sent to the bottom of the rock, Ana and Dysi to walkways that left them on opposite sides, one hundred eighty degrees apart. Tal was last, as she motioned to him to move to the top.

Tal got it. They had been moved like chess pieces to the five cardinal directions of the stone. Borras, as Prime, occupied the center. Tal was taking what would have been Borras's spot absent Kentro's death. Tal's gangplank led him a few feet above the stone's apex. He heard fingers snapping and looked down to see the HuntsMistress was snapping them at him. Once she had his attention she pantomimed him turning himself upside down and extending one of his arms downward. What the hell?

Apparently unhappy with his failure to act, she quickly mimicked the movements again and then snapped her fingers several times rapidly in succession. Crap! Tal finally realized he was supposed to hang upside down from the catwalk and touch the PO. Like it's the Blarney Stone, he thought. One of his semester term assignments back in Munedan school had been the history of the British Isles. Which included the Blarney Stone, the Stone of Eloquence. Some legends held that it was a part of the Lia Fail, the "Fatal Stone" upon which Irish kings were crowned. Of course others said that was the Stone of Scone.

More finger-snapping pulled him back to the present. He gave Ms. Empousa the high sign to let her know he got the message. He knelt and felt along the rim of the walkway. The lip was about four inches high and curled back up around itself. He should be able to hook his feet up under there and lower himself down to touch the rock. What's the worst that could happen, he asked himself. I fall a couple of feet and land on the rock? And then it falls out of the air after being suspended for millions of years—and crushes Notos? I'm good with that, he decided, as he lowered himself into position.

Once he was upside down he waved at the HuntsMistress. He couldn't see any of the others. He figured the same held true for the rest of his teammates. As soon as Ms. Empousa saw the entire team was in position, she walked back to the entrance, the door clicking closed behind her. As the door sealed, the torches extinguished themselves. Great, Tal thought. I'm hanging upside down like a bat and it's dark as hell in here now. I appreciate them going all green and everything to conserve their magyk but how the hell are we supposed to see? And when I get Recalled am I going to be hanging upside down like this?

Then Tal literally felt his breath taken away as the room exploded into light and motion. Holy shit, it was like being at one of those Disney three hundred sixty degree three-dimensional rides. A planetarium version of those rides. Well, a planetarium version of those rides where you had to hang upside down. And instead of one sun, there were a host of them, accompanied by bookoos of planets together with bucketloads of stars. Bucketloads! The suns were of all different sizes and burned in blues, red, oranges, and yellows. As Tal twisted his body to look at it all he saw the planets were spinning on their respective axes, and the stars pursued their studied courses across his range of vision—twirling, twinkling, before falling off a dark horizon.

Dizzied, Tal lowered his right hand to steady himself with the Prime Omphalos—and his head split wide open.

CHAPTER QUINQUAGINTA NOVEM

When he came to, Tal found himself on his hands and knees staring down at powdery white sand. Sugar sand, they called it in the Florida Panhandle. All of it a blinding white in the midday sun. Except for a patch of wet ochre-colored sand immediately beneath him. *I've been bleeding.*, he realized. He tried to take a quick survey of the damage, but his head screeched for no sudden movement while his stomach dry heaved several times to reinforce his head's position.

Try it again Tal, he told himself, *but slowly this time.* He carefully scanned his clothes. Nothing on them. He rubbed his hands together to knock most of the sand off and started feeling his face. *Slowly, Tal, go slowly. Son of a bitch!* Best he could tell he had been bleeding from his eyes. Which made sense as it felt like someone was continuing to use his temples as tympani. *That bitch Empousa! Wouldn't let us use our Pucas for the trip. She's a sadist. The pinup girl for sadists actually.*

He cautiously stood up. He felt a little nauseated but it was manageable. *Where was everyone else?* He staggered down to the water's edge and lifted a handful of water to his mouth. *Gaugh! Salt water. Okay so I'm on a beach somewhere with* saltwater, presumably an ocean. He scooped another handful and splashed it on his face. Gaugh!! That stings like a son of a bitch. He repeated the exercise several times until he felt like the saltwater had both cleansed and cauterized his eyes as well as removing any traces of dried blood from his face.

Tropical, or maybe sub-tropical, he decided. There was a pleasant breeze blowing off the water, a cloudless sky, and the temperature felt like it was in the lower eighties. Far out across the water he could see a sizeable mountain rising up from the sea. The waves were only about a foot high at the shoreline but they were hurling themselves against an underwater obstruction a couple of hundred yards out. Shoal or coral reef, Tal decided. Whichever, I wouldn't want to be on a ship heading for that.

Where am I? How long have I been here? Where's the team? How much time do we have in our reduced EPT window? Small chance I'll find them if I stand here, he decided. Which way, though? He resolved since he was clueless where he was, it made no difference, so he turned to his right and started walking up the beach.

After walking for about five minutes he'd come to a blind right angle corner, when he heard female voices. He paused to make sure that's what he was hearing. The waves were more serious on this section of the beach, and the crashing was creating substantial white noise. He cautiously stepped around a boulder a little more than head high and the first thing he saw was—breasts.

Four of them. Well more accurately, two pair. Two pair of grade "A," no-tan lines, browned in the sun, medium to medium large mammaries. Attached to two sun-drenched, water-drenched twenty-something-drenched nymphs. Both of them had hair at least down to their waists, one sea foam green and the other's hair was the color of the cloudless azure sky.

They were seated on elevated rocks, a few hundred feet out into the sea, at the end of a rip-rap promontory made of large chunks of wood and other sea detritus. It ended barely inside the reef so that after the waves broke, the remnants of spray repeatedly baptized the girls. Tal noticed a number of large pieces of timber—planed, fashioned lumber not driftwood—eddying around the reef near the women. Ship wreckage. What kind of dumbasses steer that close to rocks, he wondered. Now that I think about it, isn't it a little dangerous for those girls to be sitting way out there, exposed to the unabated force of the ocean?

Speaking of exposed, the water swirled around them continuously, advancing, then retreating. There were a couple of ebbs where it appeared to Tal there might be "not-any" bikini bottoms to match the "not-any" bikini tops. Yowsers! We haven't studied the Died and Gone to Heaven plane yet, he thought, but if there actually is one this must be it.

So what do I do? They're sitting out there in broad daylight with maybe nothing on so surely this is a topless beach and it's okay if I go ask them where I might find the rest of my team. Surely it's okay, he thought as he stepped out in full view. 'Umm,…hi," he stammered, his voice cracking. Damn it, he asked himself, when is this whole can't talk to hot chicks thing going to change? Cut yourself a little slack, Tal, these two are at a minimum half-naked. At a minimum.

The women froze immediately at the sound of his voice. In unison, they slowly turned toward Tal. The blue-haired one spoke first, "Sister, we have company."

"So I see, Marina. It has been some time since the land brought us an offering."

Offering? Kind of an unusual way to describe me, Tal thought. "Yeah, uh, hi. My name is Quint."

"Hi, Quint," the green-haired sister replied. "I'm Lorelei and this is my sister, Marina."

"Come join us, the water is refreshing," Marina said, both motioning to him and taking a deep breath.

Holy hell, Tal thought. Those are some serious racks on those chicks. What would it hurt to go out there and hang for a few minutes? An information gathering expedition, as it were. Stop being an idiot, he told himself. Every minute counts and you've already cost the team time. Get your info from them and move on. That jetty looks slippery anyway, and by the look of the water there may be a substantial riptide. "Thanks, ladies. Looks like fun but I'm in a bit of a hurry. Can you tell me what plane I'm on?"

The two girls exchanged puzzled glances. "A jester I see," Lorelei said. "Surely, you know the name of that great mountain over there." She motioned to the mountain Tal had seen when he first woke up.

He shook his head.

"You truly do not know it to be one of Heracle's Pillars?" Marina asked.

Heracles? Another name for Hercules. If we were on Earth plane, and that mountain was one of the Pillars it would be either the Rock of Gibraltar on the northern side or Jebel Moussa on the southern side. Which means I'm standing on land in the middle of the Strait of Gibraltar. There is no land there on the Earth plane. But the ancient Greeks said there used to be. Plato said that was the location for...Atlantis. "No," Tal replied calmly. "I didn't know that."

"You are not of this Realm," Marina said, but as a statement this time.

" 'Fraid not," Tal replied.

The girls exchanged a look. They just did some silent code type of thing, Tal thought.

"If you are not from this plane then you haven't heard of my sister and I, Quint?" Lorelei asked breathily.

"No," he replied, a negative thought beginning to niggle.

"We haven't had anyone to talk to but ourselves for days, Quint, and we are lonely. Will you not come talk to us? For just a few minutes?" asked Marina.

"Um,...no,...thank you." In the back of Tal's mind the name Lorelei was sending up an alarum. That's never a good name in Earth tales. Bail on the breasts, buddy, he told himself firmly. Those breasts are dangerous. Bail.

"I think maybe Quint would stay with us for awhile if we sang for him, Marina," Lorelei said.

"Yes, let's," Marina replied. And with that she began ululating softly while Lorelei sang what seemed to be disconnected syllables but in perfect harmony with Marina. Their voices were pitched totally in sync with each other, the sound ebbing and flowing with the waves that caressed their bodies.

Then it hit him. Oh shit! They're not comely nymphs. They're sirens. Mermaid sirens. Naked teeth-gnashing flesh-rending evil mermaid sirens full of bad intentions. And I'm a dead man. I've got nobody to lash me to a mast. He frantically rifled his pockets, even though he knew there was nothing in them he could use to stop his ears.

The song continued, a song to him, for him, because there was no other person in the world but him. They were singing the song of the leviathans that swam hundreds of leagues beneath the surface. The song of the sailfish as they joyfully erupted into the midday sun, flinging their glistening iridescent bodies through the air. The song of the pale, lonely moon as it bestowed its unrequited glimmer on its lover, the ebon nighttime sea. It was the song of all of those things, and it was so beautiful it made Tal want to step closer to them, to be more intimate, to become part of the rhythm of life of which they sang.

"Stop it, Tal," he yelled at himself. He not only surprised himself with the outburst, he startled the two mermaids who momentarily lost the threads of songmagyk they were weaving to entrap him. Because that's what it is, Tal realized, magyk. Notos is right, I'm a stupid Munedan with no magyk to defeat them. Think, Tal, think. Once they get cranked up again you're going to become mermaid sushi. Well technically it would be sushi for mermaids.

He saw Marina take a deep breath. Damn that girl can breathe artistically. Focus, Tal. It takes the two of them together to create their spell. Something about the harmony of their two voices. Bingo! That's it, he realized. They're a duo. And their victims' responses have always been attempted denial or aversion. I may not have any magyk of my own but I can totally disrupt theirs. I hope. As soon as Lorelei joined her sister, right when he started to feel the compulsion, Tal started walking toward them. As he walked he looked down and noticed that much of the jetty structure was made of cracked and broken bones. A shiver went through him as he realized they had built the walkway from their victims' splintered bones.

The sisters again sang to him of the mysteries of the seven seas, then added those of the measureless stars, and how all of it—including them—could all be his. When Tal was almost halfway across the walkway, where he knew they could hear him, he used all of his waning willpower to stop walking. Then with his voice pitched in perfect counter melody to both of theirs, he sang as he'd never sung before, as if he was singing for his life— because he was, "Winter is here again, oh Lord," and continued on with the rest of the first verse.

He heard one of them stumble a little at his unexpected response to their aural seduction. He made himself relax his vocal chords, so he could place even more emotion into his voice as he started the refrain, "Wheel in the sky keeps on turnin'." He kept on, listening to their song, and countering it with his.

Lorelei broke first, her voice changing to a discordant owl-screech. "Stop it! Stop it! You filthy stinking biped. Stop it!" With that she flung herself backwards into the swirling water, her long tail slapping the water for emphasis. Tal didn't stop because Marina had not yet given up. He repeated the chorus several more times, until Marina apparently also realized there would be no filet of Tal on today's bill of fare. She abruptly became silent and dove headfirst into the angry waves.

The adrenaline that had been coursing through his body suddenly left the building, leaving Tal feeling faint. For a quick minute he thought about sitting down, then realized he was still surrounded by water, and therefore in danger in the event the pulchritudinous sirens decided to take another shot at him.

He walked briskly back toward the sandy beach. Once there he continued to the tree line at which point he decided he was safe enough to stop and rest for a minute. It wasn't until then he noticed his entire body was shaking. He was soaking wet. It's shock, Tal, he told himself. You don't have time to give in, and there's no one here to help you, so fight it. He was thirsty, and starting to get hungry.

Prioritize, he told himself. Beat the shock by ordering your thoughts. Okay, first thing—when I get back home, I'm sending a candy bouquet with a thank you note to Steve Perry and the rest of Journey to tell them thanks, because "Wheel in the Sky" literally saved my life. Second thing—tell Emet that never again would either of them utter the phrase, "sing for your supper." Third thing—you have to find your team, Tal.

He decided the beach might present additional trouble, so he struck out directly into the lush tropical jungle. After stumbling over a number of rotting logs and fighting through clinging liana as big around as ships' hawsers, Tal found the barest hint of a narrow path. Canopied by towering palms, he followed it as it meandered beside a fresh water rivulet, burbling its excitement at the prospect of losing itself in the sea. He knelt and cupped his hands to get a drink. As he did he heard music. Oh, please, let it be an instrumental, I can't handle any more singing right now. As he kept walking along the path, the music became more distinct. It was…calliope music. Either that or Atlantis has an ice cream truck making the rounds.

The music grew louder, and soon he heard the sound of voices—talking voices, thank goodness—lots of talking voices— added to the audio mix. Please let them be vegetarians, Tal prayed. Or at least, non-Munedanivores. Another couple of minutes trudging found him at the edge of a large clearing. He was dumbfounded as he gazed at the view in front him. In the middle of the glade was a multi-storied structure made of smoky quartz colored reflective glass and shiny metal. There were a number of what looked exactly like neon signs that flashed, and pulsed, and convulsed in time to the calliope music. Huge neon signs. Some strobed, "Pandora's Box," and others, "Always Open."

Wow! And wow! Atlantis Realm has a casino.

CHAPTER SEXAGINTA

Tal stepped out of the quiet of the woods and into a vortex of Folk activity. Clearly there were a number of different Folk species on this plane. There were some plain old humanoid Folk but there were also quite a few Folk with gills and fin-like upper appendages. There were also many variations of human with some type of animal head. Bisonheads were walking with Elephantheads, and to Tal's right there was a small pack of Wolfheads. He could see the casino was a high volume center of commerce, so maybe his gang was here looking for the piece. If not, surely someone has seen them and can tell me where they are. Of course, I have zero money to pay anyone for some information.

As Tal stepped through the gaudy entrance and into Pandora's Box, the assault on his senses was amped up tenfold. Lights were blinking, flashing, strobing, back-lighting, black-lighting, high-lighting. All of it he knew was magyk-powered. A quick glance around showed no sign of electrical cords or outlets. There were ca-chings, and ding-dings, ba-bings, and cha-chings— which had a completely different sound than ca-chings. There was whooping, and hollering, and screeching, as a myriad of Folk won, lost, encouraged, and rooted for, or against. The games were not Earth plane games but the actions of the participants were the same as on Earth. There were Folk who had clearly had way too much of this Realm's intoxicants, Folk who were celebrating some event, and Folk who simply looked sad. Whether it was from a lengthy losing streak at a game of chance, or simply the totality of their lives, Tal didn't know, but he knew sad when he saw it.

The place was doing a gangbuster business. Every table had players three deep, and every ca-chinging, ding-dinging, ba-binging, or cha-chinging machine was occupied. Tal politely elbowed his way along the main aisle, looking back and forth, and repeatedly saying, "Excuse me," as he bumped into Folk. "C'mon team, where are you?" he whispered to himself. He was afraid he'd get lost if he ventured down the smaller arterial walkways, so he slowly made a circuit of the entire main thoroughfare, finding himself back at his original point of entry. Nothing. Well, plenty, but nothing giving any indication of the Omada or of a scavengyr piece.

At a loss as to his next move, he started looking for a place to sit for a minute. There was a small aisle to his left that didn't appear crowded, and since it would be a straight shot back to a familiar place he went that way. He kept on the same path and saw a little ways ahead a junction with a game booth without any players. As he got closer it looked like it might be the kind of huckstery-type thing where the casino was trying to get personal information from you by offering a chance to win two free tickets to a crappy show, or to pay a reduced amount to ride in a helicopter or on some open air amphibious vehicle in sweltering hundred degree heat. Maybe there's some bored employee I can get some info from, he thought.

When he got to the game booth he could understand why it was the only empty game in the entire casino. It was a tired, weathered wooden wheel about ten feet in diameter that looked like it had spent the better part of its long life on the outdoor Atlantis Realm County Fair circuit—right next to the deep-fried Snickers vendor—before somebody finally took pity on it and brought it indoors. At one time, it had been intricately painted. The remaining colors were clearly only haggard impersonations of the original vibrant hues, the painted figures now hard to discern one from the other. The game definitely did not fit in with the polished glitz of everything else in the establishment.

The pseudo-neon magyk sign over the booth had even given up half the ghost. Only about every second letter remained illuminated, and some of those were fitful at best. The letters were in a flowing script and looked like they spelled, "R-O-T-A F-O-R-T-U-N-A-E." Rota Fortunae. Makes sense, Tal thought, that's Latin for "Wheel of Fortune." The Wheel had tick-pegs near its outside edges, dividing the differently colored columns from each other. The booth obviously wasn't much of a profit center, there wasn't even anyone manning the game. There was, however, a bell to ring for assistance. I don't want tickets to any crappy show, Tal thought, but if there's ever been anyone walk up to this booth who truly needed assistance, it's me. He picked up the bell and shook it.

"Coming. Coming. I'll be right there." Tal heard the female voice before its owner appeared from behind the booth. The voice-owner was svelte, about five foot, six inches tall. Tal quickly guesstimated her age somewhere around sixty or sixty-five. Her light brown hair was sprinkled with salt and pulled back into a chignon. His Mom wore her hair back like that sometimes and had told him what it was called. Her face had the appropriate number of lines but they weren't deeply etched, rather they seemed to bob on top of the genuine smile she sent Tal's way. She wore a long flowing white gown, very much looking like it had been borrowed from some Greek Antiquities special exhibit at the Metropolitan Museum of Art. There was one other thing a little odd about her ensemble—she was wearing a coal-black blindfold. Even in a casino that was a trifle outré.

"Good afternoon, may I help you?" she asked, as she walked to the counter without any hesitation relating to her apparent inability to see. Her dulcet alto voice was as pleasant as the smile that crinkled up beneath her blindfold.

"Um,…hi. I'm Quint…" he started.

"Yes, I know," she replied. Even though he was certain she couldn't see his doubtful expression she continued, "Actually, you are Quint of Omada."

Tal looked around to see if anyone else was paying attention. Nope. It's like this piece of the casino was in its own little bubble. "How do you know who I am?" he asked.

She smiled again, while waving her arm above her head toward the top of the wheel. "What does the sign say, Quint?"

"The English translation is, 'Wheel of Fortune.' "

"So if this is the Wheel of Fortune, who am I?"

Think, Tal. Mythology, but which species? Greek or Roman. Themis, the Greek goddess of divine justice is often shown blindfolded. The woman's outfit could be Roman as well as Grecian, for all I know. This booth has a Latin name, so think Roman. Got it. "If this is the Rota Fortunae, you must be Fortuna."

She laughed softly, as she nodded her head in agreement. "Very good. For our brief Time together today, I have chosen to appear as Fortuna."

Tal wagged his head a bit. "I'm not sure I understand. Are you, or aren't you, Fortuna?"

"I have already answered that question, Dust Child," she replied politely, but firmly. "Do you wish me to spin the Wheel of Fortune for you?"

How does she know I'm a Munedan, Tal wondered. Maybe…he started to sniff under his arm but stopped himself just in time. "I don't have any money," Tal replied.

"Risking your future is the only currency needed to spend this Wheel," Fortuna replied.

Okay, this isn't funny, Tal thought. I don't have time to waste. If she can help me find my team or a scavengyr piece, that's one thing, but she's not acting like this is only a second rate casino game. Magyk obviously works on this plane. What if I'm actually rolling the bones on my future by playing? "Are you saying that whatever this rickety Wheel tells me will happen is absolutely going to happen?"

Fortuna laughed loudly, pleasantly but loudly. "Philosophers of every ilk on every plane have debated the answer to that question for millennia."

"Well?" he pressed. "What's the answer?"

"Let me see if I can find an easy way to explain it. You know there is a special book at Hunts School."

"Yes. The Book. Word is that from day one it has contained the name of every student who will ever be admitted."

"It does," she said confidently. "However, the page with a student's name on it isn't visible to anyone at the school until the student actually makes the choice to attend the school."

"So you're saying it was predetermined I would attend Hunts School? That I would be Omada? That whoever is going to win the Tyrning will win the Tyrning?"

Again that soft, generous smile. Tal wasn't sure how her smile could be enigmatic with a blindfold hiding half her face, but it was. "When Barton Sellars and his friends threw you out of the back of their truck, did they have any idea there was a book at Hunts School with your name in it?"

I'm going to put aside for the moment the fact she knows I got thrown out of a truck, Tal thought. "Of course not. How could they?"

"Did you know about The Book when you decided to step into the Ladies' Restroom at the Gas Station?"

Great, the word is apparently out that I've been frequenting girls' bathrooms. I'll bet it's that bigmouth Air Hose spreading the word. "No."

"I'm trying to point out to you that just because Amarantos is all-knowing—you did realize The Book is simply a tangible manifestation of the UnFading Spirit's omniscience, didn't you?"

No, I missed that one. "Well, duh. Of course."

"Just because Amarantos knows what choice you, or Borras, or Väst…"

Väst. She is so damn hot, Tal thought.

"Yes, she is 'hot,' but you need to focus, Taliesin."

Wait. What? Did I say Väst was hot out loud?

Fortuna paused and looked at him a moment. It's like she's waiting for me to catch up on something I missed, Tal thought. There was something, but it's lost in the shuffle of Väst's hotness.

"Omniscient foreknowledge does not automatically preclude free will," she said. " 'The race is not to the swift, nor the battle to the strong...; but time and chance happeneth to them all'."

"Hey, I know that quotation. It's from the Bible."

"From Ecclesiastes, to be precise."

"It's a good thing Myrddin isn't here. He'd probably claim he wrote it."

"He did actually," came the reply. "Quint, lean forward and touch the center of the Wheel."

Tal did as directed. He had to get all the way up on his tiptoes to be able to lean far enough and high enough to touch the center. As soon as his finger made contact there was a static spark and the Wheel transformed. It was still a wheel but it wasn't an abused funhouse relic anymore. It shimmered with color. All kinds of colors. In distinct patterns.

"Does the Wheel look familiar now?" she asked.

I've never been to Atlantis Realm before so I don't know how it could look familiar, Tal thought. He gave the Wheel a hard look anyway. Okay, the circle part was kind of familiar. Something about the composition of the patterns and the way they intersected each other also and the intact center kind of sort of rang a bell. From where, though? When? His mind started flipping through its immense catalog of stored pictures. Yes! Found it! He hadn't noticed it before because of the Wheel's vertical orientation. To the smallest detail it was an exact replica of the one Mertin Wilt made on the floor of the—"Kalachakra. It's a Kalachakra."

"Not just any Kalachakra, Quint. Once you touched the Wheel, it became your Kalachakra."

"Pardon?"

"It is the Time Wheel of your life."

Wait…what? Tal wondered. That means the entire time I was talking to Mertin Wilt, a/k/a the Myrddin, he was nonchalantly drawing my life…and my death on the dirty scuffed up linoleum tiled floor of Nemeton High?

"Your Journey time runs short," Fortuna gently reminded him. "Do you wish me to spin the Wheel for you?"

"I still don't understand, Fortuna. I say yes, and then what happens?"

"You will ask the Wheel a question?"

"About?"

"About any potential future occurrence."

"And then I'll get a 'yes' or 'no' answer?"

Again that gentle laugh. "No, Child of the Dust. The answers to the meaningful moments in life are rarely so simple as a yes or a no."

"So, I could ask the Wheel what day I'm going to die, or how I'm going to die?"

"If that is what you wish to know," she replied. "How would knowing either of those things improve your life, or anyone else's?"

"I get it, this is all about that whole enjoy the Journey mindset thingy."

Fortuna softly nodded her response.

"So, whatever question I ask, the response will be about some event that is definitely going to happen?"

"If you can correctly interpret the Wheel's response, you will learn what would have happened absent your foreknowledge. What was a certainty will become a possibility—which might still happen—or your knowledge of that former certainty may occasion a different actuality."

"So, I may not like what I find out, and the bad thing might still happen. Or, simply by knowing about an event, I might prevent the occurrence of a good thing," Tal said.

"Correct. There is an entire universe of questions. You might not ask what. You might ask a when, or an if, or a how."

"Do you have any Tylenol?"

"No. Do you wish me to spin the Wheel? I am offering you a privilege sought by all who have ever lived, but granted to only precious few."

Puzzled as to what would be a worthwhile question, Tal moved his hand slowly around his chin in the universally recognized pondering motion. One question? What's the perfect question? One opportunity to learn something that might change the future of all of the Realms. Damn you Gas Pumps for laying that heavy trip on me.

That's it, he realized. The important question is not about me. Not about whether I survive, or get a full-ride scholarship, or if Väst and I hook up, or if Elle and I hook up. Or even when I die. Although I have to admit I would really like to know when I'm going to croak.

Those were the burning questions only a few weeks ago, and they're all "if" questions. I'm more than myself now, he realized. For the first time ever I'm part of a team. The team—that from everything I've seen so far—should be the one that governs the Folk Realms and protects the Earth plane for the next three hundred years. The perfect question isn't an "if," nor a "when," or a "what." It's a "how." "Yes, Fortuna. I'd like for you to spin the wheel for me, please."

In response, Fortuna leaned over and lightly touched the side of the Wheel, which began rotating. Slowly at first, then faster and faster, the colors becoming a seamless rainbow circle, the lines in the patterns aligning and realigning, seeming almost as if they were tracing words in the air. No, they were actually tracing words in midair—'Seek the Center.'

"Ask your question now," Fortuna intoned.

Let this be the right question, Tal prayed. "Please show me how I can help the Omada win this Tyrning?"

There was a bright flash as if phosphorous had been ignited. As the Wheel slowed, Tal could see it had returned to its original time-worn self. Great, just great, he thought. I broke the Wheel of Fortune. The Wheel continued slowing, yet it was different than when he first arrived. Now each potential stopping tick-peg had a worn out legend for all of the possible results. There was one for "date of death," which was blacked out. There was a narrow column that said, "college." And any number of other columns: "relationship(s), wealth, happiness, family, and 'Nobel prize'."

The Wheel hadn't stopped at any of those possibilities. It had stopped on the thinnest sliver of a sliver of a category. It was so narrow the letters had to be teeny-tiny even to fit vertically within the column. What the hell? It looked liked it said, "Go Fish."

"Aahh," Fortuna said. "Your answer is 'Go Fish'." She reached under the counter and pulled out a large, cracked plastic bin chock full to the brim with all manner of cheap beads and grimcrackeries.

What the hell? I could have found out if I was going to win a Nobel prize and instead I'm going to pull some crap out of tired Tupperware? "I would like a do-over," Tal announced. "I want a mulligan."

"Fate offers no mulligans," Fortuna responded, as she gently shook the box full of second-rate dime store items. "Close your eyes, reach deep into the box and select only one item."

I knew this wasn't legit, Tal told himself. At least since it's a fake there wasn't any possibility I might actually screw the future all to heck and back, Tal decided, as he closed his eyes, reached deep into the box and started rummaging. Twice his fingers closed on irregular shaped objects. He felt them all over trying to ascertain what he was getting. That's ridiculous, he decided. Go with it, concentrate on Borras and the rest of the Omada. His fingers slid off of something rounded and smooth and he started to move on before abruptly stopping. Static electricity had discharged when he touched that one piece. He touched it again. Nothing this time, but I know it happened, he told himself as his fist closed around the object and lifted it up out of the box. I know this is the right decision. I just know it.

"You may open your eyes now," Fortuna said.

Tal did so, looking at the object in his hands. It was a shiny translucent bubble, like out of a gumball machine. Inside was a pair of wings. That was it. A pair of the fake pilot's wings kids got from airline stewardesses to try to bribe them into not crying when their ears stop up. Except only about one-tenth the size, so that they would fit into a small clear plastic bubble. For a gumball machine. A tiny scratched plastic bubble was supposedly the universe-saving answer to his perfect question?

"Really? I asked what potentially was the most important question I'll ever ask and this is all I get as my answer?"

"It is the Wheel's answer to the question you asked, Quint," she replied.

"That's great," he said shoving the junk deep into his front pocket. So this whole Wheel of Fortune thing was a joke. Fortuna was only an employee at a casino. How did she know all those details about me? She must have some type of mind reading magyk. There's a reason everyone else in this place knew not to waste their time at this game, Tal told himself.

Not a word, he quickly resolved. To any of the Omada. I really tried to do the right thing and I'm not catching hell from Notos because I spent the whole Journey getting a baby-sized pair of plastic wings. I'll tell Emet, but that's it. No one else. Ever.

"I'm sorry if I was rude, Fortuna," he said. "You're only doing your job. It's not your fault I got a crap response. I'm mad at myself for wasting time playing games when I was supposed to be looking for my team."

"Ah, the Omada?" she asked.

Tal nodded affirmance.

"Does the Omada have one really large guy, two women, and another guy who looks like he's spent the last month eating nothing but sour apples?"

"Yes," Tal replied quickly.

"Follow that path to the Exhibition Hall," she said pointed off to Tal's left. "It's about a two-minute walk. I saw them go that way about an hour ago."

"Thank you," Tal said, again mentally kicking himself in the head for spending all that time with Fortuna, and for buying into that whole 'some splintered plywood Wheel knows the future' ridiculousness. As he neared the next curve in the walkway he turned back to look at Fortuna. He wasn't the least bit surprised that she and the Wheel were no longer there. Where the Wheel had been, there was an absolutely packed table with a card game. Magyk, he thought, it really is some funky shit.

He weathered a huge tide of Folk leaving the Exhibition Hall. He couldn't make out individual words but the loudness of the speech, the overt gesticulation of upper limbs, and the pitch of the voices indicated a high level of excitement. Whatever it is, it's over, he thought. They're all leaving.

As he took a left through the door and into the hall he noticed both his feet were tingling. Kind of the same feeling as when one of them fell asleep. Except it was both of them. He cleared the doorway and looked up into—

Bedlam. Lots of people scurrying. People with white lab coats—medical personnel—who were carrying almost half a dozen unconscious Folk out on gurneys. There were another half-dozen Folk moaning—in some cases screaming—that were still being triaged inside a boxing ring.

The tingling in his feet moved up to his knees. It's the Recall, he realized. Damn it. Then in the far left corner of the ring he saw the Omada, huddled around Borras. Well actually, Borras, if he had been serially mugged about eight hours a day every day for about a fortnight. There was skin missing in several places on his face. His left earlobe was dangling by a fold of skin. His left eye was swollen completely shut, the ostrich egg-sized purpling flesh over it ripe with blood. Ana was wiping his face with a well-bloodied rag. When the giant opened his mouth to speak to her, Tal saw a couple of his index card sized front teeth were either jaggedly broken in half, or missing altogether.

It was actually Borras who saw him first. "Quint," he breathed loudly. Louder than usual, Tal thought, as the lower half of Borras's nose was at a right angle to the upper half.

He saw Dysi laying prostrate on the mat of the ring. Notos looked his normal self. "Of course, he shows up now," Notos said, with as much venom as he could muster. "Way to be a team player, Munedan."

Tal felt the tingling move up to his waist. Its amplitude had changed from a somewhat unpleasant tingle to hot skin-poking needles.

"Quint," Anatolia said, "Thank Amarantos. Quickly get up here. Now."

Tal did as commanded. Anatolia was about five shades paler than her normal complexion. The needles poking him heated up as they moved up to his chest. As he approached his team he saw Notos and Dysi absently rubbing their midsections. They feel it too.

"Tal," Ana urged, "Over here. Hurry. Borras cannot go back in this shape, the Recall would kill him. Even if it didn't, he would be placed on the maimed list. We can't afford to lose our Prime."

"What do I need to do?" Tal asked.

"I have already used all of the lyfeforce I am able to give to heal him. So has Dysi. You must consent to the same." As Tal started to reply she quickly added, "Quint, you are human. I'm not sure how much I can take without killing you."

Without a second's hesitation, Tal responded, as he reached out to touch Anatolia's shoulder. "I consent."

Tal felt two sensations simultaneously. The Recall needles turned into poison fire-tipped darts and moved from his chest into his head, so that it felt like expanding flaming skewers were being driven from the inside of his skull out through the backs of his eyeballs. The other sensation was an overwhelming lassitude, as if he didn't even have enough energy to draw his next breath. Right before his peripheral vision closed and the room faded to black, he saw Borras with a huge smile on his broken face, holding a ring up for Tal to see.

"Got it," the giant whispered. "The Ring of Gyges."

Tal's last thought before total blackness was that he really, really hoped that wasn't a ripped off chunk of someone's finger inside the Ring.

CHAPTER SIXTY-ONE

"Uhhhh," Tal groaned, as he lay in his bed completely spent. He couldn't remember the last time he'd been this tired. He'd fallen asleep—maybe passed out was a better way to put it—immediately after Emet had hoisted him onto his back for the trip home from the gas station. Tal had meant to give both Gas Pumps a piece of his mind, but he'd simply been too tired. He'd finally regained some strength after two large helpings of his Mom's chicken spaghetti and about half a loaf of Texas toast. Luckily his mouth had been so full of food at the table the normal family chatter about the day's activities had been curtailed. Even with all of the food at dinner he'd had to make a pretty serious dent in his and Emet's secret candy bar cache before he'd felt full.

The hot shower had also helped. After that he'd turned off all of his bedroom lights and told the folks he was hitting the rack early, so he and Emet could get caught up. With his narrative and Emet's follow-up questions, it had taken almost two hours to cover everything. Tal was so drained mentally and physically he'd even forgotten about his Crackerjack box toy until he shucked off his jeans to take the shower. Actually he was surprised when he did find it. Besides his clothing, no Earth stuff went to Hunts

School and other than his Hunts School backpack and textbooks there hadn't been any items that crossed back with him through the Gas Station.

He gave the plastic bubble to Emet to take it to the attic for safekeeping. Why, he wasn't sure. Seemed prudent since it was technically an alien artifact. As exhausted as Tal was, his brain still wouldn't stop retracing the day. Apparently his subconscious was refusing to submit to sleep status until his conscious brain recognized some unnoticed fact or facts.

Ms. Empousa had given all five of the Omada a thorough visual review before escorting them out of the chamber. Borras still had some scrapes and bruises. All of them, excepting Notos, were still wobbly and holding on to each other, but they passed muster. Tal was pleased to find he wasn't precariously hanging upside down after the Recall, all five of them were standing in the center of the Prime Omphalos. While still in the chamber, the HuntsMistress took out her clipboard and asked Borras if the Omada had secured a scavengyr piece and if so what it was. He showed her the ring, and she had him put it on one of his carrot-sized fingers. He winked out of sight, then back again when he took it off. They had been required to declare a category for their piece—Defense was their answer.

Once they were sequestered in the Omada team room, Tal had gotten the expected ass-chewing from Notos. Apparently it was his fault for being human, which was the only explanation for why he didn't land with the others. Team members were always dropped at the same location. After his reaming, Tal told them all about being dumped on the beach and about his sing-off with the flesh-eating siren mermaids. He also told them about walking through the woods and wandering through the casino. He omitted the whole Wheel of Fortune scene. Not only was it embarrassing that all he got was a plastic bauble but he simply couldn't take any more of Notos's guff at that point.

The other three had taken turns filling Tal in on the events leading up to Borras ending up in the ring at the Exhibition Hall. They had landed in the entry hall of the casino.

It was the axis mundi for the Atlantis Realm, and the reason the casino had been built at that location.

After waiting a few minutes to see if Tal was going to show up, they'd split up into pairs and even though it took quite a while they managed to cover the entire casino. As none of them had any money they weren't able to wager on any of the games in an effort to get some conversation started with at least one of the locals. The few employees they ran into were singularly unhelpful.

They had all been depressed at that point. With no idea where Tal was or if he was even alive, they knew their time was running short before the Recall and that they hadn't seen any indication there was a scavengyr piece nearby. They'd finally voted to split up individually and strike out for other parts of the island until the Recall.

As they were heading back toward the main entrance, Dysi saw a pathway to her right that they were all certain hadn't been there before. They walked a little ways down it and came to a booth with an attractive woman hawking tickets for the casino's daily magyk show. The woman was unusual in appearance in that she had multiple filigreed whorls of dot tattoos which circled across her forehead and down her temples.

Tal knew from their description it was the Wheel's location and asked if the employee's name was Fortuna. Ana told him no, the woman's name was Kore. She told them she was a human, indentured long ago in Atlantis. Kore was her Atlantean name, as she said she'd given up her human name. Tal had asked Borras if they'd inquired how a human came to be enslaved on Atlantis plane and Borras said they were so flustered at that point they hadn't delved into that issue.

They quickly told Kore who they were and why they were on Atlantis plane. Kore told them it was fortunate they'd run into her. She was pulling a double that day, and the booth was her second shift. Her first shift had been at the Exhibition Hall. There was a fight about to start. It was the reason the casino was so packed. It was to be a "winner take all" match and "all" happened to be a powerful invisibility ring.

They all knew that was the scavengyr piece and ran like leaves before a twister to the Exhibition Hall. Once there, Notos spied the registration table. The fight promoter was sallow-faced and snarkish, one of the species of Folk who had gills and finlike arms. He advised the fight was starting in five minutes, was a Battle Royale, and would continue until only one person was left standing. Absolutely no magyk was allowed in the arena. Other than that there were no rules: kicking, biting, gouging, were all allowed. It didn't matter if you killed an opponent or only incapacitated him. It was all allowed. Sourpuss confirmed the prize was in fact a magyk ring.

Borras immediately stepped up and tried to enter but the entry fee was fifty gold staters. The Omada were sunk. It didn't matter if that was a lot of money or only a little, they had none. As Notos quickly surveyed the room it appeared the entry fee must be a sizeable amount as there were large syndicates of Folk clustered around the individual fighters.

Made sense Tal thought, there's no telling how much a quality magyk ring would trade for on the open market. The ring was the reason the Omada had been sent to Atlantis Realm. It had seemed within his team's grasp but that was only an illusion.

Then from behind them they'd heard a female voice. "I'll pay their fee." Anatolia was the first to turn. It was Kore.

If possible, the promoter's face had become even more dour. "Where would the likes of you get fifty gold staters? That'd be more than a hundred years of pay," he had responded, the sarcasm spooned thick on every individual word.

"What has the likes of me got to spend money on?" Kore replied, as she dropped a burlap sack as big as Borras's hand on the table. It had landed heavily and burst open, dozens of rough finished, irregularly shaped gold coins spilling out on the table.

"Stupid bitch," the promoter replied as he snatched the coins up and started stacking them. "You just threw that money away. This idiot don't stand a chance." With that he'd turned to Borras. "You got two minutes to get ready," he said tersely. "If you're not in the ring when the bell sounds, you forfeit the match—and the entry fee." Turning to Kore he'd snarled, "Your break must be almost over. Get back to work or I'll take it out of your thin Munedan skin."

Borras had nodded his appreciation to Kore and then taken off for the ring with Notos in close pursuit. Ana said she and Dysi stayed behind to thank Kore. They reminded her they had no way to repay her, they couldn't sell the ring because they needed the ring for the Hunts, and they had no likely means of returning to the Atlantis plane to compensate her.

Kore's response was more than a little cryptic, "Remember, whatever treasyre your mind may conjure, it all be dross compared to love. 'Seek the Center' always." Then she'd bent over and kissed them both on their foreheads, told them she hoped they found their missing teammate, and then walked out of the Exhibition Hall.

Dysi picked up the story, beginning with the ringing of the bell. There had been about twenty-five fighters. Both of the girls almost hurled as Dysi described the details of the fight to Tal. It has been that brutal. "No holds barred" with Folk who have wolf fangs and claws and others with razor sharp fins was a completely different proposition than "no holds barred" on the Earth plane. And a lot of the combatants decided the easiest way to take an opponent out was simply to kill him.

Most of the combatants apparently didn't see plain human looking Borras as a threat early in the match so the alliances first took out each other and the ones they presumed to be the deadlier enemies. It reached a point however where it became apparent that Borras stood a chance of winning. Ana said at that point a gang of four mismatched species coordinated their attack on him to take him out. Permanently.

Neither of the girls could bear to finish that part of the story and, even though Notos had been using most all of his energy up to that point to nurse his grudge against Tal, he finished the story for them. He said Borras stood in the ring like a hero out of legend, taking everything they could throw at him, trying not to permanently maim anyone while they were all trying to rip his throat out. He'd grabbed a wolf-head and a tiger-head in each hand and slammed them together so hard all of the capillaries in their eyes exploded and they fell to the floor screaming, blue blood cascading down their faces. That was when Borras almost lost his left ear, and took two or three claw rips, each of which would have been fatal for any Munedan or even a lesser Folk. Even toward the end, when it was mostly his blood that he and his opponents were slipping in, Borras had refused to go down. He refused to be anything but—indomitable. The Omada could all tell he was going to do whatever it took to win the scavengyr piece.

Next, Borras punched a lion-head in the larynx so hard the fellow crumpled like single-ply toilet paper, unable to even whimper. It was the last two opponents though that did Borras the most damage. A bear-head and a fish-face with stiletto-like fins. They had realized he was going to win if they didn't stop him. One got in front and the other behind and they slashed him, and slashed him. Again and again. The rest of the team could see Borras was out on his feet. He'd lost so much blood that Ana didn't know if she could fix him when the match was over and she could use her healmagyk.

It ended when Borras unexpectedly sidestepped Tuna's powerful jab, which caused the powerful spiked fins to spear Bear, who extended his claws trying to stop him. Borras quickly stepped behind Tuna and fell forward on top of him, driving Tuna's fins all the way through Bear, whose four-inch claws easily pierced Tuna's heart.

As soon as the referee signaled the fight was over, Ana was through the ropes and into the ring laying hands on Borras. She had just enough of her own lyfeforce to keep him from bleeding out and dying on the spot. She motioned to Dysi and Notos who quickly realized what she needed and they leapt to her in the ring. Dysi immediately consented, and Ana drew her down as far as she dared. It was enough to keep Borras alive but it would have all been for naught if Tal hadn't shown up right before the Recall. Tal thought about asking why Notos wasn't asked to contribute but decided to let it lie.

Tal had realized at that point in the story he had in fact asked the perfect question of the Wheel of Fortune. If it had been the real Wheel of Fortune. But it was only a stupid bullshit carnie Wheel of Fortune. He'd been wrong about Fortuna too. She wasn't a Glinda the Good Witch magykal being, she was only some smooth talking casino hack with a really slick shtick.

Rolling over in his bed for about the hundredth time, Tal's conscious finally relinquished its sleep filibuster when his subconscious brain finally produced the requested information, the factoid that had been keeping him awake despite his exhaustion.

It was arguably no big magykal or investigative feat for Fortuna to learn all of the names of the members of Omada. Clearly that was something a fast-talking carnie with some magykal chops could have discovered and Fortuna had called him by his Omada name every single time. Except one time. When she called me Taliesin.

CHAPTER SEXAGINTA DUO

They were all sitting quietly in homeroom waiting for Ms. Empousa. She was already ten minutes late, which was unusual There was more tension in the room than there was oxygen More silence too. With all the extra tension and extra silence there really wasn't a whole lot of space left for oxygen. As Tal looked around he saw there were only four students at both the Hak'éí and Shuzoku tables. The Aile station was completely empty.

When Tal had finally gotten out of bed he'd thought he was fully recovered from the preceding day, but after running up and down the stairs a couple of times for breakfast and participating in cover chatter he realized he was still only operating at about fifty percent. He'd told the folks at breakfast he was going to school extra early to check on a chemistry lab experiment. That way Emet could help him get to the Gas Station this morning. It bothered him every time he lied to his parents but it was necessary. Worlds were at stake, including the Earth plane. Besides, every time he got close to mentioning something about his school activities he started coughing up virtual hairballs. He made a promise to himself. When this whole thing was over he'd tell them everything. Well, maybe not the parts involving Väst.

Tal went out the window, and Emet exited through the front door before grabbing their bicycle from the garage. The bicycle wouldn't support them both comfortably so Emet pedaled it at warp speed to the school, locked it up, and then sprinted to catch up with Tal. To save Tal's strength, Emet piggybacked him the rest of the way to the Gas Station.

The classroom door creaked, pulling Tal from his reverie. The HuntsMistress strode in, bringing another couple of dump truck loads of tension with her. Guess we didn't need oxygen for breathing anyway, he thought.

"Listen up, I'm not planning on repeating myself." Man was she ever in a fell mood today, Tal thought. "Seven of the nine teams returned with a scavengyr piece. The team rankings as of today—from all of your test and Combat scores, together with your first Journey results, are as follows: Pleme is in first place." She stopped and shot Sredina a double-barreled laser of a stare. It looked like she was daring the Prime Direction to show any emotion. Any, whatsoever. But she got nothing. Sredina and her entire crew could have been store manikins. There wasn't an eye twitch, not a single extra breath. "The rest of the teams, in rank order are Bùluò, Släkt, Shuzoku, Ayllu, Kabila, Omada, Hak'éí, and Aile."

That had to be a sword Släkt was toting, Tal concluded. Even so they dropped to third, and they're only getting one more Journey.

Ms. Empousa walked around her desk, then decided to sit behind it before continuing. "Nahookos of the Hak'éí and Higashi of the Shuzoku are in the infirmary. The Hak'éí had the misfortune of running into the Amadan Dubh and Nahookos got overlooked."

Tal looked at Borras, who while keeping his head up to avoid drawing attention, wrote, "the Fairy Fool" and "evil eye" on his notepad.

"Nahookos was unconscious when he returned from the Journey and he remains in a coma. The Shuzoku ran into a pod of rabid Spriggans. Higashi lost his right arm below the elbow to a fairy barb. The physicks believe they can restore both to full health but it is extremely complicated magyk and will take the rest of this term. Therefore, those two individuals have been placed on the disabled list and those teams are now down to four presently active members."

Ms. Empousa paused to gather her thoughts before she continued. "As you are aware, the Aile and the Pleme were assigned overlapping Journey times and ended up being sent to the same Realm. They apparently ran into each other trying to secure the same piece. The Pleme returned with the scavengyr piece, the Aile returned without their Prime Direction."

Merkez! Tal barely caught himself before he shouted it out loud. First Bati and now Merkez. Two of the most honorable students at this school. Dead. He looked at Sredina of the Pleme. She had a satisfied grin on her face. They did it, Tal realized. It was a sword, they found it first, and they killed Merkez. The Pleme are only a half-notch better than the Släkt, he thought. Maybe not even that.

Ms. Empousa continued, "Oh, one final thing. I have made the decision that nonuse of the Pucas will continue for the two remaining scavengyr hunts. You are excused."

CHAPTER SEXAGINTA TRES

The students had a couple of hours of free time before they were due for the team strategy session. Normally, Tal would have gone and gotten Piras for some practice or headed to the school library, which Tal had learned was modeled after the famed ancient Library at Alexandria. Or the modeling might have been vice-versa. Today he needed some time away from thinking, and from his teammates—tension was high. He'd decided to find one of his music groups and let the music carry him away from all the negative waves surrounding him. He was cruising toward the Greek temple section, daydreaming about Elle, when Väst appeared. He actually tried to tell her no. Twice.

"Sing for me, Dust Child," she said the third time, the request now a demand.

Heaven help him he had no choice but to comply. It wasn't only that he wanted to—which he did, very badly—he absolutely had to. And away they went. And he sang for her. And she kissed him. A lot. And before he knew it the gong summoned them both to their team rooms.

CHAPTER SIXTY-FOUR

It didn't take Tal long that evening to debrief Emet on his day. The team meeting had been brief. Their goal was a weapon. Period. Borras would focus on asking the Prime Omphalos to send them to a Realm with at least one qualifying weapon. The rest of the team time had been spent going through a check down list in case Tal didn't land with the rest of Omada again.

Emet had the reverse day. He aced the tests in both Physics and Accounting. Tal almost found himself a little jealous until he realized that it was some kind of crazy to be jealous of yourself. Elle had typed a note telling him which schools she was applying to, and what it appeared the odds were for her in getting scholarship offers from each of them. Tal admired the fact she didn't want to use any of her parent's money, she wanted to earn her education with her own brain. She also mentioned she was going out with her family tonight to some elderly relative's house so there wouldn't be time for any phone conversation. As much as Tal wanted to hear her voice, he realized his sleep deficit needed to be addressed. He told Emet he was crashing early, and Emet headed out and up.

CHAPTER SEXAGINTA QUINQUE

Tal watched as his teammates took their assigned directional positions around the edges of the Prime Omphalos, with Borras again stepping into the center. Tal was the last to step into place, before kneeling and then hanging upside down. Under Ms. Empousa's watchful eye, Borras had the team members sing out, and when he was sure they were all properly positioned, the chamber became silent. Tal knew Borras was focusing his thoughts on the object category they had selected—Weapon. There was a brilliant white hot flash, and...

BREATHE, his lungs were screaming at his brain. Tal couldn't hold his breath much longer. Someone had kicked him in the head with a boot heel, and that someone was now standing on his neck, holding his head underwater. He knew what would happen if he inhaled, but his lungs were out-screaming his brain. He gasped a half-breath and immediately started choking on the sediment-filled water coursing through his nose and mouth. Hellava Journey, he thought. I got sent to drown in a murky cesspool.

Suddenly a hand latched onto the back of his collar and catapulted him into the air. He went from being submersed in water, to drowning in a chilly deluge of rain. Desperate for air, Tal hard-retched several times, expelling the brackish water. He looked to his right and saw he'd been saved by a soldier wearing medieval-style armor. His new friend had skewered Tal's now former assailant with his sword, and said now former assailant was lying face up in the drowning pool, a dark maroon stain spreading like an oil sheen across the water's raindrop pocked surface. "Human" came the random thought. That blood is red, not blue. The dead guy's a Munedan.

Then the noise hit him. Men were screaming. Lots of men. Lots of screaming. Lots of screaming men. Men were running in every direction. Lots of men. Lots of men running in every direction. Tal's brain was finally able to start sorting freeze frame images. Muddy dented armor. Horses squealing in agony—from fractured limbs, or from arrows sticking out of their bodies, or from both. Swords slashing—up and down, left and right. All of them slicing the rain, some of them weighted down with chunks of hacked flesh. The smell of urine and shit. The metal-taste-in-your-mouth smell of blood. Lots of blood. Red blood. There were men missing limbs, passed out or dead on the ground. Interspersed with the incoherent screaming, Tal heard the pleading prayers of men who knew they were dying, of men promising the Almighty anything, everything to keep from dying today. Holy hell, the Prime Omphalos sent us into the middle of a battle.

CHAPTER SEXAGINTA SEX

"Hurry up!" the soldier yelled at Tal, while turning his head from side to side looking for would be attackers. "Bollocks man, why aren't you wearing your armor? If that bastard hadn't been trying to kill you I wouldn't have known you were on our side." Tal stood there frozen. The guy grabbed Tal's head, and leaned forward, looking him directly in the eye. "Snap out of it, soldier! I don't have time to babysit you, I'm expected back at the command tent." Tal didn't move. "You're clearly in no condition to fight." The guy looked back over his right shoulder. "I have to go, but I'll stay and cover you until you reach those trees. Go!" He slapped Tal across the back of his shoulders with the flat of his broadsword.

Getting sword-bitch-slapped kicked Tal's brain into gear. He grabbed a quick breath, and then did his best to sprint through the muck. He couldn't run, in fact it felt like he was barely moving. The mud sucked at his shoes, as the rain did its best to beat him down. He dodged sideways several times to avoid ongoing swordfights, before making it to the underbrush surrounding the trees.

Tal looked around the thicket. It was about fifteen feet in diameter. Apparently the trees were out of the direct area of combat. They were thick enough to provide some respite from the torrential rain. Even with the shelter of the trees, it felt like someone was dropping bucket after bucket of ice water on him.

"Where am I?" he asked himself. Tal could feel his heart rate increasing, knew panic was trying to take over. "No, no, no," he told himself, "and quit talking out loud to yourself, someone will hear you." He got enough of a grip to start thinking it through. I'm going to do what we've been taught to do, what Borras makes us do—I'll do the drill. The Prime Omphalos is configured to send the teams someplace with one or more scavengyr pieces. Borras announced we were Journeying for a weapon. That means there is an available weapon somewhere within three hours EPT.

I need to figure out where I am. Maybe I'll figure it out if I can decide who all these people are that are fighting. I've seen hundreds already, and none of them seemed to be members of the other teams. Where's my team? The PO is supposed to drop us off together. Unless of course you're a Munedan. So, what first, he asked himself. Find the team. No, he decided, that's not what Borras would instruct me to do. He would tell me to find the weapon before the Recall.

What do I know about this place? That soldier was speaking English. In fact, all of the yelling and crying had been English. Not American English, more like really formal "thees and thous" English. Actually, when you factored in the horses, the armor, and the weaponry, it's Medieval English. Tal couldn't think of any Folk planes they'd studied that currently waged battle in an Earth Middle Ages manner. Plus there was the fact that it appeared to be red-blooded humans doing all the dying.

The tempo of the rain increased from downpour to double-time downpour, reducing his visibility to only a few feet. I can't stay in this hidey-hole and have any hope of finding the piece, Tal decided. There are at least two armies. I don't know which one it is, but odds are that someone in one of those two armies has the sword we need. Decision made.

Tal stepped out of the shrubbery into a howling wind. After going only a short distance, he heard some yelling. In response he leapt prostrate into a pool of water that had pooled against a waist-high wall. Tal looked back at the shouter, and saw two squadrons of soldiers laboriously slogging toward each other. They ended up fighting only a few feet from him, on the other side of the wall. He peeked over the wall in time to see one soldier thrust his dagger through an opponent's eye. When he withdrew his sword it plucked the eyeball out intact, like a meatball on a fondue stick. As that soldier stared at his prize, a mace swung downward cratering the back of his helmet. He collapsed, dropping the eyeball, as nondiscrete portions of his own facial bones and tissue erupted out of his helmet visor.

Brutal, is the only word for it, Tal thought. This was nothing like the pseudo-violence of video games or slasher flicks. The sound that metal makes when it cracks bone, the gurgling men make as they slowly drown in their own blood. The overwhelming stench in the air as they involuntarily shit themselves in the final convulsions of their muscles. Brutal. Tal didn't even realize he had already thrown up again until he found himself dry heaving into the surrounding ankle-high pool of water.

The slaughter went back and forth, until each side had killed all but one of the other's soldiers. Tal took a quick glance back over the wall and saw the last two combatants flailing away at each other. Their struggle brought them closer and closer to Tal's position. Then right when one slashed his sword down through the other's gorget, the other thrust his sword upward through the armhole of the cuirass covering the other's chest. Okay fine, Tal admitted to himself, I've spent way too much time jousting at Renaissance Faires with the Society for Creative Anachronism.

Now impaled on each other's weapons, the combatants continued to flail at each other, finally falling over the wall immediately to Tal's left. Tal stayed motionless for at least several more minutes. Neither of the soldiers moved. They've killed each other, he realized. What do I do now? He knew what Notos would do. He'd say something like, "Look Quint, you need to get with the program. This isn't fun and games—it's the Hunts. And the Hunts are like life. Some people win, some people lose. Everyone only gets one trip through—some die in their sleep after living to a ripe old age, and some die young. Violently." And then he'd call him a dumbass Munedan if he didn't immediately appropriate some armor.

He'd be right too, Tal realized. Those guys don't need their armor anymore, and I do. The rain finally decreased to a sprinkle, as Tal started removing the armor of the guy on top. It took Tal some effort to get the guy's helmet off, it was bashed all different ways. Tal stripped the guy of everything except his underclothes, before reassembling the pieces. He pulled the mail hauberk shirt over his head and shrugged a couple of times until he got it all straightened out. The cuirass covering his chest and back had leather straps on each side to cinch it closed. He strapped the greaves to his shins, and the cuisses to his thighs. The pauldrons went over his shoulders, like high school football pads. Everything was oversized for him but hopefully no one would notice. He pulled the coif, the mail hood, over his head, and finally pulled the braces up over his forearms. He couldn't make himself put on the helmet, it had brain yogurt splattered all around the inside. He reached down, grabbed a handful of mud, and smeared it over the small portion of his face that wasn't already covered by the coif. Then, he pulled the metal gauntlets over his hands.

He looked at both swords, just to be sure. Nothing special. So he finished looting the top guy by taking his sword. Damn it's heavy, he thought, I'm used to swinging one of these with Piras to help me. Thanks for nothing HuntsMistress! He decided to follow the wall. As he crept forward, it looked to him like the wall wound its way up to a fort on top of a small hill. Based on the colors of the fighter's shield, it appeared the other dead soldier's side seemed to be holding the fort. As Tal watched, he saw significant reinforcements for the defenders arriving from the west. Based on the armor, Tal's dead guy's side was attempting their siege from the east. Following the wall put Tal on a north-easterly track, at a forty-five degree angle from the bulk of the two armies. It also continued to provide cover. There were plenty of outliers fighting each other. He had made it about half a mile before he saw he was about to run into trouble. Two small groups were approaching each other, and there was nothing he could do to avoid both of them. They were still pretty far off. Tal doubted with the mist now rising from the ground, that they'd seen him yet.

Great. I'm out here by myself. Looks like its time to play possum. If I get killed before the Recall it doesn't help anyone. The Omada would be back to four, teetering on the edge of elimination. And I'd be dead. I know I need to try to make up for my mistakes, but I can't do that very well if I'm dead. The other four must have landed together. That should give them a better chance of staying alive and scoring a sword. Play possum, he told himself, as he lowered his face into the freezing mud.

Damn it, he screamed in his head. Damn it. Unbelievable, I actually fell asleep in the middle of a battlefield. How long was I out? How much time before the Recall? Tal realized he had no way of obtaining that information. He cautiously turned his head, first to the left, then to the right. He had been asleep long enough for that last group of soldiers to skirmish and move on. There was no longer any excuse for not trying to find the scavengyr piece. I'm not helpless. I can't fight as well as when Piras is helping, but I know the basics. He went ahead and ditched the sword, it was simply too heavy. I'll score a dagger off one of the dead guys.

It would make things a lot easier if I had some magyk like everyone else. Wait a minute, he thought, I do. He reached down with his left hand and pulled off his right gauntlet. Aurora's ring. What was it she said? It was good for three wishes, but I'd need it four times. If I'm not alive, I won't get a chance to use the ring any times. He didn't even know how he should ask, or for what exactly. He turned the ring one time, just because it felt right. As he did the ring turned into a rainbow band and illuminated itself from within, its multitude of colors flowing over and through each other. "Amarantos…please…um…please help me 'Seek the Center.' Then he stayed perfectly still for at least a minute. Listening…looking…nothing. Great! I got a lemon magyk ring. Batting two for two. I got a pair of plastic wings from the Wheel of Fortune and a fake magyk ring from the Lady Aurora. Wonder if there is such a thing as customer service to return defective magyk rings.

At least the rain let up while I was snoozing. He decided the suit of armor was also too heavy and had to go, so he ditched everything except the hauberk and the coif. The hauberk might save him from a stray arrow. Although the wall was low, it provided cover, so he followed it as it angled up to the fort, toward what he hoped was the rear of one of the armies. He stopped at a clump of corpses to retrieve a dagger. Tal kept the wall to his right, and off to his left was a harvested wheat field, or that's what it was before the day's deluge of biblical proportions. Now it looked like a freshwater marsh.

The sun appeared, finally paroled from its cloud prison, and as it brightened the sky a rainbow appeared in the mist. A spectacular rainbow, with each individual color etched like cut glass. It's beautiful, Aurora, it truly is, Tal thought, but I'm not counting that as the answer to one of my three wishes.

Tal followed the wall a dozen more steps, before stopping to look at the rainbow again. As he watched, the arc of the rainbow changed. One end remained lost in the horizon but the other end moved until it curved down into the middle of the harvested field. At that moment Tal saw something rise vertically out of the water at the terminus of the rainbow. Long and narrow, the object prismed the rainbow, reflecting it a hundred different directions. Must be an optical illusion Tal thought, a mirage. He checked around to see if there were any combatants near—there weren't. When he looked back, the rainbow was still there. It's only a couple of hundred yards away, and I'm already sopping wet—guess it won't hurt to go check it out. I mean how many times in your life do you get to actually see if there is a pot of gold at the end of the rainbow?

Tal started sloshing toward the spot, turning his head repeatedly to keep watch. He was completely exposed—with no escape route—if somebody came up on him. As he got closer he saw the bottom of the object was a large irregularly shaped granite boulder. Actually, it kind of looked like a miniature version of the Prime Omphalos. A sculpture of an oversized hand rose up out of the boulder. The stone hand gripped a metal sword, pointing it skyward. The rainbow ended at the sword's tip, which was what had been refracting the rainbow.

No freakin' way, Tal told himself. There is no way a sword held by a hand in a stone rose out of this eighteen-inch deep lake. Because if that just happened, and if this whole thing is not some "held down in the water and almost murdered" near-death delusion, then that sword would have to be…Excalibur.

He quickened his step, the water splashing almost to his knees as he tried to run through it. When he reached the rock he checked out the sword—a blade of polished steel with a rune pattern that kept appearing and disappearing, the hilt was midnight black and inlaid with the threads of a red gemstone. Yep, it's Excalibur. But it's retired. I saw Arthrys with Excalibur only a little more than a month ago in Myrddin's Pentacle. It can't possibly be here. Unless it's a duplicate…or unless Arthrys has died. Oh, shit.

Tal walked around the rock. There were words carved into the rough stone on the far side:

Through countless choosings,
across legions of lives,
I am the Sword of Many Names.
Eversore the Destroyer.
The Flaming Blade of Uriel.
One day I shall be called Dies Irae—The Day of Wrath.
Given freely I may be, by force never taken.

Take me up— if you 'Seek the Center'.
If not, leave me stay—else your soul I'll take.

What the heck is that all about, Tal wondered. Wait a minute. My wish was that Amarantos help me to 'Seek the Center'? Everyone keeps saying that's what we are supposed to be doing and I'm still not sure what it means. Before this sword gets to snatch your soul, do you have to be 'Seeking the Center' one hundred percent of the time, or is it good enough to seek it a mere preponderance of the time? Is it some type of balancing test, he wondered. If so, I'm probably okay, but if it's a screw up once and you're done thing I'm cooked. And I think I'd be better off keeping my soul. Pretty sure.

Stop it, Tal told himself. Gather all available information, and make an informed decision. The Prime Omphalos sent us here, which means there has to be a qualifying weapon on this plane. There is no mention in any of the literature of there being duplicate Excaliburs, so this sword has to be the Excalibur. Excalibur would be an eligible weapon, except Arthrys has it and it's therefore retired. Arthrys clearly doesn't have it right now, so that means for whatever reason it's not retired, which, therefore, makes it an eligible weapon. We need a sword for our weapon. Decision made.

Stretch out your hand he told himself. Countermand that order, another part of his brain said, because you really, really need your soul. You owe it to the Omada, Tal. 'Seek the Center' and take the sword. Slowly, almost imperceptibly, he reached up until he touched the sword. There was no flash of hellfire. Can you be soulless and not know it, he wondered.

Tal closed his hand around the sword's hilt right above the stone hand's grasp, and as he did, the hand opened, releasing the weapon to him. Tal lifted the sword, and took several steps backwards. As he moved, the boulder sank slowly beneath the water's surface until finally the hand was swallowed. As the water stilled, the rainbow gradually disappeared.

Now that Tal actually held the sword he realized he felt different. He felt…well, he felt…powerful. Like he could do anything, to anybody. He swung the sword slowly. It seemed light as a feather, not heavy like the sword he'd picked up earlier. He swung it quickly through the air several times. The hilt seemed to have molded itself to fit his grip perfectly. I wouldn't even need Piras if I used this sword, he thought. I hope some enemy soldiers find me now. Excalibur would slice through an entire squad. Hell with that, through a whole company. What're you going to say to me now, Notos, when I cruise back from Recall swinging this bad boy? What, cat got your tongue, Notos?

Tal started walking back toward the wall, his mind racing. With Excalibur I'm invincible. All manner of grand thoughts flitted through his mind, leaving only to be replaced with even grander ones. Barton Sellars and his goons would shit bricks if I showed up swinging Excalibur. How would he like it if I had him pinned to the locker with the tip of my sword. It wouldn't take me long to teach Notos a thing or two about respect. How could all the girls not love me now? Elle would be all over me. Väst wouldn't be able to let me out of her sight.

I bet I could win the Scavengyr Hunt single-handed, Tal decided. Little old Stupid Non-Magykal Dust Child Me. Now that I think about it, maybe it would be better if I was the Omada Prime. Borras is nice, but he's not tough enough, and I'm clearly smarter. Makes more sense. I'm sure I can do a much better job of running the team. Now that I think about it, it would probably be best for all of the worlds if I'm the new Archon. Who's going to tell me no while I'm swinging this badass sword? It's amazing how I can see so clearly now what's best for everyone. With Excalibur, I can fix everything that's wrong with everybody. Everywhere. World peace? Not a problem. Even if I have to force people to do what I tell them. If I have to, I'll kill a few thousand who don't want to get with the program, and that should shut the rest up.

As Tal finally reached the wall his stomach went all queasy on him. He set Excalibur on top of the wall, before hopping up on top to sit for a moment. As soon as the sword left his grasp, a still, small voice within him told him Excalibur had some major juju and it wanted to call the shots. It's not Excalibur now, the voice reminded him. Right now it's called the Sword of Many Names. Its name is Excalibur when Arthrys wields it. What kind of demon weapon could it be when it's not in his hands, Tal wondered.

How can it be in this Realm, anyway? I met Arthrys. Arthrys wields Excalibur, because he found it and used it during his Hunts. It was because Arthrys had Excalibur that his team won their Tyrning, and it was because of the power of Excalibur that he became Archon. During his three hundred year rule both the Folk and human worlds prospered. Alberich and his two predecessors based their rule on Arthrys's model. What would have happened to humanity if Arthrys hadn't won? What would have happened to the Folk on all the countless other planes?

"Who dost thou battle for?" Tal didn't know how long he'd been lost daydreaming. Long enough for a squadron of soldiers to sneak up on him. One of them had the tip of his sword sticking in the back of Tal's chainmail. Tal slowly extended the fingers of his left hand toward Excalibur.

"Ah, ah, none of that," a second soldier said, whacking Tal's knuckles with the flat of his blade. "Try it again, and you'll be minus a hand."

Tal watched as four of the men leapt over the wall to completely surround him. One of them was the guy who had stuck his sword in Tal's back. "I'm going to ask you politely one more time. Who dost thou battle for? Symmoria or Släkt?"

Oh shit, Tal thought, there's other teams here. The Symmoria must be a nickname but the Släkt are here too. Damn it. I didn't think Empousa was sending us out where three teams could end up in the same Realm at the same time. "I'm Quint of Omada."

"Got a smart mouth on ya, do ya boy? This query from some guy who looked to have about twelve cavities in the five teeth remaining in his mouth. "He's having a right time jerking on you, Captain."

The captain took his sword and placed the point of it right on the edge of Tal's Adam's apple. Tal could feel a tiny bead of blood bubble up, before he felt it well over and begin tracing its path down his neck. "One last time," the captain said. "Symmoria or Släkt?"

I don't get it, Tal thought. I've seen hundreds of people fighting today. How did the Släkt get them on their side? And which team is the Symmoria? The sword point pressed harder into his throat. Think, Tal, think. If you tell them you're with the Släkt, and that's who they're with, Nord will kill you if they take you there. If it's the Symmoria, whoever that is, as least he stood a chance. Decision made. "Symmoria."

"The enemy. I thought as much," the captain replied, as Tal shrank backward.

"Awful pretty sword you got there Symmoria-lover." This from the poster child for flossing. "I think you should give it to me."

"I can't do that," Tal replied.

"Then I guess we'll have to take it," another one of the soldiers volunteered.

'Seek the Center,' Tal told himself. You've already felt what the Sword of Many Names can do when someone besides Arthrys holds it. "Then kill me if you think you can, but I'm returning this weapon to its rightful owner—Arthrys Pendragon."

"Oh, la-de-da. Arthrys Pendragon, you say?" This time, it was a fourth member of the group. "Is that someone you likes to has afternoon tea wit'?" he asked, as the entire contingent laughed at Tal. "What do ya think o' that, Victor?" he asked turning to his dentate-challenged comrade.

"I thinks that a fine, fine blade like that un deserves a right and proper swordsman," Five-Tooth replied. "Which I is, so I think I'll just 'proprate it. You know what they says, 'To Victor goes the spoils.'"

There's another platitude I'm never saying again, Tal decided. Ever.

The man reached over to pick Excalibur up off the top of the wall. The sword did not move. The man looked at Tal and back to the sword. He stepped closer to the sword, took hold of the hilt with both hands and lifted. The sword did not move.

"What's a matter, Vic? Fine steel too heavy for you?" Soldier number three asked him. He pushed Victor aside, and grasped the sword in both his hands. The sword did not move. He placed one foot against the wall for leverage and jerked as hard as he could. The sword did not move. In rapid order the members of the squad tried their hand at the sword. The sword flat refused to be moved.

The captain interrupted the action. "Stop it," he ordered his men. "It is clear," he motioned toward the Sword of Many Names, "that is a sword of power." He placed his sword back at Tal's throat. "It's also clear it has been spelled to work only for this one. Pick up the sword," he demanded. "Slowly."

The moment Tal touched the sword's hilt, he felt the blade jerk forward on its own power, moving Tal's arm so fast it was a blur as it sliced through the air, severing a thumb-sized piece of Victor's left ear lobe.

"Bloody hell! I'll kill you, you little bastard," Victor raged, as he started to pull his sword from its scabbard.

Before the man could even get his sword half-drawn, the Sword of Many Names had already completed several strokes in quick succession. First, it cut the guy's sword in half while it was still partly in the scabbard, and the next thing Tal knew the point of his sword had drawn a pencil thin line of blood horizontally across Victor's neck. My sword sliced his sword in two like it was a piece of cardboard, Tal thought.

"Yield! I yield to the magyk sword," Victor whispered, his greasy shoulder length hair falling over his face as he fell to his knees.

As Tal leaned forward to check the man out, someone clonked him on the back of his head knocking him to the ground.

Before he knew it he was calf-roped with his hands tied behind his back.

"Let's take him to Mitt, Captain. He'll know what to do with him."

Mitt? They're taking me to the Släkt? Hell, no. No question about it. Mitt will let Nord kill me to get the Sword of Many Names. It's a game-changer. If they catch the rest of the Omada before the Recall, Nord will kill them as well. All of them. *'C'mon sword,'* Tal thought, seeing if he could communicate telepathically with the sword. *'There's only ten of them, we can take them. Well, you can. C'mon.'* It was his last thought as something heavy again thunked him in the back of his head.

I'm blind was Tal's first thought when he awoke. Those bastards hit me so many times in the back of the head they've knocked me blind. After blinking a couple times, he realized there was some type of dark cloth tied tightly over his eyes. And some foul-tasting something was wadded up in his mouth. He grimaced a few times until he could move his lips a little. He realized he'd been gagged with a hemp rope. Apparently, a hemp rope that had first been dragged through a latrine. He slowly tried to move and discovered he was trussed up hand and foot, probably with more of the crap-flavored ropes. There was something hard in the palm of his left-hand. He flexed his fingers within the limited range of motion available to him. It's a sword hilt, he realized. Really strange. Why would they cinch me up like this, but still leave me holding the sword?

Tal wiggled his back a little. He was seated, and they had leaned him against a pole. He slowly raised and lowered his chin, and felt the back of his blindfold catch on a knot on the pole. He raised his chin back to where he felt the snag, hooked the blindfold and then jerked his chin down to his chest. After a half-dozen tries the cloth loosened, and with another couple of attempts, it fell off.

As the fresh air blew across it, his face felt crusty. It's dried blood, he realized. Probably from the source of his headache. He could turn his head a few degrees in each direction, and after doing so determined he was tied up to an exterior support pole for a large canvas pavilion. Torches spaced every few feet broke the darkness with an oily light, the fragile light wavering in the early evening breeze. Tal could smell the oil, rendered from some type of fish. Those torches aren't magyk, he realized. Magyk torches have no scent.

Tal could hear voices, loud voices, from within the tent. As he listened he could discern four, maybe five, separate individuals having an argument. About him.

"Bloody hell, he cut half my ear off, and then split my sword in half."

Tal heard a low rumble—like a chuckle—he thought.

"He's not one of our mortals. We know the rules. He should have been killed on the battlefield." This was a different voice.

"I agreed with Nord." A third voice in addition to the first two.

Nord? Oh hell, it is the Släkt, Tal thought. Of course Nord wants to kill me.

"There's something queer going on here." Tal was trying to keep a tally. This was a fourth voice.

"What is it, Ost?" Ost? The guy giving the directions then must be Mitt. They all sound different. Maybe it's the tent. Or getting whacked repeatedly in the head.

"Well, he's not fighting for us, but he doesn't seem to be fighting for them, either," Ost replied.

"Kill him." That was a fifth voice. "I bet we won't have any problem taking the sword then."

"Hold on Väst, we're not animals." Six. There's at least six of them.

Väst? Is she trying to kill me too? I gotta be a better kisser than that. She must have caught a cold, Tal thought. She sounds like she's a three pack a day smoker.

"There's something else." Tal could tell that was Ost. "Even when he was out cold, the sword fought us when we tried to take it."

"It's not any of the weapons in our textbooks." That was the Väst voice again. Except it wasn't her voice. I've had my tongue in that mouth, Tal thought. That's not Väst. What book was the Släkt using? References to Excalibur were all over the *Weapons* textbook.

"A Dust Child wielding an unknown sword of power during the Hunts. Now that is something novel," Mitt said. "Is that everything I need to know? Absolutely everything that happened?"

"Not quite." That was Nord. "He was rambling about the sword's owner. He said the sword belonged to...Artemis, I think it was."

"That makes no sense." That sounded like the Ost voice, Tal decided. Although all of their voices sounded different. Maybe they have some voice modulation magyk on this plane. Ost continued. "The Artemis's mandated weapon is a bow."

Another voice broke in—this time it was that Five-Tooth creep Victor. "Begging your pardon your lordships, the name t'weren't Artemis. It were some t'other name we never heard. Sounded somefin' like 'Art-ris'."

"WHAT?" Tal could see the tent walls billow from the force of Mitt's exclamation. "Bring him in here now. All of the humans leave immediately. I appreciate your good work today, but we have Folk business to discuss."

Humans fighting on this plane for Hunts teams. The Släkt have humans working for them. How long has that been going on, Tal wondered, feeling legs brush up against him as a number of people left the tent. Hands appeared from the darkness and grabbed him, roughly hauling him to his feet, and dragging him into the tent. He closed his eyes, and acted like he was still out.

"You can open your eyes, genius. We know you're awake, you took your blindfold off." It was the Nord voice.

Oh yeah, forgot, Tal thought. So much for playing possum. Good to know froggy Nord is as big a dick as regular voice Nord.

The leader turned to his four lieutenants. "Untie him, please. I'm going to ask you all to wait outside as well for a few minutes."

"But Prime...he has the sword," Nord replied.

"There's nothing to worry about. This gentleman and I are going to have a conversation." He turned to Tal. "A friendly conversation, isn't that right?"

"I can't speak for the sword but as far as I'm concerned—yeah." Tal looked around the room. There wasn't a single member of the Släkt in the tent. They used the Släkt names, but they weren't them. And Väst wasn't Väst with a head cold, Väst was a guy. What the hell?

Mitt turned back to his crew. "Nord, please escort the wounded human to the infirmary and get his ear healed." Mitt turned to the other three Folk in the room. "Söder, Ost and Väst—please check the perimeters."

As soon as the tent flap closed behind them, Mitt stood to address Tal. It was Tal's first chance to get a good look at him. Dude is like all handsome and beautiful at the same time, he thought. Tousled straw-blonde hair, blue steel eyes, all square-jawed. A young Robert Redford. He looks like he's only about twenty, but he even stands like he's supposed to be in charge. There was something familiar about him—his air of authority, his speech cadence, even the way he stands. Very, very familiar.

"I am Mitt, Prime Direction of the Släkt."

"Mitt. Right—good one," Tal replied curtly. Didn't matter if the guy was Prince Charming, his henchmen had sucker-punched him and stuck shit-cloth in his mouth. "I don't know what scam you're running buddy, but I know Mitt, and you're no Mitt."

"You are mistaken, human. The two Finalists in this year's Battle Hunt are Släkt and Symmoria. I am Mitt, Prime Direction of Släkt."

Battle Hunt? What's going on around here? "That's not right. It's first term and there are nine teams left in the Hunts, including my squad—Omada. A Battle Hunt is most definitely not this term's Hunt."

"You are Munedan?" Although it was more of a statement than a question.

"Yes."

"Yet you claim to be on a Hunts team?"

"Yes."

"Maybe Nord is right, and you are simple. There has never been a Munedan at Hunts School." He took a step toward Tal, his eyes on the Sword of Many Names. "Nord told me some things about your sword."

"I heard him. It's all true, except it's not my sword."

"Interesting. May I see it?" Mitt extended his hand out to Tal.

"No. It doesn't belong to you either."

"I see. Who did you tell my men that it belongs to?"

"This sword belongs to Arthrys, Pendragon of the Alfar."

In the infinitesimally short period of time between the present heartbeat becoming the immediate past heartbeat and the next heartbeat which might be a future heartbeat never realized, pseudo-Mitt had drawn and laid his naked sword across Tal's jugular.

"Whooaa, take it easy, dread Pirate Roberts. We're only having a friendly conversation, remember?"

The sword remained taut against Tal's skin. "I will give you one chance to tell me what kind of Folk you are and what magyk you have that you know my psuche name."

Tal was only able to keep his knees from buckling because he was uncertain whether collapsing would effectively slit his own throat. Psuche name? This Mitt is Arthrys? How? Arthrys is in Forest Fell guarding Myrddin's Pentacle. With Excalibur. He doesn't even look like Arthrys.

Duh, think Tal, he told himself. This Arthrys is a Hunts contestant. He has been made to appear human, like everyone else. You know it's him though. You knew you recognized his voice, the way he stands, you knew it when you first saw him. This is Arthrys twelve hundred years ago. He hasn't won the Hunts yet. The Sword of Many Names hasn't become Excalibur yet.

"Most folks would not describe me as a patient man," Arthrys said, as he continued to hold his sword against Tal's skin.

"Give me a second, please. I'm having an internal conversation," Tal responded in a timbre of voice he hadn't heard since he reached puberty. This sword isn't retired. We need a sword of power, and this one's a killer. Omada will win if I kill Arthrys and take the sword back with me. Well not kill him, only incapacitate him. But if I take the sword, Arthrys won't become Archon. Who knows what would happen on the Earth plane? If I would ever even make it to Hunts School? Tal felt a tingling in his toes. The Recall. No! I need more time to talk to Arthrys. I have to sort this out.

"Now," Arthrys demanded.

'Seek the Center,' Taliesin Smith. Okay, Tal thought, I know what my voice sounds like in my own head when I talk to myself. It's never been female before, and that sounded an awful lot like Fortuna. The needles were rising from his feet to his ankles. Gas Pump Duo said worlds depend upon me. Decision made. "Take this sword, Arthrys. You have to have it to win the Hunts and become Archon."

It was Arthrys turned to be confused. "Mortals have no awaymagyk. How can you know what I need to win?"

"No time to chat. I wish to make a gyft given freely to you of the Sword of Many Names. Do you consent?" Tal asked as he turned the sword around hilt-first to Arthrys. He could feel the tingling moving up his shins now.

Arthrys laid his own sword aside, and took the sword from Tal's hand. "I consent." The look on Arthrys's face as he experienced its power for the first time told Tal he'd made the correct decision.

"This weapon—it sings to me." Arthrys sheathed his new weapon. "However, this means Lailoken was wrong."

"Lailoken! Myrddin? He's here?"

"Curiouser and curiouser," Arthrys said, looking Tal over a little more carefully. "A Munedan wielding a sword of power, who claims to be on a Hunts Team, and who knows the Alfar's secret name for the Myrddin."

"I get around a bit," Tal said, as he felt the prickles heading toward his waist.

"Lailoken is not here, Munedan. As his Alfar name implies, he is Time's Fool, and has been whisked away by the UnFading One to do her bidding."

That's right, Tal thought, he kind of told me that's how it works for him. "So what did he get wrong?" Tal was starting to have trouble breathing. They were right, the second Recall was going to hurt worse than the first one.

Arthrys clearly couldn't keep his hands off of Excalibur. He pulled it back out of the sheath to admire the sword. "Lailoken prophesied the winner of the Battle Hunt would wield cut steel taken from a hand rising out of a lake."

"Gotcha covered on that," Tal said, as the needles moved toward his neck. "I got it from a hand coming up out of a lake. Kind of a sad excuse for a lake but I guess it met the minimum depth requirements."

"What is this sword's name?" Arthrys asked, as he looked at the runes carved into both sides of the blade.

"At this moment Arthrys, it is the Sword of Many Names." Tal knew he was running out of time, so he quickly told Arthrys the words written on the stone. Then it hit him. "Arthrys, what is the word for 'Cut Steel' in the Alfar tongue?"

Arthrys thought for a moment. "There are different words, different meanings. Caliburnus, mayhaps. Yes, that is one way to say it. Excalibur would be the other," he replied.

I only have a couple of minutes left, Tal thought, as his jaw first went numb and then began to ache, like the entire lower set of teeth were all abscessed. "Excalibur it is, Arthrys

Pendragon. Please remember when you are Archon, humans are Amarantos's children too."

"I will remember your words and your gyft. Is there no gyftpryce you would ask of me?"

The pain was behind Tal's eyes now. He could feel fluids seeping out and down his cheek. Only seconds to go, he realized. Really hard to concentrate now, but there was something he needed to ask Arthrys. Oh yeah, that. "Now that you mention it, there is a little something something. Do me a huge solid. Please, please don't cut my head off with Excalibur the first time you and I meet."

"Done," Arthrys replied immediately but then looked confused. "I don't understand. This is the first time we've met."

Tal realized the pain was going to be intolerable this time, the pressure in his skull was beyond belief.

"Wait!" Arthrys exclaimed. "Your name. You never told me your name."

Tal tried to answer Arthrys but before he could, the world spun counterclockwise and exploded into black.

CHAPTER SEXAGINTA SEPTEM

Head still pounding, Tal willed his eyelids to slowly peel themselves open. Even though the Omphalos chamber was fairly dark, what light there was shot splinters of pain into and through his eyes. Since it seemed the head pounding he was experiencing was about the same with eyes opened or closed, he elected to keep them open. Something was terribly wrong with his orientation though. He wasn't standing with the team, he was still hanging upside down, his left hand pressed firmly against the Prime Omphalos for support.

Notos was the first to speak, although everyone's words tumbled over each other. "Five-Hells!" Tal could tell from the echo he was still in his position at the bottom of the giant stone.

"What happened?" Dysi asked. "I felt like I started Journeying and then I bounced off of something. But I never left my spot here in the Chamber."

"Me neither," Anatolia added. "Bounced is how I'd describe it, too. Like I ran into an invisible rubber band and it threw me back."

Tal took the opportunity to carefully reach up and pull himself up onto his catwalk. It took every bit of his remaining energy though. He felt like he was eighty years old. Actually, probably more like if he was eighty years old and had just been a participant in a head on collision.

"There's no question about it," Borras said, as he stepped out of the center and began walking up his runway. "We were blocked. Although that would be an unprecedented event." He walked over to the large hourglass positioned near the exit door to the chamber. "What the hell?"

""What?" Notos asked.

"The hourglass shows almost all three hours of Journey time has elapsed. But it was only seconds and none of us went anywhere. We need to let the HuntsMistress know someone has interfered with our Journey and with the Hunts. Immediately. We have to lodge a complaint to try to obtain a redo on this Journey before it gets counted against us." He had ascended to the level of the top of the Prime Omphalos and saw Tal lying on his back on the catwalk. "What happened to you? You look terrible."

"None of the rest of us were hurt," Anatolia said solicitously as she ran from her position up to Tal's. She had to cross two skywalks and then over another one before catching one that angled up to him. She took a moment to inspect him, before turning back to Borras. "Borras, the rest of us may have remained in the Chamber without consequence but Quint is bleeding from his eyes." Tal grimaced from the pain flashing through his brain as Ana took his chin and slowly turned his head first to the left, then to the right. "He has a black eye and there's a major bruise along his jaw. There is fresh blood on his face. His hair is completely matted with dried blood from at least two deep gashes on the top and back of his head. The dried blood looks a few hours old. She turned her gaze back to Tal, "I'm sorry but while we're at Hunts School I can't do any healmagyk."

Notos had arrived at the scene. "A few hours old? How in the Five-Hells could that happen? Mortal, what have you done now?"

"I'll be okay, Ana," Tal replied. "Are y'all saying you didn't Journey?"

All of the others shook their heads in the negative.

"Are you saying you did?" Borras asked.

Tal nodded his head in the affirmative, the motion setting off echo waves of pain careening off one side of his skull before hard bouncing back to the other.

"That's just great," Notos said. "More messed up human fallout. Never in the history of Hunts School has only one team member Journeyed."

"Kentro did," Dysi said quietly.

"That's not the same thing. That wasn't a Journey. Kentro used his authority as Prime Direction to go someplace by himself," Notos replied. "If the Munedan actually Journeyed somewhere we can't even think about lodging a protest for a make-good Journey. In fact we might be disqualified from the Hunts for not all going together. Although I'm not aware of a specific rule on that point. Because it's never happened."

"Could you tell which Realm the Omphalos sent you to?" Borras asked.

"Yes. It was Earth plane."

"You mean, here?" Dysi asked. Tal nodded. "That's not a Journey, Borras," she said excitedly. "We were all on the Earth plane for our origination point."

"Now's not the time for jokes, Quint," Borras said. "We have to make a protest decision before they bring the next team in for their Journey."

"Do I look like I'm kidding?" Tal asked irritably, rubbing his temples to try to ease the throbbing.

"No, he doesn't," Anatolia said staring at the rest of the team.

"Quint, there's no question your head has taken some serious poundage, but how can we be sure you Journeyed when none of us did?" Borras asked.

"Because I gave Excalibur to Arthrys to help him become Archon," Tal replied.

"Right," Notos said. "The Prime just told you now is not the time to try to be funny. Arthrys was Archon twelve hundred years ago."

"I realize that," Tal replied.

There was a scared hush for a few seconds before Notos spoke again. "Okay smart guy, how do you even know what Excalibur looks like?" Notos asked.

"Because I saw Arthrys with it when I met him and the Myrddin at the Pentacle in Forest Fell."

"WHAT?" Dysi exclaimed.

"You've been in Forest Fell, and met with Arthrys and the Traveler and didn't think we had a right to know?" Notos asked

Borras quickly interrupted the others. "Quint, you know the Prime Omphalos does not have timemagyk?" Tal nodded. "And you are still one hundred percent sure you gave Excalibur to Arthrys?" Tal nodded again.

As the others stared at Tal in shock, Notos whispered, so softly it was more a breeze than a spoken word—"Conundrum."

CHAPTER SEXAGINTA OCTO

The other three were still too stunned by the implication to speak. Borras finally broke the silence. "Quint, this is critically important."

"One hundred percent sure," Tal replied.

Notos was about to say something else when Borras shook his head vehemently, then placed his finger over his lips, and with his other hand motioned for all of them to get in a line and follow him. Tal got it. They weren't having any more discussion until they were safely in their secure team room.

Borras led them toward the door. When he got there he turned around to give them another stern look. Tal got it, everybody follow his lead. Borras then knocked on the door.

Ms. Empousa opened the door and stepped inside the Chamber. "Report, Prime. What piece did you obtain this Journey?"

"We failed to secure a piece," Borras replied.

The HuntsMistress gave them all a disapproving look. Then, she walked over to Tal, grabbed him by the arm and turned him around a couple of times. "Prime, I think your Fifth qualifies as "maimed" and needs to go to the infirmary." She opened her notebook to write the team's demerits.

"With all due respect HuntsMistress, it's nothing," Tal replied. "Just a little tough on us Munedans without a Puca, but I'm good to go. I'll saddle up again right now for another spin around the block if you'd like."

She gave them all another hard look. Tal could tell she knew something was up but couldn't figure out exactly what. She closed her notebook without writing any demerits. "Out."

As they entered the antechamber to the Omphalos room, the Ayllu were in line, ready for their Journey. "Looks like a swing and a miss for the Omada," Nohol sniggered.

"I guess we know who's moving to the bottom of the rankings," Xaman added.

"Sure thing, dickweed," Notos replied, looking at Nohol. "Because you idiots have x-ray vision and can see exactly how many invisibility items—yes, that's plural—we picked up this time out."

As the Omada left, Tal heard Nohol and Xaman arguing about changing their strategy to go for something other than invisibility pieces for defense. Notos may be a jackass, Tal thought, but he's our jackass. They quickly walked the rest of the way to their room in silence.

When their team room door clicked closed, Notos threw himself at Tal, grabbing a handful of his t-shirt. "What you said was impossible, human," Notos said. "We all know it's impossible. I'm getting to the bottom of this, even if I have to beat it out of you."

"Leave him alone, Notos," Borras said, as he took a step toward the two of them.

"But he's lying to us. He met Arthrys in Forest Fell, my ass," Notos insisted.

Ana stepped in between Tal and Notos. "Before you attempt to inflict additional injury on our teammate, I suggest I be allowed to doctor him up as best I can from whatever it was that obviously did happen to him," Anatolia said.

"Fine," Notos said, releasing Tal's shirt and retreating to his chair.

As Ana got her medicine kit out, and started putting antiseptic on his cuts, Tal started bringing the Omada up to speed. He first told them about his trip to Forest Fell, meeting Arthrys, Perun, and the Myrddin. They were fascinated by his description of the Pentacle. Apparently even important Folk weren't allowed anywhere near it. It became clear to Tal that Arthrys's presence in Forest Fell, and the Alfar's duties in guarding the Pentacle were also secrets.

"Okay, so are you done with that part of the story?" Borras asked.

Tal thought for a few moments about telling them about his gyft from Aurora and ultimately decided against it. "Yes," he replied.

Borras looked at the other three. "I'm sure you all have a million questions, I know I do. But we only have limited time until the bell sounds, so please hold them until later. Now, Quint, tell us about your Journey."

Tal told them every detail he could remember. Everything. How hard it rained, the wall, the different soldiers fighting each other, being knocked unconscious and taken captive. He was finally interrupted—by Notos—when he got to the part where he took the sword from the stone.

"WHAT DO YOU MEAN YOU HAD A SWORD OF POWER? WHERE IS IT? WHY DIDN'T YOU BRING IT BACK WITH YOU?"

Tal wasn't sure he'd ever heard anyone yell louder than Notos was yelling right now. I hope this room is as soundproof as we were led to believe, Tal thought, or else this entire quadrant of the school will know we didn't score a scavengyr piece. "You don't understand."

"Damn right, I don't," Notos continued, still screaming.

Dysi interrupted. "Notos, stop. Give Quint a chance to explain. I'm sure there is a good reason. There is, isn't there, Quint?" Tal could tell from the tremble in her lower lip, that even Dysi was disappointed in him.

"There is, Dysi. I'm telling you the sword was Excalibur."

"Hold up everyone, we've missed a step," Anatolia said, while she turned Tal's head to look at the cuts on the back of it. "Quint, you said there were humans involved in the Hunt, right?"

"Yes."

Ana looked at the rest of the squad. "The Scavengyr Hunt is the only Hunt going on in all of the Moiety." She paused for a moment before adding, "At the present time."

"It's impossible, Ana," Borras replied firmly.

They were talking around him again and he didn't like it. "I'm telling you I gave the sword to Arthrys and it became Excalibur."

Borras continued trying to reason with him, "That's contrary to our History textbook, Quint. It's a well-known story. Arthrys was the one who took Excalibur from the stone. With the sword's power, his team won and he became Archon. Twelve hundred years ago. After that, Excalibur was retired."

"The book is wrong, that's not what happened," Tal replied testily.

Notos turned to Borras, "I think somebody broke your human. I guess you'll have to get us a new one. Or not."

Dysi interrupted the other two. "What Borras is telling you Quint is that it had to be one of the other swords of power." Tal could tell Dysi was trying her best to understand how he could have made such a grievous mistake.

"Damn straight," Notos said interrupting her. "All drawings of Excalibur were removed from the Hunts textbooks when it was retired. You're the only one at Hunts School right now that even knows what it looks like. Hey!" he said suddenly. "If you met Arthrys in Forest Fell, why didn't you recognize him when you went on this Journey you say you went on?"

Borras responded. "If Quint went othertyme, as he says, Excalibur would look the same both then and now. The weapon is a constant. Arthrys, however, would not. Quint would know what present day Arthrys, Pendragon of the Alfar, looks like." Borras started pacing. "He would however have no way of knowing what Arthrys looked like when he was a student here at

Hunts School." He turned and walked over to the closet, and after rummaging through the large number of books in it, pulled one out. He showed it to the group. "This is a copy of volume seven of the History of the Hunts. It's one of our old textbooks that we studied all the way back in year three. Well before Quint was ever born. Quint, have you ever seen this book?"

"No."

Borras handed the volume to Anatolia. "Ana, would you please find the page with the copy of Arthrys's Hunts' portrait on it?"

She flipped quickly through the tome. "Here," she said handing the book to Borras.

"Describe him for me, Quint," Borras asked.

Tal went back through every detail he could remember. The blonde hair, the way Arthrys stood, his air of command.

Borras showed the book to the rest of the team. Tal's description was a perfect match to the portrait.

"Five-Hells!" Notos's voice was ratcheting back up to airplane decibel levels. "A CONUNDRUM? YOU'VE GOTTEN US INVOLVED IN A CONUNDRUM." Yep, Notos was back to full volume now.

"I don't know what that is," Tal said.

"It's an impossibility, Quint," Anatolia said gently. "The Omphalos stones, all of them including the Prime, transfer Folk between planes. Their magyk does not extend to time. That would create Conundrum."

"Time travel," Borras explained. "It's a theoretical concept. The Wheel of Time only turns in one direction."

"It's against the Hunts Rules, I guess," Tal said.

"No," Dysi replied. "It's against the Lex Immortalis. Can you imagine what would happen if someone not 'Seeking the Center' could go back in time and change events?"

"The whole thing is impossible," Notos added. "Folk can't move through time. The only one who can do that is the Traveler and only then when he is sent by Amarantos."

"He has no reason to lie to us," Dysi said. "He's part of our team. We have our textbooks right here. He perfectly described Arthrys from his time as a student twelve hundred years ago. Let's do our drill, and see if we can conclusively prove or disprove Quint's statements."

"This shouldn't take long," Notos said. "You said there were at least two armies."

"Yes. But I'm pretty sure it was only two."

"Did you get a look at the crests for either of the armies," Dysi asked.

"Both of them. One side had a pennant with three crowns on a blue field. The other side's standard was three white lions on a purple background."

"That'll be in the Encyclopedia of Heraldry," Dysi said. "We got a team copy last year before the Snype Hunt. I'll get it." She got and walked over to the book closet. After rummaging through a few of the overloaded shelves, she located the book, sat back down and started thumbing through it. "This is going to take awhile, there are thousands of crests, and a lot of them are similar."

Anatolia had been reading further in the Hunts History textbook. "It says the last Hunt of Arthrys's Tyrning was a Battle Hunt."

"Right," Tal said. "Mitt, I mean Arthrys, said they were in the middle of a Battle Hunt."

"Battle Hunts were a common final Hunt during the early Tyrnings," Borras said. "Before Arthrys, when humans were treated by the Folk as slaves or property. The two final teams would Journey to some place on the Earth plane, a geas would be placed on the population making them believe the Folk team members were either gods or opposing royalty. A battle would then be fought until one team was defeated."

"And what happened to all of the humans?" Tal asked.

"Thousands died during each Battle Hunt," Notos replied.

Tal was speechless as the reality sank in, that what he saw happen today, actually happened to real people more than a thousand years ago."

"Battle Hunts were not of the Center, Quint," Borras added. "Sometimes it wasn't only a geas, sometimes compulsionmagyk was used as well."

"You mean the Folk not only hypnotized people but if that didn't work they put a special whammy on them to force them to fight and die?" Tal asked, his voice now being the elevated one.

"Just so," Notos replied quietly.

"That's murder. Who's the Brainiac that thought that was okay?"

"It is unknown," Dysi replied, glancing up from the book. "Battle Hunts were infrequently used. Arthrys is the one who finally outlawed them when he became Archon."

Anatolia stepped toward Tal. "It is solely because of Arthrys that Folk may no longer enslave the Munedan."

I don't care how mad Notos is at me, Tal told himself. It was the right thing to give the Sword of Many Names to Arthrys. Arthrys needed Excalbur to become Archon to the Folk, and King Arthur to mankind.

"Dysi?" Borras asked.

"Still looking."

Anatolia interrupted. "Quint, tell us again what the battlefield looked like."

"There was a low winding wall that went as far as I could see in both directions. It was only a few feet tall where I was, but some parts farther away looked like they might be head high."

"Was there a small hill?" Anatolia asked.

"Yes."

"And a rudimentary fort on top of the hill?"

"Yes."

She turned to Borras. "You're the geography whiz. The wall, could that have been Hadrian's Wall on the Earth plane?"

"It's possible," Borras answered, "but there are walls matching that description on many planes."

"Found one!" Dysi exclaimed. "Three crowns on a blue field was the standard used by the Släkt in the Battle Hunt four Tyrnings ago."

"Arthrys was Prime Direction of the Släkt that Tyrning," Borras said.

"That means it was Hadrian's Wall," Anatolia said, thinking out loud. "The fort on the hill is Camlann, overlooking the Salisbury Plain. That was the site of the Battle Hunt."

"I found the other pennant," Dysi exclaimed. "It was used by the Symmoria that Tyrning."

"The whole thing is impossible," Notos said. "Arthrys's time as Archon ended hundreds of years ago. It's impossible."

"Not if Quint was othertyme," Dysi whispered.

"He's Munedan," Notos replied. "Not even the Principes can magyk a Conundrum."

"I can prove it," Tal said. "Does that book tell how the Battle Hunt ended?"

She flipped through a couple of pages. "Yes."

"Y'all know I've never seen that History book."

"Go ahead, Quint," Borras said.

"The leader of the Symmoria probably challenged Arthrys to one on one combat because he felt like he had the advantage."

"Correct so far," Anatolia replied, turning the page.

"And Arthrys happened to show up on the last day swinging Excalibur for the very first time."

"Yes," she said.

I might as well have killed that other poor bastard myself, Tal thought.

Anatolia turned another page, and started reading. "The deciding point in the Battle Hunt came on the last scheduled day of fighting when the Symmoria Prime Direction was apparently mortally wounded by Arthrys. Until that time, the history suggests the Symmoria were winning on points, and were about to win the Hunt."

"Apparently mortally wounded?" Borras asked.

"There were so many hundreds of dead and dismembered Munedan, no one was able to conclusively say," Ana replied. "In fact, it was such a bloodbath they never recovered the bodies of any of the Symmoria team."

"None of them? That seems more than a little coincidental, don't you think?" Dysi asked.

"Does to me," Notos said.

Ana continued reading from the textbook. "All five were listed as KIH, and their families compensated accordingly." She apparently saw Tal's raised eyebrows. "KIH. Killed in Hunt."

"Who was the Symmoria Prime Direction that year?" Borras asked.

Anatolia looked at the book. "His psuche name was Malebranche."

"I've never heard that name before," Tal said.

"The Munedan histories generally use a different translation. He is referred to as 'Mordred,' " Borras added.

Anatolia had finished reading the Battle Hunts chapter. "Because Arthrys, as Archon, immediately imposed the magykal ban on the Earth plane, it was decided the easiest way to resolve the whole episode was to tell the surviving Munedan that Arthrys had been killed in single combat."

And thus was born the Arthurian legend, Tal thought.

"Okay," Notos said. "Assuming everything happened like he said it did, Quint assisted a Hunts team other than his own, which is a violation of the Hunts Rules, and we're busted and out of the competition."

Dysi looked up from the Heraldry Book. "You're the Parliamentarian, Notos, but I think you missed on that one."

"Twice actually," Borras said smiling.

"Fine," Notos said. "I'll bite. What did I miss?"

Anatolia closed her book. "Last time I checked, Quint is a Munedan. Dust Children are not part of the Moiety…"

"And so he is the same as a Creature as far as the Hunts," Notos said. "Good catch, Ana." He turned to Borras. "What else?"

"It was a Battle Hunt, which not only allow but require humans to assist the Hunts Finalists," Borras said.

"So there is no rule violation," Notos confirmed.

Borras turned his tennis ball sized eyes in Notos's direction. "I think you owe Quint a fairly sizeable apology."

Notos glared at Tal. "You may be right, Borras. We have a more important matter to resolve first, though."

Borras sighed. "Conundrum. How it happened, why it happened, and what it means to the Omada."

The ten-minute bell sounded summoning them to Ms. Empousa's class, leaving no time for any more private discussion.

CHAPTER SEXAGINTA NOVEM

"Although you are the sorriest group of underachievers ever to make it as Hunts Finalists, some congratulations are in order. No one got themselves killed—or substantially maimed as defined by the Rules—on the second Journey. There is one last Journey this term. Only the top five teams will advance to next term's Hunt. Three teams will be an embarrassment to themselves, their families, and their Realms. Never having been born would be a better option than losing the Hunts."

That HuntsMistress Empousa sure knows how to give an inspirational message, Tal thought.

"The third Journey is your last opportunity to make a substantial move in the rankings. Although I will tell you the team in last place right now will have to experience a miracle to make the cut. Actually that's not entirely correct," she said looking over to the Omada, "They would have to have an extra-large sized miracle to make the cut." She followed her short statement with a snicker. Tal wasn't sure he'd ever known there was such a thing as a malevolent snicker. A derisive snicker, of course. But malevolent?

"These are the rankings: Shuzoku, Kabila, Pleme, Släkt, Bùluò, Hak'éí, Ayllu, and Omada. After this class, teams in places one through five will go to your team rooms. There are second Journey prizes and winner's feasts. A much more substantial feast than after the first Journey. Teams six through eight will leave here and go immediately to the cafeteria. Chef Hestia needs the floors scrubbed with some rare kind of cleaning acid. I volunteered the losers. No Pucas, but you can wear gloves to keep the acid from peeling your dainty skin off. Now get out."

Last place, Tal thought. We're in last place. I know, I know, he replied to mental Notos in his brain. The Sword of Many Names would have put us in first. Släkt is in fourth place, but at least they're done with their Journeys.

CHAPTER SEPTUAGINTA

Most people think nose hair and cilia are the same thing—they're not. Nose hairs are the subject of many disgusting tv trimmer commercials and are the random hairs sticking out of quite a few unfortunates' noses. Truth be told, folks with lots of nose hair often have fewer problems with allergies and rhinitis. Cilia are microscopic strands. Their job is to help move mucus along through the sinuses. The point being that after three hours of scrubbing the cafeteria floors with the export from the "Realm of Hellish Acids," Tal knew with certainty he now had neither of either. All of both had been literally vaporized, as well as probably about half his lungs. The three teams finished their assigned chore though and Hestia was so happy with their work she gave them an extra hit of ambrosia, which gave Tal barely enough energy to make it home.

He and Emet had learned their lesson about communication. Tal's shower was moved until after dinner so that they could each quickly recite all of the day's events and still allow time for Tal to be downstairs for the family dinner. They'd caught a break. Emet's only contact with Elle had been across the hallway, and she'd smiled at him and pointed to her watch that she had an appointment before signaling she would call him tonight.

Tal grabbed his shower and knowing he wasn't going to last long after the phone call went ahead and started reviewing his Creatures textbook. There had been intimations by Ms. Empousa that she might have more pop tests and Tal wanted to make sure he was tuned up and ready. Besides, he was fascinated by the whole topic of draugrs. Everything about them, from their making, to their unmaking.

When Elle called they had a pleasant, normal boy-girl conversation. He reminded her she didn't have to use sign language at school, she could talk to him, he simply couldn't respond vocally. She laughed and they told each other goodnight and Tal had been right. He was physically exhausted, and he was all warm and feel-goody after their conversation, and he nodded off with draugrs on his brain.

CHAPTER SEPTUAGINTA UNUS

There had been a little extra time in Tal's morning schedule. There was no first-period homeroom, as they were all to report directly to their team rooms for a strategy session. Tal had come to Hunts School early anyway. He'd wanted to get to the room before anyone else and do whatever he could to be fully and completely prepared. He no sooner walked in the front door though, than he ran into Väst. She'd been waiting for him and waylaid him.

Before he knew it, they were in their secret trysting room, and they were doing some heavy-duty mugging down. Things were heating up to a new level—she didn't even demand that he sing for her, as she normally did. She'd told him she wanted to feel the spark all over her entire body, and then she'd started slowly unbuttoning her shirt, looking at him with that wonderful smile the entire time. He sat there mesmerized, as he realized she wore no undergarments. The now open shirt was coming off her shoulders when they'd both been surprised by the ten-minute gong.

Damn it, he thought as he'd watched her slowly rebutton her shirt. Ever so slowly, slowly, to make sure he got a long look at her firm white breasts. At the blue veins running across them right below the skin. Pulsing. It was the sexiest reverse strip tease ever. For whatever reason he couldn't tell her no. Whatever she asked of him he would do. He wouldn't have made it to his team room on time if she herself hadn't insisted on not being late.

After he left Väst, he zombied his way to the Omada room, sliding in right before the class gong tolled.

"Last one here," Notos sneered. "Figures."

"Chill, Notos," Borras responded. "Since we don't have a weapon, our strategy this Journey is rather simple. Get a weapon." Turning back to Tal he said, "It wouldn't have killed you to be here a few minutes early."

"Sorry," Tal responded. Borras was doing his usual job of managing all of the different personalities on the team, trying to achieve victory. Tal had made his job tougher, again, by being the last man in. He had to do better. He was going to have to do a better job of telling Väst no. But she has those breas…

"Okay, so we're going last and we have to go for a weapon. I'm not sure of the reason behind the change but I received a memo last night that the Journeys wouldn't be staggered this time."

Dysi spoke up. "It may be because Empousa caught a lot of heat about Merkez's death."

"That might be it," Ana said, "or it could be something a little more pointed."

"What?" Borras asked.

"I'll tell you," Notos said. "Based upon the initial rankings after the first Journey and the change in rankings announced yesterday, I calculate that four, maybe five of the teams have obtained a sword."

"And?" Borras asked.

"We're going last, Prime. No overlap means we don't get an opportunity to fight it out with the team right in front of us in the event we would have Journeyed to the same Realm for the same piece. It lessens our chance to obtain a weapon."

Borras rubbed his chin a moment. "I hadn't thought about that possibility. Good work Ana, Notos. Okay, so we're up against it guys. A hundred years of work and we're done for sure if we don't score a weapon during our three-hour Journey."

Tal saw Notos scowl at him but he didn't say anything further.

"So I instruct the Prime Omphalos we want to go to a Realm with a sword. That's done. Can we tell anything else from the change in team rankings that might help us if we can break into the top five?"

"There's something odd about Släkt being in fourth place," Anatolia said. "Notos, do you have them as one of the teams with a sword?"

"Yes," he replied.

"Do you also agree that they must have at least one other piece?"

"I do," Notos said.

"That's my guess as well," Anatolia added. "We know when we started this year they were in first place. They should be a lot higher than fourth place if they have a sword and a second scavengyr piece."

"Not if their second piece is really weak," Dysi said.

"Like one of the lesser flying carpets," Borras added. 'Enough to keep them in the top five but still vulnerable."

"Exactly," Anatolia said.

"Okay, we've had a hard few days," Borras said. "We don't leave until after lunch. Everyone go do whatever gets your heads straight for our Journey. We will meet back here fifteen minutes before Ms. Empousa is scheduled to come get us." He stopped and looked over at Tal. "No one needs to be late."

CHAPTER SEPTUAGINTA DUO

Tal felt like someone had grabbed hold of his eyeballs and twisted them backward into his sinuses—so that his irises were now facing backward into his brain. Which—by the way—was repeatedly sending him a one-word message: PAIN…PAIN…PAIN. After really concentrating on his facial muscles for a few moments he finally felt like his eyeballs were at least pointed in the right direction. Even after he was able to open his eyes and focus, his vision still seemed blurred. PAIN…PAIN…PAIN. Notos was standing—well, wobbling—next to him, and he could tell by the way Notos's head was cradled in his hands that it was an extra-strength Tylenol moment for him as well. Tal glanced at the others. Yep, every single member of the team was evidencing similar body language.

"This is not how we felt on the first Journey," Notos snarled, looking at Tal.

"You heard Professor Elphinstone," Dysi interjected. "Multiple journeys without a Puca can be dangerous."

"Quint probably made it worse. He's cocked everything else up."

Borras leaned to one side and placed his hand on the side of a large rock next to him. "Focus team. We don't know how long we have on this plane until our three-hours EPT expires. Wow!" Borras said, half-stumbling backwards. "I don't know about you guys, but I can barely stand up." Tal saw everyone else nod, acknowledging their similar status.

Borras continued. "At least we all made the Journey this time and we landed together. First thing—figure out where we are. Everyone sound off."

"There is a full moon, obscured by a low-lying haze," Anatolia said.

"It's not just any haze, Ana," Notos added, wrinkling his nose. "Smell."

Borras took a deep breath. "Salt air."

"Right. It's a sea-haar," Notos replied.

"What?" Tal asked.

"Sea-haar, a marine fog layer," Borras replied. "You can tell from the salt in the air."

"I'm guessing the temperature is in the mid-forties," Dysi said, wrapping her jacket tighter around her. "And the wind..."

"It must be gusting at twenty to twenty-five knots per hour," Notos stated.

Anatolia slowly bent down and pulled a few blooms from a small clump of flowers. "Look at that these," she said, pointing at several small vermillion blooms, ringed with black-colored berries, "these are Alpine bearberries."

Tal stood shivering, the northeast wind whipping his clothes tight up again his arms and legs. They have been studying hard for a hundred years to prepare for the Tyrning, he thought. Notos is right, they don't need a deadweight mortal like me jacking them up. Tal tried looking around to see if he could do anything to help. "There's a large obsidian stone, maybe about fourteen feet high, it's been rough carved." He started to step toward it and...wow—PAIN...PAIN...PAIN.

Anatolia took two steps before leaning against the same stone and then took half a dozen halting steps to her right, both hands outstretched into the fog. "Found something," she announced.

Tal saw her move her arms first sideways, then up and down. "It's another hewn stone. About the same size," she announced. "I got it. I see the pattern. They're standing stones. It's a henge. We're at a henge."

"Good work, Ana," Borras said. "That means the odds are we're somewhere in one of the British Isle Realms."

The wind winnowed the fog a little and as it did Tal could see even more stones standing in a complete circular pattern. There's only one way I'm going to be of any help to them, Tal thought, and that's to learn as much as I can as fast as I can. "What's a henge?"

"Do they teach mortals nothing?" Notos asked. "A henge. You know, like Stonehenge on Earth plane."

"Right, right. Just needed some context. I'm with you now," Tal replied.

"There are henges in almost every Realm," Borras added. "Standing stones, like these, arranged in a pattern."

"As far as henges go, Borras, this one is near the top of the scale on the large end," Dysi said. "There are only a couple of henges this big on any plane that still have a complete circle of standing stones."

"It has to be the Ring of Brodgar," Borras stated. "Remember there was a picture of it in eighth year. It's located on the largest of the Orkney Islands, just off the northern coast in the Scottish plane."

"Mainland is the largest island's name," Notos added.

"I don't remember ever reading of an Omphalos located in a henge," Anatolia said.

"Maybe it's because of Quint," Dysi said.

"That's a possibility," Borras said. "No one has ever satisfactorily explained all of the reasons the circles were built on any of the planes. We do know the Munedans built the henges at places of natural electricity on Earth."

"I'm obviously not up to speed on henges in general," Tal added, "but I think you're referring to magnetic lines. I remember reading a National Geographic article that Stonehenge was built at an intersection of Earth's magnetic lines. Ley lines, they're called."

"Ley lines," Borras repeated for emphasis. "If that's the deal, Notos, having Quint with us has enabled us to go somewhere none of the other teams can go. Everyone test your magyk strength."

"I'm out," Dysi said.

"Me too," Anatolia confirmed.

"Dead in the water," Notos added.

Borras closed his eyes, concentrating. "Me too. Nothing."

"Could we be on Earth plane and it's Alberich's Bane?" Anatolia said.

Borras closed his eyes and concentrated. "No, this is a different kind of magyk, it's localized."

"I still don't get it," Notos said. "There is no record of the Omphalos ever sending a Hunt group to a henge. Surely there would be a written record..."

"Oh, crap!" Tal said, as he realized what had happened. "Hey guys, I think I may have..." No one was paying any attention to him.

"There are, however, recorded instances of entire teams not returning to Hunts School," Anatolia said as quietly as she could, and still be heard over the wind's voice.

"Kentro never came back..." Dysi started to say.

"Kentro abandoned us because of her. No one is supposed to use the Omphalos alone," Notos replied angrily.

Anatolia couldn't stand it anymore, "Shut up Notos! Just shut up! I'm tired of you saying that. You know she must have placed a geas on Kentro."

"This isn't the time or place for such discussion," Borras said calmly.

Tal tried to interrupt, "I really need to tell y'all something..."

"I specifically asked the Prime Omphalos to send us to one of the Realms with a qualifying weapon," Borras stated.

"Hey guys..." Tal said, a little more stridently this time.

"We have to find a weapon this Journey or we're cut," Notos reminded them.

""What is that smell?" Dysi asked, her nose wrinkling.

Tal could smell it now too. As they had been talking the wind had steadily increased and its breath now stank of rotting fish and badly spoiled eggs.

"Listen!" Borras said. Everyone stopped talking.

Something was howling in tandem with the wind, the second noise growing louder by the minute. The scent and the sound were now overwhelming. Tal was about to start puking, and the greenish hue of Anatolia's face warned she felt the same.

"What is it, Borras?" Dysi asked.

"I know what it is…" Tal interjected.

Borras took over. "Hold on Quint. Whatever it is, this is our best defensive position. Everybody put your back against this standing stone," After seeing that everyone had complied, he turned to Tal. "Now, what is it, Quint?"

"I'm really sorry. I was studying for the final exam last night, and went back through the Creatures textbook."

"There's nothing wrong with studying, Quint."

"I was reading the chapter about…anyway I was reading a certain chapter because of some things that happened to me when I was little. But I never thought we would come see it in person."

"What have you done, Munedan?" Notos hissed. "You didn't think we'd come see what in person?"

"A draugr," came Tal's hushed reply.

CHAPTER SEPTUAGINTA TRES

"A draugr?" Anatolia asked, frantically looking around.

"No, please..." Dysi cried.

"Nice work, human!" Notos said, quickly turning his head from side to side. "You've killed us all. We have no magyk and no weapons. We can't beat a draugr without them."

"How did this happen?" Borras asked Tal.

"Right before we touched the Omphalos, I was thinking about possible questions that might be on our Creatures' final exam."

"Fool," Notos snapped.

"I'm the Prime Direction, Notos," Borras said sternly. "I announced to the Omphalos what object category our team wished to scavenge. Quint is human. He has no magyk. There's no way he could affect the Omphalos," Borras concluded locking back to Tal.

"We didn't Journey to a navel, Borras," Dysi said. "There's no Omphalos here. Even if we get away from the draugr, how do we know there's a scavengyr piece in this Realm?" Dysi asked. Tal could tell from the speed of her speech she was close to losing it.

"Stop it," Borras commanded. "Everybody stop freaking out and let's prioritize. If we put our heads together we can figure out a way to survive the draugr. Remember—do not look into its eyes. After we've lost the draugr, we can spend the rest of our time looking for a piece." He turned back to Tal, "When we get back, there are questions that need answering."

Tal found small solace in the solidity of the large stone at his back. He could tell by his friends' shoulders—and faces—that their tension was ratcheted to the breaking point. The smell kept increasing until it was unbearable. He watched as Dysi became the first to be overwhelmed, falling to her knees. Then Notos. The stench reached the point where Tal couldn't tell if it was better to breathe or not breathe, and he couldn't tell if the roaring in his ears was sound or the lack of fresh air. He started feeling light-headed, then watched as Anatolia leaned over to hold on to Borras for support, before both she and the giant succumbed and crumpled to the moist, lichen covered ground.

The noise had grown with the stench, a separate and distinct assault upon his senses. It now sounded to Tal like he was standing butt up against a freight train hurtling full bore down a tunnel. At some point the smell had taken on physical shape as a fog, a sulfurous murk with finger tendrils reaching for him. He felt like the fog was helping suck the little remaining air away.

As the noise reached a crescendo, the mist parted, and Tal saw the draugr. Ten feet tall, it was naked except for a ratty loincloth tied around its waist and a battle mace in its right hand. Its skin was a shiny black, so black that it had a blue sheen. That color is called hel-blár, Tal remembered from reading the textbook. Death-black.

CHAPTER SEPTUAGINTA QUATTUOR

"Unexpected, this is." The draugr's voice was like the sound of someone walking in stiff boots on bone-dry gravel. Actually, Tal thought, it was more like the sound of someone crunching a mouth full of grit—while walking in stiff boots on bone-dry gravel.

"Why art thou not unconscious like the other trespassers?" Somehow even the sound tasted gritty inside Tal's ears.

Tal realized he was lucky he'd assumed the subservient position and had his eyes facing downward. He would have been screwed otherwise because he was actually scared stiff. Apparently it wasn't just a folk saying, there really was such a thing. He couldn't move a single muscle, certainly couldn't make all the necessary body parts move to form words.

The draugr walked right up on him, bent low to look into Tal's face, and took a deep breath to smell him. "Odin's beard. Thou art Munedan!" He sniffed the others, one at a time. "Folk. Folk. Folk. Folk. Different kinds but all Folk. Never have I seen mortal travelling with Folk on this plane."

Okay, Tal thought to himself, I'm pretty sure there aren't any Quaker draugrs. To be truthful, Tal, until a couple of minutes ago, you were pretty sure there weren't any draugrs, period. Quit talking to yourself and focus you moron. Listen to his accent, his speech patterns. His verbiage is consistent with some type of medieval draugr. Is this another Conundrum?

"What is thy name, human?"

It was all too much; the stench, the rasping sounds—the abject terror. Tal would have started crying, except apparently his tear ducts were too scared to produce. "Quint. Quint of Omada," he stammered.

"Look at me, human," the draugr commanded. The draugr put one of its blue-black fingers under Tal's chin, and effortlessly lifted it up. He remembered Borras's warning, but there was nothing he could do. Tal found himself looking into the black of the draugr's eyes. There were no irises, no whites. No hints of browns, blues, or greens. The eyes were the black vacuum of a midnight sky stripped of its moon and stars. The blackness of charred coal, of something that was once living but was now devoid of life. Tal realized it was no longer his body voluntarily refusing to respond to his brain's directions, he was no longer in control. He had been spelled by the draugr.

"That should hold you until I decide how and when you and your companions will die."

Tal watched as the draugr threw Borras on his back as if he were a five-pound bag of dog food. Then the draugr simply sank into the earth. Okay, this is not happening, Tal thought. I don't care what that textbook said. That thing just took Borras, and sank into the earth. Actually, this land mass appears to be more rock than soil. Which would be an indicator of a possible volcanic origin centuries ago. Focus, Tal. Do not go into shock, you can't help the Omada if you go into shock. You witnessed it with your own eyes. It happened. The draugr simply sank into the rock. And most certainly killed Borras, while he was as it.

Several minutes later the draugr came back and took Notos. Dysi and Anatolia followed in quick succession. When the draugr returned the last time, he walked back over to Tal. "Speak!" he ordered.

Tal felt his facial muscles release. All of his scared, and his anger, and his worry for his friends boiled over. "You want me to speak? How's this for starters? I'll kill you for this, you son of a bitch."

The draugr's mouth bent upwards ever so slightly. "So, the Dust Child dost have some warrior sand. Alas, I am afraid thou art more than a thousand years too late to have the pleasure of killing me. Now we go to my home, and you will answer some questions for me. After that, you and your companions will make several fine dinners. Or perhaps a feast. I haven't hosted a feast for centuries."

"If you're going to kill us anyway, draugr, I'm not answering your questions."

The draugr shrugged and started walking away. "If that be your choice. I will obtain the information from your Folk friends. Folk are not the same as human. Being made of magyk, they be hard to break, but it is a fun game nonetheless. There will be much gaming and wagering on how many body parts your women will lose before their minds flee their bodies screaming."

Dysi, Anatolia. He's going to torture them because I brought them here. "So the deal is if I tell you what you want to know, you'll let them go?"

The draugr's laugh was worse than its speaking voice, if that was possible. It was like a high-speed blender filled with two-percent milk—and scree. "No, the agreement is that if you tell me what I want to know they will not be tortured. Their deaths are non-negotiable."

It's a start, Tal, he told himself. It will give me time, and them time. Time to figure out how to kill this bastard. Oh right, he reminded himself, there's the whole dead already thing. Well, time to effect an escape. "I will try to answer your questions."

The draugr turned around. "Good. We will talk at my cairn." With that the draugr threw Tal over his shoulder, and slid into the earth.

Tal knew he was screaming only because he could feel his throat vibrating. But there was no sound. There's no air to create the reverberations, he realized. None. There's no air to breathe, or hear. Only blackness, the same lifeless black as the draugr's eyes. Tal had known for years he was scared of heights but he'd never thought of himself as claustrophobic. Of course, he'd never been swallowed whole by the earth before.

CHAPTER SEPTUAGINTA QUINQUE

It was Tal's own coughing that finally roused him. The dry wracking coughing that makes your abdominal muscles spasm, and you feel like sooner or later you're going to cough up about a third of your left lung. It felt like he had dust all the way down his windpipe. As he came to, Tal found the muscles of his head and neck had been released and were back under his control, so he started looking around. He was seated in an ornate, gilded chair. He could see it had a black leather seat, with the same leather on the padded armrests and the back. He wasn't tied down, but he was paralyzed except for his head. As he scanned the room he saw dozens of flickering torches throwing patterns of light and shadow on the walls and a high rounded ceiling. Again there was the smell of fish and rendered animal fat, they were not magyk torches. The room locked to be at least several hundred feet in length. Draugr swag was strewn everywhere, most of it in haphazard piles, some of the piles taller than Tal. Gold was casually heaped in dozens of places. Pearls and precious stones, faceted and unfaceted, were laying about the hall, some of them singly, others in gem-encrusted tiaras, necklaces, and bracelets. There were hundreds of weapons as well. More than a couple looked, in the flicker of the torches, to have dried blood on them.

There were even teetering stacks of books, looking like they would topple at the slightest touch.

As Tal finished the sweep to his right, he spotted his friends lined up against the wall of the chamber. They weren't even bound, just sitting on the floor, with their backs against the wall. Motionless. Their eyes were open. Staring without blinking.

The draugr appeared from behind a particularly large mound of hammered gold bracelets and ingots. He saw that Tal was looking at the rest of the Omada. "They're all alive and unharmed. For now. But they're not going anywhere until I release them. Actually, if I release them. Right now they can't see or hear anything either. So, let's get started. Why dost these Folk have a pet human?"

"I'm not a pet," Tal replied indignantly. "I am a member of Omada, and we're one of the Finalist teams in this Tyrning's Hunts."

"Curious," the draugr said. "I didn't think humans were allowed by the Hunts Rules."

"As it wasn't specifically prohibited, it was allowed."

"And your name is in The Book?"

"So I'm told," Tal replied.

"That is of no small interest," the draugr mused. "So you and your playmates have come to steal my treasyre for one of your Hunts. I guess this term must be a Treasyre Hunt."

"No, it's a Scavengyr Hunt. And we weren't trying to steal your treasyre."

"If you are not here to steal, why art thou here?"

"It's kind of a long story that starts with being thrown out of the back of a moving truck."

"Clever. I see what thou dost. Dissemble as you wish, human, it will not stay the running of the sands of your lives. This is a house of the dead, the Recall will not come for you while you are within these walls."

"Fine. I was studying a textbook about draugrs and somehow I ended up directing the Prime Omphalos to send us here."

"Dost thou take me for some fool wight? Clearly thou dost not value your friends' lives. In all the centuries I have been, there has never been a Hunts team come this way. There is but one Omphalos on this plane and it is many days travel away, even for me." The draugr paused a moment, thinking his way through something. He continued, his voice grating in Tal's ears. "Art thou truly a member of a Hunts team?"

"Yes."

"Thou are the first Munedan to ever be admitted to Hunts School?"

"Apparently."

"You arrived at this Realm's most powerful henge."

"It is called the Ring of Brodgar, on the Earth plane."

"The original is on this plane. Brodgar is one of the most powerful henges in all the Realms. Its strength is evidenced by its mirror images in many Realms, including the Earth plane. Still," he mumbled to himself, "it dost not explain how thou summonsed me."

"Trust me, I didn't 'summons' you," Tal replied.

The draugr growled, the sound of rough grade sandpaper being rubbed slowly across even rougher grade sandpaper. "Fool human! Why else would I have left my dwelling? Still, thou art clearly not yet of the undead. How didst thou call me?" The draugr suddenly stopped talking and walked right up to Tal, taking an extremely deep breath. "Ah,…yes. I hadn't looked for it earlier or I would have noticed. Thou art tethered to an undead. Something very unusual."

"I beg your pardon," Tal asked, surprised.

The draugr breathed again, a sound like sand being poured out of a large funnel. "Yes. You have been touched by a shade."

"What?"

"A Revenant."

"Still lost."

"Hast thou been visited in the black of evening by the sliver of a shadow?"

Tal was embarrassed, and scared. How could this thing know about his nightmares? There's really no need to be embarrassed, Tal told himself. The guy is getting ready to eat me for dinner. Which I have to concede is pretty embarrassing in itself. "Yes, I have."

"A faceless creature it was?"

"Yes," Tal replied shakily, as he thought about the specter that had haunted his entire childhood.

"Your face has been given to a Crestfallyn."

That's what Notos was talking about when they came to my house. The Myrddin said something about the Crestfallyn too. Might as well see if I can get some info. "What the hell is a Crestfallyn?"

"They are abominations among the children of the UnFading Spirit."

"Where did they come from?"

"They are the remnants of a team betrayed by their Prime Direction. Dead, though not dead, they seek to be reanimated."

"I get it," Tal replied. "Crestfallyn are zombies."

"No," the draugr replied calmly, "they are not. Zombyes owe fealty to me. Crestfallyn are things that should not be. Their existence is sliced so thin they may even exercise limited magyk on the Earth plane without triggering Alberich's Bane."

"So this Prime's teammates agreed to be sliced and diced?"

"They were not asked. They had bound the contract and their Prime used their oaths against them. It was treachery of the foulest kind."

"And what do I have to do with them?"

"The Crestfallyn are still oath bound to their Prime. They unwillingly do his bidding because he has promised them when he comes into power they shall each have a new existence."

"I get it now. To have a new existence, they have to start with some human's face."

"And that human's life essence."

Even though Tal knew his body was still paralyzed, he felt himself shudder all the way down to his feet. All of these years, he'd been right. The thing existed, it was evil, and it had been planning on killing him.

"The first mortal named in The Book, who is also face-sworn to a Crestfallyn. Strangeness abounds, but strangeness dost not fill my belly. I'm hungry and your friends are food. It's time I got dinner started." The draugr walked about twenty feet away to a fire pit that was located underneath a hole in the ceiling. He began assembling the necessary components for a bonfire.

Tal looked frantically around the room, searching for something, anything that could help him. Nothing, there's nothing. I'm paralyzed anyway. Dang, the draugr must have about a billion dollars worth of treasure lying all around this place. It has everything it could possibly want. "Want," that's the key, Tal thought. I have to be able to give him something he wants, more than he wants to eat us for dinner…and maybe he doesn't have absolutely everything. Sorry, Aurora, I know what you said, but the Omada is my responsibility now, and I have to do whatever it takes. "Fine, but as I look around your quite impressive version of an episode of 'The Hoarders,' I already see that I have something you don't have."

The draugr immediately stopped working on the fire, and turned back toward Tal, with a look that was half-smile and half-sneer. "Ho! You want to treasyre bargain with me, human?"

Tal could tell from the tone of the draugr's voice and the fact he was laser focused on Tal, that treasyre bargaining was something draugrs found of great interest. "Why yes, I believe I do."

"You are wasting my time. My treasyre has been gathered from innumerable planes over hundreds of years. What could you possibly have obtained in your brief span that I don't have?"

"A magyk ring. Good for any three wishes you could possibly make. Well, actually it only has two left in the tank." That did it, Tal thought. He is totally into this, but it's more than merely treasyre bargaining. The draugr wants something badly. Really badly. Something he hasn't been able to get for himself.

The draugr took a couple of steps toward Tal. "Humans are Children of the Divine Spark. You have no magyk of your own. Where wouldst thou obtain such a ring?"

He doesn't believe me, Tal thought, but he's interested. Totally interested. "The Lady Aurora."

"What say thee?" the draugr exclaimed. "How canst a human possibly have met a Principe?"

Tal interrupted the draugr, "Arthrys took me to meet the Myrddin who introduced me to Aurora, and she gave me the ring."

The draugr appeared almost dazed by the news. No, not dazed. Surprised. There's something else to his expression, Tal thought, almost like he's hopeful about something. "Arthrys was made Archon after I was made draugr. Before magyk was forbidden on the Earth plane," the draugr whispered almost to himself. "Which made it impossible for me to save her." He turned his attention back to Tal. "If this is true, why haven't you used a wish to escape?"

Tal thought about lying and decided against it. "I have to turn the ring when I make the wish and before I realized how much trouble we were in, you paralyzed me."

"Now thou dost smell of honesty," the draugr replied. "Your entire story, a Dust Child who knows Arthrys and Myrddin and the Lady Aurora smells of honesty."

"But you accused me of lying earlier," Tal said.

"I'm undead, not stupid," the draugr replied, as he walked a few paces to his right, and sat down on a much larger, and more bejeweled version of Tal's chair. "The ring is not something you may treasyre bargain. The ring's magyk will not work for me. It was a gyft freely given from Aurora to you."

Tal would have slumped in his chair if he hadn't been paralyzed. That was all he had. There was nothing else he could use. Think, Tal, think. Got it. "Okay, I understand that. However, if you would agree to let me and my friends go, I could use one of the wishes on your behalf."

This time the draugr almost purred. Well, it would have been a purr if the sound hadn't been made by a ten-foot tall dead guy who sounded like he gargled with all of the sand from a quarter-mile stretch of beachfront property. The purring stopped as the draugr's facial lines fell. "It will not work. Magyk wishes must be made by consent, free of duress or coercion."

Tal's heart sank. He really didn't have a bargaining chip, no leverage to save his friends. He never would have guessed when this school year started he'd end up as draugr fast food.

Then unexpectedly the draugr began walking toward him. "We may still be able to treasyre bargain, Dust Child."

"With what? You know when I'm telling the truth or a lie, and I'm telling you my ring is the only thing I own you might trade me for."

"Mayhaps we may trade for treasyre you don't presently possess, but which you could obtain."

Hope leapt within Tal. "Anything. I'll go get anything to trade."

"Not anything, human. Someone. Her name is Aislinn. The tale is long in the telling, and if we are going to come to a satisfactory trade, your friends must hear my story as well." The draugr snapped his fingers. Tal saw Borras, and the others start blinking and moving their heads.

"What the Five-Hells?" Notos demanded groggily.

"Silence," the draugr demanded. "This one and I are trying to determine whether we can treasyre bargain to save your lives."

Notos's eyes got as big around as silver dollars, but he closed his mouth.

The draugr sat back in his chair. It's a throne, Tal realized. Someone's priceless throne and it's only one of a gazillion pieces of treasyre in this place. The draugr sat still for several minutes. He's having to compose himself, Tal thought. This story, it's difficult for him. It has great significance, and he wants to tell it correctly.

And then the draugr began.

CHAPTER SEPTUAGINTA SEX

"More than fifteen hundred years ago, I lived on the Earth plane. I was human, like you. My name was Arnfinn Skullcrusher and I was the eldest son of Ragnar, first Earl of Orkney, vassal to Erik Goldenhair, King of what is now called Norway. The King gave my father his title and lands because of his loyal service to the crown through many decades of war. I was my father's heir and War Chief."

"Who were you War Chief against?" Tal asked.

"Drest, High King of the Pettr, and the many tribes who swore him allegiance."

"The Pettr?" This time it was Dysi who had gotten the courage to speak.

"It means 'the painted people.' It was another name for the Picts of the Earth plane," Borras replied.

The draugr continued. "The Pict women fought alongside the men and they were every one of them just as fierce. During one of our skirmishes we captured Drest's daughter—Aislinn. Odin's ravens, but that woman could fight." He paused for a moment with the faintest tic of a smile at the memory.

"She maimed twelve of my best warriors before I knocked her unconscious with the flat of my blade. My father held her for ransom, and I was charged with seeing to her safekeeping. At first I left the food and water with her in silence. She was a royal hostage—no more, no less. After several weeks I started exchanging a few words with her, and after some time the words became sentences. Sentences became paragraphs, and one day I found myself looking forward to my minutes with her each day. We taught each other about our cultures and about our families. We talked about things dark and light and we laughed. There had been scant cause for laughter in my life before her."

"The day came when I found I could not leave because I could not stop talking to her. That was the day—for the first time in my life—that I felt everything. Where before I had sensed somewhat, now it was everything. Her skin smelled of the earth, freshly bathed by the spring shower. The touch of her mouth on mine burned hotter than the sun's fire at its zenith on Lammas Day. She moved as lithely as the leaves of autumn in their waltz with the zephyr. And when she gazed upon me, her countenance sparkled brighter than Thiassi's Eyes on a cloudless winter's eve."

"You fell in love," Anatolia said softly.

"Aye, and Aislinn felt the same. Drest continued the war for some time longer. But as we had his only daughter hostage, he ultimately had no choice but to agree to a ceasefire between our peoples. My father was able to convince King Erik that both his security interests and his treasury would be bettered if the Norse and the Picts agreed to live in peace and share the land. Subsequent negotiations led to a treaty.

"The day of the signing ceremony came. I was there to sign on behalf of my father and the king and Aislinn for her father. There was to be a celebration feast afterward. It was a special day for Aislinn and I, because after the treaty of peace between our peoples was signed, our fathers had agreed we could announce our intentions to be wed. We were unaware that Harald RedHand, one of my father's chief captains, had turned traitor and allied with the Finmen."

"Finmen?" Tal asked.

Borras responded. "They are Folk who love war more than any other. They once spent much time pillaging humans, before Arthrys outlawed magyk on Earth. Since then, they have been unable to travel to Earth plane and remain mostly in their Realm of Finfolkaheem."

"Aye," the draugr said as he continued his story, "they loved to fight. We didst not know about the Folk. In our ignorance, we believed the Finmen to be merely fierce human warriors dressed like animals. It was not uncommon battle strategy at that time, to instill fear in one's enemies."

"During the ceremony the traitors attacked. Harald and his men slaughtered my unarmed honor guard, while the Finmen attacked me. I was armed with only a ceremonial sword, and still killed more than a score of the water bastards. Aislinn, who— Freyr bless her—was never without a long knife hidden somewhere, killed another ten. That woman could fight like the Morrígan herself. Wave after wave of Finmen had at us, but in the end there wast simply too many. One of them thrust his sword straight through my belly. After I was down, the coward Harald put two arrows in my back. They proceeded to kill every one of my clan there that day. Everyone—except for me. And Aislinn. They knew my wounds were mortal, and that I would suffer for many days from my torn entrails. They deliberately denied me a warrior's death. To further shame me they propped me up against a stump to watch as they defiled every one of my men, rendering them unrecognizable, so the Valkyries would not know them to take them to Valhalla. Apparently, Harald had promised Aislinn to the Finmen chieftain as his reward. I saw Harald drag her away screaming. She was trying as hard as she could to claw his eyes out. He threw her into a skiff with a waiting Finman, and the two of them rowed her across the water to the Isle of Eynhallow. As I passed out, I saw Eynhallow disappear into the mist. Taking Harald, and Aislinn, to a place that mortals cannot find. Where I could not go."

"Rat bastards," Notos interjected.

The draugr took a deep breath before continuing. He was obviously having a difficult time retelling the story. "I don't know how long I slept, but I woke to the sweet taste of fresh water. Someone had dampened a rag, and was squeezing water into my mouth, a few drops at a time. When I could finally open my eyes, I saw it was the captain of Drest's advance guard. A couple of hours later, Drest himself arrived. He fed me a bowl of warm broth, as his men prepared funeral pyres for the fallen, both Norse and Pict. I told him about Harald and the Finmen and about Aislinn disappearing into the mist of Eynhallow. He wept. The High King of the Picts, perhaps the greatest warrior who had ever lived in those islands, fell to his knees and wept."

"He had his healer dress my wounds. They were fatal. I knew it and Drest knew it. I told him I would refuse to accompany the Valkyries until I saw Aislinn safely home, and until I had my full measure of vengeance against Harald RedHand. It was then Drest told me of an ancient Pict ritual. A dark, terrible ceremony that had been banished from use by his people for hundreds of turns of the sun. It was a ceremony that had been created to punish a man in the most horrible way possible—to deprive his soul of its opportunity to move on to eternal reward. A punishment designed to be unending, to punish a man for all eternity. The ceremony could turn a human into a dead, yet undead, creature.

"A draugr," Tal said.

"Yes, human. Though that is the Norse name, not that of the Picts. I swore to Drest that if he could find a way to help me, I would never rest until Aislinn was returned to the mortal lands, and my family's revenge unleashed on Harald. Drest urged me not to do it, but I was unrelenting in my pleas. He finally agreed and sent runners to tell the priests at Maes Howe we were coming and to begin their preparations for the ritual. Then his men placed me on a litter, and we began our journey.

"Maes Howe?" Anatolia asked.

It was Notos who answered. "It is a cairn. A burial mound built centuries before the Picts arrived in the Orkneys."

"How did you know that?" Tal asked.

"Because it is a place of the dead," Notos replied. "Can't you feel the death all around us? We are in this plane's Maes Howe now. He brought us here to kill us."

Tal noticed the draugr staring strangely at Notos for a moment. He walked over and smelled him before resuming his seat on his throne. It seemed to Tal that the draugr realized something about Notos. Whatever it was, he didn't share it with the rest of them. "Drest said his goodbyes and left me at the threshold of Maes Howe. He would not take me inside. There are apparently things even High Kings fear. The priests found me, and carried me inside.

"They told me about the procedures involved in their ritual. I was told it failed frequently, that it would only transform me if I held fast to a passion stronger than death's summons. The emotion didn't matter, it could be anger or revenge, love or hate, but it had to be something I could clasp tighter than death's pull would be upon me. They told me that if it worked—if I awoke—I would be undead until such time—if ever—that my passion was satisfied. I assented and they began."

"First, they bound me head to toe in white cloth. I couldn't move even a fraction of an inch. My eyes were propped open with splinters of bone. They withdrew most of my blood, mixed it with spelled charcoal, and drew glyphs upon my shroud with it. While they did these foul things, they muttered coarse incantations for what seemed like hours. When they were through, they left me alone, and they sealed me in the crypt. In the blackness of that Hell. Alone. The only sound was my screaming. I was screaming because of the indescribable burning as the poison from my gut wound ravaged my body. Screaming, because every time my heart beat, Aislinn's absence caused my chest to ache worse than the fire burning in my body. And I was screaming because my hatred for the traitor Harald gnawed at my mind without surcease. Finally, it was all too much, and I fell into a coma.

"When I awoke I was human no longer. Never again would I be Arnfinn. I was draugr."

"Have you seen her since then?" Dysi asked.

"No," the draugr replied. "For more than a thousand years I have watched day and night. Maes Howe exists in many Realms, including the Earth plane but not the plane of Finfolkaheem. I wait below ground each day, and at night walk sentry on many shores. Waiting. For Harald to make a mistake, or for Aislinn to escape."

"Why don't you go get her?" Borras asked.

"Eynhallow exists only on its own plane, except when temporarily made visible by the Finmen in other Realms. With Alberich's Bane it may not now appear on the Earth plane. They also know that even though I may swim through stone and rock, I may not cross living water."

"I don't mean to be indelicate, but it's been hundreds of years..." Tal said.

"Aislinn and Harald are human. They will not age as long as they are in the Realm that holds Eynhallow. They aren't even really truly alive there—it is not their proper plane."

"So you've brought us to your home?" Anatolia asked.

"Yes."

"Wait," Borras exclaimed. "You said this barrow is Maes Howe?"

"'Tis so."

"Then you are the Hogboon of Maes Howe."

"Aye, for these many centuries past."

"Hogboon?" Tal asked. "I'm guessing that means you're not any old common draugr, are you?"

"No, mortal, I am not. I am Helblad Clawfoot, Jarl of all the Draugrs and Wights of every Realm." Helblad snapped his fingers and growled a few words Tal didn't understand. "I have changed my mind. You and your friends are free to go."

CHAPTER SEPTUAGINTA SEPTEM

"What?" Tal asked, as he felt all of his muscles return to the control of his brain. He looked over at the others, who were cautiously beginning to stand and stretch. "After all of this, you're simply letting us go?"

"I find I have lost my appetite. Go thee quickly, before my hunger returns."

Tal saw Borras, and the others start shuffling towards him. As they did, his mind began whirling. Because of him the Omada only had one scavengyr piece, and this was their last opportunity to score a weapon. We're in last place, so our one piece isn't worth enough points to move to the next Hunt. Without a weapon we don't stand a chance of surviving the remaining Hunts even if we do move forward. Regardless of whether I interfered with the destination Realm, the Prime Omphalos sent us here because there is at least one qualifying piece within our original time window. Well, to quote my old friend Gas Pump No. Unus, "worlds depend on me." "No!" he declared.

"What?" Helblad asked, clearly taken aback.

Although his friends were still befuddled from the draugr's magyk they started making guttural noises that indicated displeasure with Tal's statement. Looking at them, Tal said, "Y'all are going to have to trust me on this one. This is the choice that needs to be made. It is the only way for Omada to 'Seek the Center'." He then turned back to Helblad. "I said no." Then more formally, "Quint of Omada desires to treasyre bargain with the Hogboon of Maes Howe. Unless his Highness is worried a Dust Child might get the better of him in a bargain."

Helblad reared his head back and guffawed. His laughter, as it echoed off the walls of the howe, sounded like a rockslide. "Máni's Light, I hadst forgotten the hubris of being human." He gave Tal the barest hint of a bow. "As thou wishest, mortal. I will treasyre bargain. Let us begin. What seekest thou in the bargain?"

"A weapon..." Tal began.

"Not much of a bargain. Tis a simple thing," Helblad replied. "I will save you the trouble of looking and will trade you the finest weapon in my house. It is my favorite. It earned me my human nickname—Skullcrusher." He leaned over and picked up the handle of the battle mace propped against his throne. The thing had about twenty small spikes sticking out of a round ball. The spike ball was attached to a two-foot chain, which was attached to the handle. The spike ball had a rough, mottled surface of black and dark maroon.

I don't even want to know what all the dried stuff is on the mace, Tal thought, and I gotta figure out how to smuggle some Purell into Hunts School. "Thank you Hogboon," Tal replied. "Skullcrusher is a noble weapon leaping forth from legend and would normally make a more than fair trade. I must, however, decline your generous offer. We require a sword."

With a wave of his left arm, Helblad indicated there were dozens of blades scattered throughout Maes Howe available for trade. Tal was quick to respond. "Thank you, Your Lordship, but no. The blade I desire to trade for must be one of only eleven blades in all of the Realms."

"Aha, thou hast made the bargaining much more interesting Dust Child," Helblad replied. "And you have upped the demand pryce. You have leave to search the entire treasyre of Maes Howe."

Notos interrupted. "This is futile, Quint. We didn't even Journey to an Omphalos. If Helblad will still let us go, we need to go."

The draugr nodded his acquiescence while looking back at Tal. "Thou art human and dost not fully realize the implications of bargaining with the undead. There will be no further warnings."

Tal took a moment and rethought his logic one more time. "No, Notos. The Prime Omphalos wouldn't have sent us here unless a qualifying weapon could be acquired."

Borras interrupted the conversation. "I agree with you Quint, but we are running short on time before the Recalling."

"What do we have to lose by looking until time runs out?" Dysi asked.

"Your lives," Helblad responded.

Tal's subconscious had kicked it into high gear. His mind was proffering a number of apparently stray factoids. *There are henges that exist on more than one plane. He said Maes Howe itself has a physical manifestation in many Realms. Helblad is the Hogboon of Maes Howe. The Hogboon of Maes Howe has a title…and subjects.* "Wait a minute!" Tal exclaimed. "Helblad, you said you are Jarl of all of the draugrs and wights?"

"'Tis so."

"And does your suzerainty extend over more than one Realm?"

"Aye, I am the Hogboon. Save only the Folk of the Five-Hells Realm, all of the undead on every plane owe me their fealty."

That's interesting, Tal thought. Five-Hells is an actual Realm. "Would all of the undead who owe you allegiance come at your command?"

"They must obey a call from their liege."

"How would they get here without the Prime

Omphalos?" Anatolia asked.

"Because they are undead Creatures, and this is Maes Howe," Notos promptly answered. Tal noticed that earned him another glance from Helblad.

"Tis so. If they are on a plane with a Maes Howe, the undead must come at my command," Helblad confirmed.

"Quint, what's the plan?" Borras asked.

"Without even wanting to know what other kinds of undead there might be, draugrs and wights are primarily Northern European plane Creatures," Tal replied. "The Weapons textbook described the histories of the eligible blades in great detail. Six or seven of them had their origins in Northern European planes—not counting Excalibur of course."

"Of course, we're not counting Excalibur," Notos remarked snidely. "Excalibur is retired. Because Arthrys has it. Now."

"Quiet, Notos, we're on the clock," Borras said. Turning back to Tal he said, "So, you're thinking the undead on Maes Howe planes should be asked to look through their respective treasyres and bring with them their most powerful swords?"

"Right."

"Brilliant. It's both an offensive and a defensive play. If one of the other teams is Journeying looking for a weapon they will all be here, at least for a little while."

"That is what we ask for our side of the bargain," Tal said to Helblad.

"And if I agree to this and thou dost not find one of the named swords?"

Tal put his finger to lips as he thought the possibilities through. "As I am asking you to trade for a contingency, then if the contingency is not fulfilled, I will consider the bargain to have been honored."

"That is an acceptable condition," Helblad said with the faintest hint of a grin.

"Your turn," Tal said. "What do you propose to treasyre

bargain in return?"

"You will return Aislinn safely to the Maes Howe on the Earth plane before the coronation of the new Archon."

CHAPTER SEPTUAGINTA OCTO

"Five-Hells," Notos exclaimed.

"Quint," Dysi said frantically. "Quint, look at me." Tal turned to her. "Quint, you cannot go any further with this bargain."

"She's right," Anatolia added. "Let's leave and wait outside for the Recalling."

Tal looked at his four teammates. Both Borras and Notos were leaving the decision in his hands. Tal turned back to address Helblad. "You mean by the actual coronation ceremony of the new Archon."

"That would be the bargain," Helblad confirmed.

"Or else what?" Tal asked.

"There is only one meaning of 'or else,' when you treasyre bargain with the undead," Helblad replied. "It means you forfeit your lives to me."

Tal thought about everything that had occurred so far in this crazy adventure. About how catastrophic it would be for all mankind if the Släkt won, about how he'd maybe cost Borras and the Omada their shot at winning. He thought about his Mom and Pell, his brothers, about Myrddin, and Arthrys. About Emet, Elle, and Väst. About Perun and Piras and all of the Creatures he'd met. He even thought about the Gas Pumps and the Air Hose. "I can't do it," he finally replied.

"I thought that wouldst be the case. I am disappointed that we shall not bargain. You and your clan are free to leave."

"You misunderstand me, Hogboon. I cannot accept the bargain you proposed. I will not gamble with my friends' lives. They didn't offer to trade. I did."

This time Helblad smiled. "I find your counter-bargain acceptable, Quint of Omada. This treasyre bargain is a matter of honor between me and thee. One treasyre bargain. One life. Yours."

Tal was pretty sure it was Ana who gasped and Dysi who whimpered "No," but he couldn't be sure because he was staring directly into Helblad's undead-dead-as-a-doorknob black eyes. Without blinking, without flinching, Tal replied, "I consent. Do you?"

Helblad stood, walked over to Tal, bent over at the waist, and stuck out his hand, "Yes."

As Tal shook the draugr's hand he noticed it felt like marble. Not just the hardness, the cold as well. He's like an animated block of stone. "The contract is bound," Helblad declared.

Helblad walked back over to his throne and picked up a cloth bag at its feet. He took a ball of something out of the bag and walked over to each of the Omada in turn. He gave each of them a semi-handful of a slimy wad of distilled ick. "Put this in your ears," Helblad demanded.

"What is it?" Tal asked.

"Sea-slug shite," Helblad replied.

"Pardon?" Tal asked.

The color had fled from Dysi's face. "He said we are supposed to put snail shit in our ears."

"Oh, hell, no!" Notos responded.

"If thou dost wish to retain thy sanity during the Calling of the Undead, thou shalt do as I command," Helblad responded.

Tal took a deep breath, tore his goo in half, and suppressed his gag reflex as he crammed it into both his ears. Tal watched as his teammates followed suit.

Helblad closed his eyes, and began a similar high-pitched keening to that which had originally put them all on the ground at the Ring of Brodgar. Within minutes, beings started rising from the floor. Large, small, male, female, some androgynous. Tal hadn't realized how big the great hall in this plane's Maes Howe was until he saw the torchlight reflected off of hundreds of creatures carrying several thousand burnished blades.

"I have summoned ye here to treasyre bargain with your Sovereign," Helblad's voice echoed through the Howe.

A generalized murmuring began immediately. Tal realized they were lucky the wads stuffed in their ears suppressed most of the noise. He was pretty sure the crunching and cracking and grinding would have driven him bat shit crazy within minutes. Or maybe snail shit crazy was more apropos in this situation. Based upon the snippets he could hear and understand, it was unheard of for the Hogboon—the Guardian of the Treasyre of Maes Howe—to allow the lesser undead an opportunity to acquire any of the fabled Maes Howe treasyre.

One voice spoke above the rest, "What bargain propose ye?"

"Whichever of you has the most powerful sword—as determined by this Child of the Dust," with that Helblad gestured at Tal, "I will bargain with that one." If grit could murmur, that was the noise Tal heard spread through the barrow, as the word was passed there were living beings present in Maes Howe.

"The most powerful sword is a unique object," one particularly filthy looking wight said. He had a little bit of a lisp, but Tal figured he was doing the best he could with only the one mandible, the lower one. "Lord or no, you have no right to use our oaths to force a trade upon your vassals." Tal heard quite a few grunts in assent from the mob.

"I impose nothing. This is a true treasyre bargain and

consent must be freely given. I am willing to offer something in trade clearly more valuable than any magyk blade," Helblad countered.

"Such as?" Mono-Jaw asked.

"This," Helblad said as he reached up and opened a hinge on the ball at the end of the battle mace. Tal saw him pull something out.

Whatever it is, it must be off the chart valuable for Helblad to keep it that close to him, Tal thought. He has innumerable piles of gold and jewels laying around. As Tal watched, Helblad opened his hand and started unrolling a small ball. It looks like string was Tal's first thought. No, it looks like it is a gold chain, except the gold is shining with every color of the rainbow. That's it, the best description of it is rainbow gold. Actually there were two separate pieces of the rainbow gold chain. Tal looked at his teammates. To a person they were all standing there with their mouths wide open.

"I offer in bargain one of these two pieces of Gleipnir," Helblad said, "stolen from the Asgard plane centuries ago." A hush fell over the crowd. Filthy used his disgustingly filthy hand across his equally filthy jaw to wipe away the brown drool now dripping from his just as filthy chin.

"I know that one," Tal whispered to Borras. "Gleipnir was the chain forged to keep Fenris bound until Ragnarok."

Helblad continued. "Dwarf-forged, its strength is without equal, as it was made from three impossible things. The noise a cat makes when it takes a step, the roots of a rock, and the breath of a fish."

"A fair trade," Tal heard from the far end of the hall. "Aye, a most worthy treasyre bargain," came another voice. "I will consent to that trade," cried another.

"If thou thinkest you bear a weapon worthy to bargain, get in line," Helblad instructed. For over an hour Tal and Helblad stood at the front of a receiving line, which included all make and manner of draugr and wight, as it inched forward one being at a time. With each new blade, the owner described its attributes to Helblad and Tal.

By the time the last sword was examined, the Omada could see Tal's plan had worked brilliantly. Of the eleven eligible blades, two of them lay gleaming before Helblad: Skofnung and Fragarach.

"Which should we pick?" Tal asked Helblad.

"I can be of no help. I have had no personal experience with either of those swords and know them only from legend."

"Guys?" Tal asked his teammates.

"What's the number one strength and weakness of each?" Anatolia asked.

"Any wound inflicted by 'The Answerer' causes death," Notos replied.

"What's its weakness?" Tal asked him.

"Doesn't have one," Notos said. "Kills everybody it cuts."

"That is its weakness, Notos," Dysi said. "We are charged not just to win, but to 'Seek the Center'. More often than not Fragarach is a murderer."

"And Skofnung?" Tal asked.

This time it was Borras who answered. "Skofnung has twelve berserkers magykally imbedded within it. One of whom is Bödvar Bjarki." He evidently saw Tal's puzzled look. "Bjarki is the most famous were-bear of any known plane."

"Its weakness?" Anatolia asked.

"Skofnung's hilt must never see the light of day," Borras replied.

"Or what?" Dysi asked.

"Legend does not provide the answer," Borras responded. "It may simply lose its power, or perhaps the magyk is unwound and the berserkers' spirits will be set free. Some texts say that if sunlight touches the hilt of the sword, Skofnung will turn upon its wielder."

"We need to make a decision. Fast," Dysi said.

"Maybe not," Tal replied.

"What you got in mind, Quint?" Borras asked.

"As Notos continues to remind me, we're down one piece."

"Don't forget the part where it's all your fault we're down one piece," Notos added.

"Right," Tal said. "Well, the HuntsMistress said we'd need a major miracle…"

"I see," Borras said, smiling as he caught up with Tal's thinking. "We take them both and call one of them our Wyld Thing."

"It's brilliant," Anatolia said.

"There's no need to get crazy," Notos added with his customary scowl. "The human already cost us a piece, so that would only get him back to even."

"Two of the swords? You know that would be much better than even, Notos," Dysi interjected. A scowl was the only acknowledgment she got.

Tal turned back to Helblad, "Our bargain is for only one blade, your Lordship."

"Indeed, it is," Helblad confirmed.

"It would be unfair for one of us to try to unilaterally change the deal to their advantage."

"That be so. It would dishonor the bargain," Helblad confirmed.

"Agreed. Which is why I am voluntarily giving you my consent to bargain two swords to me instead of one."

"What?" Helblad asked, the downward diagonal shape of his eyebrows indicating he was perplexed, with more than a smidgeon of anger mixed in.

"My bargain with you is to bring Aislinn back to you by the time of the new Archon's coronation ceremony," Tal said.

"Indeed."

"If I die prior to that time the Omada will have received the benefit of the bargain but you will never receive anything for your trade."

"Had not considered that possibility, but tis the bargain I have made," Helblad replied.

"Any change that increases my chances of surviving the year increases the probability of you receiving the benefit of our bargain."

"Tis so."

"My chances of surviving are greatly increased if I have access to the magyk of both Skofnung and Fragarach."

"Aye, I can see that," Helblad replied.

"So, because you are the greatest Lord of the Undead that has ever lived—then died, then been undead—I know that you would never ask me to modify our bargain exclusively for your benefit."

"Tis true."

"That is why—without you having to ask to modify our bargain—I am offering you the opportunity to bargain us both of the swords even though it gives you an advantage you do not possess under our original terms." Tal smiled broadly and stuck out his hand. "I consent. Do you?"

Helblad finally realized he'd been snookered. His chuckle sounded like he was snorting a handful of pea gravel. "Norns above, I consent. I shall be much displeased if I have to eat you, human. Much displeased indeed." He turned to the owners of the two swords, handing the piece of Gleipnir to the wight who possessed Fragarach. He then turned to the creature that owned Skofnung, it turned out to be OneJaw. "Kieklak, as treasyre bargain for your blade, I will offer you your choice of any item from the entirety of the treasyre of Maes Howe. Do you consent?"

Tal could tell from Kieklak's broad smile that Helblad was offering him a lopsided deal.

"I consent," Kieklak replied.

Helblad nodded in return, and then addressed the assembled host. "Thank you, my loyal subjects. This audience is ended, and thou art free to return to your cairns and barrows."

As Tal watched, the hundreds of creatures dematerialized into the floor of the chamber.

When they were alone again Helblad said, "You may remove the muting from your ears."

It took Tal a couple of tries to get it all. The wad had congealed into tacky ear jam. After they all complied, Tal said, "Okay, Hogboon. Time to fess up. You knew we needed a sword and that Skullcrusher wouldn't work, didn't you?"

"Mayhaps," Helblad replied grinning. "The living dost not pay attention to what they say in front of the dead. I might or might not have known this term's hunt was a Scavengyr Hunt, and that the weapons category might have been limited."

"I knew it," Tal replied. "You outsmarted me. You were never going to let us have those two pieces of Gleipnir you kept in your mace as part of our bargain."

"'Tis so. Undead and brain dead are not synonyms," Helblad replied. "Our business is concluded. It is time for your return."

"We're not sure that's going to happen," Borras replied. "We arrived at a henge, not an Omphalos, so I'm not sure we are tethered for the Recall."

"As you are living, I cannot myself take you back to the Earth Realm, but once you are back where you started, the Recall magyk will find you and take you home."

"So back to Brodgar?" Tal asked.

"Yes," Helblad confirmed.

"Through the dirt?" Tal asked. Helblad nodded. He then bent down, picked up Skofnung and handed it to Borras. After that he retrieved Fragarach and handed it to Notos. "This is particularly fitting don't you think?" he asked Notos.

"What's that supposed to mean," Tal asked.

"Nothing," Notos replied, glancing over at Helblad. "Let's get out of here."

"It is time," Helblad announced. With that he grabbed each of them one at a time, for the terrifying trip through the earth, starting with Borras and finishing with Tal.

When they were all assembled at the henge, Helblad walked to each of Tal's teammates and breathed on them in turn. As they passed out he positioned them in a heap so that each person had at least one body part touching every other person in the pile, and touching the largest stone. Helblad then motioned to Tal to walk over to the group.

"What did you do to them?" Tal asked.

"Didst thou not experience great pain in your Journey?"

"Every time so far," Tal responded. "I think it hit the others even harder this time."

"I sensed as much when first we met," Helblad replied. "There is something different about you and the Omphalos. Their lives are much at risk when you direct the Journey. I have rendered them unconscious to better their chance of surviving the Recall. I will do the same for you when the Recall begins."

"Helblad—I'm going to be honest with you. I don't have a clue as to how I'm going to hold up my end of our bargain.

"Thou be overmodest, Quint of Omada. In all of history you are the first Munedan to attend Hunts School, the first to use the Omphalos, the first to treasyre bargain with the undead. The UnFading Spirit has blessed you with many gifts. If you are going to survive the Hunts and fulfill our bargain, you must use them all."

"Umm, last time I checked everyone else has magyk. I pretty much got nothing—no super powers."

Helblad placed one of his blue-black hands on Tal's shoulder. "You may not have Folk magyk at your command, but She has given you two of her greatest gifts—a clever mind and a giving heart. If such were not the case, Child of Dust, you and your friends would be roasting on a spit on the floor of Maes Howe at this very moment."

"Not really feeling the love, big guy," Tal said smiling. "My feet are starting to tingle. It's happening."

"Remember, Folk are like humans in that they assume that if someone looks different, or talks different, they are somehow inferior beings. You will not be perceived as a threat, until it is too late. Use your gifts."

"I'll try," Tal replied.

"You must return Aislinn to me by the bargained date. Thou mayest not return to this place, Quint of Omada, until thou art ready to fulfill the trade."

"Or else?" Tal added.

"The bargain will be accelerated, and I am honor bound by the bargain. Art thou ready?"

"Should I click my heels three times?" Tal asked nervously.

"I am unaware of that human tradition, but yes, if thou art comfortable in thy masculinity, and if it helps you focus, thou mayest do so. Art thou ready?"

"Ready," Tal replied.

Helblad leaned forward and shot a breath of fetid air up Tal's nostrils at about a hundred miles a second. Tal felt like a boxcar full of green boogers was heading the wrong direction up his sinuses. Right before they would have detrained, he mercifully passed out, his last thought being about the five of them safely back, and touching the Prime Omphalos.

CHAPTER SEPTUAGINTA NOVEM

The oxygen-sucking emotion in homeroom this morning was their old companion, tension, but today excitement had also been added to the mix. Tal realized he himself was about as adrenaline-fueled nervous as he'd ever been in his life. He could only imagine what all of the others in the room must be feeling. They'd been working toward this moment for a hundred years. Their families, their Realms were counting on them. The fate of worlds depended upon which five of the remaining eight teams made the cut for the next Hunt.

The class bell gonged right as Ms. Empousa stomped into the room. There were no greetings this morning, no introductory comments, nothing. She walked straight over to the blackboard, and wrote in all capital letters, "FINAL TEAM RANKING - SCAVENGYR HUNT TERM" before turning back toward the class. "Not a word, not a single word, until after I am through writing. If I hear anything, out of any of you, your team will be demoted one position. Got it?"

Tal saw nods from every head in the room. Tiny, small nods. No one was taking a chance on inadvertently making any noise.

The HuntsMistress turned back to the board and began writing: 1. Ayllu, 2. Omada,…

Tal hadn't realized he was about to vocalize his joy until Borras's hand clamped down on his right quad so hard it momentarily banished any thought other than huge immediate pain. It worked because the moment passed and Tal regained his self-control. He smile-grimaced at Borras to let him know he was good and the steel clamp was released. We did it, Tal thought, the two swords catapulted us from last to second.

Ms. Empousa continued writing on the board—3. Pleme, 4. Kabila, 5. Shuzoku, 6. Släkt, 7. Bùluò, 8. Hak'éí.

When the HuntsMistress finished and turned back toward the class, the excitement finally released into an excited babble. Dysi and Ana hugged each other, Borras was beaming, and Notos momentarily forgot to scowl. Tal was doing the Snoopy happy dance inside. Need a major miracle? You best talk to Quint, because he's the man. Suck it, Släkt! Squinty, you are out of the game. You just got your ticket punched back to your home plane, the rest of the known universe is safe from the likes of you.

Then it hit him. Väst. She's no longer a competitor. We can be together every day if we want. We don't have to sneak around. It's completely okay now if I go ahead and finish falling in love with her.

Tal looked across the room toward the Släkt table. Odd, Nord was smiling. They're in sixth-place and out of the Hunts. Done. Finis. Kaput. What could he possibly be smiling about? And Väst is deliberately looking down, refusing to make eye contact with me. What the hell?

"I am releasing you early. The top five teams may return to their team rooms where they will find winner's prizes for each team member. Those teams will have the rest of the day off to celebrate and heal. The losers will first return to their team rooms and then to their dormitory suites to clear out all of their personal belongings. You are no longer Hunts competitors, you are losers. Your team names are dissolved, and you will return to being known by your original student identification numbers. Starting tomorrow you will report to non-Hunts curriculum classes to finish out the school year."

Ouch, Tal thought. Somebody needs to give the HuntsMistress the old "it's all about the journey speech." Out of the corner of his eye he saw Mitt's hand shoot up into the air.

"Yes?" Ms. Empousa asked.

"As the sixth-place team we claim challenge pursuant to Rule 15 of the Hunts Rules."

That does it, Tal decided. I'm getting a copy of those Rules before the end of the day. Wait a minute, now Ms. Empousa is smiling. If she likes it, it must be bad. He looked at Borras who gave him the smallest head shake to let Tal know he needed to remain still.

Ms. Empousa walked behind her desk, to her ledger. "Rule 15.1 of the Hunts Rules allows the first runner up of any Hunt the ability to issue Combat Challenge for a roster spot. If such challenge is made, Rule 15.2 allows any other lower ranked teams to also enter the contest, making the Combat Challenge a battle royale.

Combat Challenge? Could be worse, Tal thought. The Släkt might or might not weasel back into this thing, which sucks for Shuzoku, but we're firmly in second place. Repeat Snocpy happy dance.

"Does Bùluò wish to enter?" Ms. Empousa asked.

Tal saw Zhong look at the Släkt, particularly at Nord, who was practically slavering he was so happy about the challenge. Zhong then leaned over and he and the rest of his team conferred. Tal heard some snippets of a heated conversation and there were some aggressive hand gestures by Bei, their Second Prime. Finally, Zhong looked up at Ms. Empousa and shook his head no.

"The Bùluò decline. Hak'éí?"

The Hak'éí had used the time to confer so they were ready with their response. Ulh-Ne-Ih lifted his right fist and pointed his thumb down.

"The Hak'éí decline as well," she confirmed, before walking back over to the blackboard and erasing both the Bùluò and Hak'éí team names. She then pivoted back to the class. "As we have additional Hunts matters to discuss, the losers need to pick up their books and leave immediately. I'll have your tables removed promptly after this class is over." The members of both teams, shoulders uniformly lowered, complied with her directions and shuffled out the door.

Damn that bitch is harsh, Tal thought. Seems like those squads gave it up awful easy, though. After a hundred years of hard work and with the leadership of the known universe at stake it seems like both teams would have chosen to stay and play. I mean after everything that's already happened, what's a bloody nose and some bruised knuckles?

"Shuzoku," the HuntsMistress announced. Chuusin and his crew turned their full attention to her. "Your winners' prizes will be removed from your team room as will your feast. You haven't earned them yet. Please..."

"HuntsMistress!"

Holy hell, somebody interrupted Ms. Empousa. She's going to skin them alive. No really, Tal told himself, they probably do actually skin people here.

"What is it Släkt?"

"Our challenge is not issued to Shuzoku, HuntsMistress. It's to Omada," Mitt stated.

"Five-Hells," Notos blurted out before Borras could get him back under control.

"We've checked the rules and precedent, and it is our right," Mitt concluded.

"Looks like you're winners after all, Shuzoku," Ms. Empousa said. When she saw the relief on the Shuzoku faces she added, "For now anyway." Then she turned to the Omada table, "Omada, the winners' prizes will be removed from your team room as well as the special celebration feast. Instead of taking the day off you are now required to spend the day making strategy decisions and choosing a Champion for the Combat Challenge. Choose well. It is, of course, a fight to the death."

"To the death," and "what the hell," kept repeating themselves in Tal's mind as he picked his stuff up and followed Borras out of the classroom.

CHAPTER OCTOGINTA

"It doesn't make any sense," Notos growled for about the tenth time since they'd arrived at their team room a couple of hours ago. "Technically it's allowed under the Rules. I've looked through every one of the historical annotations though, and there has never been an instance where a challenge was made other than to the lowest team that made the Hunt cut."

"Which makes sense," Dysi added. "If your goal is to make it to the next Hunt, logic dictates you pick the weakest opponent and try to take them out."

"We're ranked number two based primarily on two things," Anatolia said. "First, the strength of our scavengyr pieces and, second, Quint's second place standing in Combat. Why? Why choose us?"

"We've been asking ourselves the same question for hours now," Borras interjected. "We only have a couple of hours left before the school day is over and Quint heads home."

"The Släkt aren't hobbled with a Munedan so they'll be planning all night," Notos stated tersely.

Borras cut Notos off. "A good case can be made that we are only making the cut because we are 'hobbled' with a

Munedan. Let's get to strategizing. I'll go first. It's an easy decision. I should be our Champion."

"Why you?" Ana asked.

"Physically, there is no question I am the strongest and fittest person on our team," Borras replied.

"That's not true when you factor in the Pucas. Quint is head and shoulders above the rest of us, and I'm not that far behind him," Dysi said.

"You can't be our Champion, Borras," Notos said quietly. "Omada will not advance out of the next round if you aren't our Prime."

"If our Champion is defeated, we won't advance from this Hunt," Borras responded.

"Odds are that is a correct statement," Notos said, agreeing with his Prime. "There are factors though, such as default by a qualifying team, which although unlikely might return us to the competition. We all know that given the nature of this Challenge, I should be the one to stand for Omada."

"I don't understand your reasoning," Tal said.

"You really are dense, aren't you?" Notos said.

"It is precisely for that reason, Notos, that you cannot risk yourself," Anatolia said solemnly. "Omada needs you almost as much as Borras. My combat scores are not much lower than Quint's and Dysi's. I will be our Champion."

"Don't be ridiculous," Dysi said. "Your healmagyk has already saved one of our lives and it will do so again if the need arises. Plus, you've already sacrificed yourself once. It is my turn. I demand to be selected Champion."

Look at the four of them, arguing to be the team member that might die tomorrow. Dysi's right. Ana already sacrificed herself once—to make Emet so that I could be on the team. Notos is correct this time. Omada will not win if Borras isn't at the helm. Both Dysi and Notos have magyk which might help the team in the next two Hunts. Of course, the decision I'm about to make risks two lives—Emet's and mine. I hate to leave him out of the dialogue, but his logic-based conclusion on the matter would be the same as mine.

"Everyone stop talking," Tal said. To his surprise they all did, even Notos. "Let's cut to the chase. There is no magyk, other than the scavengyr pieces, allowed in the Combat Challenge. So in that respect we are all equal. Piras and I have repeatedly beat the shit out of every opponent, save only Kita and she's not competing tomorrow. That includes Piras and me smacking all of y'all in practice over and over. So it doesn't matter who Släkt chooses, they can't put anybody in the competition better than Piras and me. Our scavengyr pieces are head and shoulders better than theirs—we ended up in second and they ended up in sixth. And, if Notos is right, and by some fluke circumstance we lose to Släkt tomorrow and still end up in the competition, I have no magyk to help on the next two Hunts, whatever they might be. So, I'm the Champion. Agreed?"

Tal looked at each of his four teammates in turn. Notos, then Dysi, then Anatolia, and finally Borras. All of them wanted to tell him he wasn't the best candidate. He could tell Borras wanted to overrule him but that his obligation as Prime wouldn't allow him to ignore Tal's logic. Omada deserves to win the Tyrning—with or without me.

"Good, now that that little matter is settled, if y'all don't mind I think I'm going to head out early. I'd like to spend some time with my family before I…well, before the competition tomorrow." With that, Tal picked up his backpack and walked out of the team room, feeling more alone than he'd ever felt in his entire life.

CHAPTER EIGHTY-ONE

With his early out, Tal was most of the way home before Emet showed up. It gave them the time and opportunity to leisurely walk and talk together as opposed to their normal harried race against the clock. He gave Emet a full accounting of the day and of his actions and why he had volunteered. When a couple of minutes had passed with Emet still making no move to type something on his cellphone, Tal went ahead and asked him the question that had been first in his mind all the way home. He motioned for Emet to get his phone out.

"Are you mad at me?" Tal asked.

Tal watched Emet type his response. He really could type like a madman. 'You know I'm incapable of feeling emotion.'

"Fine. You know exactly what I mean."

'Yes, I do,' came the response. 'It was the logical decision, Tal. It is what I would have done if I were in your place.'

"But if you were in my place and you died, it wouldn't cost me my life," Tal replied.

'All life is a gift,' Emet replied. 'In my specific case, my life is a gift—from you. If you had not chosen to 'Seek the Center' by joining Omada, I would not be here today. I cannot say that I trust your decision-making process because trust requires an emotional component I do not possess. I can say you are the most intelligent person I know and, thus far, the logic and reasoning underpinning your decisions has been unassailable.'

"How did one so young become so wise?" Tal asked.

'Actually, if we're talking about knowledge, life experiences remembered, and physical maturity, we are exactly the same age,' Emet replied.

Tal laughed and gave Emet a hug. Funny, Tal thought, Emet seems like a completely separate person now. No longer Pinocchio, but a real boy. I guess hugging him was probably some subconscious attempt to hug myself for self-assurance, but it sure felt like I was hugging my brother. An emotionally challenged brother maybe, but a brother nonetheless.

They split up a few blocks from the house. Tal went ahead to silently nod his afternoon greetings and to go upstairs to give Emet the "all clear" sign to shinny up the oak. They spent about fifteen minutes going back and forth about the day's activities at Nemeton High before Tal went downstairs. First, he played basketball with Remy and Romy for over half an hour. They played until they were all three dirty with sweat, finally collapsing laughing on the side yard grass. He had been so busy lately he hadn't had a chance to spend any real time with them.

"You guys are getting big all of a sudden," Tal told them.

"We're going to be as tall as you real soon, Tal," Remy replied.

"And then you're going down hard," Romy added.

"I love you both, you know that don't you?" Tal asked.

"Uh-huh," they both replied, their attention already turning back to the basketball goal.

Tal ran upstairs to shower and shave before dinner. When he went back down he engaged in the appropriate amount of dinner table chatter about what had happened to Emet at Nemeton High. He was able to snag a large dessert plate for Emet before he went back up. The two of them communicated back and forth until Tal was pretty certain he'd heard the last of dinner being cleared away. He knew that meant Thea and Pell would be sitting around the table having coffee.

"Here goes nothing," he told Emet.

'That is an inaccurate statement, but I understand the colloquialism so I'm going to let it go,' Emet typed back, right before Tal headed downstairs with the empty plate.

"What's up?" he asked his folks when he got to the bottom rung on the staircase.

"Nothing important," Pell replied, "Come join us."

"Yes," his Mom added. "After dinner Tal is a rare sighting these days," she said motioning for him to hand her some plates so she could put then in the sink to soak.

"I know, I'm sorry. I've been"—man, he hated lying to them—"I've been really busy."

"I'll say," his Mom said. "As much as you come and go, a body would almost swear there's two of you."

"Yes, ma'am," Tal replied, keeping his head down.

"Not that we aren't glad to have your company," Pell said, "but I feel like there's a special purpose for this visit."

"Nope," Tal replied. "Just realized I hadn't told you both lately that I love you."

"Oh, Pell," his Mom cried. "I think he's doing marijuana."

"I'm not doing marijuana, Mom," Tal replied.

"Are you sick? Is that it? There's something wrong with you we don't know about, isn't there?"

"No, Mom," he replied.

"Everything's okay at school?"

"Yes."

"You haven't, you haven't gotten a girl…"

"No, Mom."

Pell reached over and placed his hand on Thea's forearm. "It's okay, Thea. Contrary to articles in women's magazines, men do actually sometimes express their feelings out loud."

She gently slapped Pell's hand away.

"Like this," Pell continued. "I love you with all my heart, Thea Smith."

His Mom smiled. A huge smile. "I love you too, Pell." Then back to Tal, "Is that really what you wanted to tell us?"

"Yes."

She got up and ran over and hugged her eldest so hard he almost couldn't breathe. Then she ran back over to the cookie jar. "One good turn deserves another, Tal. Take three or four of these. I made them an hour ago so they're still warm."

Tal crossed the room and hugged his Mom really hard before taking the proffered chocolate chip cookies.

"Ahem," Pell said, his hand outstretched. "One good turn..."

"Your good turn, Pell Smith, is that I don't give you any of these so you don't have to buy new pants."

Tal knew what was going to happen as soon as he walked up the stairs. Right before the stairwell blocked his view he looked back. He was right. His Mom was sitting in Pell's lap, smiling and talking to him—and handing him a cookie. Not sure how to put it into words, Tal thought, but that right there is 'Seeking the Center.'

He handed Emet the cookies as soon as he got upstairs. "One more goodbye left, I guess."

Emet nodded.

"Why don't you hand me the phone and head upstairs. I have a feeling I'm going to pass out as soon as I get this done."

Emet handed the phone to Tal. Then he touched his index finger to Tal's chest, before reversing it to touch his own, and then holding it upright, and vigorously nodding yes.

"Thanks, Em," Tal said before Emet headed out the window, "You are right. We are two, but at the same time, one. I know you'll always have my back."

Get a grip, Tal, she's only a girl, he told himself one more time before typing. 'Got time to talk?' Tal texted.

There was an immediate typed response. 'Give me a minute and I'll call you. I just got out of the shower, my hair is in desperate need of attention, and I'm currently dripping wet, wearing only my towel.'

Wow, Tal thought. She's standing there, all five foot ten of her, her hair is probably all tied up in a towel on top of her head, and she's wearing a towel…and nothing else. Fifteen yard penalty for unnecessary taunting.

'Hello? Earth to Tal?'

'Um, yeah, that's great. Call me in a few minutes when you have some clothes on.'

His cell rang about five minutes later. He jumped on it. "Hey."

"Hey. So what's up?"

"Nothing. Just felt like talking, I guess."

"I guess the only difference between you talking and you not talking is the verbal communication itself but sometimes you seem like a completely different person in the evening. So tomorrow morning, you are still silently walking me to Calculus, aren't you?" she asked.

Tal heard Emet thump his ceiling. Twice. Twice for yes was their code. "Of course."

"How long are you expecting this top secret experiment of yours to continue?"

"I was thinking I'd have enough data by the end of this semester," Tal replied.

"So you might actually be doing daylight talking by Christmas?" she asked excitedly.

"I think so," Tal responded.

"Excellent. Although you know it hasn't been that terrible."

"What hasn't?" he asked.

"Not talking with you during the day…"

"And she scores a knockout blow to his male ego," Tal replied.

"You didn't let me finish. It's been nice having to pay attention other than with my ears. I've learned how you stand when you're perplexed, you get this funny crease down the middle of your forehead when you're puzzled. If you're tense, all of your movements become slow and deliberate. When we text back and forth during the day you're funny, and intelligent, and you're kind. I've gotten to know the uncensored Tal, and I like him very much. It's been nice to learn about all of you, not just the portion most folks are willing to disclose when they speak."

"Male ego back online and fully operational," Tal replied smiling to himself. I've gotten to know you the same way Elle, he thought. From Emet and I talking about you every night until you're the last thing I think about before falling asleep. And the first thing the next morning.

"Tal—"

"Yes?"

"Since you obviously aren't willing to put yourself out there, I guess I'm going to have to assume the risk. How about you and me going out Saturday night? On a date?"

Tal caught himself right before he woke up the whole house yelling, "HELL YES!," that there was nothing he'd rather do in the entire world than go out with her, to be with her, to hold her, to kiss her. But reality clonked him first. Tal, you may not be around Saturday night. Both you and Emet may not be around by midafternoon tomorrow. Even though it was Barton's fault, and she's forgiven me, I already no-showed her one time. I can't do it to her again, he thought. She's too special. Elle is someone I could wake up the day after tomorrow and realize I'm in love with. If I'm alive the day after tomorrow.

"Speaking-in-the-evening Tal?" she asked timidly. "Courtesy requires a verbal response."

"I know it does, Elle. And trust me, there's nowhere I'd rather be on Saturday night than with you, but I may have a previous commitment."

"Oh."

That was it. The sum total of her response. Shit! Shit! Shit! I know that particular inflection of that two-letter word, I've felt it myself way too many times. Her feelings are hurt. She thinks I'm going out with someone else, or that I don't really give a flip about her. She thinks absolutely everything except for how I really feel. About her. "Elle, listen…"

She cut him off. "It's okay, Tal. Late notice and all that. I should have known better than to ask. I just thought we had something…it doesn't matter what I thought. I'll see you at school in the morning."

The phone clicked before Tal could respond. He went ahead and said the words anyway. "The truth is Elle, I picked a really lousy time to engage in a death duel. Right when I found somebody…I guess it may not matter now what I found."

His last thought before his body gave it up for the day was, "This whole 'Seek the Center' thing can be a real pain in the ass."

CHAPTER OCTOGINTA DUO

Another procession. Apparently every big trip out to the back forty required a procession. This time there were two rows of two front door Keeper clones, followed by a single Keeper with a huge golden tympani strapped to his chest. The honor guard marched in perfect synchronization to the slow cadence provided by the drummer. Tal and the rest of the Omada marched equally slowly in between those groups. He kept expecting someone to yell, "Dead man walking!" He almost yelled it himself a couple of times, just to cut the silence.

The silence continued as the Omada were guided single-file through the twisting corridors in the bowels of the Coliseum. In fact, there hadn't been a word said since they'd left their team room. Finally, their honor guard ushered them into the holding room designated for the Omada. As Tal crossed the threshold he immediately saw it was decked to the nines in gladiator décor—which apparently required a floor covered with rushes, dead animal pelts on the wall, and greasy lit torches shoved in wall sconces. Tal knew the torches were spelled to look like they did, they could just as easily have provided the same quality of light as all of the other light fixtures at Hunts School. The tableau was clearly designed to foment a killing mood mindset. The Släkt's room must be similarly appointed. That's exactly what Nord needs, Tal thought. Murder-themed decorations.

They each took a seat and glumly stared at each other. In complete silence. So they all about jumped right out of their skins when a trumpet blast shattered the silence. After the fourth tantara, the sentries watching over the team withdrew back through the entry door. As soon as it closed behind them, a garage-door sized piece of the far wall dematerialized. Sunlight poured into the chamber, spilling over the Omada. As the light struck them, tears began to fall. Anatolia started sobbing first. Borras was next, followed quickly by Dysi. Even Notos looked grim. Not that he doesn't always look grim, Tal thought, but this is like a "concerned for me" kind of grim. If that's even possible.

"C'mon Notos, you're starting to scare me a little here," Tal said. "Don't you be getting all sentimental on me. Fate of the world rests on my shoulders, and all that. 'Seek the Center.' Go team!" Notos continued to stare at Tal, the moisture threatening to reach flood stage over the levies of his lower lids. Tal looked at him and nodded. "Notos. Stop it. I really need for you to believe it too. We are here, all of us, all of this, we are doing it for one reason. Right?"

" 'Seek the Center,' Munedan," Notos finally replied, wiping what would have eventually become a tear from his left eye. "May the UnFading Spirit guide your steps this day."

"Good." Tal didn't feel good, but there was no need making his team feel worse. "This is why we've been training. You know we have the advantage. We have strong pieces, theirs are sad." His teammates glumly stared at him. "C'mon guys. I'm the only human ever paired with a Puca. With Piras helping me, they'll never lay a glove on me."

Notos interrupted him. "It is not a glove you need to worry about. It is a sword protruding through your chest…or your arms being lopped off…or being decapitated that should be your concern." There's the Notos we all know and, love, Tal thought.

This whole thing about actually killing another person was about to transform from concept to reality, and one side of reality might be his own death. Squinty is the best combatant they have, Tal thought. He and his Puca placed fourth in Combat, none of the other Släkt were even in the top ten. Plus, as much as Nord hated Tal, he would kill to be the Släkt champion. After everything Squinty had done so far and was clearly willing to do, if anyone needed to be put down, like a rabid skunk, for the good of many worlds, it was Nord.

The trumpet's call sounded again—three times this time. Tal sensed that was their signal to enter the arena. The team formed rank behind Tal, and he began walking toward the opening. As they stepped through the threshold, Tal did his best to get his battle fury on. As to what a battle fury might actually be, he was clueless. Amped up road rage maybe. A Red Bull or five would have been of great assistance, he decided.

Tal shielded his eyes as he stepped into the incandescent glare of morning and was greeted with a bone-rattling roar from the crowd. As his pupils adjusted, Tal swiveled his head so he could see the entirety of the stadium. It was jam-packed with tens of thousands of Folk and Creatures. He could see skin of every hue, cloth of every color, moving and swaying, forming a breathing tapestry. Tal felt his teammates also pause as they stepped into view and saw what awaited them. As soon as they had all stepped onto the arena floor the wall rematerialized behind them.

As his eyes adjusted to the light, Tal looked across the stadium to see who it was he was going to have to kill today. The Släkt half of the stadium floor was in deep shadow. Tal took the chance to scope out the layout. His best guess was that as the sun moved during the morning, a rotating half of the stadium floor would always be in the shadow. Just as he had hoped, it was Squinty standing in front. Even though he's tried to kill me, I don't know that I can make myself say he deserves to die, Tal thought. But I can rationalize putting him down for the good of the known universe—and to keep from dying.

"Champions, step forward." It was Ms. Empousa's voice, magykly enhanced so it could be heard throughout the entire stadium. Tal could feel the crowd's excited breathing, anticipating what was to come. Each collective breath seemed to come a little faster, then faster still.

Even though he was already in front of his team, Tal took a step forward. As he watched the group across the arena, he saw Squinty smirk at him. What's he got to smirk about, Tal wondered. While glaring right at Tal, Nord took a giant step backward. They were sandbagging me to throw me off, Tal realized. Oh God, no, their champion, it's—

Väst.

CHAPTER OCTOGINTA TRES

Ms. Empousa's voice again reverberated throughout the Coliseum. "The teams will now have ten minutes to work on final strategy."

Tal turned back to his team. "I can't do this."

"As Prime I would gladly shoulder this burden, Quint As would any of your teammates," Borras responded kindly. Tal saw the other three nod in affirmance. "The selection was made and announced. A change now would cause a forfeit. We have no choice. You have no choice." The last was said with compassion, but also firmness. Tal had seen it before from Borras. When he had pushed Ana to create Emet. When he'd restrained himself from helping Tal save Väst. When he had left everything he had out in the ring in Atlantis. He was fulfilling his responsibilities as Omada Prime, even though it was tearing him up.

"You don't understand. Me and Väst, well we've kind of hooked up."

"WHAT? YOU DID WHAT?" As Tal watched Notos yell, he thought he might actually self-combust this time.

"Um, yeah, we may or may not have been mugging down on numerous occasions."

Borras, Anatolia, and Dysi simply stood there, mouths wide open. Notos was bouncing madly around the other three in a tight circle. "YOU DID WHAT?"

"You know—made out."

"WHAT? WHAT? WHAT?" Notos couldn't stop himself repeating the word over and over.

Tal realized at that moment that someone could actually be hopping mad. Notos was jumping on one foot, and then the other, and with each foot change screaming the word, 'WHAT?"

The girls were angry as well. "Quint, didn't we tell you any type of personal interaction with members of another team was a really bad idea?" Anatolia asked him.

Dysi's anger wasn't directed only at Tal. "That fucking bitch! She did it again. She used compulsionmagk on you too."

Tal knew Dysi hated Väst. Unconditionally hated her. But he was lost about the whole compulsionmagyk thing. Last time he'd heard anything about that the Omada were in their team room talking about Battle Hunts. Besides, none of the students could use their magyk. Why would Väst be any different?

Dysi wasn't done yet. "I'm going to kill her low-life scheming ass. We all brought our Pucas. Notos, think of an exception to the Rules so I can be the Omada champion. The universe will be better off without that harlot. First, she gets Kentro killed, and now she's doing it all over again to Quint. I'm not going to let her. I will kill her…then I'll cut her into quarters…and then I'll kill her again." Dysi finally ran out of steam and collapsed to her knees sobbing.

Borras stepped over to Dysi, and after kneeling, placed his massive right hand on her petite shoulder. "Dysi, stop it. We only have a few minutes and you're wasting it. You know we can't change the champion designation. Even if we could, it wouldn't make sense. There's absolutely no magyk allowed other than our scavengyr pieces that are selected. Quint and Piras are head and shoulders better than the rest of us. They have the best chance of winning this challenge. They have to do it."

"Borras?" Tal begged.

Anatolia stepped forward. "Quint, I don't want to be insensitive, and I would also gladly take this responsibility if I could, but you had absolutely no business engaging in a physical relationship with someone on a competing team. Unless you were willing to kill them afterward. You bound the contract. That means you must be prepared to kill the opponent. This is how it has been for millennia."

"Don't give me that crap," Tal snapped. "There hasn't even been a Combat Challenge for more than ten thousand years." As Tal saw Anatolia recoil from his anger, it abated as quickly as it had flamed. "I'm sorry, Ana. You're absolutely right. All of you told me early on there was a no fraternization rule." He looked to the group. "My entire life I've been the plain vanilla guy, the best friend, only the 'someone to help you with your homework' guy. I never had a hot chick interested in me before. Now, all of a sudden I have two girlfriends. Which isn't going to be a problem much longer, I guess, since I'm supposed to go kill one of them. Or die myself."

"I don't see how you can possibly believe you aren't special," Borras told him. "You are the first Munedan ever allowed at Hunts School. You're on a Hunts Finalist team. There is a Combat Challenge today, the first in ten millennia. Bards are already composing their lays. If one of the two teams in this challenge goes on to win the Hunts, that team will be the legend above all legends."

"That's great, Borras, be sure and carve that on my tombstone—He Was A Part Of The Best Lay Ever."

"Quint," Anatolia said, as she grasped his chin gently with her right hand. "Quint, look at me. It never mattered which of the Släkt you fought this day. They are like us, like all the rest of us—a team. They win as a team, or they lose as a team. Each of us risks our life every day to be in the Hunts. We do it to 'Seek the Center'."

"You have to remember that," Dysi added, finally standing back up. "If you die, we not only lose a friend, Omada is out of the Hunts. You've seen the other remaining teams. Do you

469

want any of them to have control over our Realms, or the human plane, for the next three hundred years? Do you trust the Slӓkt to 'Seek the Center'?"

The trumpet sounded again. This time with only two blasts. "Three minutes," Ms. Empousa's voice announced.

Notos had finally calmed down enough to speak. He walked over to Tal, leaned over and whispered in his ear. "Quint, I want you to listen to me. Here's the bottom line—someone is going to die today. It's either you, or it's her. Period. Every one of us here made a choice, we are all here of our own free will."

Choice. Free will. There has to be a way, Tal thought. What was it Helblad told me? I have a clever mind and a giving heart. I need one of those light bulbs of inspiration to ding over my head right now. Like that's going to happen, you moron, and who would even see it in this bright sunlight? I guess if I was standing over there in the dark half of the arena with the Slӓkt someone could see it. That's it, Tal thought, shadows—there's plenty of shadows in the dark half of the arena. There may be a way out of this death dilemma. *Choice. Free will.* "Borras?"

"Yes?"

"When you said absolutely no magyk other than the scavengyr pieces, I'm guessing that even a low-level glamour on our swords so they each look like the other one isn't possible?" Tal asked.

"A temporary glamour on two very similar objects might fall below the prohibition level of Alberich's Bane, but would probably be stopped by the additional warding on the Hunts School campus," Borras responded. "Notos?"

"Odds are even if it wasn't prohibited by the Bane, it would be against the Hunts Rules and could get us disqualified. Plus, everyone on Slӓkt would know we were using magyk for something."

"Figured as much," Tal replied. "Fine. We'll do this the Munedan way. Borras, I need for you to go over to our team table and completely wrap both our swords in one of those red blankets."

"Even the hilts?" Borras asked.

"Take special care to make sure the hilts are wrapped tightly," Tal responded.

"May I ask why?"

"We don't have time." Borras was clearly clueless, but he nodded to Dysi to go with him and walked over to the Omada objects table. Once there, Borras got one of the blankets and wrapped Skofnung. Dysi also carefully wrapped Fragarach in one.

Tal turned to Notos. "Notos?"

"Yes?"

"This is really important. Skofnung is the sword, on the end of the table. Fragarach is the one next to it. Whichever sword I ask you to bring me, I want you to bring me the other one."

"Why don't you walk over there and pick it up yourself?"

Anatolia grabbed Notos's arm. "Do as he asks, Notos. Quint is the one putting his life on the line for the team today."

"Fine, but there's no question which one to use. Fragarach is easily the superior weapon. You'd have to be a major Dunser to ask for Skofnung."

"Notos," Tal replied. "I'm counting on you. No matter what happens. Skofnung is at the end of the table. Fragarach on the right. Whichever one I ask for, you have to bring me the other one."

"If that is what you require."

As Borras and Dysi walked back over, Notos added, "Remember, Munedan, when it's our turn to pick a category we voted to choose 'Defense' first. Then it doesn't matter which of the other two categories she picks. With Fragarach, your Puca and the Ring of Gyges we should have this thing in the bag."

Before Tal could respond, the trumpet sounded, a single long note that reverberated throughout the vast arena. Then Ms. Empousa announced, "The teams will approach the middle of the arena for final combat instructions."

"Okay, troops," Tal announced, "let's go see who gets to die today."

As they approached the center Tal noted the stadium floor was now split right down the middle between sun and shade. Tal looked up toward the sun. The sunlight was going to rotate as the day wore on, but his first thought was confirmed, it looked like half the floor would always be in darkness.

At some unseen signal from Ms. Empousa, the members of the other six finalist teams spread themselves out in a wide circle encompassing the entire arena floor. The two combatant teams' tables were across the circle from each, with space next to each table to be filled in by the non-combatant members of Omada and Släkt. The Omada table was beautifully draped in a deep cherry red, the team's color. The Släkt table was similarly adorned but in royal purple cloth.

Ms. Empousa continued with the final fight directions. "First, the combatants will arm themselves with their weapons." Tal saw all four of the Släkt other than Väst huddle around their objects table. Tal mentally crossed his fingers. Please let Notos just be himself, today of all days, Tal prayed.

The two bundled swords were right next to each other. Tal deliberately pointed right in the middle of them. "Second Prime, please bring me the sword we discussed." Notos took a step to the table but then looked back at Tal, clueless as to which sword Tal wanted. In a somewhat louder voice Tal said, "Now is not the day for you to be your normal dumbass self, Notos, bring me the sword I instructed you to bring me." Tal could see Notos was still perplexed, but now his ears were turning red at being talked down to by a Munedan. Tal heard a few snickers go up from the non-combatant teams. He could tell Notos heard them too.

This time Tal made sure his voice was loud enough to be heard by everyone on the stadium floor, including all of the Släkt. "Damn it Notos, you halfwit." Tal saw Notos recoil at the jibe. "Skofnung. Just like we talked about, bring me Skofnung. Damn, you are the most pitiful excuse for a Second Prime ever."

Notos's entire body was rigid with fury. He grabbed one of the bundles so fast Tal couldn't tell whether it was the one on the right or the left. He ran over to Tal and threw the wrapped sword at him without saying a word. Tal caught it, making sure it stayed wrapped.

Across the floor, Tal heard Nord snickering at that "halfwit" Notos taking orders from a Dust Child. He also heard Mitt repeat his words to the rest of their team, "Skofnung. The Munedan said their sword is Skofnung." Tal watched as the Släkt all began whispering, modifying their strategy to address the power of Skofnung.

Tal realized his charade had worked. The Släkt were convinced he held Skofnung. Tal hoped Notos hadn't been so angry he'd forgotten their plan. The entire time Tal had been working his charade with Notos, Väst had held her hands behind her back. Mitt walked up behind her to give her their weapon, so that Tal couldn't see any of the details of the Släkt sword. They were going to give Väst every advantage they could. Tal started rolling the inventory of remaining swords together with their attributes through his brain. Kladenets, Mistleteinn,…"

"As the challenged team, Omada get first choice of one of the three remaining categories."

Here goes nothing, Tal thought. I hope I'm half as clever as I think I am. Notos is about to go ballistic. "Omada choose Wyld Thing."

Out of the corner of his eye Tal saw Notos explode, immediately jumping back into hopping mad mode. "WHAT? That's not what we discussed. You were supposed to pick…"

At that moment Borras stomped on Notos' right instep so forcefully that Tal thought he heard a couple of small foot bones cracking.

"Silence," Ms. Empousa said, looking at Notos. "One more word from a non-champion and I will declare a forfeit by Omada. She then addressed the two combatants. "Omada has chosen. The Wyld Thing objects shall remain on the team tables. Which of the two remaining categories does Släkt choose?"

As Väst stepped forward to announce her team's selection, Tal could see her eyes were red-rimmed and swollen.

She doesn't want to kill me, he realized. But she will. She has to, she has to help her team win the Hunts. "Släkt pick Defense."

Perfect, Tal thought, this couldn't have worked out any better. I get both swords, Piras, and the Ring of Gyges. I am so not going to die today.

"The Släkt have chosen Defense. The defensive objects shall remain on the tables."

"No, HuntsMistress," Väst stated. "That is not our team's choice. The Släkt selection of Defense is a negative selection pursuant to Rule 15.3. There will be no defensive object used in the challenge."

The stadium had been ebbing and flowing with the dialogue on the arena floor. When Väst made her pronouncement, it was as if everyone present inhaled at the same time. Leaving no oxygen for Tal. Even for a Combat Challenge this must be unusual, Tal realized.

Deal with it, Tal, he told himself, as he watched Borras remove from their table the large case they'd used to disguise the tiny Ring of Gyges. It's not going to be a problem. We were overmatched in that category anyway if that's the Helm of Hades sitting on their table. Guess they outfoxed themselves. I've watched Väst and her Puca in practice. They're good, but nowhere as good as Piras makes me. He turned to Dysi. "Okay let's get this party started. Please get Piras off the table and hand it to me."

Ms. Empousa raised her right hand. "Stop. The negative selection under the Rules means no defensive weapon. Which includes Pucas."

"Oh, shit!" Tal realized he'd said that aloud, but no one heard him as the entire stadium roared at the news.

Ms. Empousa continued. "Today's Combat Challenge is mortal combat using blades and Wyld Thing pieces. No other pieces will be allowed. At the sound of the trumpet, the match will begin."

Tal turned back to look at the Omada. They all put on a fake smile for him, even Notos made an effort. Then they took their positions on the end of the Omada team table, still presently in the sunlight, while the Släkt completed the circle on the far side.

The trumpet blared, this time a short, staccato note that seemed to say, "Die!" Tal knew in his gut the next time it sounded someone would be dead. Either Väst, or him.

Väst walked over to the Släkt object table and picked up an object. It was the Helm of Hades. She then walked back to the center of the arena to meet him. What's up with that, Tal wondered. She doesn't get to use it.

As they'd been instructed, they both turned and bowed to the Ruling Council, before turning back to each other. Väst began to walk slowly in a clockwise circle, so Tal followed suit.

"Umm, your hair looks nice today," he said. Vast didn't respond. *Idiot!* Well, no one ever told me what the proper conversational etiquette is when you're about to have a fight to the death with someone that you've gone to first base with. Repeatedly. Someone you might actually—that you might—you might be in love with. Tal took the opportunity to scope out Väst's gear. He still couldn't tell about the sword, but she was definitely carrying the Helm of Hades in her other hand.

"I get it. You're going to use your defensive weapon and forfeit the challenge."

"Sorry," she said with a wan smile. "For strategy purposes, Mitt designated the Helm as our Wyld Thing."

Game. Set. Match. You've been outplayed, Tal told himself. The Släkt have outplayed you at every step. Your second object is another sword and she's about to go all invisible on you. "Väst, you know without our Pucas, it's going to be hard for you to even lift your sword."

As close as they were now, he could clearly see she'd not only been crying but that she still was. "I'm sorry, Quint, but you're wrong." With that she turned her sword sideways so he could see the entire thing.

It was Heaven's Will. Holy hell, Tal thought, as his stomach clenched. It gives her the strength of a thousand men.

That's why they were in second place at the end of the first Journey. She has Heaven's Will and the Helmet of Hades. He was only now beginning to comprehend the full measure of the Släkt's evilness. "The Helm was worth a lot of points as a Defense piece. Your team intentionally took the low score on the Helm by calling it a Wyld Card?" he asked.

Väst nodded. Slowly.

"The Släkt didn't want to be in the top five, did they?"

She shook her head side to side. Slowly.

"The Släkt's plan all along was to only finish high enough to issue a Combat Challenge to one of the strong teams, so that your team could kill someone on one of the strongest teams and take them out of the Hunts."

Väst slowly nodded her head.

"All of our times together, you knew it might be you and me in this fight?" Tal asked, his voice breaking on him.

Väst grew noticeably paler as she nodded her head, and continued to circle him. As they did, Tal stopped for a moment to tear the blanket on his sword into pieces, leaving only the hilt wrapped. He also tried to shift their dance so they'd remain predominantly in the shadows. Whenever his feet took him to sunlight he raised the sword behind his head so that his hand and the hilt remained out of the light. His original purpose for camouflaging the true identity of the swords was gone. He had been prepared to use Fragarach against Nord, he couldn't use it against Väst. If he even scratched her with it, she would die.

His instincts told him, however, that he needed to maintain the subterfuge. Keep her going slowly in a circle, he thought, buy yourself some time to think.

"I don't want to kill you, Quint," she said. "I owe you my life."

"There's that. And I thought the whole sticking our tongues down each others throats was working out fairly well for us too." He looked at her and could tell behind her red-rimmed eyes she was blushing. "Let's stop it, Väst. You and me. Here. Now. Let's change the Rules."

"I can't," she said starting to cry. "Don't you see. I don't have any choice, but to do this. To do any of this," pointing first at him, then herself to show him she meant including their time together.

"There's always a choice," Tal replied.

"That's what I'm trying to tell you, Quint. I don't have a choice. I haven't had a choice since…" Väst choked as if she had something in her throat. "I don't…" She began coughing violently. Then abruptly she stopped circling. "One of us has to kill the other. Now. I have to try to kill you, Quint. You need to kill me first, if you can. I want you to. I think I'm in l…" She started shaking uncontrollably. Tal stopped circling for the moment, even though he heard the crowd screaming for blood.

Väst regained her composure. pointed her sword straight up to the heavens, and said, "Your power to me."

As Tal watched, Väst began to stretch. Like really stretch, one body part at a time. Like a Fantastic Four Reed Richards Mr. Fantastic kind of stretchy thing. She kept growing until she must have been ten or eleven feet tall. Think, Tal, think. Heaven's Will Whoever uses it will grow to the size of a giant."

"Goodbye, Quint," she said sadly as she put the helmet on her now ridiculously large head, and promptly winked out of sight.

I need a few moments, Tal thought quickly. He ran back past his team to the portion of the wall they'd used to enter the arena. As he watched, he saw Väst's size-seventy footprints march toward him across the sand. She's slow right now, Tal noticed. She isn't used to walking or moving that oversized body. As the footprints got within striking distance, Tal leaped to his left and rolled. As he did he felt a whoosh of air as the sword went by his ear before it carved a slice a foot deep out of the arena floor.

Tal felt, but couldn't see, a back and forth sawing movement. She's slammed the blade so hard into the ground that she's stuck it in the bedrock. Quickly, Tal, told himself. You need a plan. If I could reach my table to switch Fragarach for

Skofnung then I could have twelve berserkers to help me. No, the Släkt had ten minutes as a team to help her strategize for Skofnung. They're prepared for it. She is expecting you to unleash twelve crazed killers on her and she has a plan. They've outthought you on every decision so far. Plus, she's huge and invisible. No matter how berserk the berserkers are, it would be kind of hard for them to go all medieval against an invisible opponent with the strength of a thousand men.

Tal felt the air move again as the ground finally relinquished Heaven's Will. How can I win when I can't even cut her without killing her? I refuse to believe one of us has to die. Use your brain, Tal. What else is Fragarach besides certain death? It's also called "the Answerer." That doesn't help right now. What else? Whoever holds Fragarach, he reminded himself, is master of the winds. Tal saw her footprints move to a new stance. She is going to swing again. I need space for this to work, he realized, leaping to his feet and sprinting to the middle of the arena. As he did he felt motion behind his back. She's swinging sideways now to avoid the ground. Suddenly he felt a breeze on his left side. He looked and saw a steady stream of crimson flowing down the left side of his trousers. Beginning right above the waistline. Really flowing. She must have nicked me with the tip of her sword. Faster, Tal faster. You're running out of time.

He was limping by the time he reached the middle of the arena. He could feel the blood pooling in his left tennis shoe. Woozy, he thought, I'm feeling a little lightheaded. Mom's going to be mad about my torn jeans. Concentrate, Tal. Which wind do I invoke, he wondered as he saw the footsteps begin to turn his way. You're on the clock, Tal. Call them all, stupid. Call the name of every freaking wind you know.

"Sirocco, I call upon you, stop my enemy where she stands." Instantly, from the stands behind him came a scorching scream as the hot desert wind swept past him, seizing every grain of sand from the arena floor as it passed him, enveloping Väst in an impenetrable thermal blanket of sand. He could see Väst now that the sand was tightly molded against her. Tal could feel the blowback from the wind's heat. It had to be more than one hundred and twenty degrees. Tal was pretty sure he could hear her screaming his name as she roasted alive inside the sand cocoon. He couldn't stop now. He had to find a way to end this.

"Now, Mistral! I summon you to…to…take her strength. All of it." Slivers of ice flew from Fragarach's tip as the Mistral fell upon them from the upper reaches of the atmosphere. The icy wind storm continued until Väst's giant sand covered form was also encased in a foot-thick sheathe of ice, her sword caught in mid-sweep toward Tal. The heat had melted and refrozen the ice on her face. He could see her achingly blue eyes, reflected across a thousand crystal facets, and he was pretty sure that those were tears frozen on her impossibly beautiful face.

He continued to wrestle with himself. I will kill her if I keep going. But I bound the contract to Omada. The Släkt cannot be allowed to win the Hunts. I can't stop now, Tal told himself. Actually, he wasn't sure he could stop. He wasn't sure he wanted to stop. One part of him acknowledged he was getting more and more lightheaded from the loss of blood. The other part seemed to be conceding itself to the sword's power. It was the same but different from when he'd held Excalibur. The Answerer was making it perfectly clear it intended to kill Väst.

Almost as if it was someone else speaking the words he heard himself say, "Monsoon! Typhoon! Cyclone! I call you all, by the power of Fragarach, to vanquish my enemy. Three whirlpools appeared on the ground in front of Tal. He watched as each of the whirlpools slowly became cylinders about fifteen feet in diameter. They continued to rise before him until they must have been at least fifty feet tall, spinning hundreds of miles an hour. In unison they rolled into Väst, melting the Mistral ice, washing away the Sirocco sand. Tens of thousands of gallons of water spinning faster and faster, the cylinders constricting as they spun. Three pirouettes of death, combining their force.

Tal could barely make out Väst's words from within the tumult. "Stop, Quint. Please stop. I'm drowning, I give up. I surrender." She's pleading with me for her life, Tal thought. It's

Väst, you idiot. You may be in love with her, but she is one of the Släkt. Tal heard her gasping as the enormous water column started leaning, and he watched as she toppled heavily to the ground.

"Stop," Tal screamed. The wind and water still surrounded her. "I am master here, Sword, and I say enough. Stop!" The sword bucked involuntarily in his hands. The winds ceased and everything fell away from Väst. Everyone in the arena, crowd and participant, was silent. Väst lay unconscious on her back, normal sized, on the floor of the arena. Tal stood there, swaying. I must have lost more blood than I thought. I can barely stand. No, that's only part of it. It's Fragarach too. All that magyk needed a power source and apparently it was me. Tal could barely hear the crowd as it started chanting—"Death! Death! Death!"

What do they want from me? I've won. Surely, I'm not supposed to kill an unconscious combatant, who's kind of my girlfriend, except for the part where she's also one of my mortal enemies. I think I may lo…I think I may lo…I am so tired…I'm really, really tired. Tal took a step toward Väst to check on her. Fragarach bumped against his leg, tangling his ankles, and he stumbled. As he fell, Fragarach, with a mind of its own, used Tal's arm to hoist itself high above his head and then drive itself straight through Väst's chest. Tal barely had the strength to remove the sword, and as he did, blue blood spurted from the gaping wound in her heart. Every beat, spurting, pumping more blood. Overwhelmed, Tal fell on her, placing both his hands over the three-inch hole in her chest, trying to staunch the flowing river of blue.

In his next heartbeat, Tal saw the rest of the Släkt race toward them. All of them, except for Mitt. Tal saw Mitt run across the circle to the Omada table and grab the other wrapped sword. He tore the cloth off the sword, and without even looking at the sword he began running toward Tal.

The next few seconds were a sensory blur—both sound and motion. Somewhere on the periphery of his senses the crowd was screaming, out of control. There was more yelling, closer to him. Tal heard Borras yelling, "No!" as he began running with his giant steps to intercept Mitt. Mitt was screaming syllables that didn't even form words. Except that the word "kill" was repeated over and over. Mitt was racing toward Tal as fast as he could, moving now from the shaded area, and into the light.

"Don't, that's…" Tal croaked right before Mitt's sword arm crossed into the sunlit portion of the arena. As soon as the sunlight touched the hilt, Tal saw Skofnung break Mitt's right arm as it took control. It buried itself point-first in the sand of the arena floor, like some kind of dowsing rod. Mitt began screaming when he saw the bones of his forearm sticking jaggedly out of the skin. Mist began pouring from Skofnung's hilt. Tal saw Mitt using his remaining good arm to try to pry his right hand off of the hilt of the sword, but the mist wouldn't let him. The sword isn't letting him go, Tal thought. The mist grew exponentially, before breaking apart, and congealing into a number of separate pieces.

Wraiths, Tal realized. Twelve wraiths. One ghost, in particular, kept getting bigger and bigger, until it was larger than Borras. Tal realized he was lightheaded from loss of blood, and probably in shock, but the extremely large spook looked more like a bear than a man. Mitt was screaming for help at the top of his lungs. His left hand was waving frantically for help. From anybody. Mitt's right hand was still stuck to the hilt of Skofnung, and his blood was pouring down the sword's blade. Tal saw spectators swarming like ants over the lowest wall of the stadium onto the arena floor.

Tal watched as the man-bear reached out and snapped Mitt's right hand off at the wrist. Mitt somehow remained standing. The apparition then handed the sword with Mitt's hand still clasped around the hilt to one of the other ghosts, which used it to slash Mitt's right leg. As soon as it did so, it disappeared into the sword. The next ghost in line grabbed the sword in mid-air and laid Mitt's left forearm open. It screamed in delight, and was sucked into the sword. Tal could hear Mitt screaming, saw blue fluid soaking through his shirt and pants. Every time Mitt was stabbed or slashed, another ghost dissipated. Mitt was now down on his knees, bent over, sobbing. Finally, only the man-bear remained. He picked Skofnung up off the blood-soaked sand, cranked his arm all the way behind his head and swung the sword so fast it was a blur. The sword lopped Mitt's head off, sending it flying thirty feet across the arena. As it landed with a thud on top of the Släkt team table, the were-bear dissolved into the sword, which promptly fell over on the arena floor.

It couldn't have taken more than a minute, Tal thought. What those things did to Mitt, not even a minute. *Väst*. Tal turned back to her.

"Quint," she feebly tried to reach up to him, but her arm only rose several inches.

"I'm sorry Väst, I'm so sorry. I didn't mean...I didn't want...Väst, I..."

"Quint..."

"Help her!" he screamed. But everyone stood there, doing nothing. It's because of those damn Hunts Rules, Tal realized. There is no magyk on campus. No Folk can interfere in the Hunts. The Ruling Council could intervene but they won't. Not until this is over. Which means they're all going to let her die because of their stupid Rules.

"No," he yelled. "She will not die because of me." Suddenly he remembered what Helblad said. *A clever mind and a giving heart.* He could see Aurora's words scroll across his brain like the credits on a movie screen. *"Four times before the Tyrning shall you have need of my ring, but only thrice may help it bring. Choose well Taliesin, and only when your need is clear, for by your choices you will doom someone dear."*

It will not be Väst, not this day. He grabbed the ring, turned it once, and was enveloped in a bright flash. "Aurora—UnFading Spirit—whoever out there may be listening. Help her. Please. It is my wish that Väst be made whole."

Tal recognized he was blacking out. The logic part of his brain advised him it was shutting things down. Right before everything went black, Tal was pretty sure he saw a rainbow curtain descend to the stadium floor, and that when the curtain opened—Perun stepped out.

CHAPTER OCTOGINTA QUATTUOR

Tal woke to a familiar smell. Before he even tried to move, his brain was already cataloguing it, comparing it against all known scents. Then he sat up. Then he promptly leaned over, and hurled into the bucket fortuitously placed by his bed. Woozy, he had no choice but to lay back down. When he did he realized his left side was absolutely killing him. From a horizontal non-nauseous position he started turning his head to look at his surroundings. He could see a row of a dozen beds, precisely placed and symmetrically spaced. White curtains covered the windows, and even whiter linen sheets were tucked tightly on the beds.

His brain whirred to a stop—it knew that smell very well. It was the smell of leftover pain, with an overlay of doctor's waiting room antiseptic. Now mingled of course with the bouquet of fresh vomit. What the hell? I'm in the infirmary. He struggled to sit up, mashing two of the pillows behind his back for support.

The swinging doors at the left far end of the room swung inward. Doctors apparently didn't wear scrubs in the Folk worlds but he knew medical types when he saw them. Tal could almost see more leftover pain sticking, like toilet paper, to their shoes.

The taller of the two, noticing Tal was awake, stopped and whispered in the other man's ear. That guy took off like he had a rocket strapped to his ass.

Tal opened his mouth to speak and realized it was so dry his lips were stuck together. The doctor-type walked over to the side of Tal's bed, and poured him a glass of water from a pitcher, added a straw, and placed it in Tal's mouth. Only a few sips later he took the glass away.

"Hey!"

"That's enough for now. You're going to have to take things slowly until we get the go ahead to heal you."

"Where?" he semi-gasped.

"You're in the Hunts School Infirmary. I'm Moros, Chief Physick."

"What...happened?"

"I am not at liberty to speak with you about any Hunts matters. Crouch has gone to get the HuntsMistress, and the Archon. They will be here within the hour. You should rest further until then."

"Have them bring me a couple of quarter pounders with cheese, would ya, Doc? And a Dr. Pepper. My mouth feels really, really dry." Tal realized as consciousness left him that the doctor had drugged the water.

"Hey! Quit pushing on me!"

"Wake up, Quint of Omada. It is time to wake up."

I know that voice, Tal thought. That's Ms. Empousa. "Did you bring the quarter pounders with..."

A male voice chimed in. "Arise. There are serious matters to discuss."

Tal knew that mellifluous voice as well and immediately tried to sit up. Before he knew it he was leaning over the side of the bed, vomiting into the bucket. Again. Except the bucket was no longer there, and in its place were the sandaled feet of the...Archon.

"Why has the Munedan not been healed?" Alberich demanded of the medical staff.

Moros lowered his eyes and his shoulders drooped a little. "The HuntsMistress told us only to maintain him until a decision was reached."

"Enough," Alberich pronounced, waiving his hand in a full circle before Tal's face. Tal suddenly felt like a million bucks. As he quickly sat up he noticed the vomit was even gone from Alberich's sandals. Must be good to be Archon, Tal thought.

"I'm sorry, your Majesty." He started to get out of the bed before Alberich motioned for him to remain where he was. Alberich motioned again and the doctor-types brought chairs for he and Ms. Empousa. Alberich then signaled the physicks they could go attend to other business. They promptly left.

As soon as the medical staff was out of earshot, Ms. Empousa let Tal have it with both barrels. "Cheaters. You and the rest of Omada are cheaters. I am declaring you disqualified."

Tal was unable to stop himself from exploding. "What the hell? Cheaters? What are you talking about?"

"Omada violated the Hunts Rules. Transportation was not one of the combat categories and you used the Omada Transportation piece during the Combat Challenge."

"No, I didn't. We didn't score a Transportation piece and you know it." Careful, he told himself. She is the HuntsMistress and there are two more Hunts…if we make the cut on this one.

Tal saw the Archon frowning as he tried to put the pieces of the puzzle together. "Then how do you explain what happened?" the HuntsMistress asked.

"Before I can explain to you what happened, you're going to have to tell me what happened," Tal replied.

Ms. Empousa lit into him like a firecracker. "Now you listen here, mortal, I don't have to…"

Alberich raised both hands, palms downward before slowly lowering them. As he did, the HuntsMistress eased up, closed her mouth, and sat back in her chair. "Lilith, the boy was both mortally injured and magykworn at the time."

The HuntsMistress turned her anger toward the Archon. "We all saw what happened and felt the magyk. We're not only on the Earth plane, we're on Hunts School campus which is double-warded. He is not a member of the Ruling Council. Five-Hells, he's not even Folk. He's a Munedan, for Spirit's sake. Yet he was able to open a portal." She turned back to Tal. "How did you do it? How did you open a portal in the middle of the Coliseum?"

"Clueless," Tal replied.

"And I guess you're also clueless as to why the Chieftain of the Cooshies appeared?"

"No, I know why Perun appeared."

"Perun?" she asked astonished. "Perun? You're on a first name basis with that…that…Creature?"

"That Creature, HuntsMistress," Tal replied, saying her title with exactly the same sneer in his voice. "was Perun, Chieftain of all of the Cooshies." He saw Ms. Empousa's astonishment give way to speechlessness, which was quickly squelched and replaced with renewed anger.

"HuntsMistress," the Archon softly interjected, "let's get back to telling the boy what all the rest of us saw happen."

"Lord Alberich, clearly some Folk have violated the Hunts Rules and are helping the mortal."

"You are jumping to a conclusion," he replied. Calm, Tal thought, he is always calm.

"There is no way some simple-minded Creatures were able to accomplish this."

"Lilith, your bigotry does not serve the Moiety well."

"And your time as Archon is almost done," she replied curtly. "The Hunts Rules require that a member of one of the challenge teams die."

"A member of Släkt did die."

"He killed himself by grabbing one of the other team's pieces in violation of the Rules. Quint was Omada Champion. The Rules require that the Omada Champion kill one of the Släkt."

"Quint of Omada?"

"Yes, Lord Alberich?"

"Was it an intentional subterfuge that both Fragarach and Skofnung were covered with identical blankets?"

"Yes, sir."

"Whose scheme was that?"

"Mine, sir."

"And switching the swords, was that a designed deceit?"

"Yes, sir."

"This trickery, whose idea was it?"

"Mine, your Lordship."

"To further your gambit you used one of your unknowing teammates by belittling him in front of the entire stadium?"

"Yes, sir."

"Was that also part of your plan? To help sell your ruse?"

"Yes, sir."

"Well played, although you should be prepared to suffer the consequences when you return to your team room." He glanced over at Ms. Empousa before looking back to Tal. "When he returns to his team room, right now."

"Yes, sir," Tal said, smiling a little.

"Who says he or any of Omada will be going to their team room?" the HuntsMistress barked.

"It is clear from this young man's statements he is responsible for Mitt's death."

"That's ridiculous. Mitt killed himself. This has never happened in the history of the Hunts. A combatant has never saved the life of the person on the other team. I am declaring a forfeit by Omada. They are out."

"There is no forfeit." If someone could make breath into words of granite, the Archon just did, Tal thought..

"Archon, I am the HuntsMistress." The solidity of Ms. Empousa's words couldn't even come close to that of the Archon's.

"The Council has the authority to overrule you by a majority vote. I have the votes."

"Omada cheated. Magyk was used." There was now the slightest quiver in her voice, almost but not quite into the petulant range.

"The Rules prohibit using magyk to win the Challenge, Lilith. Quint ingeniously used his allowed scavengyr pieces to defeat his opponent. As you may recall he was dying too, and he didn't use magyk to save himself. Which would have been a violation of the Rules."

I was dying, Tal asked himself. Damn, I wasn't even smart enough to use a wish to save myself.

The Archon wasn't through. "He knew Väst was within seconds of dying. He knew the Rules prohibited those of us allowed to wield magyk on-campus from interfering until the Challenge was over. Until she was dead."

Now that I was smart enough to think about, Tal thought, mentally patting himself on the back.

"Whatever magyk was used was not used to win the challenge, it was employed to save a life." The Archon turned his attention back to Tal. "Clearly the actions of someone 'Seeking the Center.' How a Child of the Dust was able to use any magyk, much less such powerful magyk on the Hunts Campus is not Hunts business, Lilith. This matter is of grave importance. It is Moiety business and will be investigated by the Council."

Tal could see Ms. Empousa had concluded she couldn't defeat Alberich on that point. "Fine, you're the Archon. For a little longer anyway. However, decisions must be made. The Hunts must be successfully concluded. Part of my responsibility is to help insure the Folk maintain faith in the integrity of the Hunts. The Munedan killed a member of the opposing team who was not that team's Champion. So Släkt is down a team member in a situation not specifically covered by the Rules."

"I have a suggestion," Alberich said, while smoothing a wrinkle out of his robe.

"I'm listening, Archon."

"You have previously stated the Släkt violated the Hunts Rules by grabbing another team's scavengyr piece?"

"Absolutely," she replied. "Punishment has already been levied for that violation."

"My point, HuntsMistress, is that by your own words you believe both teams in the Combat Challenge violated the Hunts Rules."

She stopped to think for a moment. "That is correct."

"As Archon I am giving you the authority to declare a tie."

Ms. Empousa paused for a moment. "So you're saying for the first time ever, we will have six teams move to the Second Hunt."

"Yes."

Tal watched as she rolled that idea around in her head. She's trying to screw us, I just know it, he thought.

Then she smiled. In Tal's brief experience with the HuntsMistress, a smile was never good for his side. "In a true tie situation the teams would be left in the same status as before the contest."

"This is true," Alberich conceded.

"Släkt are disadvantaged, being a man down."

"I agree," Alberich responded. "Advise Släkt they may choose a fifth member from any of the eliminated teams."

After considering his words for a few seconds, Ms. Empousa nodded in agreement. "I will advise the teams of my decision."

"Excellent," Alberich said as he stood up to leave. Turning his attention back to Tal, he added, "I'll have some fresh clothes brought for you momentarily, Omada Fifth. Something suitable for your team's winner's feast."

"Thank you, sir," Tal replied, smiling as he watched Alberich and the HuntsMistress leave. Go ahead, he told himself, have a self-congratulatory conversation, with yourself. Thank you, I think I will.

Nice work, Tal, you won the first Combat Challenge in over ten millennia.

Why, thank you for noticing, Tal.

And you saved Väst's life—for the second time.

I certainly did, didn't I?

Oh yes, and if she was grateful before, she will be twice as grateful now.

I guess you're right. Hadn't thought about that.

Because of your bargain with Helblad, your team is still in the competition.

I'm pretty proud of that treasyre bargain.

And well you should be. You should be really enjoying your journey about now.

Oh, I am. I really am.

Good. Because you've executed flawlessly in all respects.

Stop it before you make me blush.

No, really, what could possibly go wrong from here on out?

Ditto that. Really, what could possibly go wrong?

You're the best, you really are.

Oh, stop it.

No, you really are. I mean the way you totally humiliated Notos in front of the entire school as well as the most important Folk from every known Realm. Oh, that was rich...

Oh, yeah, well about that...

I'm sure it will be fine, he's always seemed to be a very forgiving sort, don't you think?

I guess there might be a little problem with...

And you were so honest with the rest of your team when you told them you and Väst are engaged in a prohibited affair.

You don't think they're going to still be angry about...

Surely there won't be any horrible arguments with the rest of your team about that little bitty transgression.

They'll let me explain, won't they?

And look at you, you have become such a player. Stringing both Elle about Väst along.

They're never going to meet. They're on different planes. You don't think that me dating both of them can possibly become a problem, do you?

What? A small love triangle like that one? What could possibly go wrong with that?

I think I'm starting to feel sick again.

No, no, no. You've accomplished so many other things as well. You've done all this and still have one wish left in your magyk ring.

That's true. That's a positive.

Sure it is, it means you're only going to doom one person that's important to you.

Oh yeah, I almost forgot…

I'm sure the fact you lied to your teammates about the ring won't be a trust issue with them either.

I didn't exactly lie, it was more of a sin of omission, but they're probably going to be more than a little pissed about…

And hey, it's no big deal if you can't figure out how to get Aislinn to Helblad by Coronation Day. He's only going to kill you and eat you.

Yep, definitely feeling a little sick to my stomach.

Buck up, Tal. You have to get to the feast. Where I'm sure the Omada, as well as the rest of the entire known universe, will want to personally thank you for single-handedly fixing things so that Nord is now the Släkt's Prime Direction.

HOLY CRAP!